STOP ME

MICHELLE JESTER

RopeSwing

Press

an imprint of
Rope Swing Publishing

RopeSwing

Press

an imprint of
Rope Swing Publishing

To my parents, who sacrificed so much
to raise and protect me, and to my second set
of parents, my in-laws, who love me as
one of their own.

I love you.

RopeSwing

Press

Foreword from the Author

It's difficult to share my stories, mainly because while, yes, they are fiction, the feelings involved are very real. Revenge is a desire that every one of us experience at some point in our lives, and many feel it would be the only solid resolution.

I like to include trigger warnings because I'd rather be safe than sorry when it comes to certain content. Some people appreciate them, some don't. If you are one that doesn't and feel they are a spoiler, please pass over them. I would certainly rather protect those that the content may trigger, than prevent slight reveals.

In either case, whether you read the warning or not, I also hope you enjoy and thank you for reading!! To see more of my books or join my quarterly newsletter feel free to visit:

www.michellejester.net

Michelle

CONTENT WARNING

This novel contains material that is disturbing as to include a trigger warning and stress indicator. Reader should be cautioned that this novel does go into specific detailed accounts and contain elements of violence, murder, rape, and neglect.

CHAPTER 1

PRESENT

"In revenge and in love, woman is more
barbarous than man."
-Friedrich Wilhelm Nietzsche

"Thank you." Jeselle politely said as the waitress placed the food in front of her. She watched the server walk away, "They really shouldn't allow ugly people to serve food. It's disturbing."

"I'll make the call. She'll be unemployed by morning."

"As I was saying, Dennis," she stated matter-of-factly, "this deal would benefit both of us. You more financially, but I'll get the satisfaction that I have run the old tyrant out of business."

"I'm the one who thought of the plan in the first place," Dennis said without emotion, "besides I didn't say *no*, Jess, I simply need to think on it. He still has powerful connections, and I don't want to make any of them my enemies," Dennis stopped talking while the waitress returned and placed the plate of food in front of him.

"Need anything else?" the waitress asked, her words as empty as her eyes. She hadn't made eye contact even once, Jeselle noticed.

"No, thank you," Dennis said politely and watched as the woman sluggishly walked away.

"By the way, Dennis, don't call me that again," Jeselle said with a cool tone, "I don't know how many times I've asked you, but now I'm telling you, I'm not Jess anymore."

"I wish you would consider leaving her alone," he was eyeing the waitress, "It's obvious she's having a hard enough time as it is for the simple fact that she's reduced to working in a dump like this. Plus, it's a waste of our time. Are we seriously going to eat here?"

"Dennis, hideous people like her shouldn't ever be allowed to work with the public, period. The food looks awful enough without having to watch her deliver it."

"Then, why else are we here, *Jeselle*?" he placed emphasis on her name. "You wouldn't need to order the food to have her fired."

"If she's lucky, I might let her keep this job," she said coolly, then quickly added, "Oh, who am I kidding, make the call."

She saw a slight flicker of amusement in his

eyes. "You remain so calm and collected while you annihilate someone's life."

"Consider it a public service."

Dennis laughed. "Well, be careful. In a few days we will likely be sending ourselves down the river, socially anyway."

Jeselle made a condescending noise that always forced Dennis into laughter. "Dear Dennis, if it does, it will only be a temporary hurdle. Many of those socially upstanding people will need you after all is said and done."

"I worry that it may backfire. I'm concerned Stryker could get a bad name from it and profits will suffer," he said honestly.

"Dennis, you found a way to deem every single employee essential, down to the very man who shines your shoes during the crisis stages of COVID, I imagine you'll find a way to recover."

"Still, we'll lose a lot of support," he stated.

"They are not your friends now anyway, so what do you really have to lose?"

"Tracy will never forgive me," Dennis sounded almost melancholy.

"Do you care?" Jeselle showed signs of agitation, "You both haven't really talked much since high school, have you?"

"Some."

Jeselle smiled, "Besides, it's good business in the long run and let's not forget, I have an interest in Stryker Steel as well. Also, like you said when you hatched this ingenious plan, you'll be the hero after you save the company and all those employees get to keep their jobs."

"True."

"If that isn't enough you can simply think of your mother's money. That should help," her smile faded.

"Okay, let's do it," Dennis declared as he slid out of the booth, leaving the plate of uneaten food. "It'll be worth the backlash simply to see old man Brantley crumble."

Jeselle looked up at him and blinked her eyelids dramatically, "Do you really want to leave me to pay this check? You know how I hate to tip dreadful people."

"You are so honest that it can't even be offensive," he laughed. "I know I want this, only worried it'll truly destroy the old man."

"Now, now dear Dennis, you've been working toward this day for so long. Think of how proud Daddy Dearest Theodore will be of you. Oh, and let's not forget the spoils of war you want, Uncle Brantley's sweet little wife. Didn't you say you had plans to have Raini in your bed within the week?"

Dennis's mouth curved upward, he snatched the bill off the table and winked at Jeselle as he glided away.

Jeselle watched Dennis walk toward the waitress. The repulsive woman would be unemployed by morning.

Good riddance.

STOP ME

* * *

No sooner had Dennis closed the door to his Mercedes, he made the call. "All done. We're proceeding with the plan. Brantley won't know what hit him. Be ready," he smirked.

"Are you sure you can trust her with this?" a deep voice flowed through the phone.

"I don't know how many times I need to assure you, George, I'm perfectly positive. She's brutal, but she's also brutally honest."

"And you're sure she wouldn't betray you, even for that kind of money?" George asked.

"We have a bond that is unbreakable, even for money," Dennis said evenly.

"Okay. Count me in. I'll front half, but that's it."

"Seems Dad might be paying you too much after all," he laughed, "Unfortunately, I'll need the majority of the investment up front," Dennis started the car and the call resounded through the premium surround sound speakers. "I'm temporarily running a bit low on capital."

"Fine. Be sure I get a return."

"Oh, I'm sure. If there is one thing I know more than Jeselle's loyalty, it's her greed. Once she ran the numbers, she knew. She never invests in anything that doesn't have a high return on investment. Still remind me to tell Dad we pay you way too much."

Both men's laughter echoed through the parking garage as Dennis rolled down the window, shifted the car into gear, and squealed out.

Best move his dad ever made was hiring George.

CHAPTER 2

PRESENT

Reflections off a ceiling always caught Camilla off guard.

Why do people put mirrors on the ceiling anyway? Unless they're above a bed? Then again, even there, typically only one person enjoys it. Seems so…solitary.

It also seemed a huge waste of money. Lots of money. While wasting money wasn't necessarily a negative thing, excessive waste was, especially when it wasn't her wasting it. Finding herself at thirty-four years old and job hunting for the first time in her life was also excessive.

A prim, little beauty with soft, wavy brown

hair falling around her shoulders walked toward Camilla, "Ms. Parsons will see you now."

She sweetly delivered the message. Also, a waste.

Camilla walked behind the wispy brown haired guide, excited to finally be there.

At the gate of a new life. She realized she hadn't dreaded it nearly as much as she had before she'd talked to Dennis.

She noticed all the walls were reflective and pristine. Must be expensive to clean, everything so ostentatious. She should've expected that Jeselle would surround herself with mirrors. Ever since they had reacquainted after high school she had noticed Jeselle couldn't pass a mirror without looking into it and with good reason ... she was breathtaking. Camilla let out a slight laugh when she entered the elevator, also covered from top to bottom in reflective plate. She followed and watched as the perky guide used a security card to enter and exit doors, hallways, and another corridor of elevators, until finally she stood before a set of double doors, her own likeness shining back at her, of course.

A shallow, dull, slightly plumper image of herself. Marriage and divorce tended to do that to a person.

"Walk in Ms. Harrison, Ms. Parsons is waiting." Camilla waited as the image of the brown pixie drifted away from her in the mirror's reflection before opening the doors.

Inside she found a massive office. Camilla

noticed the rich, brown walls first. It was evident that they were expensive. Camilla did notice something significant about the walls though, they didn't contain mirrors.

"It's Honduran mahogany,"

Camilla jumped and turned quickly to face Jeselle, "Jess!"

"It was reclaimed from the historical courtroom that used to occupy this land," Jeselle said from across the large room.

"I remember that building," Camilla moved forward and wrapped a tight hug around her as soon as they were close enough.

Jeselle inwardly cringed. It didn't show on the outside, of course, years of practicing and honing. Most people would never know the irony of that room. The significance didn't matter to anyone else anyway.

"How are you? I heard what happened with Rick," Jeselle's sincerity was obvious, "I was so sorry to hear it."

"Yes, well, traded in for a younger, newer model. You know, same old story," Camilla said with a note of sadness.

"Yes, I do. Matter of fact, I see it all the time. Hence, why I never married. They all want something they don't have." Shrugging it off with a touch of arrogance, she motioned for Camilla to sit in a cozy corner of the massive office. "Blueberry muffin?"

"Oh, no, have to watch the weight," Camilla said as she patted her thighs.

"It's been too long since we actually spoke. Social fundraisers simply aren't the same. What have you been doing with yourself?"

"Oh, you know, raising kids, running the house and campaigns. It all took so much time."

"So, you gave all of yourself to your family and Rick," she covered Camilla's hand with her own and leaned in, "and retained nothing for you. Is that right?" The description was clear.

"Yes."

"Dennis said the kids are nearly grown?"

"Yes, off to college, paid for by their father, of course. I wasn't awarded anything. I have to be out of the house by the end of this month; with only my belongings. I really couldn't afford the attorneys like he could. You know. And that's ... well ... why I'm here. I have nowhere else to go."

"Say no more. First, a job. Seeing as you ran very successful campaigns for his two terms in office, managed his crazy social schedule, and raised his three bright children, I'd say you're exactly the perfect fit here. As it happens, I have a corporate condo in the heart of the city that you can use until you get on your feet, or lease it if you choose to stay. The city is so addicting," Jeselle smiled brightly.

Camilla broke down in sobs. "Thank you! I owe you, Jeselle! Thank you, oh thank you! I was worried, you know, because..." Camilla hesitated a bit, "I didn't know where else to turn."

"You do your job. That is all you owe me. Besides, Dennis is a dear friend, and I'd never let his sister suffer."

"You know Dennis and I grew apart over the years," Camilla hesitated in her speech, "So I really appreciate this."

"You can remedy that Camilla. Now is the time to draw close to your family. Your brother loves you. It is a plus, too, to know Rick won't have the last laugh! You can't merely leave your faithful wife after fourteen years of marriage. Especially after having her raise your three children from your first marriage. Trust me on this Camilla, I imagine once Rick hears you are working for one of his largest contributors from his last campaign, as you well know, he'll cringe a time or two over the loss."

That made Camilla laugh for the first time since she was told she'd be tossed from her mansion in Wellgrove Estates.

* * *

Jeselle walked into the elevator. As the doors closed, she stepped closer to her reflection, took in four deep breaths and released them slowly as she simply stared into her own likeness.

She thought of her mom and dad.

Jeselle lifted her hand and softly moved a piece of hair away from her face. Soon the elevator came to a slow stop, and she turned toward the doors.

Once they opened, the crowd that she found waiting immediately cleared a path for her.

"Hello, everyone," she said.

The crowd replied with various greetings, all warm and friendly.

Friendly, she thought.

Everyone was motivated by something. Something they needed or wanted: a job, a compliment, a donation, and that was fine with Jeselle. She was motivated also. Knowing that about others simply made it easier to understand how everything fit together into the world. Many people are honest about their needs, some aren't.

Somehow, Jeselle had the gift of discerning the lies people told her most of the time.

Maybe it was from years of watching. Maybe it all boiled down to one day: her biggest lesson. Maybe it was all luck. Sometimes, it was as simple as perceiving what a person would get out of a situation to find the truth.

Jeselle knew early on that doing something good for someone else in front of a crowd, likely gained the reward of the admiration a person received. Possibly, it was getting the admiration so they could then use it to get something else from the onlookers.

Therefore, the truth of a person is often found in the outcome. Jeselle never liked to wait that long. Once the outcome was seen, it was too late to use the truth anyway.

In her freshman year of college, Jeselle often thought how odd it was to see who landed on top

STOP ME

in the world. It wasn't always the good ones, or always the bad ones. However, there did seem to be a system of some sort.

While having lunch in the college cafeteria one day, she considered the salt shaker. It always gets top billing over the pepper shaker. Since alphabetically pepper should come first, it made her wonder: who decided salt should come first? Even by its proper name, pepper should still be first. While salt was used for decades earlier than pepper, there still should've been some sort of order to it.

Someone along the way decided which came first.

It could be that salt was deemed more important, and let's face it, it really is. It preserves as well as enhances the flavor of food. Whereas pepper only makes food taste more like pepper.

So maybe usefulness made it more important?

Jeselle wondered if that was why salt got top billing. She started to focus obsessively for an answer. After classes, each day she went to the library on campus and researched. She learned that while all spices at one point in history were associated with wealth, that all changed when new mining techniques made salt much more accessible and affordable. Salt was in abundance and could be found easily all throughout the world. It required less processing and could be manufactured twenty-four hours a day, three hundred sixty-five days a year. That, of course, made salt much more efficient to acquire, and in turn cheaper to sell and purchase. She found that salt, then, sold for the low price of about twelve dollars per fifty pounds.

So accessibility, hence popularity, made it more important?

Yet, pepper had to be imported mostly from India and Vietnam, it was seasonal, had to be harvested, dried and required much more preparation time and effort before you reached a final product. Like most things, the more quality a product, the harder it is to acquire, which always made it most desirable. Since pepper sold for around four hundred twenty dollars per fifty pounds, it should've taken top billing because it brought in the most money per pound.

The perceived value was what should've made it more important.

Only, it didn't.

Jeselle looked deeper and deeper until finally, she found it. On the surface, or the gross, pepper seemed much more valuable, salt seemed nearly worthless.

It was all in the profit margins. That was where the truth reigned.

The outcome.

Salt had a much larger net profit margin at approximately twenty-five percent; pepper had a dismal net profit margin of around eight percent. Hence, the net profit is far greater for salt, than it is for pepper.

So, money decides; not the gross monies, the net. That was the key.

Of course, over the years she'd learned some

things really didn't have to do with money, but that day in college, that was when Jeselle decided. That was the day when all the dollar signs lined up and she understood for the first time, that top billing boiled down to the bottom line: *profit.*

As she started to exit the glass doors that led to the street, a person caught Jeselle's attention. A young woman stood off to the side. In the past, when Jeselle saw someone who reminded her of her mother, it made her angry; she didn't want to remember all that goodness. Now she realized, to see, one had to look; because remembering was what helped her to maintain her focus.

Jeselle stopped, causing a line to form behind her in the large doorway. She was accustomed to it; she was the boss after all. Who would dare walk around her? She watched the young woman slowly look up from her phone. The girl appeared startled to find Jeselle staring back at her. Then just as quickly, she launched herself away from the large column she had been resting against and made it to Jeselle within seconds.

Noise, white noise encircled Jeselle. She could see the girl standing in front of her talking, but couldn't hear her. Up close she really didn't resemble her mother at all, but her honey brown hair was the precise color. The woman looked so youthful and happy; like her mother had when she was younger. When they'd first moved to Baton Rouge.

"Shut up," Jeselle said, lifting a hand.

The girl immediately stopped talking and her

15

eyes grew wide.

Jeselle then turned and started walking toward her driver, who was waiting by the street.

She heard the pleading in the young girl's voice all the way to the car. Jeselle finally stopped and turned to face her, "What kind of experience do you have?"

The girl seemed somewhat timid, "I work hard and I learn quickly ... but I don't ... um, have any experience," her voice trailed off softly.

"None?"

"No. None," she answered honestly.

"What do you have going for you other than working hard and learning quickly?"

"I- I- um, nothing ... I guess," the girl seemed perplexed by the question.

"Then why do you expect me to give you a job?"

"Well," the girl fumbled through her large, floppy purse and pulled out a magazine, "I read your story. How, if it weren't for Mr. Vinton giving you a break, you wouldn't be here," she quickly stated.

Jeselle narrowed her eyes skeptically, "and you want a break?"

"Just to get in," she rushed her words, "I'll work. I'll work so hard. I know I don't look like much, but I will, work, that is." The girl brushed her jacket down a bit and noticed a piece of dried food, which she hastily scratched off with her stubby finger nail.

Jeselle huffed, frustrated, "Many people say they'll work hard or do whatever it takes when they are desperate. Then after they get the results they desire, they rest in their snug little job. I fire people like that every day, young lady." Jeselle bent toward her, "My philosophy is: work hard to get the job so you appreciate it."

"I will. I can, I mean! You, um, you didn't though. Respectfully," the girl pointed to the magazine, "you said you asked Mr. Vinton for a job and he gave you one. And you worked hard every day to prove you deserved it. I will," she seemed more sure-footed than before, even stood a bit taller.

"What is your name?" Jeselle asked, her eyes narrowing again.

"It's Rose."

"Great, a Titanic baby," Jeselle looked to the driver who held her door open, then back to the young girl.

"I'm sorry? Titanic baby?"

"Yes, you were born late 1997 or somewhere early 1998, is that correct?"

"Yes!" Rose seemed excited, "How-"

"The movie. If there is one thing certain I've come to realize through the years, it is that many mothers lack imagination once they've deemed a current movie their favorite," Jeselle stated plainly.

Rose blushed and looked down at her feet.

"And, Rose, you are wrong, you do have something very valuable going for you: honesty," Jeselle snapped. "Now, let's see if you have the only other trait that I hold valuable in this world…" Jeselle slid one stiletto-embossed foot into the car, "loyalty," she snapped. "Be here tomorrow morning at eight a.m. sharp. Use the password 'mirrors' to get through first floor reception."

"Yes ma'am! Thank you!"

Right before the door closed Jeselle added, "Don't thank me just yet."

As the car pulled away from the curb. Jeselle took a glance back and saw Rose jump into the air, smiling.

Righting the world of all the misguided decisions on who should take top billing and who shouldn't had become Jeselle's only true mission.

CHAPTER 3

PRESENT

"The thing is not to leave unfinished
business; make every day count."
-Wally Amos

The food smelled delicious; no doubt he'd had the latest trendy chef prepare it. If Jeselle knew the only sure thing about Dennis, other than the fact that he wanted everything, she knew he was also not a cook. He met her in the large foyer and helped her with her coat. The butler showed up at precisely that moment and removed the coat from Dennis's arm.

"I don't know why I keep you around, Stuart," Dennis said curtly.

"Yes, sir," the older man responded dryly.

"Do you think it's too difficult to answer the door?"

"Sometimes, Sir," again his words were dry which made Dennis laugh.

"That is why I keep him around," Dennis looked at Jeselle, "he entertains me."

"Which chef prepared that wonderful smell?" she asked.

"I had Aucoin come in this time. Impressed?" he asked her.

"Of course, I am. You never cease to impress me, Dennis."

He stopped and stared at her for a moment, a serious emotion passed over his face; then just as rapidly, it was gone.

Immediately a memory surfaced; a memory she squelched until later.

"What is it? The dinner?"

"The best." Dennis gave her a sly smile and gestured for her to move forward. They were seated, and the food was served immediately.

"Smells incredible."

"Jeselle, I know what we are about to do tomorrow, and I had hoped to do this in a different way, but I don't think I can wait."

Jeselle lifted her glass of tea to her lips just as Dennis laid a small gift-wrapped box on the table in front of her. She laughed.

"Why are you laughing?" he asked.

"Dennis," she took a sip of her tea, "let me guess, this is the engagement ring and your thoughts were that we'd, what? Join our wealth the day before we acquire majority voting shares in Briggs

International," she tipped her glass toward him, "and be king and queen? And then, let's see, you'd be one of the richest men in the city. Is that it?"

"Jeselle, you make loving you so hard." It was obvious he was hurt.

"And what? After we wed, you'd still have Brantley's wife in your bed? That was your plan, no? Oh, Dennis," she leaned forward and placed her hand over his, "you are one of my oldest friends, actually, you are my longest lasting friend, and I am not willing to risk that."

"We wouldn't be risking our friendship, Jeselle. It would be more of a melding of resources."

"Like? A business transaction? No, thank you. Sincerely, Dennis. I don't need more resources. I need more friendships."

"And I will be that, too," he insisted. "I already am. Haven't I been there for you, always?" He lifted a brow. Jeselle could see he was getting angry. Rejection often did that to people.

She patted his hand affectionately, "Yes, you have. You have been there for me, but truly, I can't. You know why."

"We wouldn't have to do that; sex doesn't make a marriage."

"Then it's settled, we remain friends." Jeselle slowly moved the box back toward Dennis and smiled softly.

"I'm saying, I wouldn't need that."

"Dennis, your four ex-wives, and the very short length of each marriage, testify with me when I say,

I think sex is too important to you to *not* have it. So, can we agree that it is best to continue as we are?"

He could see she wasn't going to change her mind. "You know I'll ask again."

"Yes, and you know I'll say no again."

They ate in silence. As soon as dinner was over Dennis stood, "Stuart will see you out."

She smiled inside at his display of pettiness, "No need, I can see myself out. We have a big day tomorrow, and I'd hate to spoil it with too much negativity, so let me put this bluntly for you, Dennis," she placed her fork down slowly and just as slowly she pushed her chair back and stood. "I have never led you on in any way and you know it. If my not wanting to marry you stays a source of contention then maybe we shouldn't be friends at all." His head jolted up, as shock spread across his features. She moved away from the table and toward the door closest to the foyer. "I thought you'd finally gotten the notion out of your head, however, your display of scorn here during dinner has proven to me otherwise. If you feel I owe you marriage in exchange for our friendship, to be quite frank, I don't need anything that expensive."

She nearly smiled when she saw the hurt pass across his face, replaced by desperation. He had always been so predictable. Well, almost always. If she hadn't expected this tonight, she might not have been so cruel. She knew with him things had to be nipped in the bud as quickly as possible before they flowered. "It would be regrettable, but losing your friendship wouldn't change my mind, and that is how I must look at all of my decisions. I don't want to lose you, but I will never marry you. I know you too well."

He walked toward her with such force that when he stopped in front of her, she felt the air move around her.

"Jeselle Kate Parsons, you will marry me one day. I will prove to you that I love you the way I have never loved another woman. I am loyal to you. Yes, I am hurt by your repeated rejections, but I think it's obvious by now that I can take it. You will say yes one day, and I will gladly wait for it. See you tomorrow evening."

When she finally made it home and crawled into bed, she recalled the memory that she had earlier tucked away.

She flashed back to standing in her mother's kitchen. Dennis had just driven her home after school and her mom had gone on a quick run to the grocery store. Freshman year was hard for her. Jeselle was cutting carrots in preparation for dinner when Dennis leaned into her back and whispered in her ear. "You know I've fallen in love with you, don't you?"

Jeselle collapsed to the floor and started crying. He bent down in front of her and apologized. He was frantic, explained that he had only wanted to be close to her. He ran to get a paper towel and wet it quickly. Dennis softly started blotting her forehead.

"I'm sorry, Jess. I'm so sorry. I thought…"

She quit crying, took the paper towel away from him, and looked up to where he hovered above her. Unexpectedly, he leaned in to kiss her. She backed away.

"I, I can't do *that*," she stated softly.

"Kiss me?" he questioned, as a small smile formed on his lips. "It'll make you feel better."

"No," she whispered honestly, "It'll make *you* feel better. Me? I can't, don't want to… do anything like that," Jeselle tripped over her words.

"It's just a kiss, Jess."

"It's not just a kiss."

He sat back onto the floor, "We've kissed plenty."

She looked down at her hands where she was wringing the paper towel in her lap, "That was before. I don't want that now. I don't think I'll ever want it."

Tears started to build in his eyes, but then he stood and left.

The next day everything went back to normal. Dennis picked her up for school, walked her to her classroom, they ate lunch together with the rest of the group, and it was as if the afternoon before had never happened.

Which was fine to Jeselle. She had gotten accustomed to pretending. Those days taught her how to put on a smile and fake it.

CHAPTER 4

PRESENT

"Goodness is about character…More than
anything else, it is about how we treat
other people."
  —Dennis Prager

Jeselle opened the double doors wider than usual, and surveyed the area, knowing what she'd find. Rose was seated closest to the receptionist desk, smiling back at her.

"Come in," Jeselle waved her hand to motion the young girl forward. Then she elevated her voice a notch or two higher, "Karli, bring the packet please."

Rose followed Jeselle into the office.

"No mirrors," Rose said as she entered.

Jeselle stopped and turned toward Rose, "You are correct. Do you want to know why?"

"I … um, think so, maybe," Rose answered.

"Well, do you, or don't you?"

"I do, but only," Rose hesitated again, "if you want to tell me,"

"I didn't ask you if you thought I wanted you to know, I asked if you wanted to know. Here, come sit." Jeselle motioned toward a set of sofas in one corner.

The moment Rose sat down she exclaimed, "Wow, these are really comfortable." She bounced up and down a few times, which made Jeselle want to smile.

"Stop bouncing like a child," she snapped instead, "Have you never sat on a comfortable sofa?"

"Sorry," color immediately flooded Rose's cheeks.

The click of the doors closing startled Rose and she looked to find Karli walking toward them with a tray and package.

"Here is the packet, Ms. Parsons," Karli smiled at Rose, knowing what was about to happen. Karli had found herself in that very same situation only a few years earlier.

"Thank you, Karli. Don't buzz anyone else in for the rest of the day except for Milly and her crew to get us ready for tonight. Also, Dennis will be here later to escort me; he can wait in the main lobby."

"Do you want me to at least have him escorted to the fifth-floor lobby for you?"

"No," Jeselle said immediately, "That would be for *him*, not me. He needs to wait in the main lobby until I go down."

STOP ME

Karli nodded and didn't skip a beat, she'd learned through the years not to.

"And have Rose added to the list as well."

"Absolutely," Karli smiled warmly.

Jeselle waited until Karli had closed the doors firmly to turn back toward Rose.

"Here," she extended the packet, "in here is everything you need to start. Open it up, and we'll quickly go through it. Blueberry muffin?"

Rose opened the packet and poured the contents into her own lap and then eagerly grabbed a muffin and took a large bite.

"There is the company manual of conduct, of course. A general map of the entire building. I do rent out space on the second and third floors, however, I won't be renewing their lease come summer since we could use that space now." Jeselle observed that each time she mentioned an item Rose sifted through the pile to find it.

Good. Detailed.

She also noticed the crumbs that fell into Rose's lap with each new bite. "There is a temporary lanyard with your passcard on it, guard it carefully until you can get the photo ID later this afternoon. If you do ever lose your passcard, you must alert Lakshmi, the head of security, at once. Do not wait. You will not be fired for making a mistake or having a mishap, you will be fired for covering it up. I have given you full access, except this floor."

"Full? Like I can go anywhere in the building except this floor?" Rose was surprised.

"Yes. What did you expect?"

"I, don't know. I guess…" Rose stumbled over the food in her mouth, "I guess I thought I'd have to, I don't know, water the plants or something at first."

"And you see that as a menial job? Watering the plants?"

"Yes, ma'am, but I'll do it!"

"Well, let us pause for a moment," Jeselle set her coffee cup down, "Plants provide oxygen to our lungs, which then in turn supply that oxygen to our blood with enough to feed our organs. So, dead plants would mean less oxygen. Is that not important?"

"Oh, no ma'am," Rose exclaimed placing her unfinished muffin on a side table, "I mean yes, ma'am that is important," The confusion was honestly written across her face.

"Considering God is the ultimate waterer of plants, I suspect it's quite an important job. Think on the janitorial staff. Many people believe that scrubbing toilets or taking out the garbage is the bottom of the line, the lowest job, correct?"

"I, yes, I think," she laughed awkwardly, "scrubbing toilets, yeah."

"If there was no one to scrub toilets they would grow increasingly dirty with waste and bacteria. Even a good toilet that flushes well will still build up waste. More and more of it clings to what is already there until you have a disgusting bowl of filth. Now that's not healthy at all. Think on the garbage in our offices, my father used to say that the societal breakdown is felt first in its garbage. It compiles as well, much like that toilet, only if we never took out the garbage it would pile around us. The lunch from the week before starts to decay and smell. Before long the entire office would be a cesspool of disease. Isn't that important?"

"Yes, ma'am," Rose was obviously deflated.

"I'm not saying that to call you ignorant. I am saying that so you don't remain ignorant. All jobs are important, and we want to respect them and the people that do them. However, the ones that seem at the bottom should actually be at the top. Be sure you always respect the ones who clean up your waste. *It's a dirty job but somebody's got to do it*, is no joke. If you knew what I pay the janitorial staff, you'd beg for that job."

"Yes, ma'am."

"And some of them do have access up here, which you do not." Jeselle could see her point was driven home and she continued, "Okay, you'll be buzzed up here each day by Karli-"

"Up here? Like I'll come up here?"

"Yes, Rose you did ask me for a job. Do you not want it?"

"I do, I only...I didn't think I'd be working directly with you, up here."

"Don't get too excited yet, I suspect after the first week you'll wish you hadn't asked."

"I won't," she said resolutely.

Good. Backbone.

Jeselle did smile then. "Karli will show you to

your office. You will start out learning from her. She may seem like a mere receptionist, however, she holds the keys to my office, literally. She is my gatekeeper. She has gatekeepers for her and they have gatekeepers for them and so on. I suspect once you learn your way around, you'll make a fine gatekeeper as well. In that packet is also a 'house card.' We have a deli, assorted coffee and food shops around the left side of the main lobby. As a part of your salary, you'll get a card each week which can be used at any of the shops. It'll only have a hundred on it so use it wisely. Also there is a parking pass. That is for the executive parking garage listed on the map. For clarity, the janitorial staff parks there as well. The only executive who ever had a problem with that was fired due to his own arrogance over the matter."

"Yes, ma'am."

"There is a list of administrators that work on the floor right below ours. It includes pictures of each person as well as their bio. You'll deal with each of these individuals, sometimes on my behalf. I expect that within the week you'll know each one."

"Yes, ma'am."

"You don't need to keep saying 'yes, ma'am.' I assume by you staying here that it is already understood between us that you agree."

"Yes … oh, okay," Rose nodded nervously.

"Where do you live currently?"

"I, I am still living with my parents. I don't want to, I just haven't really gotten on my own yet. I know

I'm old and should be in my own place, but they are trying to help me and since I graduated college and wanted to save some money, but I haven't really..."

"Stop," Jeselle lifted her hand. "I don't need your life story, simply a direct answer will do. We have several leases around the area. We can work that out of your pay if you want. Karli will go over all of that with you."

"I don't know that I'll be able to afford it. I don't even know what the job pays yet."

"Did that matter when you asked me for a job?"

"No, ma'am."

"Did that matter when you thought you were going to be watering plants?"

"No, it didn't matter," she said softly.

Good. Honesty.

"Then when Karli tells you what your salary will be, don't be disappointed. You may be working for less pay than the *plant waterers* around here, but you'll move up quickly." Jeselle stood from the sofa and looked down at Rose, "I don't believe one can pay for integrity or loyalty; it is or it isn't. Don't let me down, Rose."

"I won't!"

"Oh, and the last thing, in that smaller envelope is a five-hundred-dollar prepaid Visa Debit. Go and buy yourself some new clothes. Start with some of the basics like a pair of black and navy pants or skirts. A couple of jackets. A few shirts. That should start you off nicely. Nothing that sports heavy cleavage or excessive leg, I am all about individuality; however I also am about professionalism."

Rose started to get up. She messily grabbed all the contents from her lap and shoved them back in their original envelope as crumbs fell to the floor.

"Also, wear a bib or something when you drink or eat. You seem to have a problem with spilling things." Jeselle looked down at Rose's coffee stained shirt.

Color flooded Rose's cheeks again. Jeselle could tell she had wanted so badly to say "yes ma'am," but she had stopped herself.

Good. Quick learner.

"Do you have a formal dress?" Jeselle asked.

"A formal … like a prom dress?"

"Precisely."

"Yes, I do," Rose's brows drew together in question.

"Go home and get it. You'll be attending the Business Gala tonight with us."

"You want me … I mean, I'd love to, but are you sure you want me to go? I've never gone to anything like that before."

"I never say anything I don't mean, Rose," Jeselle paused for a moment, "If I told you one of the housekeepers was going also, would that make you feel better?"

Rose smiled then. First time she'd smiled the entire time she'd been in Jeselle's office. She looked so sweet and relaxed.

"You may go see Karli now." Jeselle walked to her desk and watched as Rose scurried to the door, then turned around to get what remained of her blueberry muffin. Just as Rose managed to open one of the doors, she looked back at Jeselle.

"Wait. Um, the mirrors. I do want to know why."

Good. Thorough.

"It is thought that in mourning, a person should cover the mirrors so that they aren't staring their demons in the face. Demons such as guilt, anger, and regret. It is said that the mourner sees that perhaps they didn't do enough for the lost loved ones, or didn't say all they needed to say; reminds them that they have loose ends or unfinished business. It is believed that mourning should not be the time someone needs to face those things. Those thoughts are said to be evil spirits or ghosts that haunt the mourner, rob them of rest. So, mourners cover their mirrors to avoid seeing any unfinished business, while they focus on the loss itself."

Rose let go of the door and it closed. She turned fully toward Jeselle. Even from across the large room, Jeselle could hear Rose's breathing hitch.

"So, no mirrors in here, means you are in mourning?"

"Something like that."

"Your parents?" Rose asked. In the moments of quiet Rose added, "The article in the magazine."

Good. Observant.

"Yes."

"No mirrors in here, but mirrors everywhere else?"

"Yes. In here I can mourn and experience the

loss, but out there I face my demons, stay focused. I still have unfinished business to accomplish, and I can't rest until it's done."

CHAPTER 5

PRESENT

"Bear today whate'er today may bring, Tis
the only way to make tomorrow sing."
-Richard Le Gallienne

At a quarter after five, Jeselle made her way
down to the main lobby. Her elegant, black ball
gown had been simply stated on purpose so that
the jewels from Easton's City Collection excelled
above anything else about her. Dennis had shown
up at four thirty, eager to get to the gala. She exited
the elevator and made her way through the large,
highly polished, black path to the front lobby. The
marble reflected her movements off the mirrored
walls and vice versa.

The moment she came into view, Dennis stood
meticulously dressed in his perfectly fitted Brioni

tuxedo, and nervously rushed toward her.

"What the hell, Jeselle!" he whispered indignantly, "They wouldn't let me up to see you!"

"I know," she stated coolly.

It clicked and she saw the mask of his confusion turn to anger then to regret. "Last night."

"Are you ready? The car will be around in a moment," she said.

"Jeselle, do not punish me for loving you," he said, a touch of sincerity lined his words.

"Dennis, you love yourself far more than you love me, and money falls in line after you," Jeselle stated in her usual cool tone as she glided past him, "While I don't mind taking third billing, let's at least be honest about it, shall we?"

Dennis stopped, bent forward bracing his hands on his knees, and laughed. She paused and turned back to him and winked.

"You are something else." he quipped, "See how well you know me? We are genuine soul mates, I tell you."

"Yes, we may very well be." She looked back at him over her shoulder, her eyebrows lifted.

"You know I look out for myself and of course I love money, but I would never screw you over for either," he was still smiling as he moved forward to stand near her.

"That's because I have far more of it than you do," she smiled wider.

"Far more of me? Or money?" he said as he slipped his hand around her waist to escort her through the glass doors.

"Yes."

He laughed again. They sat in silence as her driver weaved through traffic. It wasn't until they were nearing the event center that he reached over and took her hand.

"This is life-changing. This moment," he said.

"Yes. Indeed, it is."

"These people will be out for our blood by the ten o'clock news."

"No, Dennis, they'll need us too much."

"Well, at least we can enjoy this last social event before then."

Jeselle considered his statement; she stared out the window as the event center, the one she'd bought several years before, came into view. An unexpected flood in the area due to unrepaired drainage issues where two rivers meet, coupled with heavier than normal rainfall, deemed the property pennies on the dollar. She bought the property and restored it. Making sure, ever since, to donate a set number of days per year to the state of Louisiana's big events, resulting in it becoming everyone else's top pick to hold conferences. After all, if it's good enough for the state…

She took a deep breath. Having received the award for the Louisiana Governor's Business Person of the Year again, her third in a row, was tantamount to accepting the Oscars for Louisiana business.

Several years prior, she'd received the Louisiana Businesswoman of the Year award, which she'd been awarded a few times through the years. However, Businesswoman of the Year was laughable to Jeselle. It truly was simply like getting a pat on the back, probably more the backside, from all the men in business, the ones who believe themselves to be the serious business people. It was really them saying that they deemed you worthy in…let's see…knitting. You were good in your sub-category, simply not quite good enough in theirs.

No, Business Person of the Year was the top and today's award made the rest of the day line up nicely in Jeselle's mind.

With her recent new hire, dear, poor, victimized Camilla Stryker Harrison, ex-wife of cheating Representative Rick Harrison, Jeselle was on the verge of sainthood. Actually. It would be closer to "fait accompli" as soon as she leaked the details of his torrid, wretched affair that had lasted nearly two-and-a-half years. The one in which he used campaign funds to pay for trysts with his lover. Also, of course, it would be leaked that the whole time he was using his authority against his much younger sex partner, he was also using his meager wife to do all of his grunt work for his bid to the House. She had the connections, after all.

She audibly laughed at that.

"What's so funny?" she heard Dennis ask from the seat beside her.

"Today is a good day." She really could put on the best show; then again, she always had. Well, she always had since middle school anyway. She opened the door and started to exit when Dennis grabbed her hand again.

"We are the best team."

She smiled warmly at him, "Yes, Dennis, we are."

And he basked in her affection.

***

They mingled well together. Dennis did indeed think they made the best couple. He caught glimpses every now and then in the mirrors that surrounded them on all sides and thought often how incredible they looked together. Anyone who was anyone in Louisiana business was there to honor Jeselle, the woman on his arm. The one he received light pats from when she found something someone said to be funny. She was the most beautiful woman he'd ever known. Of course, her ruthless business practices, and all the money it brought her didn't hurt her case. Which in his mind, was more the work of his parents. If they hadn't paid for her well-being, where would she be? If they hadn't helped her after her mother died, she'd be penniless. So truly her money was his money. Being in love with her was the cherry on top.

"Jeselle!" a loud voice intruded on Dennis's thoughts.

"Cindy," Jeselle greeted and kissed a cheek of the enemy.

"How are you? I was so glad to see you won it again. Who would've thought it in middle school, right?"

Cindy was notorious for her jabs at people. Her nose was so high in the air, Dennis thought, it was a wonder she didn't drown when it rained. He knew that smile wouldn't be there by midnight though.

He greeted the woman, "Cindy, how are you? Where's that husband of yours? I'm assuming Tracy came with?"

"Of course, he did," Cindy said in her condescending way, "although something's got him in an awful mood. He's talking to his father over there," Cindy lifted her glass of champagne in the air as she pointed toward the stage.

Dennis wanted to break into a dance as he watched Brantley Briggs and his son in a heated discussion. Dennis had planned this day for so long, it was hard for him to believe it had finally come. Or hard to believe he had been afraid of it only a few days before. Sometimes success is like that, you want it and are willing to do just about anything to acquire it, and then when it's within your grasp, you hesitate. Dennis was fairly sure it wasn't fear of completing the goal, but it was fear that there would be nothing left to grasp for.

When his father turned over the reins of Stryker Steel Corp to him, Theodore never imagined how well Dennis would do. Come later that evening, Theodore Stryker would be prouder of his son than he had ever been in his life.

"Why I think you are right, they don't look very happy. Huh," Dennis seemed genuinely concerned, "I think I'll go over and say hello."

He noticed Jeselle smile slightly and relished in her approval. As he strode away, Cindy stopped a waiter walking past them and grabbed another glass of champagne.

"So, Jess, I see you are doing a lot. Tracy said you bought the old library. Seems you are racking up the real estate." Cindy tipped the glass back and drank a large gulp.

"Only the important ones," Jeselle responded.

"Well, if they are so important, why do you tear most of them down?" Cindy's voice was laced with sarcasm.

"To make them unimportant," Jeselle said, noticing the slight flicker of recognition in Cindy's eyes. Also, how quickly Cindy composed herself again; she's also had years of practice. Jeselle moved into Cindy a bit and touched her forearm, "Start anew, Cindy."

Cindy stiffened.

"I'm not talking about the past," Jeselle said softly, "I'm talking about the now."

Cindy looked away from her, "I don't know what you mean. You always were so judgmental. I swear Jeselle, it's pathetic."

"I want to say that I know; we all do. Everyone knows what he is like. If you need us —"

Cindy walked away abruptly. And just like that, her fate was sealed.

Not that it hadn't been already, but sometimes Jeselle heard her mother's voice echoing through her brain to forgive and give people a chance.

Not these people, Momma.

CHAPTER 6

PRESENT

"What the hell is she wearing?" Dennis said with horror. Jeselle looked up to see Rose and Karli approaching the table. Rose had on a flouncy, overly stated, hot pink dress. The sleeves stood much taller than her shoulders in a fog of pink netting and the material jumped as she walked, which delighted Jeselle immensely.

Camilla openly choked on her gulp of wine, "That is awful."

Dennis patted Camilla on her back, "Sister dear, if you are going to die, please go sit by someone else."

"This is incredible," Rose hurried the rest of the way to the table and took a seat.

"I love coming to them, too," Karli said, leaning toward Rose as she seated herself. "I remember my first time, I thought it was a dream. But Jeselle actually has a purpose for it. They know she wouldn't invite you if you weren't important."

"That's true," an older woman sitting next to Jeselle agreed, "but it does make me feel important too." The woman giggled.

"I am really nervous, like what if I put my fork back in the wrong place or something?" Rose said as she lightly touched the fork on the table in front of her, and it made Jeselle smile.

"Here is a quick lesson for you," Jeselle said, "My mother–"

"God rest her soul," the woman sitting next to Jeselle said.

Jeselle looked at the woman and smiled again. Then she lifted a fork and shifted her attention back to Rose, "My mother told me something growing up that I have never forgotten. You won't either."

"Dear heavens, couldn't you have given her this lesson at the office?" Dennis said condescendingly which, Jeselle noticed, caused Rose's head to fall in embarrassment.

"Pick your head up, Rose," Jeselle barked. Rose lifted her head. "Do not listen to him," Jeselle used her calm voice, "He doesn't know about real people, he's been spoon fed his entire life. Don't let people like Dennis, here," she put a hand on his leg under the table and squeezed, "make you feel any less important than they are. Matter of fact, I'd say you are more important than those people." Jeselle squeezed harder.

Rose's eyes widened and she looked from Jeselle to Dennis and back again.

The lady sitting next to Jeselle laughed under her breath. Rose looked over at Karli, who wore a big smile on her face.

"Now, as I was saying, here is a basic lesson you'll never forget. How many letters in the word left?"

"Fo- four," Rose replied hesitantly.

"How many letters in fork?" Jeselle lifted the hand that held the fork slightly higher in the air.

"Four," Rose replied more confidently.

"So, your fork goes to the left of the plate." Jeselle placed the fork back to the left of her plate. "Now, how many letters in the word right?" Again, she lifted her hand, this time her right one.

"Five."

"And how many in the word knife?" she lifted the spoon and knife together.

"Five."

"And how many in spoon?"

"Five."

Then your knife and spoon go to the right side of the plate. Jeselle set them back down. "In alphabetical order. Fork, knife, spoon." Jeselle touched each one slightly as she named it. She perceived the moment that Rose grasped the information and she relaxed.

"That's it? It's that easy?"

"Well, for the basics, but before long I'll have you able to set an eighteen-course dinner with ease." Jeselle looked pointedly at Rose, "Anything that makes you feel uncomfortable, or feel like you don't fit in, is simply information and *that* you can learn. The more information you learn, the more you will be tempted to be like Dennis here. Don't, it's a trap. If someone is deliberately trying to make you feel like you don't fit in," she looked over at Dennis, "Well, that is simply arrogance." Jeselle turned to Rose again, "And arrogance can be taken down, with only one piece of information. Do you understand, Rose?"

"I do. Thank you."

The best part of the evening, Jeselle thought, was detecting that Rose really did understand.

The older woman next to Jeselle put her hand across the table, "I am Isabel."

"I'm Rose," she put her hand out to meet with the woman's. "I'm new. I don't really know the name of my position yet, but I'm just happy to be here."

"I am always happy to be here. I'm in housekeeping."

Rose looked to Jeselle in surprise. Then, they both smiled at one another.

"I see Cindy and Tracy have an open space," Camilla stated rather arrogantly, "I may go sit with them."

Jeselle took a small sip of water, "Camilla?"

"Yes?" Camilla answered.

"Do you like your new job at *E. Rindre*?"

"I do, so far," she answered.

"Good. Did Briggs International offer you a job when you were at your lowest?"

"No," Camilla was instantly humiliated.

"Did sweet brother here offer you one at Stryker?"

Camilla shifted her gaze to Dennis, "No."

Jeselle looked toward Cindy and Tracy's table, "That table is the Briggs International Steel table, Stryker Steel doesn't have a table, this table is the *E. Rindre's* table. Where do you prefer to sit?"

Camilla shrank down into her seat just as Rose started to stand and everyone turned to her. "Oh, I have to use the bathroom," Rose stated rather loudly. Suddenly, Camilla felt better about herself and sat straighter.

Jeselle watched the coarse, sheer, bright pink fabric as it bounced its way through the large room. She smiled every time someone gasped in horror as Rose passed their table.

Dennis leaned into Jeselle's personal space, something he was notorious for doing, since his silver spoon made him feel he owned all the space he wanted, "I'm going to go poke old man Briggs and his pathetic son a bit more." Dennis closed the extra few inches between them and kissed her quickly on the cheek.

"Have fun," Jeselle said.

"So, Camilla, how is the job, really? Are you

enjoying it?" Isabel asked.

"Oh, you know, it's only been a few days, but can one really enjoy working?" she laughed facetiously, "But when one doesn't have a choice; one must do what one must."

"Camilla, it's surprising you have so much self-importance left." Jeselle took another sip of her water.

The instrumental music started to fade, the lights around the tables dimmed, and the stage lights went up.

"Welcome to the annual Louisiana Business Gala. This year I am honored to introduce the recipient of the Business Person of the Year for the third year in a row," The governor started. "After turning nineteen and in her sophomore year of college, Jeselle Parsons started her climb from a copy assistant at Vinton Publishing and Media to senior editor in only two years. After graduating, she went to work full time, and when owner, Mason Vinton decided to go into semi-retirement he helped Jeselle start her parent company, *E. Rindre Corp.* The first company she acquired was his and, with his approval, of course, she renamed the publishing company *Mind.E Publishing & Media.* Mason remained on as a consultant until his death."

"It's easy to recognize one of Jeselle's subsidiary businesses because of the silent signature 'dot-capital-E' following each name. She stated in an interview given in 2013 to *People* magazine that naming her businesses with the capital E was something she uses in honor of her parents. Throughout the years, Jeselle has acquired several other failing companies from the brink of ruin through her investment firm *Tag.E Investments* and developed them all into powerhouses for Louisiana: all of them renamed and rebranded."

"Through *Husk.E Construction* Jeselle has restored several historical buildings, bringing them back to their glory days and getting them listed on the national registry of historical sites." The governor continued, "She has made a name for herself through the conservation of materials by purchasing other buildings in disrepair and reclaiming as much of the original materials as she could or donating them to non-profits in an effort to reuse and recycle." He paused and took a deep breath. "Many know of her tragic past and admire her for using her resources in forming the non-profit *Geno Prett.E Suicide Alliance*, which funds suicide hotlines and counseling throughout the world."

"In a brilliant public relations campaign to revamp downtown, Jeselle bought two buildings on each side of an alleyway, at the time nicknamed 'Prostitution Way.' She was driven to do so because of a tragic story that had stayed with her since she was a child. In 2002 Trudy Michaels, who was a certified nurse's assistant at a local hospital, and thought to have been a prostitute in the evenings to help with the expenses of raising her three small children and putting herself through nursing school, was murdered in the alley. Ms. Parsons has stated over the years that it was that incident, at the age of fourteen, which caused her to want to work to help others. Once she was able, she bought the two buildings, hence the alley between them. She converted the buildings into centers for education and financial freedom for former prostitutes, naming it *Haevn.E Foundation*."

"In the alley itself, she paid to convert it into a small park and commissioned a large mural by a street artist with the likeness of the woman in it as well as other citizens. One of those citizens is our very own, Dennis Stryker of Stryker Steel Corp." the governor pointed towards Dennis, who had returned to his seat next to Jeselle, "Another is Mason Vinton, the man that gave Jeselle that first opportunity."

Jeselle looked over at Dennis. He smiled warmly and grabbed her hand. She knew how proud he was to be one of the citizens on the mural.

"Her own office building is located only blocks away from that park, and it's said you can frequently find her there having lunch. Jeselle now owns several additional prosperous businesses and has recently opened *Lett.E Learning Center*, which provides free, online career diplomas and certifications from virtual classes and virtual assignments to all people. She is far ahead of her time and has helped the city of Baton Rouge and the State of Louisiana through her enormous growth. Everyone join hands with me to welcome the Louisiana Business Person of the Year, Ms. Jeselle Parsons."

STOP ME

Dennis stood to hug her and then escorted Jeselle to the stage. She shook hands with the governor before taking her place at the microphone. She allowed the crowd to clap as she looked over the sea of people who filled the room. In the hundreds of faces she took note of the few who didn't clap or smile. Her 'frenemies,' Dennis liked to call them. Then she saw some of the others, the fakers like she, who smiled and clapped, but didn't mean it. Then her gaze rested upon Dennis.

"Thank you," she gracefully motioned for everyone to sit. "Thank you, everyone," Jeselle said as she waited for the crowd to take their seats. She smiled and continued, "No one ever makes it on their own. I am incredibly honored to be here, yet I also have to share that honor with a few of the people who helped pave the way. Of course, always, first and foremost my parents, Sherrill and Jessica Parsons. They taught me that remorse can be stifling," then she laughed and joked, "so I learned not to have much of it." The crowd laughed along with Jeselle, with the exception of a few.

Dennis didn't laugh.

"Seriously though, this award is shared with my parents, because they were amazing. My dad taught me a lot about standing up for the truth, no matter the consequences. My mom, taught me about having the strength to start over. They both taught me about working hard and taking care of others. I also share this award with Mason Vinton, for giving me a chance I didn't deserve and teaching me why all positions in life are valuable. Lastly, to Dennis Stryker," Jeselle pointed toward Dennis, "who continues to be my biggest fan, thank you." Jeselle used both of her hands to blow him a kiss and was inwardly amused by the tight smile that suddenly appeared on his face.

"I humbly accept this honor and hope to live up to the standards it represents." Jeselle received a standing ovation.

Throughout the rest of the dinner Dennis sulked like a child. He ate in silence and barely mingled. When people stopped by the table to congratulate Jeselle, Dennis would take another bite of food and feign not being able to talk. Only after her driver had shut them in the backseat to leave did Dennis say anything.

"My God, Jeselle! You made me sound like a damn puppy," he morphed his voice into a sweet, soft, feminine drawl, "I'd like to thank my biggest fan for his adoring worship." Then his sneer returned, "I am Dennis Stryker, for God's sakes!"

"You sound more like a scolded child to me."

"Is this payback for my putting down on that new pipsqueak you hired? Dear God Jeselle, that dress."

"What would you have rathered I'd said?"

"Oh, I don't know how about 'to my best friend for his strength.' Or 'to the Stryker family, for getting me where I am today!' Thankfully Dad wasn't there to witness it."

"Dennis," Jeselle laughed nonchalantly, "are

you seriously saying I should attribute Theodore for where I am now? For which part? The putting the house in my mother's name out of guilt after dad died? For giving mom a job where she worked her fingers to the bone scrubbing Stryker company toilets?" Jeselle laughed again, this time in amusement, "Or do you think I owe your father for my good grades? Do I then owe him for Mason Vinton giving me the job? Oh, wait, I know, I should've thanked him for—"

"You have made your point," Dennis said dryly.

"Oh, dear, dear, Dennis, I don't think I have. Thank him … oh I don't know, maybe for the cover-up?"

"Stop it, Jeselle," Dennis looked to the driver and then back at her.

"Are you not my biggest fan?" she smiled as she reached over and placed her hand over his, "You tell me that so often. How proud you are of me dragging myself up by the proverbial bootstraps and clawing my way to the top? Is that not the accolades you feed me? Are they untrue then?" she waved her hand as if to dismiss him, "Dennis, your pride is boundless. Sometimes, I wonder if you only keep me around to use for your evil intentions."

"Of course I am," his mood changed quickly, he winked, "your most loyal fan that is. Just…just don't make me sound like a pubescent boy ogling the high school cheerleader next time, will you?"

"Then stop ogling," she smiled adoringly, which in turn made him smile. "Besides, in about an hour when the news airs, you'll be Man of the Hour, the true Powerhouse."

He smiled wide then, "I will, won't I?"

"Yes, and my fifteen minutes of fame will be over," Jeselle turned to look out the window as they continued driving through the city streets.

In about an hour the wheels would start turning.

Finally.

CHAPTER 7

PRESENT

"True enemies aren't always the ones who
hate each other."
-Elie Wiesel

"Did you see that girl's dress?" Cindy leaned against Tracy's shoulder as he stared at the buildings passing quickly through the window of the limousine.

He nodded.

"I think Jeselle purposefully made her wear it to keep the attention on her table all night," Cindy added.

"It worked. Personally, I think all eyes should've been on you. You are always the tastiest piece in a room."

"Thank you," Cindy pouted. "I spent ten

thousand dollars on this dress and was outdone by a ten-dollar piece of pink polyester netting."

"Did you see how smug Dennis was?" Tracy's tone shifted to angry.

"He's always that way, exactly like his dad," she affirmed. "What were you and Brantley in such a heated discussion over earlier?"

"Nothing that can't be managed," Tracy replied.

"But everything is okay?"

He shrugged her off his shoulder and turned toward her in frustration, "You'll still be able to afford to shop, if that's what you are asking Cindy. I swear."

"So, it *is* money?"

"Yes, like I said it's nothing to worry about. I sold some stocks, but several other shareholders sold some also within the past few weeks. I hadn't known that or I wouldn't have done it."

"You sold some of *our stocks*? In Briggs?"

"Not our stocks, Love, my stocks," Tracy said with indifference. "You have never earned a penny in your life. I'd be happy if you'd at least give me a child."

She took the blow like it had been a physical one.

"Don't start crying. It's pathetic."

Tracy's phone rang and he answered it.

"Wait, what? Are you sure?" Tracy sat upright in the seat of the car. This time it looked as if Tracy had taken the blow. His face turned pale and he downed the rest of his scotch. "Dad, that can't be true. How did this happen?"

"What?" Cindy whispered, "*What?*"

"Dad, I, yes sir. I am, sorry. Yes sir. I'll get them back, yes, sir." Tracy clicked to end the call and turned to stare back out of the window.

Cindy knew not to ask anything else.

***

"Todd, definitely not true. I just left the gala. Tracy and Dennis were talking like they always have," Camilla spoke into the air of her car.

"It broke on the evening news a few seconds ago. Hostile takeover is what they said, but you know the news: anything to get headlines. I called William before you and he said they probably bought a majority voting shares."

"They? You mean Father, too?"

Todd laughed, "No, get this, Jeselle bought stocks, under her investment company, Tag.E. So Jeselle and Dennis now own between them a majority of Briggs International Steel. Isn't that hilarious?"

"I guess…"

"It's definitely your old man Theo pushing this one. He's wanted to get ahold of those shares for years."

Camilla took a deep breath, "Cindy's had her nose in the air toward me since Rick kicked me out."

"She always was the worst. It always made her so sexy."

"You only want to be the one to help her pick up all the little pieces when Tracy finally gets caught doing one of his many illegal activities and goes off to prison," Camilla laughed.

"Sounds like a plan."

"You always were so jealous of them. That why you've been married three times, Todd? Can't find anyone to replace Cindy?"

"It's an honest question, and who am I kidding, yes," he stated bluntly and they both laughed again. "I hope he doesn't break anything surgery can't fix."

"That's terrible," Camilla said, but her words contained a hint of amusement.

"How's life with Jeselle?"

"Great, she's wonderful. Gave me sole reign over events and I have a full staff."

"Wow, that was nice."

"I'm not going to lie, I was worried asking her, pride more than anything else, but Dennis said she would help me and he was right."

"Still, can't repay nearly what you sunk into Rick's campaign over the years."

Camilla took the right turn that led to her new apartment building. "I sunk my entire inheritance into it. But a job's a job and she's letting me use one of the corporate apartments and it's really nice so at least I don't feel like I'm poor."

"Are you … poor?"

"Todd, you know I am. The way the gossip in this city works, I'm surprised there isn't a detailed list posted on a website somewhere of all he took from me."

"Well, at least he let you take your personal belongings. You could always sell a pair of your Manolo's. With such a tight prenup I'm surprised you were left with the Valentino on your back."

"You know he fabricated that prenup, Todd. All of my money: gone. I only hope you can help me prove it like you promised."

"Promise is a strong word, sweet, entitled Cam. I already told you I would take your case, but I can't do it for free."

"I don't have a lot now, but I told you when we win, I'll pay you," she said nonchalantly. "You are one of the best. I need your ruthlessness. You've seen all those records I gave you of him withdrawing from my inheritance!"

"Without your knowledge?"

"Well, let's say, without my signature."

"That'll do for now, but you'd better be ready to back that up. I love ya, Cam and you know that, but I can't wait in hopes of winning. We may not. I do know one way you can start payback though."

"I'll do whatever I need to, to hang Rick out to dry," Camilla said.

"Good, let's start with … I don't have a wife at the moment."

Camilla parked her car and left the motor running so as not to cut off the call. "You want me to be your wife?" Camilla laughed, but inwardly she was flattered. "I'm barely divorced."

"No, Camilla," he said bluntly, "I've learned

being an over-priced, highly-sought, oh what was your wording… 'ruthless' attorney keeps me too busy to maintain a wife, but I do need some of the perks having one brings."

"Like what? Managing your affairs for you? I already have a job," Camilla thought more on it, "but, if the pay is substantially more I would consider –"

He laughed, "Think, more domestically," he waited for her to get it.

"Todd Parrish, are you… are you asking me to sleep with you?"

"It's not like we haven't had sex before," he said as he yawned.

"That was high school," the hurt came through in her voice, "I needed you."

"Yes, poor us, me in love with Cindy and you in love with Tracy. Aren't we a pair? So, the way I see it, you need me again."

"Todd, are you joking?" she asked softly, the humiliation spreading through her bones.

"No, Camilla. I am most certainly not."

"I'm…I'm not a prostitute," indignance pouring through her words.

"Are you not? Seems you've been selling yourself for years, only this time, you'll get something out of the deal. I'm not as boring as Rick," he laughed. "and if I'm as good as I think I am, both in and out of bed, you'll get to stick it to him better than he ever did to you. It's simple, you need me and I need you. See you soon, Cam."

STOP ME

He disconnected the call.

Camilla turned off her car, sat there and cried.

*** *** ***

Todd looked at the phone in his hand for a few minutes. The picture for the contact was an older one, but Camilla had somehow managed to keep her looks through the years. He knew he may have had a fixation on Cindy, likely because she mercilessly teased him in high school and he never actually got her into bed, but it was Camilla he truly yearned for through the years. He never could pinpoint if he loved her or if it was because she was so good in bed, but being Theodore Stryker's daughter certainly didn't hurt.

When she first married that douchebag DA, the whole group knew why, she was a pawn in her father's game. A game Theodore intended to win for himself, not any of his family. Theodore Stryker sold his own daughter to ensure that his name stayed clear of blemish. The simple fact that it helped them in the process didn't matter. Todd had wondered often when they were younger if Theodore was even aware that he had a daughter, because all he ever talked about was his son. His pride and joy. And no matter what the function was, he always toasted to Dennis.

Every country club function, Dennis.

Every company party, Dennis.

Every family barbeque, Dennis.

Every big birthday bash, Dennis, no matter whose birthday it was.

Dennis, Dennis, Dennis, it was always about Dennis.

When Todd became a successful attorney, Theodore decided he was again worthy to be included on invitation lists. Todd resented that, considering his parents were quite as wealthy and just as prominent in the city as the old man was when they were alive. Todd also thought back often to when his father had passed, not even two full years after his mother. Todd stood to inherit everything. He was finally on top. Then, the week after the funeral, Theodore announced Dennis would take the reins of Stryker Steel.

It was all about Dennis, and Theodore couldn't stand to see one of his son's peers rise above him in any way. The very day probate was settled and everything signed into Todd's name, was suspiciously the same day Dennis Stryker was officially announced as head of Stryker Steel.

Todd smiled, he knew in the future he would pick up all the pieces in poor little Camilla's life and earn enough of her trust to marry. He'd make a decent husband. She would have all the money her heart desired. The clout she was raised to need. And then Todd, being the savvy attorney he is, would end up part owner of the Stryker family fortune.

And if the Gods were generous, he'd end up with much, much more than Dennis.

CHAPTER 8

PRESENT

"When we live at each other's mercy, we
had better learn to be merciful."
-William Coffin

Cindy sat up in the bed and looked around her room through the small openings of her swollen eyelids. She leaned forward to pick up her phone to check the time, knowing things were going to get bad today.

Eleven thirty already, she thought as she winced from the pain. Then she replayed the night before and remembered why. Brantley had been waiting for them when they got home. He'd called Tracy in the limo as soon as he found out it was Dennis and Jeselle who had acquired the stocks. Tracy assured his dad that he'd get them back somehow, but

Brantley knew better than to trust his son.

His pathetic son, as he'd called him many times throughout the night. After Brantley finally berated his son enough for his satisfaction, and they'd hatched a plan, he left.

Then it was her turn to be berated. Difference was, Tracy didn't only use his voice, he used his fists.

She remembered several key points that the Brantley Briggs had made. Exclamations like 'We're through!' and 'I'm mortgaged up to my ass!' Briggs, Sr. said the weak link was Jeselle, get to her. Otherwise they were dead in the water. Tracy had promised.

Maybe Tracy would let her go to the doctor this morning. She touched her swollen face. He likely wouldn't. If only she could get away. When she had talked to Camilla at the Gala the night before, Camilla said she'd gotten an upscale four bedroom condo in the city and would love to have her over soon. Maybe an old-fashioned slumber party, Camilla had said.

Cindy wondered how Camilla could afford such an extravagant place given all the rumors, but obviously Camilla hadn't lost as much in the divorce as the rumors said she had. *Maybe a roommate for a bit?* Cindy almost said, but hadn't dared. At least Tracy wasn't around for that conversation, so she could hide out with Camilla for a few days and he'd never suspect it. She knew Camilla wouldn't turn her away.

STOP ME

Cindy moved slowly, wincing again at the pain in her side. She got to her closet and slid one of the large doors open. She walked slowly to the back, past all of her designer clothes, shoes, and stopped in front of the wall of purses. She bent slightly, took in a deep breath, and pulled an oversized Prada Vitello Daino tote from the back of one of the shelves. It had her emergency kit in it. The one she'd packed and unpacked so many times throughout the years. If she and Tracy still shared a room, she'd never have been able to keep it ready.

She crept her way through the hallway. She knew the tenth step down the staircase creaked, and the fourteenth one snapped. The tenth one was what happened to wood after it settled. The fourteenth one was what happened after her head was planted in it two years before. She wanted to have it fixed, but Tracy thought it was a good reminder to them both of what happens to a disobedient wife.

She shuttered in pain as she reached the bottom. Cindy took a slow, deep breath. She waited and listened, wanting to hear something. If she heard Tracy in the study, then she was free. If not, maybe he went out or was still in bed.

She decided to walk normal, well, normal for having been chastised the night before.

Head down, walk slow.

The slow part would be easy since she probably had a broken rib or two. She checked her phone one last time to be sure it was on silent, then she made her way to the back of the large mansion.

It was eerily quiet. Usually he would send the staff home with pay after one of their fights, but the house was never this quiet.

Maybe her senses were heightened in accordance with her fear.

* * *

Sifting through the pile on his secretary's desk, William Reims grew frustrated. He knew it was there somewhere. He lifted the first pile of papers and flipped through them quickly, then the second pile. He wondered often why he even kept her, then he thought about all of those quick lunches she took in his office. Still, he needed her to at least attempt to be organized.

The door opened and Desiree walked in.

"Will, what are you doing?"

"I can't find the-" he looked up at her and momentarily forgot what he was saying, She had a low cut shirt on and her breasts were pushed up so high he was surprised her chin wasn't resting on them. Her skirt seemed higher than normal also. She walked around him and leaned over the desk in front of him. He slipped his hand under the fabric.

"No, undies," he commented, the words came out raspy.

Desiree looked back over her shoulder at him and smiled, "Just for you, Will."

The excitement shot through him. He unzipped

his trousers and vigorously took what she offered.

It was times like this that he wished the guys could see. Maybe, he'd tape it one day and send them a clip. He made sure they always saw him in public with the next model or debutant, but to be getting it at the office any time he wanted, that would make them all bow down in worship. William stood. Desiree adjusted her skirt and turned toward him.

"What were you looking for?"

He broke out of his daze, "I need the stock breakdown Jeselle sent over. I thought it was on my desk, but I can't find it."

"It was," she paused and tapped her chin with a slender, perfectly manicured nail, "maybe it got thrown away?"

He turned and stormed back into his office.

He needed to find that breakdown for Brantley Briggs or he was going to be toast by evening. When Brantley had called him the night before at home right after the news aired, William answered, as always. But something in Brantley's voice startled him.

Desperation.

William had never heard that sound in the old man's voice before.

"You listen to me, William, I need to know who sold their stocks to them. I want the name of who sold their stocks, and I want to know exactly how much Dennis owns and how much Jeselle owns. I can deal with Jeselle. She's been more trouble than her life is worth. I've got a plan for her, but if Dennis owns more than me, I won't survive it. Do you hear me?"

"Yes, I'm, I'm shocked. How did that happen?"

"I've got a stupid, useless son who has a high maintenance wife, for one. Thorns in my side, the both of them. I need to know who else sold. I don't know…get me those numbers! I need them by noon."

When the call had ended William found he couldn't go to sleep. He owed Brantley Briggs, and his debt had come due.

He had quickly texted: **Dennis: hey man, caught the news. stellar move. let me know if I can move anything into your portfolio. you know how much I'd love to stick the old goat. you are my hero.**

Immediately, Dennis responded: **He deserves it. Can't wipe the smile off dads face. Having more money than old prick briggs has been his dream since the split.**

William had waited a few minutes to respond: **about time someone did it. you know me, got to know, how much more DO you have?**

Dennis: **I'll get the numbers dropped off tomorrow. Not in text. Let's say much more.**

After William read Dennis's text, he texted Todd: **did you see the news-dennis stuck it to tracy. owns voting majority in briggs now. Gonna be a good day.**

Now, in his office, William had to find that breakdown Jeselle had delivered, or it wasn't going to be a good day after all. He knew he couldn't ask Jeselle for it again, too obvious.

It had to be there somewhere.

STOP ME

* * *

Her own office was one of Jeselle's crowning achievements.

The size alone enabled it to house so many neat little pats on the back to herself. Like the beautiful huge chunk of plaster moulding from the old police station that sat dutifully under her matte glass top table. She still reveled in the satisfaction she got from trading the city a much larger, newer building for the old run down station. For the better of the city, of course.

The wall sconces that adorned the sitting area by the sofas, she had personally ripped from the historic walls of the old courthouse and DA's office. Again, in trade for the betterment of the city.

They added more ambiance than anyone who sat around them would ever know.

Tree branches, treated to preserve their truths, hung from the ceiling here and there. Tassels of frayed rope were encompassed around paintings, curtains, and pillows. It looked as though she were following the trendy, rustic interior design that had started to hit the elite. Only she didn't care about keeping up with the latest anything. She had those pulled from the same place she had the tree limbs. Although no one else really knew their significance, she did. It thrilled her to watch Dennis move a pillow every time he sat on an office sofa or chair. Sometimes, he even paused to admire one of the handmade satin pillows with the wildly rustic tassels dangling about. He appreciated how expensive they must've been.

To her, their presence was actually priceless.

At one time, she thought that maybe her office wasn't the place for such things, that maybe she should sprinkle them around the rest of her buildings. But, no, she realized the moment the mirrors took on their significance, so did all the successes. That was what she had spread around her office, bits of all her successes.

No matter which old decrepit piece of this city's history she could grab, she did and made a fortune doing it. Euphoric wasn't even a strong enough word to describe the feeling she had when she walked into her office and saw the products of her own achievements. In taking down building after building, everyone hailed her as a saint for restoring or repurposing, but these were simply personal victories. They weren't her favorite victories, only her favorite so far.

Soon, she thought.

"Ms. Parsons, Dennis is at main lobby reception demanding to see you."

Jeselle laughed remembering that she had last given the order the day before that he wasn't to make it past the main lobby. "Karli, it's okay, he can come up again."

"I'll let them know."

Jeselle hung up the phone and leaned back in her chair. She was remembering several years before when Dennis had asked to get permission to go all the way up to the twelfth floor, her floor, because he was humiliated having to stop on the fifth, like so many others. He was better than everyone else, she recalled him saying. He had also mentioned it in passing through the years. He wondered when he'd ever get a full pass straight to her.

His exact words not so long ago were, *"Isabel, a maid, has access up there and I don't. It's downright chastening."*

Jeselle smiled again picturing his face at her response, *"Dennis, she works for me. If you want to come work for me, I'll give you access to my floor."*

After having been held at the main lobby reception last night, she doubted he'd complain again about only making it to the fifth floor.

Karli opened the door and escorted Dennis in.

"I'm growing weary of this, Jeselle. I am on cloud nine this morning only to come here and be treated like a nobody."

Jeselle rose from her desk and went over to hug him, "I know, dear," she whispered in his ear, "I am sorry. It was awful of me to forget. It won't happen again."

"Why are you smiling?" he whispered back.

"How do you know I am?"

"I can feel the smile on my cheek, sweet Jeselle," his whisper turned coarse.

"There, this should heal it," she turned her face slowly and kissed his cheek softly.

Dennis quickly moved so that their lips touched

briefly before she pulled away.

"Why are you here?" she asked making her way over to one of the sofas.

"I came to gloat of course," he laughed. "No, seriously, I came to talk about the next step. Dad was so proud. He has been on the phone all morning talking to everyone about how I put the screws to Brantley."

"Now, Dennis," she mockingly chastised him, "is that any way to talk about your uncle?"

"That man hasn't been my uncle since the day he screwed over my mother."

"True, I agree."

"I heard Dad telling Mother that her brother was now paying the piper thanks to their brilliant son." Dennis proudly straightened his tie.

"How is your mom?"

"She doesn't really get out of bed much anymore, you know that. I think that's why it was so important to get back at Brantley, you know? She was so crushed, Jeselle."

"I remember her crying the day she found out about it. It still haunts me."

"Me as well, Jeselle. Worst part is, I'm worried that retribution won't be enough to heal her. Thank God you were there that day. I don't know what I would've done without you," just then Dennis hopped a bit closer on the sofa toward her, "but not anymore. Soon, I will have ruined Briggs International Steel. I'll have run it into the ground and absorbed all of its assets for pennies. Then, maybe I'll convince you to marry me," his upper-class eyebrows waggled.

"No, you won't, Dennis."

"At least give me some hope," he said seriously.

"Dennis, that day, at your house, do you remember what your dad said to me?"

"No."

"He said, 'You need to leave, young lady, this is a family matter.' "

"Oh right, of course, it was the first time I'd ever talked back to my dad. What of it?"

"When you said, 'Don't you ever talk to her that way again. She is family.' I knew. I knew that day I had you on my side."

"Not to mention the house," he reminded her.

"Yes, the house, too."

"Jeselle, I've paid my penance. I wish I could change the past, but I can't. That first day we met, even you being twelve, I knew it was you. I am on your side, Jeselle. I always have been."

"No, Dennis, not always."

"You know…I always felt so weak compared to Tracy. Not anymore. We are now co-owners of Briggs International Steel. Together we are going to conquer the world. You must leave the rest behind. For us."

"Yes, Dennis, if I must," she dutifully replied.

"Thank you."

She saw the victory in his expression. He must feel like a true king today, having conquered everything.

CHAPTER 9

PAST

"It's humbling to start fresh. It takes a lot of courage. But it can be reinvigorating."
-Jennifer Ritchie Payette

"Hey, you're new," the cute guy moved next to Jeselle in the hall.

"Yes," she answered sweetly.

"Tracy was right, you are cute."

"Th- Thank you," Jeselle blushed slightly.

"Is it true you're from California? Know any famous people? I heard you can walk down the street and see famous people hanging around. Is that true?"

Jeselle laughed slightly, "I don't know, I think that's probably more around LA. We lived in Bakersfield. My dad's company got bought out and he was transferred here. I'm maybe not as exciting as the rumors say."

"Oh, okay. Makes sense." The boy put his hand in front of her, "I'm Dennis. I've already decided to be your best friend," he winked.

Jeselle thought what her mom said was true. This could be a new start for her. A new adventure. She didn't have a choice anyway. She had hated the idea when they first broke the news to her. She had friends, good ones that she hadn't wanted to leave.

She took Dennis's hand and he squeezed it slightly.

"Your hands are so soft," he said.

She blushed.

He immediately loved that about her, sweet and genuine.

Every day that week, Dennis found her at lunch and sat with her. She had worried she wouldn't make new friends, especially in the middle of a school year, but Dennis made it easy to relax. He was confident, which wasn't like the other boys she knew from Bakersfield. Jeselle found it comforting, somehow.

She'd talked to her best friend, Mariah, from Bakersfield every night, and it made moving seem less miserable.

At school on Friday, Dennis brought along a few others and introduced her.

"Jess, this is Tracy. He's my best friend and cousin. His dad and my mother are brother-sister."

Jeselle went to shake his hand, he looked at it

and laughed, "Yeah, hey."

She quickly dropped her hand.

"Don't worry about him, he's the mean one." Dennis shoved Tracy. "This is Cindy, she is Tracy's girlfriend."

Jeselle looked at the girl standing next to Tracy and beheld one of the most beautiful beings she'd ever seen. "Hi, I'm Jess," she lifted her hand to wave this time.

"Lame. I kinda already heard your name, but cool."

Jeselle realized they'd heard it when Dennis first introduced her. Embarrassed she blushed, which made Dennis smile. Soon, another girl stepped forward and pointed to Cindy, "And she's the mean one, too. They make the perfect couple. I'm Camilla," the fair-haired girl smiled at Jeselle, "I'm Dennis's sister."

"And this," Dennis continued, "is Melanie."

"Hi," Jeselle said.

"Hey." Jeselle mostly noticed the large volume of freckles the girl had on her face. They were cute with the girls' orangy-red hair.

Dennis sat next to Jeselle and put his arm around her, "Todd and William have next lunch shift, but I'll introduce you to them this weekend. We are all going to the river. Want to join?"

"Sure, I mean, I have to ask my parents, but I'm sure I can. As long as they meet whoever's parents are driving it should be okay."

Tracy laughed, "Great, a fresh one." Cindy

punched him in the arm, but not very hard Jeselle noticed.

Jeselle looked at Dennis in question.

"The river is around the back of the subdivision," he shook his head and smiled, "We all walk there. Don't worry, you'll get it." She relaxed in Dennis's arm.

That afternoon Dennis met Jeselle in the parking lot. He stood with her until her mom drove up.

"That's my mom," Jeselle said.

When the car stopped in front of them, he leaned over and opened the door for her.

"Hi," he lifted a hand, "Mrs. Parsons, I'm Dennis Stryker, good to meet you."

"Stryker?" her mother questioned, "Any relation to the owners of Stryker Steel?"

"Yep," he smiled wide, "That's my dad." Dennis looked at Jeselle and winked.

"Well, Dennis, it is certainly good to meet you. Jeselle's dad works at Stryker."

"So, Jess," he smiled more confidently, which Jeselle would've denied was possible only a few seconds earlier, "you are already part of the Stryker family."

As they drove away her mom said, "He's cute."

"Yes he is. So cute."

"See, Jessie, I told you it would be okay."

Jeselle couldn't think about anything else for the rest of the day. None of the boys at her old school ever looked at her that way. She fell asleep thinking of the moment Dennis slid his arm around her. It was almost as if he was telling everybody that she was his.

After only a week, she certainly felt like she was.

***

"Jeselle, telephone!" her mom's voice extended up the stairs.

The house was much larger than their old one. It was a corporate house, one of several that belonged to Stryker. "Made it much easier to move," she remembered her mom saying. It was in an exclusive neighborhood, 'old Baton Rouge money' the lady at the supermarket had said to her mom one day.

"Be careful, those old Baton Rouge money people stick together," the cashier said.

"Well, we don't plan on infiltrating anywhere we don't belong," her mother replied.

"If you livin' there, you already have, honey. Keep watch at your back."

Her mother didn't pay it another thought.

"Okay!" Jeselle yelled back down the stairs, "I'll take it up here!"

Jeselle ran to the phone expecting it to be her best friend, Mariah.

"Hey!" she answered excitedly.

"Well, good morning gorgeous," the deep voice replied.

She knew immediately it was Dennis. "Hey."

"Are you ready for the river?"

"Oh, I didn't ask. I forgot. I'm sorry."

"Well, go ask now, I'll wait."

"Okay, hold on," Jeselle placed the phone down and ran as fast as she could down the stairs and through the kitchen until she found her mom and dad sitting on the large back patio.

She stopped in front of her mom and bent forward to catch her breath.

"Goodness, Jessie, are you okay?" her mom asked.

"Yes, oh, hold," she put her hand up for a second. "That's Dennis," she started jumping a bit, "he wanted to know if I can go to the river with some friends. And before you say no," she rushed out, "the river is a small one at the back of the subdivision. They all walk there."

"I don't know," her mom said wearily, "it's a pretty big subdivision. Sherrill, what do you think?"

"This is the Stryker boy?"

"Yes!" Jeselle answered.

"I guess, if it's him. I know where to find him if you're out too late anyway," her dad chuckled.

"Oh, thank you! Thank you!" she hugged both her mom and dad and ran back up the stairs to tell Dennis she could go.

Twenty minutes later Dennis had formally met her mom and dad. He shook her dad's hand like a man, then they left.

"It's not too far," he reached over as they were walking and took Jeselle's hand in his. She smiled and felt it all the way down deep in her body. It seemed to kick start her nervous system.

"The other guys will be there, William and Todd. We're really only a bunch of messed up kids," he laughed then continued, "Todd thinks he's in love with Cindy, which she seems to like. I don't know if you remember, but Cindy is Tracy's girlfriend. She kisses Tracy sometimes and looks at Todd while she does it. She's just playing with him though."

"That's sad."

"Not really, Todd and Camilla hook up every now and then. Tracy thinks Camilla has a crush on him, but nobody else thinks so. Everybody thinks he's saying that to get back at Cindy."

"You mean, like have sex?" Jeselle asked.

Dennis laughed, "Yeah."

"Seems kind of young," Jeselle felt awkward.

"It's not," Dennis said matter-of-factly.

"Isn't Camilla your sister?"

"Yes, she is, why?" he seemed unconcerned.

"You don't mind that one of your friends sleeps with your sister?"

"No, it's her choice. I don't care."

"They, I mean, I hate asking, but Tracy doesn't care that Todd likes Cindy?"

"Oh no, Tracy loves it because he can lord it over Todd. Tracy gets off on it. Matter of fact, every time he and Cindy break up, almost every few weeks, Cindy flirts with Todd. Soon as Todd shows her any attention in return, Tracy gets jealous and begs Cindy back."

"That is sad."

"No, it's kind of funny, to be honest. Once you're around them for a while you'll start thinking it's funny too. Now, on to William. We all think William is a flaming gay. He swears he isn't, but he is never interested in any girls. We gave him the chance to sleep with Belinda at the beginning of this year, she's the town tramp," he leaned closer to Jeselle and tapped his shoulder into hers, "stay clear of her for sure. Any way, he didn't."

"That's ... that's..."

"I know, but hey, what can you do, some people think they are gay."

Jeselle stopped which caused Dennis to stop as well, "I'm not ... that's not why I was...not sad that he is gay, sad that he has friends that feel that way about him."

"Oh, Jess, you are too sweet. Do you think people are 'born that way?' "

"I think that's beside the point. I think we ought to care for people for being people, not for being straight or a virgin. Love them because they are people."

"Wait," he laughed slightly as he got closer, "are you defending Belinda? Jess, she sleeps around."

"What does your sister do?" Jeselle saw the realization dawn on his face.

"That's ... different, she only sleeps with Todd," he reasoned, "But Belinda, she sleeps with anybody, especially other girls' boyfriends? She's total trash," he tried to slip his hands into hers, but she backed away.

"I'm saying, it's sad that's all. You don't think it's sad that you are laughing about using a girl by getting her to sleep with a friend who you think is gay, to what, out him? Or make him do something he isn't comfortable with, gay or not? And then call her trash for—for helping you?"

"No, no, well … I don't know. I think you are making a bigger deal out of it than it is. William didn't care. He thought it was funny too. The girl obviously didn't care because she went into the next room and slept with Tracy. Making her enemy number one to Cindy," he said it like it was a side note. "I think you are giving her a little too much credit, Jess. The girl isn't even our friend."

"And yet you are still friends with Tracy, and he slept with her."

"Yeah, Jess, seriously, the girl threw herself at him, that's what she does."

"But the guys don't have to participate. That makes them worse, just saying, because they are taking advantage of her. She may be doing it because she needs love, or connection, or something, I don't know, maybe she likes sex. I mean, is that bad? Don't guys talk bad about girls who don't like it?"

"Well, yeah, but…look I don't want to fight with you. That does kind of make sense. Maybe I've been too hard on her."

"And William?"

"Maybe…" he grabbed one of her hands, "you're right. No, no, you're right. You know, you are really smart, Ms. Parsons," he bowed before her and she smiled. "and sweet. Come on, let's go swim!"

Jeselle took off running with Dennis. They made their way through the neighborhood and down a small trail in the woods. Suddenly, Dennis slowed and tugged Jeselle off the path into a shaded area. He looked directly into her eyes.

"You are beautiful, Jess. I am so glad you are here. You make me see things in a different way." He brushed a stray hair away from her face and she shivered. Dennis was amused by it. He bent slightly and touched his lips to hers. Again and again. Soft, warm, sweet kisses. She was flushed by the time he pulled away. A slight smile adorned his face.

"How many times have you kissed, Jess?"

She hesitated, "With a boy, you mean?"

"Yeah."

"This."

He moved closer to her until his body was touching hers. He wrapped one hand around her, below her waist, "I'm your first?"

"Yes."

"That makes me so happy. You are so beautiful." He leaned in, put his lips barely onto hers, and waited. Finally, she pressed forward.

That moment was when Dennis knew he had to make her his.

* * *

"That's weird. Take off your shirt," Melanie snapped.

"I don't really feel comfortable," Jeselle said.

Tracy yelled as he jumped off a rope swing into the water, startling Jeselle.

"Did you wear a bathing suit?" Melanie asked.

"Yes," Jeselle said.

"Are you fat?"

"No!" Jeselle replied defensively.

Cindy rushed over and sat on the blanket.

"You're wet, Cindy! Get off the blanket," Melanie yelled.

Cindy laughed as she shook her head, tossing water all around her, including on Jeselle and Melanie.

"Cindy, you are so stupid!" Melanie jumped off the blanket and stomped away. "Ugh!"

"Don't listen to her," Cindy turned to Jeselle, "If you aren't comfortable taking off your shirt, then leave it on. Want to go jump with me? It's fun."

"I do, but I'm kind of scared too."

"You are supposed to be. That's why it's exhilarating! Being scared is what makes it better," Cindy said. "Come on."

Cindy grabbed Jeselle's hand and led her to the rope. "I'll get on first and wrap my legs around it, then you climb on top of me and wrap your legs around me. On the count of three we'll both slip off the rope, but still hold onto each other. That way you don't have to do it alone."

Jeselle smiled, "Okay. Thank you." She felt bad for ever thinking Cindy was mean. She followed until they were close to a huge rope that was dangling from a thick tree limb. Dennis was leaning against the tree watching. Tracy held the rope while Cindy took her position on it and wrapped her legs around it.

"Hot, babe," he said to Cindy. Tracy leaned down and full open mouth kissed Cindy. He grabbed the back of her hair and pulled her head back a bit while he deepened the kiss. Jeselle crossed her arms and looked away, uncomfortable. "You are such a good rider," Tracy added as he slapped Cindy hard on the butt, "You know I love a good show."

Cindy laughed then turned her head toward Jeselle, "Your turn. Just get on top and wrap your legs around me.

"Hell yeah," Tracy said.

Jeselle did what Cindy said, which seemed like it would've been easy, only it wasn't. She struggled to get on top of Cindy.

"You aren't going to hurt me," Cindy said, "jump up here."

"Here, I'll push you up," Tracy said with a wide grin.

"No," they all heard Dennis say, "I'll help her."

"Oh," Tracy teased, "don't want me to get to third before you?"

"Something like that," Dennis replied.

Dennis helped her up by putting his arms under hers and letting her lift herself by pushing against him. Soon she was straddling Cindy.

Tracy raised his voice, "Now rub it on her," he laughed.

"Tracy, you are so lewd," William yelled from the water below. "Okay girls, I'm your spotter, I'm ready when you are."

"Bet you wouldn't think it was so lewd if I was wrapping my legs around you, though, would you pretty boy?" Tracy yelled down at William right before he pushed them hard and the rope swung over the water.

"We can swing a few times, let you get used to it. It's okay." Cindy said.

"Yeah, I'd like that," Jeselle replied.

They passed over solid ground and Tracy pushed again.

After a few passes they agreed to let go. Jeselle screamed on the way down. Once she popped above water, she was ready to do it again. Soon, Jeselle was laughing and jumping by herself.

She felt free.

Todd joined them, and they all swam and laughed together. Jeselle had never had so much fun before. Dennis found her near the edge of the water, getting ready to get out again.

"Stay with me?"

"Sure," Jeselle answered. "Thank you for inviting me. This is so fun!"

"You are hereby cordially invited to all friend activities," he smiled. "Here, turn sideways and wrap your arms around my neck, we'll float together."

She did and they floated until dusk.

As soon as Jeselle got home she ran straight to

the back patio where she knew her mom and dad would be enjoying the cool spring night with a glass of iced tea, and told them about her day.

"See, Jessie, you worried for nothing," her mom said, "I know moving was hard, but now you've found some friends. Exactly like I said, right?"

"Yes!" Jeselle replied.

"Mariah called a few times."

"Okay! I can't wait to tell her about today!" Jeselle nearly squealed as she jumped up to go inside.

"Remember, you'll always find friends everywhere you go, if you simply look for them," her mom repeated the phrase she'd said to her throughout her life, "Be wise in which friends you keep and which you don't."

"How will I know who to keep?"

"You'll learn. My best advice is to be yourself."

That Monday morning when Jeselle walked into the kitchen to grab a Coke before she left for school, she saw that her mom had left a note under a magnet on the refrigerator, like she used to do in Bakersfield. Until that moment, Jeselle hadn't realized how much her mother's handwriting felt like home, how much she'd missed it over the week they'd been there. Jeselle smiled, grabbed it and shoved it into her backpack.

CHAPTER 10

PRESENT

"A journey of a thousand miles begins
with a single step."
—Lao Tzu

In the week after the stock buy hit the news, Jeselle had been exhausted with interview requests about the alleged move to takeover Briggs International. Of course, all the calls were deflected to Stryker Steel's Public Relations department. No doubt Dennis was loving it.

The coffee in her hand was steaming through the opening in the lid as Jeselle walked around the block. "Good morning, Jed."

"Good mornin' to you, Jeselle," he reached up and took the coffee she offered.

"You coming for lunch today?" she asked.

"When have I ever missed a lunch with you?"

"You better not. They have a new Panini I want to try," she looked down on him sitting against the wall, "I noticed the key card wasn't used the last few days."

"I know, Ms. Jeselle," Jed lowered his head, "It's warm out. No need."

"Oh, it's Ms. Jeselle, now?" she lowered herself until she was eye-to-eye with him and leisurely placed her hand over his, "Jed, you still need a soft place to sleep."

"I don't need that, 'cept in the winter and can't take it for free."

"Okay," she decided not to argue today, "Don't forget I could always use some flowers around this place. It would make this tall hunk of glass and metal look a lot better. See you in the park at noon," Jeselle stood and started to walk off.

"Don't be upset, Jeselle. I'm good. You learn quick how much you really need, simply takes one card to tumble that house of cards unless you buildin' it on the rock. Don't go chasin' after all that stuff that don't matter."

She walked again, approached and bent down, "Jed, I promise you, I don't do anything that doesn't matter." They smiled at one another, she patted his arm, and then left.

On the walk back around to her building she noticed Rose hopping out of a shiny black sedan. The back seat of the car. Jeselle narrowed her eyes in suspicion and stopped to watch. Rose fumbled with her heavy purse, smiled and waved bye to the driver, then started for the front doors of the office building in haste. Jeselle let her go and for several minutes she remained propped against the wall thinking.

Rose definitely didn't have the money for a personal driver. Plus, she had just moved into one of the corporate condos; she could easily have walked the few blocks to work. So, who was driving her to and from work every day?

Immediately, Jeselle doubted her own instincts, something that made her extremely uncomfortable. The girl really was too innocent. Too vulnerable. Exactly the type of person Jeselle would be drawn to. Also, the type of person who would be a prime target of her enemies. The entire walk through the large lobby, the wait for the elevators, the time it took to travel up the twelve floors and into her private office area, only gave Jeselle more time to grow increasingly skeptical. Everyone had seen her in her pink gown at the Gala, the week before.

She couldn't remember the last time she'd misjudged someone. Not since she was thirteen. Something didn't feel right all of a sudden.

She passed by Karli's desk, "Get Rose in my office immediately."

"Yes, right away."

No sooner than she'd sat at her desk, the door opened to her office and Rose stepped in.

"Ms. Parsons? You asked to see me?" Rose's voice was the same innocent voice that she always had.

"Yes, Rose, come sit."

She watched as Rose tripped twice on her way through the large space until she finally managed to sit in front of her desk.

Jeselle didn't speak, she simply stared at Rose. Rose's eyebrows went up, then down, then crinkled in question.

"Ms. Parsons? Is everything okay?" Rose fiddled nervously. She looked down at her suit jacket, checking for food or coffee stains.

"Rose," she took a deep breath, assessing the young woman, "how do you get to and from work?"

"Ma'am?"

"A question, Rose, how do you get to and from work every day?"

"I walk, usually."

"And not usually?"

"I don't—"

"The car today, your own?" Jeselle asked.

"Oh, no, I—"

"So, who drives you?"

"I, well, it's whoev—" Rose started getting nervous.

"Rose, stop fidgeting. Who drives you?"

"Whoever is working, I guess?"

Jeselle's eyes narrowed. "Whoever is working, where?"

"Uber or Lyft. There aren't a lot of drivers here, so I get whoever takes me."

Jeselle took another deep breath, "The driver

today?"

"Oh, um," Rose lifted her phone and opened to a picture, "his name was Chris." She turned the phone so that Jeselle could see it. "I always screenshot the driver info and send to my mom, in case I turn up missing," Rose shrugged. "You never know."

Jeselle was taken off guard, but grew relieved, then agitated. "Well, for one, I let you rent a corporate condo at a very low rate, so you would be close enough to walk. I was confused to see you getting out of a car. A very nice car."

"Oh, yeah, well, again, not many around here, so I take who I can get. It was really expensive." Rose flipped through her phone, "Wow, I paid forty-eight dollars for that trip. That sucks, but I had to go early and bring my parents a few groceries."

"You woke up early, to..." Jeselle stopped, waited. "Why can't your parents get their own groceries?"

"Oh, it's Dad. He isn't in the best of health. Momma doesn't want to leave him alone. When I lived with them it was easy because she could go to the store anytime I was home, but now, well, they don't have anyone else and it's only me. They are the best parents and I hate that maybe me moving out made it harder..."

"Stop. Take a deep breath." They both took one. "Do you own a car?"

"No, but I'm saving. Momma said I could use theirs, but I don't want to leave her without one. I'm good."

STOP ME

For the first time in a very long time, Jeselle wanted to hear the rest of the story. She picked up the phone, "Karli, clear both Rose's and my schedules today, have Isabel come in here and please have the Bean Bean bring up three, hold a sec," Jeselle moved the phone away and looked at Rose, "latte?"

"Sure!"

"Karli? Three lattes and whatever you want. Also, find a grocery delivery service in..." Jeselle moved the phone away from her mouth again, "Where do your parents live?"

"Right over the bridge in Brusly," Rose answered.

"Somewhere that delivers to Brusly. Once you find them, give them Rose's number please. Yes, thank you, that's all for now."

Jeselle hung up the phone. "I am having a delivery service call you so that you can get them in touch with your mother. Anytime she needs groceries, have her call them."

"No offense, Ms. Parsons, but that, well, I don't understand. I wasn't late," Rose said meaningfully.

"No, you weren't. To be honest, I saw you getting out of that car and worried you weren't who I thought you were. Still...I have my reservations."

"I'm really confused."

"I have a lot of enemies, Rose. *Frenemies*, I call them. They are nice to your face, but they are not your friend."

"Yeah, I had one of those in high school," Rose shook her head in understanding.

Jeselle sat for a second looking at Rose before

she spoke again, "Tell me more about that, your frenemy from high school."

"Oh boy, she was really nice to me in ninth grade. She didn't ask me to hang out at school, but I had her in physical science. She asked if she could come over to my house, do homework together and I thought 'yeah, that was cool.' My momma tried to tell me that there are people out there who will use you. She did, but I knew it. I mean, I knew she was using me, but I didn't care. Not really. Not enough to make her stop coming over. I figured if I did a little extra homework to feel the way I did around her, then it was worth it." Rose looked around the office, "I bet you were really popular in high school."

"And, what happened with your frenemy?"

"She taught me how to put on makeup and fix my hair, which I was glad about. Then one day at the end of freshman year, I was leaving Principal Shelton's office to run an errand for him, and I passed by her and another girl. I said hello, probably more out of habit because she seemed like kind of my friend, you know?"

"I do know. Go on."

"Trisha said 'eeew, gross' and the other girl and her laughed. I don't know why, but I was shocked by it. I made it inside the bathroom before I started crying." Rose sighed, "Wow, I hadn't thought of her in years."

"And do you know why she said that?"

"Why she said 'eeew, gross?' "

"Yes."

"Because she didn't want her friend to know we were friends, I think."

"There are typically two reasons people do those sorts of things. One: they worry if they are their real selves, they would be you. Therefore, they put up the mask of acting as though you are lower than they are so as not to be the low one themselves. Or two: they are truly so arrogant and spoiled that they actually believe they are better than you. Both types of people are awful, but many people pity the first person when, in truth, the first is worse because they know the truth and yet live life denying who they are to get ahead. They will likely be traitors for money, mortgaged to the hilt; buy name brand shoes they hate to wear, and do just about anything to keep up with the Joneses, as they say. They may change at some point and be better people, but I don't see it happen often."

"The second one, however, doesn't know the truth. They believe they are, in fact, better than other people. Many of the second type can learn they are no better than anyone else simply by being brought down a notch or two. Some have to be brought to zero. Once the second type has faced whatever misfortune they must to learn this, they then take one of two roads: the path of the first person, where they deny the truth they've learned and still act better than others, even though they know the truth, or a new path to change and help the people they were arrogant against in the first place. The first one though, will still lie, and cheat, and do whatever they must to save face. They will blame their hardships on other people and likely never learn to simply be who they are. Only two roads for people who do things like that, Rose, do you hear me? There are only two. Which do you think your frenemy was?"

"Number one," Rose said quietly, "because even though she used me for homework, we really did have fun together."

"Precisely. Do you know where she is today?"

"Oh no, I haven't talked to her since that day. She never tried to come over again. I did feel kind of sorry for her though, because I would notice every now and then she'd look at me, kind of unhappy. I think she missed me."

"No pity for her. She chose. In my opinion, she lost."

Rose sat up a bit straighter, a soft, humble curve appeared at the edges of her lips. The door opened and Isabel entered.

"Jeselle? You okay?"

"Yes, Isabel, come in, sit. The lattes are on the way." Jeselle stood and walked around her desk to hug the older woman. "You remember Rose from the Gala."

"Yes, hello honey. How do you like it here?"

"I love it!" Rose replied earnestly.

"Let's go over to the sofas and we'll visit." Jeselle motioned them to the seating area.

Rose looked confused as she did what Jeselle asked.

The lattes arrived not long after and they were

all comfortably seated when Jeselle spoke again. "Isabel, how did you and I meet?"

"We doing that story?" she laughed and then looked toward Rose, "This is for you honey, so listen. Jeselle's momma worked as a housekeeper with me at Stryker Steel oh, what?" she looked back at Jeselle momentarily, "almost twenty years ago. She was a hard worker, and I loved her." Isabel pointed toward Jeselle, "her momma and I became friends and one day she asked me and my kids over to their house for supper. When I showed up I was in shock. Here this woman, a housekeeper, and she's got this big house in Old Wellgrove Estates, right down the street from our boss. You'd never know it. She was the most humble thing."

Rose listened intently.

"When I said something to her about her house, her fooling all of us, she replied it was legally hers, but it wasn't really her house, since Mr. Stryker paid for it. Wanna know why?"

"Yes," Rose sat forward, getting closer to Isabel.

"Cause Mr. Stryker felt guilty for Jeselle's daddy killing himself."

Rose sat back then, wide-eyed. She appeared scared.

"Now, you probably read that about her daddy, but I bet you didn't read that Theodore Stryker took care of Jeselle by giving her momma a job and paying off the house afterward. Why do you think a man as attention seeking and powerful as Mr. Stryker, who is definitely not known for being a generous man, wouldn't want that kind of PR? Cause people would've wondered why he did it."

"Why?" Rose whispered.

"That's Jeselle's story, but I know this, as soon as her momma died in that accident, Jeselle asked me and my kids to come move in. She could've been declared an adult, but instead she had me appoiunted as her legal guardian."

Rose looked at Jeselle, "How old were you?"

"I was sixteen, almost seventeen, and halfway through my junior year of high school."

"You didn't have any other family?"

"No," Jeselle answered.

"And now, to the one thing she brought me up here to tell you," Isabel winked at Jeselle and continued, "cause I've told this story a time or two, when she left that house to go to college, Jeselle wanted me and my girls to stay in it indefinitely. I thought maybe she could sell it, but, no. She declared that moment, that soon enough she'd have money to buy a hundred of those houses. Said if anybody deserved it in this world it was me, for being such a good friend to her and her momma." Isabel teared up.

"As soon as she was able, she wanted me to quit working and let her pay my bills, but that isn't my way, so she stole me from Stryker Steel for little over triple the pay and I have been head of housekeeping for her ever since."

"Wow," Rose sat forward again. Then Jeselle could see her wheels starting to turn as she pondered.

"Okay…"

"What does that have to do with you?" Jeselle asked.

"Yeah," Rose answered.

Jeselle leaned toward Rose, "From this day forward, if you need help, ask me. I am loyal, but I am also skeptical. I have enough frenemies; I'm not looking for more. However, they are always looking for ways to use someone loyal to me, against me. If you find yourself in trouble, come to me. Take no favors from anyone. Owe no one."

"I, I am not, I won't, owe I mean, I promise," Rose put up her hand in oath.

"Rose, put your hand down," Jeselle snapped, "Now," having noticed the look on Rose's face, "is there anything you need to tell me?"

CHAPTER 11

PRESENT

Dennis walked with a bit more swagger that week than he usually did. He was on top of the world, after all. Seeing the admiration on Jeselle's face the morning after had put the cherry on top of an already big, fat cake. He now controlled the majority vote in Briggs International. His mother tried to tell him that revenge wasn't the point, it was the betrayal, but even she'd gotten out of bed in a much better mood the previous week than she had in years.

His dad, who had pushed him so hard to be better and better his whole life, that morning, for the first time, hugged him tight and said he was proud. All he ever wanted was for his dad to say that to him. Sure, Theodore Stryker had said it many times through the years, to others. Good PR. Dennis knew it was more a hope than a truth, but that morning, the day after the announcement on the news, it was true. Dennis had done something no one else had been able to do, bring Brantley Briggs to his knees.

He had Jeselle to thank. If she hadn't found the weak links in Briggs stock owners and gobbled up the shares before anyone was the wiser, he never would've made it this far. Of course, it was his plan, so he did take the credit.

Now, his intent to marry her doubled. Dennis knew once he was able to get her walls down, he'd have it all. Everything he'd ever wanted and more. All the Briggs stocks, all Jeselle's assets, well half at least. And with Todd being his lead attorney, there was no way he'd go wrong. He'd never require a prenup from Jeselle, like he had the other wives. He knew their marriage would last. Women wanted love, something he was unable to give the others. He would definitely give Jeselle all his love, because he did love her. It was only a perk that she was worth ten times more than he was.

And she loved him, of that he was sure. If it weren't for him, she'd have had a much tougher life. Dennis knew deep down, past her pride, that she knew she never would've made it this far without him.

He walked past Isabel in the lobby, bending

over tending to a large leafy plant, "Well, well, did you get demoted, maid lady?" he said playfully, "I thought you were head of housekeeping here. Why else would you leave Stryker?"

"Can it, rich boy, you know how much I love working with the plant life," she looked back over her shoulder at him and smiled. He smiled back.

"Yeah, well, you better be more loyal to Jeselle than you were to my father," he said, keeping the smile on his face, but she could see it was empty now. "I'm watching you."

"Watch your mouth and don't mind me; I'm happy right where I am."

"I'm sure you are," he kept his smile steady, "cleaning after the rich doesn't hurt nearly as bad while you are living in that big house in Wellgrove does it, Ms. Isabel?"

She stopped picking the dead leaves off the plant and stood to look Dennis in the eye, "It doesn't. I could scrub every toilet with my bare hand all day every day having the satisfaction of knowing that someone as *lowly* as me is living right down the street to someone as 'important' as you."

He laughed then, "Isabel, I seriously don't know if you are kidding, but it's funny nonetheless. I do miss our little talks sometimes."

She got closer to him and adjusted his tie.

"Be careful, it's Stefano Ricci," he said.

At that, Isabel tugged on the tie forcefully, "Sometimes, Dennis, I think you are more upset with me for leaving you, than your father's company."

STOP ME

A moment passed in silence, Dennis cleared his throat, "Well, no worries, Isabel, I was old enough by then to stop having maids as friends anyway. We're good."

She smoothed the fabric on his collar, "I remember your ninth birthday. You were so happy to see me. I thought that very day that I'd do anything to keep you safe. I even envisioned one day being over your household staff."

"Yeah, well, I'm not nine anymore."

"No, you are not. But you still got the good in you, you simply have to let it control all the bad," she offered.

"And you think I let the bad rule me? Do you feel that way about Jeselle, too?"

"I think you two follow the same paths, but she already knows how I feel."

"Yet you value yourself so much that you think giving me your opinion matters?" Dennis asked.

"No, I value *you* enough to think it matters," she patted his arm.

"Don't mistake me," he bent and kissed her forehead, "I'm thankful you were so kind to me, growing up. But I'm not that kid anymore."

Then Dennis turned and walked through the lobby, his swagger growing with each step. He felt as though he owned the place already. Jeselle had done a good job of putting him in check by revoking his access to the upper floors the day of the Gala and the next morning, but Dennis figured he needed the ego check anyway. Jeselle always knew what he needed. Kept him humble. Well, as humble as he could be, he thought, which wasn't very much.

He stepped into the line at The Bean Bean and watched how quickly they worked to get people in and out. The coffee was always good. The shop was always busy. He wondered what Jeselle charged them in rent each month to be in her prestigious buildings shop area. Had to be quite a chunk of change. He coupled that with the other active businesses that lined the area and figured that monthly rent alone might barely pay for one of his suits. He laughed outwardly and a few of the people in line ahead of him turned to see what was so funny.

Too bad this was one of those small businesses without stock options. Maybe he should address the owner and offer a partnership. He could see those shops giving the out-of-state shops a run for their money. Then again, while the people in Louisiana could be so loyal, they could also be so vacillating. The thoughts about the coffee shop industry left him as soon as he heard his name.

"Mr. Stryker, what can I get for you today?"

"Same," he offered. He got enjoyment when employees couldn't remember what his usual was; watching them squirm was always fun. He got more enjoyment when they remembered.

"Oh, I, I don't, remember, I'm sorry," the young male stuttered.

"No matter," he waved his hand, "I certainly don't expect you to remember everyone's order."

The attendant sighed with relief, "Yeah, that

would be hard."

"Undeniably. Although, you do recollect my name," he stepped forward and bridged the gap the previous customers had left while he was thinking of ways to make more money. "I tell you what," he pulled out his wallet and slid a hundred-dollar bill out of it, "here, a tip for you, in hopes you'll retain my usual for next time. Do you think that would be incentive enough to remember?"

"Yes, sir!"

"Great, I'll take a Black Eye."

"A, black eye, sir?"

"Yes, a Black Eye, you know a coffee with two shots of espresso."

Dennis knew money led the world. Power wasn't too far behind. Unfortunately, power was fairly useless without money. Take his sisters' ex-husband as example number one. Starting out as an assistant district attorney gave him power, however marrying Camilla gave him money. Soon after marrying her, Rick Harrison became one of the most powerful state representatives in Louisiana. Representative to the rich, as well as being rich himself, proved to be quite an asset in his dad's pocket. Too bad he had to use Camilla the way he did. Too bad he forgot, power without money meant nothing. And using Theodore Stryker meant everything.

Soon, Rick Harrison would realize.

Dennis walked through the side doors that led to an outdoor area. He sat, he pulled his phone out to text Jeselle.

lunch?

have plans. Dinner? she replied quickly.

better - time?

come up here after work, we'll decide together.

Dennis smiled again, *yep he was on top of the world.*

CHAPTER 12

PRESENT

"The language of friendship is not words but meanings."
-Henry David Thoreau

"Where are we going?" Rose asked. She had to walk fast to keep up with Jeselle.

"We are going to lunch," Jeselle replied.

"Yeah, I know," she laughed through the heavy breathing, "but like where are we going to lunch?"

"The park."

Rose followed her around the block, thinking more than once that her flats were no match to Jeselle's stilettos. When they turned the last corner, Rose stopped. The small park was bright with a mix of sunlight and color.

"Wow."

The plot of land stood between two buildings. They were buildings Rose had seen before, of course, when she briefly came to the city. One of them was slightly visible from across the river where she was from, but she'd never seen it like this. Even in the articles she'd read about it, they never published the full beauty.

"This. This is Prostitution Way, isn't it?"

Jeselle looked back at Rose, who was still standing in the entry to the Alley.

"Well, we don't call it that anymore. It's called The Alley."

"The Alley," Rose let the name play on her lips, "I love this. Wow, the flowers are so beautiful."

On one side of The Alley there was a small row of brightly colored flowers. Along the path there were benches that led to a couple of picnic tables at the back and a trellis full of vines.

Rose walked forward slowly. One large wall of the building on the right had the mural Jeselle had commissioned displaying different citizens. The painting had a police officer, standing strong with his arms folded. A nurse stood beside him, a bloodied shirt dangling in one hand. Another man with his hands grasping a steering wheel was sitting on a bench right behind the nurse. Two men, one carrying a large steel pipe on his shoulders, which looked like Dennis Stryker, and the other definitely Mason Vinton holding a large book. There was a woman with the face of her mom leaning on a wall in the background, between Dennis and Mason.

Lastly, in the forefront was a woman kneeling down running her fingers over her reflection in a water puddle. The reflection was rippled, but you could clearly see she had two different faces, split down the middle.

"That," Jeselle startled Rose, "is obviously Mason Vinton."

"Yeah," Rose pointed, "and that's Mr. Stryker?"

"It is."

"Our lunch date, Jed, should be here soon," Jeselle patted Rose's arm, "I'm going to go lay out the food."

Jeselle noticed that Rose stayed behind looking at the mural. After everything was unpacked Jeselle sat at the picnic table and observed her as she moved along the wall, soaking in each part of the large painting. Rose touched parts of it like it meant something more to her than simply paint and brick. Jeselle saw Rose jump backward when she reached the small plaque dedicated to the exact spot where the nurse's aide, Trudy, was found murdered. The plaque read *"Tryd.E Park in dedication to Trudy Michaels, murdered here for doing nothing more than trying."*

That never changed. People always took a step back when they first read it. When they first saw the outline of where the body was found. After that they always walked around it. Jeselle intended for it to be that meaningful, and she was glad to see Rose's reaction. It confirmed a few things to Jeselle, but most importantly, it drove home that her instincts weren't wrong about Rose after all.

"Good afternoon," Jed said as he rounded the corner. He walked right past Rose and straight to Jeselle.

"Newbie?"

"Yes," Jeselle answered him.

"Good one?"

"Yeah, I think she is." Jeselle looked up at Rose walking toward them.

"Not totally sure?"

"No," she looked back at Jed, "Am I ever?"

"Woman, you are always sure of your actions. What gives?"

Jeselle had intentionally set their places on the opposite side of the table and next to one another so she could watch Rose's reactions to Jed.

A few minutes after Rose sat, it was obvious she was struggling with the smell Jed emanated. She tried to eat a couple of times, but ended up not actually taking a bite.

"So, Jed, right?" Rose asked.

"Yep, Jed Reynolds. Good to meet you, Ms. Rose." He took one hand off his Panini and extended it toward her. She shook his hand readily and smiled.

"So, you are here a lot?"

"Some. Usually you'll find me across from your building just past the main church, turn the corner and go under the walkway."

"You, you, live there. Under the walkway?"

Jed laughed, "Nah, I live everywhere, but the walkway is a safe place to stay during the day and they can find me easily when they need work done. I do some grooming of the church's courtyard, some flowers," he looked up at Rose and grew serious, "You know in exchange for food."

Rose shifted her body slightly toward Jeselle, but kept her eyes on Jed, "You any good? I mean, maybe if you worked for Jeselle, did some of her... 'grooming' she could pay you. I mean, if she needs it."

"Who do you think keeps this place up?" Jed replied.

Jeselle could see the confusion spread over Rose's features.

"Jed has a story to tell. It doesn't feel happy when you hear it, but you should, if you want to."

"I do," Rose quickly replied.

"I'll take that as my cue," Jed said. "I was in my mid-thirties, still young and on top of the world. Not as far at the top as Jeselle here, but close. I had it all. Great wife, nice house. We hadn't had kids yet, but we decided to start. Looked forward to it. I had a thriving landscaping business, almost a hundred employees. My sweet Darla went in to get her checkup and they found the lump. Back then, wasn't much they could do, so I watched the love of my life dwindle to nothing before my eyes and die. My business died right along with her."

Jeselle saw Rose's breathing slow.

"Lost my house. Traveled aimlessly for a while with some pictures of us together, a razor, canteen of water, and a bar of soap in my backpack. Took odd jobs here and there. Until one day I landed in big Baton Rouge. Got off the bus and started walking. I had a beef jerky to last me a few days and filled the canteen before leaving the bus station. I walked along the city streets for a bit, until I came upon that church, the one across the street from your office. It was so beautiful. Red brick, tall steeple. Something about it was comfortable. You following?"

"Yes."

"I walked along that walkway, no grass, no bushes, flowers, nothing but brown dried up grass. I felt like it needed me," Jed whispered the last sentence.

Rose leaned closer. The odor radiating off of Jed no longer mattered.

"And?" she asked.

"And I walked into the church and sat down. As soon as I sat, I started crying. I tell you I cried for hours. Prayed too. Don't even know what I prayed other than for God to help me. When I saw the sun had started to go down through the stained-glass windows, I stood to leave. Right as I was standing, I saw a man at the front of the church, by the altar. He was standing along with me. He startled me at first 'cause I didn't know he was there. When I looked at him though, I could see he had been crying, too. I guessed I was crying so loud myself that I couldn't hear him, but I was worried, could tell he had been sobbing." Jed stopped. He pulled out an old, dirty handkerchief from his weathered jacket pocket and wiped his eyes. Rose was simply staring at him, waiting for him to continue. "So, I asked him if he was okay. He waited a second and replied, 'You okay?' I answered that I was. And you know what he said?"

"What?" she whispered her question.

"He said, 'then I'm okay too.' I was some confused about it. I shook my head though, turned and headed for the doors to leave. I was almost to them when he said 'If you ever need someone to pray with you again, I'm here every day.'"

They all sat in silence for a few minutes. The wind picked up a bit and blew a gentle breeze through The Alley.

Rose began to cry. Jed offered her his handkerchief and she glared at it for a moment too long, wide-eyed, which caused Jed and Jeselle to laugh.

"Jed, I'm getting you handkerchiefs for Christmas," Jeselle said through her laughter.

"Don't you go getting me anything fancy, I'll only be blowing my nose on it."

"Yea, but your nose deserves the best," Jeselle smiled.

"No, that's where you wrong, none of us deserve anything."

Jeselle started to stand, "Respectfully, Jed, I disagree; some people truly do deserve what they get."

He pointed his finger to her, "You never gonna get what you looking for, girl. You gonna lose some of ya'self."

"Jed, I've already lost myself. So, the way I see it, I have nothing left to lose."

Jeselle wrapped up her garbage, put it inside her tote and walked out of the park, Rose soon followed in her footsteps.

CHAPTER 13

PAST

"Why does she have to come again?" Melanie asked as the final bell rang for lunch period. "She doesn't fit in."

Tracy laughed, "You are just jealous cause she's prettier than you. I swear you girls are so damn transparent it's laughable."

"Tracy, stop being mean," Cindy slapped him playfully on the chest then looked at Melanie, "You are as pretty as the next girl."

"That's not exactly a compliment, besides, I'm not jealous," Melanie snapped.

"It wasn't intended as one. I mean, let's be

honest, you are kind of jealous of other girls," Cindy replied.

"Well, I'd rather be jealous than a pincushion for this prick," Melanie pointed to Tracy.

Tracy laughed, "You've been my willing pincushion a time or two there Lanie, so watch your dirty little mouth."

"Speak of the devil," Cindy whispered loud enough for Dennis and Jeselle to hear as they approached the group in the commons.

Jeselle lowered her head in embarrassment. Dennis held her hand and tugged it a bit. When she looked at him and he smiled it made her feel better.

"Not that Cindy doesn't like you," Melanie addressed Jeselle directly, "We only worry you don't belong, you know, in our group."

"Come on Melanie, seriously," William pleaded.

"Well, I say she does," Dennis spoke up, "and so does Tracy here, right Tracy?"

"Yeah," he looked her up and down, "she fits."

Melanie laughed. Cindy huffed.

"Tracy," Dennis said in obvious warning.

"What, *Dennis*?" Tracy sat up and stiffened, "What?"

"Nothing, come on Jess. See you guys at the river tomorrow," Dennis said over his shoulder. As they walked away from the group Camilla passed them, "Hey, where are you going?"

"Tracy is in a mood, thought I'd avoid it today," Dennis answered.

"Oh great, can I come with you then? Not sure I

can handle it either."

"Sure," Jeselle answered.

They walked through the commons and out the side entrance to a small grassy area.

"Here?" Dennis asked them both and they agreed. Jeselle noticed neither of them had a lunch, but she was starving so she reached into her backpack and retrieved the small brown bag. "Peanut butter and jelly anyone?" she asked, pulling out the plastic covered sandwich.

"Ewww, gross, and have my breath smell like peanut butter for the rest of the day? No, thanks," Camilla cringed.

Jeselle slowly put the clearly wrapped package back into the lunch bag and reached for the apple juice. Dennis smiled and leaned forward to grab a small piece of paper that was stuck to the side of the bottle. When Jeselle noticed it was one of her mother's notes she quickly took it from Dennis, unzipped the front pocket of her backpack and shoved it inside.

"Why does Tracy always have to act like such a butt?" Camilla asked.

Jeselle smiled wide, "He does, doesn't he?"

"Because he knows he can get away with it," Dennis had noticed the question immediately in Jeselle's expression, "His dad, our Uncle Brantley, still holds control over Mom's trust until she turns like, forty-five. When Mother first married Dad, before I was born obviously, Uncle Brantley didn't like Dad working at Briggs. He thought Dad was sticking his nose where it didn't belong, but it did belong. Dad had worked there for years. That's how he met Mom, but once they married, things changed because Dad became part owner. Which Uncle Brantley hated. Mother had never cared how any of it was run and Uncle Brantley loved it that way. But Dad knew the business of steel and wanted to take his rightful place."

He noticed the shocked look on Jeselle face, "Our parents tell us everything. I think they probably shouldn't, but they do. Family grudges run deep." Dennis looked at Camilla briefly, "Unfortunately, my grandfather had placed a contingency that no one knew about except Uncle Brantley, since Mother never showed much interest, that if she ever married, Uncle Brantley could buy her out at market value."

"Ouch, I think I see what's coming," Jeselle said.

"But, it's worse than simply that. Uncle Brantley didn't do it right away; he waited until steel dipped dramatically low in market value and bought Mom out at a rock bottom price. Dad was so mad."

"I still remember that day," Camilla said.

"But you guys are doing great, right? I mean look where you live," Jeselle placed her hands, palms up, in the air.

"Yeah, but still, it's not even nearly what Uncle Brantley took from Mom. Dad can't seem to let it go."

"How long ago was that?"

"We were, I think, ten," Dennis said.

"No, no, eight, remember our eighth birthday

party?" Camilla's voice was full of dismay.

"Oh yeah, we were eight," Dennis said.

"Wait, you were both eight? You are twins?"

"We are in the same grade, Jess," Camilla said, "duh…"

"That's cool, so what happened at your eighth birthday party?" Jeselle asked Camilla.

"Mother insisted we invite Uncle Brantley. She said he was only being smart about business and who could hate him for that? He showed up with Tracy."

"Where was Tracy's mom?"

"She was long gone. Left them years before."

"Oh, that's sad."

"Yeah, more like self-preservation," Dennis laughed. "I mean Tracy and me are cool, he's my best friend, but he's still a douche sometimes, and Uncle Brantley is one all the time."

"So, what happened at the party?" Jeselle asked.

"Camilla was opening one of her gifts in front of everybody, it was from Uncle Brantley."

"It was awful," Camilla added.

"It was a roll of one-dollar bills, which Camilla thought was cool until she read the card aloud. It said 'better learn to use these for when your Dad's company goes belly up.'"

"That's terrible!" Jeselle was shocked.

"I don't think they expected Camilla to read it out loud. In any case they laughed it off as a joke, but everybody was tense after that and people started leaving."

"I'm so sorry," Jeselle said to Camilla.

"I'm over it, mostly. I mean, you're right, Dad is doing good, so, we get the last laugh."

"Yeah, we do. But needless to say, Uncle Brantley is still in control of Mom's trust, for a couple more years anyway, so Tracy knows he can get away with a lot," Dennis said.

* * *

"Is Camilla not coming?" Jeselle asked Dennis on the walk toward the river.

"She's already with Melanie. She spent the night there last night."

"Oh, so they are close?"

"Joined at the hip, Mother says. That's Camilla's best friend," Dennis said.

"That's good."

"Yeah, Melanie can be snobby, but don't be fooled, so can Camilla."

"They don't seem like they would be best friends."

"Wait until you get to know Camilla better," he laughed.

They walked hand-in-hand through the neighborhood which consisted of expansive plots with large houses, all set acres away from the road for privacy. The house Jeselle and her parents were living in was much larger than the one they had in Bakersfield, but everyone said the cost of living was much lower in Louisiana, so money went much further. Many of the houses had gated fences. As they walked, Jeselle could see most of the houses off in the distance getting bigger and bigger and farther and farther away from the street. They were taking a different route than they had the last time Dennis had led her to the river.

"Where is your house? Momma said it looked pretty from the road."

He lifted his hand and pointed off in the distance, "See that house right through there with the black roof?" Dennis asked.

"That one, the big cream-colored one?"

"The one and only."

"Well, I'd say you and your family are doing just fine without Uncle Brantley's money," Jeselle laughed.

"Our money," Dennis snapped quickly, "It's our money he stole, not his."

"Sorry," Jeselle looked down at her hand in his.

"I'm sorry, I didn't mean to get angry at you," Dennis stopped walking and grabbed her other hand also. "You are special, Jess, you aren't like the people here."

She slowly pulled her hands away from his, "So you think I don't belong here, too?"

"No, I didn't mean that. It's that, you are so sweet, is all."

"And you are saying nobody here is?"

"Not in this neighborhood," he said definitively.

They didn't talk for a few moments as they stood

staring at one another. Dennis leaned into Jeselle. He pulled her close and kissed her, standing there in the middle of the road. When she pulled back a little, he smiled softly.

"Why do you like me?" Jeselle asked.

"Ask me something else; I've already answered that one."

"Why do houses in neighborhoods get bigger as you get closer to the back? I've always wondered that."

His smile grew, "Privacy and lot size," he said confidently. "I listen when dad talks business sometimes. I plan to be a successful president of Stryker Steel one day."

"That's awesome," Jeselle said.

"Yes, it is. Come on, let's go. The others will wonder where we are."

The walk seemed much longer than the one they had taken before, but Jeselle figured Dennis wanted more time with her and it made her happy to think that. They talked, laughed, and held hands all the way to a different trail that led to the river.

"When can I come to your house?" she asked Dennis.

"Whenever you want. Want to come for dinner?"

"I'd have to ask my mom," Jeselle said.

"I can walk you home for you to ask."

"Won't it be too late by then? I thought you usually missed dinners on Saturday when you walked me home," she questioned.

"I do, but we don't have to miss. I can get a

driver to come get us. I'll call when we get there."

"Oh, wow, yeah, so that's normal," Jeselle laughed.

"I never said we were normal," he replied.

But it sounded more ominous to her than he likely intended.

It should've been a warning.

CHAPTER 14

PRESENT

"I want his head on a stake! Do you hear me Tracy! I don't care what you have to do! That snide little piece of crap. How did he get the take on us?" Brantley Briggs yelled at his son.

"Dad, I don't know. I've got William looking into it to see who sold to-"

Brantley interrupted his son, "I want to know so I can bury each one of them, but I couldn't care less about that than I do about taking back the control of Briggs. Do you hear me, boy?"

"Yes, sir!" Tracy said loudly.

Cindy listened at the door, her bag in her hand.

She knew if they came out and found her, she would be in big trouble, but she couldn't tear herself away from the door to the study. This was her second attempt to leave in the two weeks since the gala. The first time, Tracy had found her in the kitchen. She'd dropped her bag into the garbage compacter the moment she heard him walk down the hall toward the kitchen. He'd hugged her roughly, causing her to flinch. Her side had been hurt so badly that every move she made caused pain.

"I'm sorry, Cindy," he'd said. "You made me so mad. You can't push me like that."

"I know, I'm sorry," she knew it was the only thing to say.

"Okay, good girl. Here, let me love you." Tracy started to remove her shirt, she winced.

"I, I don't, I'm not sure I can. Tracy, I think my ribs are broken." Cindy started to cry, gasping again and again through the pain. After what felt like hours of tortuous "love" Tracy called his usual, trusted on-call doctor to come check her out.

She touched the wrapping that covered her midsection. She was leaving for sure today. She'd gotten almost to the back door when she heard the yelling. She knew she should at least try to hide her bag in the hall closet, but the thought of bending down caused nausea.

"Do it! I'll be damned if I owe anything to that boy of Theodore's. He's pathetic. Always has been. And Jeselle! Who the hell does she think she is? Is this some sort of revenge? Well, I can remedy that with one phone call. When she finds out her precious Dennis knew about all of it, let's see how quick she turns."

"Good, Dad! Good plan."

"Shut up! You better redeem yourself somehow through this, Tracy. I'm sick of it. You've been worthless since the day you were born. Get me *something*. William couldn't find out who had what. I need those numbers. Prove to me you can do something worthwhile. How many other stockholders are out there? I need everything I can get. I at least need to control what's left."

Cindy knew Tracy would need a punching bag after the meeting with his dad, so she had to go as quickly as she could. She made her way slowly down the hall to the back door, slipped her car keys off the door and made her way through the expansive walkway to the garage. The security monitors were off in the kitchen, because she'd purposefully turned them off on her way through. Easing the door open, she stopped to take a breath before getting into her car. She knew she had to do it all quickly. She had thought about all of the steps over and over for so long, she repeated every task in her head like a daily mantra.

Start car, open garage door, punch the gate button and go, as fast as I can.

She prepared herself for the pain of the actions and started her car. Finally, she did go as fast as she could. She looked into the rearview mirror as she passed through the gate, but no one was following her.

She was free.

* * *

"How's the new little footling doing after her big debut?"

"Camilla, you mean?" Jeselle said with amusement.

"Touché," Dennis laughed, "You know who I mean, the poor girl."

"Don't call her that," Jeselle said coolly, "Let's not forget your meager beginnings."

"I've never been poor!" he was offended.

"Oh, that's right, you are the spoiled little rich boy who's gotten everything he ever wanted," she said drearily.

"Good trap, but not everything," he looked at her sitting behind her desk, "not yet, anyway."

"Dear Heavens, Dennis, are you referring to me?" Jeselle seemed amused, "Please do move on."

"I can't," he stated honestly.

"Are you seriously going to tell me after all you have acquired you still aren't happy?"

"I realize there is truly only one thing I want to acquire," again, his honesty was apparent.

"That's only because you don't have me. Dennis, I would bore you within minutes of saying 'I do,' which by the way, 'I don't,'" she continued, "You believe me to be blind? I see the way you look at all the adoring women who throw themselves at you. Why in the world would I think I could ever be enough?"

"Is that it, then? You feel unworthy," he thoughtfully slapped his own forehead in earnest, "Of course, Jeselle. Why did I not see this?" he walked around her desk and lifted her from her chair, "You are worthy to be with me. I am sorry I haven't done enough through the years to let you know that." He meant every word.

"Do stop, Dennis, before you dig a hole you are unable to get out of," she laughed. "Let's at least put our nuptial talk aside for the moment, there is work to do."

She could see the hope spring in his expression, "Okay then, I shall take that as a positive sign. What next?"

"We need to go to lunch, did you find her?" Jeselle asked.

"I did, Melanie is working at the la Rousse du Coup," he said as he lifted the file that he had brought with him from the corner of her desk.

"How in the world did she get a job there? I thought we might've finally had her at the bottom."

"It seems not. In any case, at least we'll get a good lunch out of this one. George said she just started, but seems happier than she has in a while."

"Well, we are moving backwards," Jeselle said.

"We don't have to keep doing this, you know."

She took a deep breath, "It is curious that you should have a crisis of conscience now that you have the part of the puzzle you wanted."

The phone rang out and Jeselle leaned forward to answer it, but Dennis placed his hand over hers, "I'm not. I am saying this for you. You don't have to do this. I'm with you no matter what."

He lifted his hand and she answered. "It's who?" she asked Karli on the other end.

"It's Brantley Briggs," Karli replied.

"Okay, good. Make him hold for two minutes and if he's still on the line, put him through."

Jeselle replaced the receiver and looked up at Dennis, "It's him. Do not say one word. Do not even breathe. I'll put him on speaker. I mean it Dennis." Jeselle pointed at him.

"I won't, Jess. Hell, I didn't come this far to watch it all fall apart. I didn't expect him to call you so soon though. I thought at least a month. Huh, he must be pretty desperate to call after only fifteen days."

Jeselle laughed at his satisfaction.

"Man, Jeselle," Dennis leaned over the desk toward her "I love this. I love watching them squirm."

"Dennis, you are one very sinister man."

He smiled wider.

The phone rang out and Jeselle clicked the speaker, "Hello, Brantley. How are you doing, partner?"

There was a pause and Dennis made the motion of a chuckle without making a sound. Jeselle knew Brantley was literally seething on the other end of the phone.

"Yes, partner, what a delight. It was a shock, I must admit, at first to hear of your stock buy, but Jeselle, you are a smart business woman, and I am thrilled to see the direction we can go together."

"Yes, well, with Dennis of course. Have you talked to him?"

"That's the reason for my call. See there is some bad blood, you probably know the basics of it, and I am worried that Dennis won't want to play fair."

"Oh, I don't know Brantley, I think it's only business for him, I mean you are Stryker Steel's biggest competitor. Makes sense," Jeselle said.

"I'm not going to lie," Brantley's voice took on a tone of contrition, "I thought this might be about, well, you know?"

"What about it?"

"Well, I hate to bring it up, being so distasteful. I hate to see you in bed with Dennis, in a manner of words, of course."

Words he knew would hit home. Only they didn't.

"Of course," she replied smoothly.

"He, well, I have been concerned about your friendship with him through the years, seeing that, that he was so involved in it."

"Brantley, um," Jeselle made a concerted effort to sound unsteady, which made Dennis give her a thumbs up, "I don't know what you mean."

"Yeah, I knew it," Brantley made his voice sound so pitiful, "You didn't know. I'm sorry, little Jess, that I haven't called you before now."

"I really don't know what you mean, Brantley."

"Well, it's too much to go into over the phone. Theodore and I made some mistakes back then. Him more than me! You know…your dad."

"Brantley, I am not trying to be rude, but Theodore has really been there for me through the years," Jeselle said.

"To keep you close, no doubt. I have the proof of it."

Dennis unquestionably jolted when Brantley said that.

"Yes, well, this is strange timing. I don't know if I should believe you though, Brantley. You've done things also," Jeselle smiled up at Dennis and it clearly made him relax again. He put another thumbs up, but this time it was a less steady gesture.

"I understand, but proof is proof. I've never done anything, but try to protect my good name. I didn't push your father to, to…*ahem*. And I sure didn't think so low of your mother to hire her to clean my crap. Give me the chance to prove it."

"Well, this is unsettling, of course," Jeselle stuttered, "but what does this have to do with Dennis?"

"Jeselle, he bought all that stock for his dad. Payback for some perceived wrong that doesn't exist."

Jeselle saw Dennis' entire body tighten.

"If it were that nefarious a plan, Brantley, Dennis never would've let me buy so much more than him." She smiled up at Dennis and blew him a kiss. He relaxed again.

"So, you do own more than he does?"

Jeselle could hear the drool already forming at the corner of Brantley's mouth. "Yes. Look, I'll meet with you, but again, strange timing. How come you never came to me before?"

"I'll admit I wanted to, but thought to leave the past in the past. Considered Dennis no threat to me. Now I see how hard of a grudge he has … and Jeselle, he won't let anything get in his way. I'm concerned for you. I think you need the truth."

"I'll have to check with Karli. Can I call you back Monday?"

Brantley Briggs paused for a long while, but Jeselle stayed silent. He was intentionally trying to intimidate her into filling the voided air with a better answer than Monday.

First lesson she learned from Vinton Mason, *the first person who talks, loses.*

"Jeselle, you there?"

Bingo.

"Oh yes, yes, I'm still here," she said innocently enough.

"Well, then, I guess call me Monday."

"Talk to you then." Jeselle clicked the button to end the call. Then for good measure, she unplugged the line from the back of the phone. She sat back in her chair and said nothing.

Time passed slowly.

"What are you thinking?" Dennis finally asked.

Bingo again.

"I think hook, line, and sinker. We've got him," Jeselle laughed.

"Yes!" She could see the relief flood Dennis. Then, his fear returned. "You know, Jeselle, I didn't have anything to do with all of that. I mean, of course you know, but you know, right?"

"Dennis, please don't get weak on me now. Of course I do. Who has been a devoted companion to me all these years? You. I have already faced the role you played and we've moved past that, haven't we?" she said in her usual dry tone.

"Well, not fully, since you aren't yet my wife, but yes, I'd say we've made a great team through the years."

"We are two peas in a pod, Dennis. Cut from the same cloth. Cast from the same mold. Of like minds. Bosom buddies."

"I like that last one," his eyebrows darted up and down a few times.

"Do be serious," Jeselle said, but it was with a smile.

"Jeselle, I know you will be my wife one day, and I intend to make it so."

"Again, Dennis, I thought you had high hopes for Brantley's young wife. In a month or so, she will finally be yours," Jeselle reminded him.

"That's simply the spoils of war, you said it yourself."

Jeselle stood and rounded her desk to stand directly in front of Dennis, "Then what would I be?" Jeselle asked.

"The endgame."

She slowly put a hand to his cheek. He closed his eyes and leaned into it.

"But the endgame still has pieces on the board, Dennis. I'd hate to leave anything to chance."

"Oh Jeselle, nothing is to chance with us. I know you love me. Do you disagree with me?"

"No, I wouldn't think to disagree with you, Dennis."

He grabbed Jeselle and kissed her, hard and strong. Not a peck kiss, not a soft kiss, a full, opened mouth, passionate kiss. He hadn't tried that in years.

She started to push away. "Dennis…" she whispered.

He stiffened, then realized what he'd done, "I'm sorry Jeselle, I, I swore I would never take … I am sorry."

"You are forgiven, this once though." Jeselle went around her desk, picked up her purse and business tote. Dennis escorted her out of her office, down the first set of elevators, through the lobby on the fifth floor to the last set of elevators and through the main lobby without a word spoken between them. When the receptionist motioned that her driver had pulled around, he then escorted her to the car and opened the door. Moments later, Jeselle was gone.

Dennis stood there for a few minutes waiting for his driver, as he rubbed his chin. He regretted doing it. Then it hit him with full satisfaction that when Jeselle had pushed him away, she'd done so because she was tempted, not repulsed. She enjoyed his kiss.

Guilt he could work with. His driver pulled around also and as he stepped into the back seat, he smiled.

Yes, being on top of the world felt good.

CHAPTER 15

PRESENT

"Cindy!" Camilla exclaimed as she opened the door. Even through the tiny peephole she could see the bruises on Cindy's face. "What happened?"

"Tracy, he, I couldn't get away before now."

"Here," Camilla reached for Cindy, "let me help you in."

"Ouch!" Cindy gasped, "Sorry, I have to take it slow, my ribs are broken."

"Cindy! This is horrible. You have to call the police!"

"I can't," Cindy walked slowly through the foyer

of the condo. As she did, she noticed how magnificent it was. All the furnishings were expensive. A Daum Ultra Violet vase she used to own sat under what Cindy thought looked to be a Luxxu mirror hanging on one of the large foyer walls. Cindy stopped at the edge of the foyer. She knew, without a doubt, that she was looking at the very same Maison Valentina console table that was on full display in her own living room.

Not her living room, anymore.

She quickly felt the jealousy rise up in her but tamped it down, "I have nowhere else to go."

"Here, come sit," Camilla motioned through the living room, "Tracy always was so awful! Will…will he come here?"

"No, he doesn't know where I am. He'd never think I was with you, since we don't really talk anymore."

"I'm so glad you came here. Can I get you anything?"

"Water would be great."

"Cindy, I have three extra bedrooms, take your pick. You can stay as long as you need," Camilla offered.

Cindy was shocked to feel tears streaming down her face. She was thankful. Really thankful. She hadn't expected that feeling. It wasn't something Cindy felt often.

"Thank you, so much," Cindy expressed.

"Absolutely, but don't tell anyone you are here. I mean it. Trust no one."

"Do you think the doorman will tell him?" Cindy seemed concerned all of a sudden.

"Oh no. They all work for Jeselle, and if there is anything I know now, it's how sickeningly loyal all of her people are. But hey, good for us."

"You don't mean, Jeselle owns this building?" Cindy asked.

"Yes, I rent from her. You know I work for her now."

"I did, yes, but, I didn't know she owned residential properties."

"Oh yes, Jeselle owns many properties. I was surprised myself to see it. It's very nice."

"She must pay very well," Cindy stated.

"Well, Cindy, unlike all the rumors, I'm not totally broke," Camilla laughed, but her own lie rang in her ears.

* * *

"It's all pretenses. You know in this world even when you're down you must fake it, Tracy. If the lions smell blood, they attack," Brantley took a deep breath, then finished the Glenfarclas John Grant 60-year-old Single Malt Scotch Whisky in one gulp, "We really don't need this right now. I can't be voted out of my own company, Son."

"I know, I know," Tracy sounded desperate too.

"I warned you she was a spoiled brat. Do whatever, promise whatever, get her back in the family. I understand why you think you have to do it, Son. I understand having to keep the women in line, but you must learn to do it with little trinkets instead of fists. I'd have kept your mother if I had learned that lesson early enough. All women respond better to little goodies," Brantley stood. "I'll get Ken on it. He'll find her within the day." Brantley pointed at his son, still sitting looking pathetic, "You better be ready to beg. Know you can do this son, for us all."

As soon as his dad left, Tracy got up, walked slowly upstairs and down the hall toward Cindy's room. He stood in the doorway for a few minutes, then he slowly went into the closet and started taking all the clothes off the racks, armfuls at a time. He took every pair of shoes, every purse, bag, and suitcase. He piled them all on the bed. He went back and opened each well-crafted drawer, still full of expensive jewelry. At least he knew that she had intended to return. That would make it much easier.

He picked up handfuls and took them to the bed also. Back and forth he went until her entire closet had been emptied and piled high on her king-sized mattress.

He wouldn't be begging, but she would.

* * *

Dennis sat on the side patio of Jeselle's office building sipping his coffee. Everything was going well, better than he had expected. He wasn't really sure if it was because of the win over Brantley or the power it brought them, but something had shifted a few nights before with Jeselle. He kept remembering the look on her face when she pulled away. Desire. Guilt. Yeah, guilt because she desired him. Finally. He could use both of those, he had become the master of it over the years.

He wasn't shocked at how the little things seem to satisfy him since that kiss. For example, that the new attendant at The Bean Bean remembered his usual. Money gets you that. It gets you power. Recognition. He'd always known it.

For some reason, he thought back about Isabel and his ninth birthday.

His dad was at work, as usual. His mother was shopping with Camilla and he had sat around all day waiting for them. Getting bored, he had asked one of the new drivers to take him to see his dad. Maybe his father would remember that it was his birthday.

As expected, the driver agreed and Dennis rode the entire way to see his dad with anticipation. He'd just forgotten, that's all. His mother was likely buying him loads of gifts all day. The car pulled up in front of his dad's office building.

He stepped into the lobby of the building feeling elated to be out of the house. He'd been to the office so many times, it was a second home. The receptionist rode with him to his dad's floor. She was new also. He had gotten used to it.

It's the nature of being a firm boss, Son, Dennis

remembered his father telling him, *you'll lose a few, but the ones that are left, stay loyal.*

With such a high turnover of employees Dennis soon realized that his dad didn't have an abundance of loyal people.

As soon as he saw his dad's office door he rushed ahead. The receptionist cried out for him to stop, but he'd already made it past his dad's assistant and through the double doors. He stood there and watched in confusion as his dad scrambled to zip his pants while a woman rushed past him buttoning her shirt.

"Son, Son, come in. What are you doing here?"

"Who was that, Dad?"

"Oh, a worker. She, she's a … a seamstress. She was uh, trying to get measurements. Who cares who she was. Come in, come in."

"Okay," Dennis felt lonely, but he didn't really know exactly why. He looked back at the receptionist who had escorted him, and she smiled sadly.

"Sorry, Mr. Stryker. I tried to stop him," she said.

"No, no, it's okay. He's always welcome here," his dad looked at him with pride. "So, you came to work with your ole' dad, huh?"

"Kind of."

"Late to get started. Dennis, you must always start early. It's already late afternoon. Well, no mind, let's get to work then."

"Wait," Dennis said, "…it's my birthday."

"Don't matter. Nobody gets a day off simply 'cause it's their birthday. Must get the work done,

Son," his dad patted him on the back. "Got a few calls to make." His father went around the desk, sat, and picked up the phone.

Dennis watched the clock. Ten Minutes, twenty minutes, forty minutes. Finally, after an hour and fifteen minutes Dennis got up and left his dad's office.

His dad hadn't even noticed.

He went down the elevators and through the lobby. He was going to tell the receptionist to get his driver, but then he saw Isabel tending to one of the plants in the big atrium lobby.

"Hey, Ms. Isabel!" he said walking up to her.

"Hey there, Dennis. How are you today? Wow," she stood up and took a step back a bit, "You have grown probably two inches since I saw you! You growing so fast."

Dennis laughed, "I saw you, like, last week."

"Well, then you are growing extra fast. How are you today?"

"Uh, okay."

"Just okay? Honey, come sit. What's wrong with ya?" Isabel could see something was troubling him.

"It's my birthday."

"Well, that's a good thing. My, oh my, you are grown. You are, what, nine?"

"Yes, ma'am," Dennis's face lit up.

"You drink coffee?"

Dennis looked toward the ceiling, "No."

"Well, follow me."

Dennis did. She led him through a maze of

hallways, tapping people along the way. Each time she tapped one, they followed. By the time she opened a room all the way toward the back of the large building they'd amassed about twenty people.

"You ever been in our breakroom before?" she asked Dennis.

"No, ma'am," he said as he looked around the small area. There were two round tables, a small sink, a mini refrigerator that sat on top of a small counter and a coffee maker.

"We have all our special coffee birthday parties back here."

He looked mortified, "Coffee birthday parties?"

"Yep, go take a seat."

He sat and a few others sat around him. They were laughing and talking while Isabel made a fresh pot of coffee. She watered his down with a bit too much milk, but by the time she served him he was laughing and talking with everybody else. They each told a joke. When it came time for Dennis to tell his, he got nervous.

"Don't you be all shy with us," one of the men said, "tell us your favorite joke."

"Dad says my favorite one isn't funny."

"Well, if you think it's funny, tell it," another older man said.

"Okay," he paused worried about what they would think, "Knock, knock."

They all answered like a chorus, "Who's there?"

"Impatient cow."

"Impatien-"

"MOOOO!" Dennis laughed and pointed to them, "gotcha."

They all laughed with him, and he felt happy.

"That was a mighty fine joke," another worker said.

"That's a good one," another said.

"Okay, party is over. We all got work to do." Isabel broke it up, "Want to come work with me?"

"Pulling dead leaves out of plants?"

"Pretty much," she replied with a smile.

"Sure!" Dennis jumped up and hugged her, "Thanks, Ms. Isabel, this is the best birthday party I've ever had."

He followed her around plucking leaves, watering plants, and wiping down leather chairs and sofas in the large front lobby.

"Here, sit with me again, Ms. Isabel is tired." She plopped down on one of the chairs far off in the corner away from the front desk, and he sat on the arm of it. "What's eating at you?"

Dennis looked back at her, "My parents forgot my birthday."

"Oh, yeah that sucks, but it happens. Remind them."

"I did. That's why I came here. Dad was getting fitted for a new suit by some lady and I interrupted, even though he didn't seem *too* aggravated, I could still tell he was somewhat. I told him it was my birthday. He said birthdays aren't days off and we still have to work on them. Then he got on the phone making boring calls, so I left."

"Well, I sure am glad you ran into me," Isabel said, "I needed that coffee break."

Dennis smiled, "And the joke!" he put his finger in the air.

"The joke was the best part," Isabel smiled.

He leapt into her lap and hugged her again.

"You gonna be alright Dennis. You got the good in you. Don't let the bad take the lead over the good. You must be sure the good in you is always more powerful than the bad."

"Okay," he said, but he didn't know what she meant. Not really.

Noise of a chair being scrapped across the brick pavers in the patio area brought Dennis back to present day. He took a deep, sorrowful breath and stood. He figured he'd go up and say hello to Jeselle while he was here anyway. Dennis had always felt like he owned the building, since he knew that one day he'd convince Jeselle to marry him. Since the night of the kiss, he had no question.

He would make Jeselle happy, give her the space she required and he would be sure they stayed king and queen. They deserved to be at the top.

Dennis unlocked his phone, tapped on the third contact in his favorites, and took another sip of coffee.

"Hey." George answered.

"Any word?" Dennis asked.

"Nothing. The board is being very tight-lipped about it all. I know Brantley has quite a few enemies on it though, they aren't talking. Blame them?"

"Not at all," Dennis laughed, "Hell, they know his reach and more than likely he's threatened them on exactly how low he's willing to stoop. Do any of them seem scared?"

"Can't get close enough to find out." George said.

"Okay. Let me know if you learn anything." Dennis disconnected the call. He supposed he'd have to go into the office after all.

No rest for the wicked.

CHAPTER 16

PAST

"I long, as does every human being, to be
at home wherever I find myself."
—Maya Angelou

"Dennis, stop it!" Melanie squealed as she ran toward the others by the riverside.

"Oh Lanie, you ought to know you can't outrun Eastdale's own star athlete." Cindy laughed. Dennis caught Melanie and playfully lifted her in the air.

"I can't wait until this year is over," Tracy nuzzled his face into Cindy's neck as he pressed his erection against her backside. "Come in the bushes with me. It's been three weeks already."

"Stop Tracy! I told you I want to wait. Make sure our relationship is right. We jumped back in too quick."

"I'm not going to wait forever, Cindy!" he stepped back from her, "Do you know how many girls want go out with me?" When she didn't immediately reply he walked around her and grabbed her chin and squeezed. "Did you hear me?"

"Tracy," Todd said, "Dude, give it a rest already. Geez, you act like she's really going to be with anybody else. Dude, she's hooked already."

"Yeah, she is," Tracy said as he pulled her face toward him. He punished her with a kiss, making sure to force her mouth open with his hand so he could kiss her properly. He also locked eyes with Todd as he did it.

"Why is Camilla with Jeselle?" Melanie asked when she saw her best friend rushing to join them with the other girl in tow.

"I don't know," Todd said, "Jealous? Looks like your best friend found another bestie."

"Not true, Melanie," Dennis said, "Camilla stayed the night at Jeselle's last night."

"Really?" Melanie was obviously pissed, "She told me she couldn't stay over at my house."

"Maybe they're doing it. You put out for her, Lanie?" Tracy asked and then laughed.

"Tracy, what is wrong with you?" Melanie asked. "I swear you are a creepy serial killer in the making."

"Maybe you'll be my first victim," he retorted.

"Shut up!" Melanie said.

"Melanie, it's not like that. I asked her to, to be friendly," Dennis watched the blonde bounce her way toward them. She had a smile that could freaking light up the sky if it were nighttime.

"You're using your sister to get laid? It's pathetic you are making Camilla be her friend." Melanie said disgustedly, "Wow, Dennis, I think you've fallen to a new low. Like, Tracy-low."

"Welcome to the club man," Tracy said.

"Shut it, both of you. I'm not doing that. I wouldn't do that to her. She's special."

Melanie, Cindy, and Tracy all exchanged concerned looks with one another.

"Hey everybody!" Camilla waved as she tried to catch her breath. "We had so much fun! Next time," Camilla looked at Melanie, "you have to come."

"Bushes, babe?" Tracy asked Cindy.

"Yeah, okay," Cindy replied defeated, and they disappeared in the wooded area.

"Rabbits," Todd sneered.

"Yeah," Camilla laughed and turned toward Jeselle, "They do it a lot."

"Do it?" Jeselle looked confused at first, then it hit her, "Oh."

"Please tell me you didn't spend the night at this geek's house, Cam," Melanie said before hooking her arm into Todd's.

Camilla lost her smile. Jeselle noticed the change was immediate.

"Well, I thought," Camilla offered in her own defense, "it would be fun. Now the score will be even for a change. Four girls. Four boys."

"It didn't need to be even," Melanie said flatly,

"We can control these pricks."

"You can, can you?" Todd asked motioning Dennis toward Melanie.

"Guys, cut it out," Melanie said as one got in front of her and the other behind her. They both started playfully grinding on her, until Melanie giggled for them to stop.

"That's what you get when you mess with us." Todd told Jeselle.

"Oh wow, she's blushing," Camilla pointed out and the others laughed.

Soon Tracy and Cindy joined the group again and they all swam in the river until dusk. Jeselle felt odd at first, but then slowly she started to feel welcome again.

Mainly by Dennis, and that was all that mattered anyway.

That week at school was unusual. They all still met for lunch, but Melanie kept looking at Jeselle like she was repulsed by her. She guessed it was because Camilla had spent that night with her the weekend before. Dennis told Jeselle how upset Melanie had been. For that matter, Camilla really wasn't talking much to Jeselle anymore. She saw Melanie and Camilla whispering, then they laughed and looked at her. It was obvious they were being rude, but the fact that it was on purpose made it worse.

STOP ME

Only because it was Camilla.

Cindy plopped down next to Jeselle, "Hey, what's up, Jess?"

"Nothing," she answered.

"If it's the girls, don't worry about it, they are just snobby. They think because their parents are rich that they can treat anybody any way they want." Cindy bit one of her own nails.

"Cindy, aren't your parents rich also? I mean you live in the neighborhood, go to this school." Jeselle motioned around her.

"Yeah, we're okay, but not like them. Mom and me live in the front of the neighborhood, like you. She works for Briggs. That's how I met Tracy, at a company picnic."

"Cool. What does your mom do?"

"She's his HR admin something or another, I don't really know. I know she's important enough to keep close. We live in a Briggs house."

"We live in a Stryker house," Jeselle and Cindy laughed, "Dad wanted to move, but Mr. Theodore wouldn't have it, said it was part of the incentives or whatever."

"So, Tracy said your dad does some big, important job for Stryker. What does he do?"

"I have no idea."

They both laughed again.

"Well, try to fit in, okay. It's good for your dad. My mom always gets so mad when I break up with Tracy."

Jeselle looked at Cindy then, "Do you love him?"

"Yeah, I guess. I mean there is definitely something between us, mostly it seems like anger," Cindy laughed.

"Passion," Jeselle said.

"Huh?"

"It's passion. I mean that can be anger too, but Camilla said you and Tracy do it a lot, so probably passion."

"Right. True. I also like who he is. I mean it has the best perks. I get to go on vacations with his family. They all know we're gonna marry one day. I don't think Mr. Brantley likes me too much, but Tracy's stepmom does."

"That's good that she does," Jeselle said.

"Yeah. Have you met Mr. Stryker?"

"No, not yet. I was supposed to go over there a few weeks ago, but his dad had an emergency at work, so I couldn't."

"Well, be soft spoken and girly. That'll help."

"Why?" Jeselle's eyebrows stitched together.

"…You may live in our neighborhood, but trust me, we're different, and they know it."

The conversation trailed off, and they sat watching the boys play football. Every now and then Dennis would look over at Jeselle and smile. He had the best smile. Seemed most of the girls in the school thought that too. Tracy ran over a few times and kissed Cindy.

Jeselle found herself wishing Dennis would do the same to her.

Right before the bell rang Melanie and Camilla

started to walk off, Camilla looked back at Jeselle once, and it was evident that she was sorry.

Remorse was written all over Camilla's face.

* * *

That following weekend was full. The annual Halloween celebration was held in a huge park in the neighborhood, one that in all the months she'd lived there, Jeselle had never seen. It didn't surprise her though, because the whole neighborhood was misleading. It was actually more like a small town. Gated entry on both ends with security guards. Night patrols. A small grocery. At Eastdale most of the kids had rich parents, and it hadn't taken Jeselle long to learn that. They had a few scholarship kids, but it was obvious who they were. They all basically sat together and were outsiders. Jeselle wasn't an outsider, but sometimes she felt like one.

Dennis explained to her that the block parties, always hosted by Briggs and Stryker, were held twice a year. One for Memorial Day and one for Halloween. All the neighbors were invited to the park, and there were carnival games, painting stations, and fun water rides for all ages. It was a fully-catered barbeque with servers.

"How come we never come here on the weekends?" Jeselle asked Dennis and Camilla.

"Because it's lame," Camilla answered, "Why do you care? Do you run anything around here?"

"Knock it off, Camilla. The more time you spend with Lanie, the more you sound like her."

"Yeah well, like minds. Rather…like money," Camilla huffed and walked away.

It was apparent Jeselle was hurt by Camilla's comment. "It's pretty is all I was saying."

"I know," Dennis put his arm around her shoulders. "Don't worry about Camilla. The park though, is kind of lame," he laughed. "All the old people hang out here on the weekends. No one goes to the river, but us."

"How come though? They don't know about it?"

"Oh, they know. They also know Uncle Brantley owns it. He owns that whole tract of wooded area along the river through the neighborhood. He was going to make it into lots, sell for high profit listed as river lined property, but Tracy pitched a fit. It was his river and he didn't want his dad to sell it off. So, he didn't."

"Wow, must be nice to own a river."

"I'll buy you a river one day," Dennis leaned in and kissed Jeselle on the cheek.

"I'd like that," she smiled, feeling confident again.

It wasn't long before the whole group showed up. After a couple of hours Tracy suggested they all go to the river. When Jeselle asked her dad if she could go, he said it was okay, but only after the presentation, because Mr. Stryker wanted everyone there for it. Dennis agreed, so they all stayed. Luckily, it wasn't long before Dennis's dad took the stage on the large gazebo platform.

"There have been a growing number of quality control changes at Stryker in the past year. One of them was the acquisition of Bangle Corp out of Bakersfield. Through that we have expanded our operations and saved that area from massive layoffs. In acquiring Bangle, we also attained the best quality control department in the steel piping industry. We moved that department here and strategically retained the head and developer of many of its processes, Mr. Sherrill Dale Parsons." Mr. Stryker motioned toward Jeselle's dad and many clapped.

Jeselle leaned into Cindy and whispered, "Quality control person," and they both snickered.

"We will soon be able to buy those processes," Theodore looked down at Jeselle's dad with one eyebrow raised and Jeselle's dad smiled and nodded, "so we can then offer those processes for lease to other steel companies, such as Briggs International," Dennis's dad pointed toward Brantley in the crowd. Brantley lifted a hand.

Although he nodded his head in agreement, Jeselle thought he looked angrier than anything else, but from all she'd heard about the man, it seemed appropriate.

The presentation didn't last long, and soon they were at the river together. Tracy and Cindy had disappeared into the woods again. Camilla, Melanie, Todd, and William were all jumping from the rope swing to see who could make the biggest splash for one hundred dollars. Jeselle was wading with Dennis.

"Why does your uncle always look so mad?"

"Because he always is. If you are referring to today though, that is the one-upmanship they have going on. Dad bought Bangle for the quality control department. He'd hatched the takeover as soon as they won some important congressional environmental award. I imagine a lot of people hatched plans that day, but Dad is smarter. He bought stocks every time they became available, courted major stockholders into selling. He paid a bundle, too. Worth it. Especially since he came up with the idea of leasing the services and processes to other companies. He'll make twenty times the fortune he spent. Uncle Brantley was ticked. Still is, but he doesn't have a choice, he's gonna have to lease it, too."

"That's a little unfair, though."

"No, Babe, it is business. It's okay."

"What about you and Tracy? You don't get mad at each other about stuff like that? Your dads doing that kind of stuff to each other?"

"No indeed, we think it's funny. I mean what do we care? I love Dad, but he only cares about business. So, let them fight it out."

"I guess so," Jeselle replied, something still didn't feel quite right, but she couldn't put a finger on it.

But she did know it had something to do with her dad, not theirs.

CHAPTER 17

PRESENT

People said she was calloused, but they would say she was much worse if they knew it all. Business after business seemed to melt into her hands so easily. All of them had been gobbled up, torn down. Not out of good intentions, out of revenge, fury.

Jeselle thought of each one.

The middle school, where she first learned that people could be calculating.

The hospital, where she first learned that people could be manipulated.

The police station, where they could be intimidated.

The courthouse, where they could be bought.

The river, where they could be cruel.

The Alley, where they could be silenced.

All of her little lessons were taught very well. The good that prevailed out of it all, was her mom's voice, her dad's. She would've preferred to have seen the properties left empty, reminders that the buildings were torn down in a righteous rage. Yet, somehow she grew a greater resolve than revenge.

She grew a purpose.

The old middle school, torn down and *Lett.E Learning Center*, free education for all to acquire career skills, was built in its place. After COVID, all of the classes moved online, which was a blessing in disguise, because then more people could enroll.

The hospital, demolished and replaced with a sponsor-driven, free medical facility where money didn't make your illness more significant than another's, or conversely less significant.

The old police station, annihilated and on top of the ruins Jeselle erected *Geno Prett.E Alliance for Suicide Prevention*, for people to ascertain how to deal with loss, trauma, and loneliness.

The old courthouse, her main business building, destroyed to then house *E. Rindre Corp, Mind.E Publishing & Media, Husk.E Contruction,* and *Tag.E Investments,* where people still discovered every day that some things can't be bought.

The river, the entire portion that ran through the exclusive Wellgrove Estates was all part of her own enormous back yard, where she hosted quarterly family functions for all of her business and non-profit employees and their families. To Jeselle, it was one of the most important places of transformation: a place of peace and refuge instead of turmoil and pain.

And of course, Prostitution Way, where Jeselle erected The Alley as well as the *Haevn.E Foundation*, so people could seek rest, help, and a voice.

Righting wrongs.

Changing and rearranging the order of billing.

Jeselle agreed that she indeed was calloused. However, unlike all the people who manipulated and cheated the world for their own gain, Jeselle was calloused enough to do it *for* the ones who had been manipulated and cheated. While ultimately, revenge and fury were her driving forces.

Getting revenge was simply the net profit.

***

He walked through the side door and proceeded toward the elevators.

"Mr. Styker!" he heard his name come from behind.

"Oh, Mr. Styker!"

He turned to see one of the receptionists trailing behind him. He sighed, "I swear, Jeselle," he cursed under his breath. If she'd blocked him from the fifth floor again, he would explode.

"Yes?" he answered her.

"Ms. Parsons isn't in," the girl batted her eyelashes and smiled, "I just didn't want you to waste your time going up."

He smiled back, the smile he knew melted young girls like her, eager, young girls who loved being wined and dined by a man on his level. He'd had many of them.

"Okay, well, I'll simply catch her later."

"She's probably in the park, you know, having lunch like every Wednesday." Girls like her were also so helpful.

"Sure, yes. I, of course," he tapped his forehead lightly, "I'm the worst at remembering all of her escapades." He moved a touch closer and saw a shiver run through the girl. "What is your name?"

"I'm, it's, Rachel. I'm Rachel," she giggled lightly.

"Thank you, Rachel."

"You are welcome, sir."

Dennis made his way around the lobby, because he needed to see his image on the wall. He understood why Jeselle put mirrors everywhere, to bask in it. The wealth. The luxury. Dennis couldn't wait to call both the City Square buildings his.

Jeselle was at the park. Perfect fit for the recent events. He had been worried when Brantley had called Jeselle, but he also knew her need for retribution was far greater than anything Briggs could say to her. He did love that Jeselle went to the park so often, kept the Briggs betrayal fresh in her mind. He was sad that it hurt her, but in the end it would be beneficial to him.

Dennis took the next block slowly, reveling in the beautiful day. When he turned the corner that he thought led to The Alley, he saw that it didn't. He backed up and peered down the street.

"Where the hell is it?" he cursed loudly.

Not that he was much of a betting man, but he could've bet it was right here. Then again, all alleys look similar. Giving himself a break, he reflected on the fact that he had only been there twice; once for the dedication and once for the piece in the news about his likeness on the mural. He began walking again and after a few turns he finally found The Alley. When he spotted Jeselle sitting with the homeless man again, Dennis grew angry. He'd warned her about that. Not only could the man hurt her, but he was homeless for God's sake.

She spotted him and smiled, "Dennis, come back here!"

He thought how young she looked, how much like his Jess, when she smiled like that. He made his way quickly, avoiding the place where the nurse's aide was murdered and sat by Jeselle.

"We are starting on our pizza," she stated, "Want a slice?"

"No."

"Hi," Jed extended his hand across the table to shake Dennis' hand, "I'm Jed. Good to finally meet you, I've looked at your face enough on that wall."

Dennis grimaced at Jed's filthy hand without taking it.

"Dennis!" Jeselle scolded.

"Hey, man, I get it, you don't want to shake my hand, that's okay. I am not offended." Jed said.

"No offense intended. I simply have to eat with my hands. You know, pizza." Dennis responded.

"Dennis, stop it," Jeselle commanded.

"Look Jeselle, I have warned you about people like this. Does he ask you for money? Do you *give* him money?" Dennis talked as if Jed weren't even there.

"Dennis, you are beyond your boundary right now. Jed is my friend, and you will certainly not mistreat him."

Dennis could see that she was determined, so he reluctantly shifted to Jed, "I apologize. Seems my pride is much bigger than my common decency." Dennis put his hand out in offering and Jed shook it.

"I am so sorry, Jed," Jeselle said.

"No need. I know exactly who I am," he said in response, eyeballing Dennis wiping off the bench before he sat.

They all basically ate in silence. Jed felt it was best if he left so he finished his second slice and stood.

"Wait, you can't leave," Jeselle pleaded.

"Oh, I have to go now. It's okay dear. I'll see you next week."

"Jed…" she said in defeat.

"It was sure good to finally meet you, Mr. Stryker," Jed put his hand out again and Dennis, although hesitant, shook it. Jed held firm, pulling him in a little bit closer, "No, to answer both of your questions. She doesn't give me money and I certainly don't ask for it."

The moment Jed turned the corner Jeselle stood abruptly, "You are unconscionable." She started walking to the entrance of The Alley.

"Jeselle, I'm the worst. I am sorry. I forget sometimes."

"Forget?" she rounded one of the flowering bushes, "Forget to be human?"

"Forget that you weren't really raised in this."

"In what?" she yelled.

"Money, wealth. I mean, do we really mingle with homeless people? Prostitutes? Come on Jeselle, it's dangerous."

She again presented her façade, the one, she thought, she'd perfected through the years, "Yes, very well," she paused, "I see your argument."

"Thank you!" he said in return.

"I am far wealthier than you, Dennis. Kindly do your duty and pick up my pizza box, cups, napkins, and the other stuff from the lunch I brought and discard it. Also, don't come by my office for," she looked at a nonexistent watch on her wrist, "say the rest of the week. If by chance you do, I will have blocked you from getting any further than the main lobby, all because, let's face it, you are far beneath me."

"Okay, Jeselle," he laughed amusedly, "I get your point."

"No, no, you never do. See Dennis, you get what

your point is, which is why you say you get what my point is, so you can ultimately have your way. Not today. Today you have ruined my lunch, offended a dear friend, and called the very reason this park is in existence a mockery. You, of all people should understand. Et tu, Brute?"

"Jeselle, I am not your traitor," he rushed over to her.

She outwardly relaxed her demeanor. "Okay, Dennis."

"You are so distrusting."

"Do you blame me?"

"No," Dennis said, "I don't. Look, don't shut me out. I am sorry. I'll fix it. I'll give Jed a job! There. Done."

"Dennis. I need you to see that it isn't always about bringing people to where you can accept them. Sometimes, it is simply accepting them the way they are, where they are. Then, if on their own terms, you can help them, do so."

He hugged her, "Jeselle, dear, that is all the same thing."

Jeselle knew there was no explaining it in a way he would understand. She'd been trying to since the eighth grade.

CHAPTER 18

PAST

"Vulnerability is not weakness. And that
myth is profoundly dangerous."
-Brené Brown

The park was beautiful. Yes, her friends were right, there were a lot of old people there, but it was safe. Jeselle sat on one of the park benches and watched the geese float around the pond. It was peaceful. Christmas was a couple of weeks away, and Jeselle worried over how life would change when summer came. Melanie still didn't seem to like her very much, which by default, meant Camilla didn't either. However, Jeselle knew Camilla did like her, because each time she went to dinner at the Stryker's, Camilla sat next to her, and talked to her as though they were best friends. In front of Melanie, they weren't.

Still, it was fun to hang out with the gang and be a part of something special. Tracy and Cindy were weird, but they were fun too. William and Todd were really nice and they always went out of their way to correct Melanie when she said something belittling to Jeselle. Cindy was right about one thing, it was obvious that she and Jeselle didn't really belong in the group, but they were lucky to be there. No one really said it, but it was obvious that they all felt that way.

Williams's dad was some notable, influential guy who handled nearly everyone's investments in Wellgrove Estates. Jeselle overheard her dad telling her mom on the back patio one evening that William's dad also handled the governor's and several other wealthy business people's money. She felt weird that her mom and dad were even talking about it, but understood once she heard her mothers concerns over Jeselle always hanging out with them on the weekends.

"They just seem so much older than the other kids back home. Don't you think?" her mother asked her father.

"I think you worry too much. It's a different world here, but they are all well-mannered. Don't over think it, Jessica. This is a good opportunity for Jessie," he said.

Jeselle knew that her dad was trying to convince her mom that the kids were brought-up well, from wholesome families. She learned a lot from standing right inside the screen door that led to the back patio at night, listening to her mom and dad talk.

Information like the house they lived in, which really belonged to Stryker Steel, was worth a lot of money. Not as much as those in the back, of course, but they were still more expensive than the average house in Louisiana. She heard that her dad had asked Mr. Stryker if he could buy it, but apparently, he wanted much more than her dad was willing to part with, which told Jeselle that maybe they wouldn't be there much longer. Tears sprang to her eyes at the thought of moving out of the Estates.

Todd's dad was an attorney, so was his mom. He talked about being one too, all the time. The other friends got really tired of hearing about it, but Jeselle was happy for him. She wished that she knew what she wanted to do as a career. All the friends already knew. Each one of them was so sure. Jeselle wasn't sure of much, except that she really did like Dennis a lot, and she liked living in Wellgrove Estates.

"Hey, why did you want me to meet you here at the park?"

She looked up and had to block the sun from her eyes, "I don't know. I felt like coming here. I mean, it's free, and it's awesome."

"So is the river," Dennis said.

"Yeah, but I like it here, too."

Dennis sat next to her on the bench and put his arm around her shoulders. It felt natural. She wouldn't have believed she could feel this comfortable with someone, especially after only three months.

Then again, three months was a long time.

"The guys are going to be waiting for us," Dennis said.

"Yeah, I know. Just wanted a minute with you, by ourselves."

Dennis didn't move, but Jeselle felt him tense a bit, "I would like time alone, really alone with you, Jess."

Her face grew warm, "Me, too."

"I was thinking, maybe you could come to the house for more than dinner, to spend the whole day," he said.

"I'd love that," she replied.

"We have a guest house out back that we mainly use for parties. We could grab some stuff from the kitchen, cook maybe, and watch movies."

"I'd love that. Nobody else?"

"Only you and me," he smiled.

"I'd *really* love that," she laughed. Finally, Jeselle thought, some alone time, more than they get on their walks to the river. Hanging out with everyone was fun, mostly, but time alone with Dennis would be easy.

"Something else, Dad asked me to ask you...he said you were much younger than all of us. Like, how old are you?"

"I, I turn thirteen in February."

"Yeah, wow so you are younger. I'm already fourteen."

Jeselle laughed, "I know, I was at your crazy big birthday party. So?"

"So, how come you are only twelve and in the eighth grade?"

"It's something about my birthday being in February and my mom getting me into kindergarten early. In California, you can get an early entrance test for your kid, and my birthday was only a few months past the deadline, plus I'd already been in pre-k for two years, so I passed. It's a little weird, I guess, but," she lifted her brows and leaned toward him, "if mine would've been only a few months earlier…"

"And mine a little later…"

"We'd have been the same age," she finished.

"Yeah, twelve sounds really young."

She laughed nervously, "Yeah, I guess. Do I seem twelve?"

"No, that's why I was so shocked when Dad brought it up."

"Does it matter though, to you?" she hesitated. She knew already that it did or he wouldn't be asking.

He turned fully to her and she met his actions so that they were facing one another.

"I want us to always be honest with each other, okay?"

"Okay," she felt something bad coming.

"I was a little bothered by it. That really sounds young when you say it, not even a teenager yet, but you seem more mature than any of the other girls, so that makes up for it. Is that alright?"

"It's honest. I mean, I turn thirteen in only two

months."

"That's good. Maybe we should wait on the alone thing until after your birthday," he suggested.

She cocked her head in confusion, "Why?"

He smiled, amused, and then placed his hands gently on her face, "Jess, sweet Jess, you are beautiful, and so sweet it makes me ache for you."

She giggled, "Ache for me? Sounds like something out of a romance novel."

"Maybe you aren't so mature," he joked, but it hurt her feelings to some degree.

They walked to the river, holding hands and laughing. Jeselle thought about their conversation all day. She noticed more about the other girls. Cindy already had breasts about as big as Jeselle's moms. Melanie and Camilla weren't too far behind. Jeselle looked down at her own a few times and realized that hers were much smaller. They had grown a lot over the last year, but still they were much smaller by comparison. Maybe that was why his dad had asked about her age. Once that realization hit her, it made her much more uncomfortable.

Dennis chuckled and Jeselle sprang from her own thoughts. The water flowed around them as she waded with him, sitting sideways, snug in his lap with one arm around his shoulders.

"Honesty?" he asked.

"Yes," she replied.

"I'll tell you what Mom told Camilla last summer, they'll grow. Stop worrying about them."

Jeselle blushed. It had to have been a full body

blush because all of a sudden, the water felt much colder. Dennis chuckled again.

"Jess, you are perfect. I am sorry I mentioned the age thing earlier. You are perfect for me. Okay?"

"Okay," she felt shy.

"And sweet," he placed a soft kiss on her lips, then another. She responded like she always had and returned his affection.

"Let's go down the river a bit, okay?"

"Okay," she whispered. She started to slide off his lap, but he stopped her.

"Don't. Stay. I'll do it."

He used his arms to move them with the lazy current. Tracy could be heard in the background making lewd comments about what they were going to go do. Finally they floated around a small bend in the river and Dennis stopped. He anchored them against the bank and kissed her softly again. Then, he kissed her deeper and deeper. She responded so naturally. She felt something hard on the side of her thigh between them and looked down through the muddied water.

He smiled at her, "You do know about that, right?"

"Of course." He could see the innocence pouring off her. She knew about it, but she didn't *know* about it.

"Can you do me a favor?"

"Okay," she answered.

"You have on your bathing suit under there, right?"

"Yes."

He placed another small kiss on her lips before whispering, "Can I see it?" His breath caressed her lips and she found herself totally mesmerized.

"Yes."

He helped her remove her t-shirt and kissed her neck as it was going over her head. Then he kissed lower on her chest. He pulled back a little and stared.

"They are perfect." He lifted his eyes to meet hers, "You are perfect."

He kissed her deeper than he ever had. Soft, warm kisses. Jeselle felt so relaxed, like she could simply fall back into the water and drift away. He lifted one of her legs around him and shifted her body weight so that she straddled him, then he moved slightly against her. She gasped. Dennis smiled. Slowly he trailed kisses down her neck and then up again, trailing them all the way to her ear as he moved against her.

"You like that, my sweet Jess?" he whispered in her ear.

She moved against him and he groaned.

"Yes, I think you do."

"Why are you smiling?" she whispered.

"Who says I am?" he softly replied in her ear before he slightly licked her earlobe.

"I can feel it on my face," she answered.

"I'm happy," he said before he took the soft part of the ear into his mouth and sucked on it.

She pressed hard against him.

"She does have boobies!" Tracy's voice carried

down to them, so did all the laughter.

Jeselle looked up quickly and saw all of them hanging over the edge of the embankment, laughing. She tried to put her wet shirt back on, but couldn't. The fabric was stuck together, so she simply covered her chest with it.

"Guys," Dennis raised his voice slightly so they could hear him, but his tone seemed very nonchalant to Jeselle, "Come on!"

"Jess has boobies, Jess has boobies," Tracy chanted.

Jeselle started crying. She didn't want to, but she couldn't stop it.

"Oh no, poor wittle Jess is cwying," Melanie said.

"Don't cry," Dennis touched the side of her cheek, "They are just kidding. We're all friends here, Jess," Dennis tried to reassure her. "They really wouldn't be picking with you if you weren't their friend."

* * *

"You're home awfully early," her mom said.

Jeselle immediately started crying. Her mom put the knife down and rushed to her.

"Jessie, babe you okay?"

"Yes, had a bad day."

"Let's go out on the porch and talk. I'll grab some tea."

Jeselle grabbed one of the small blankets on the way outside.

"Here sweetie, take the cup. You okay?"

"No. I don't even know why though. I don't ever take my shirt off at the river, because I don't have any," she covered her chest with her hands. "I feel like all the other girls have so much. I mean they are technically still only one year older than me."

She saw her mother let out a slow breath and relax a little, "Dear, a lot can happen in a year, but I have to be honest with you by saying, you may never get large ones. I know how you feel, because I've been there." Her mom took a seat across from her.

"But I hardly have any!"

"Compared to the others, right?" Jeselle nodded to her mother, "You can't compare yourself to other girls, Jessie. You'll never be happy if you do that. Start now, while you are young, loving exactly who you are. God made you perfectly. However, they will fill in some."

"I, I took my shirt off today and they laughed at me," she continued crying.

"The girls did?" her mother looked confused.

"Well, yes."

"I'm concerned that ... maybe that these kids are too ... I don't know, they seem much older. Don't you think so?" her mother asked.

"Mom they are older. that's not anything new to me. All the kids in my class have always been a little older."

"I guess, I mean even older than they are."

"Tracy said 'oh look she's got boobies' and the others laughed. I don't think that's too mature." Jeselle said with a touch of humor.

"Oh honey, that was likely embarrassing, and I see how that would hurt you, but, again, is that something kids your age talk about? It worries me that he'd say anything about them at all."

"True," Jeselle took in a deep breath, "I don't know. I guess I was comparing myself to the girls, especially Cindy because she's closer to my age and she already wears a B cup."

"Honey, I wear a B cup, and I'm an adult," her mother said.

"I want a B cup." Jeselle pouted.

"Love yourself, Jeselle. If I can give you any advice that you should take with you everywhere you go, for the rest of your life, it is to love yourself. You know what, when I was younger, I didn't have 'large' breasts, but now at my age, most women's breasts are starting to sag. Mine aren't. That's a plus!"

Jeselle laughed.

"Love yourself in every stage of your life."

CHAPTER 19

PRESENT

"It isn't what we say or think that
defines us, but what we do."
—Jane Austen

Cindy sat in the living room looking out at the city through the large plate glass windows. Downtown Baton Rouge was a fairly clean city. Not a lot of buildings, yet city enough to feel good about being there. She had been to much larger cities over the years. Stayed in nice hotels, ate at the best restaurants. Still, something about small Baton Rouge was in her blood. Probably because here she was somebody; everywhere else, her money was.

Baton Rouge, with one of the highest murder rates in the country, always became a topic when they were out of town. She knew though, it was only dangerous in certain parts of the city, and they never went to those parts.

The places Cindy went didn't have murder rates. They had return rates, tax rates, and star ratings. Cindy sat back and took in a deep breath. Tracy had called repeatedly. At first, he was angry, threatened her. Then he started pleading. Then crying, apologizing.

Right where he needed to be, she thought.

Cindy went into the large kitchen and poured another cup of coffee. She was scared at first, mainly because he had never stayed this mad for this long. She'd especially never stayed away this long. She started to think he'd never relent. Then the day before, he broke. She was sure this time would be different. She felt it.

Cindy picked up the phone from the sofa and stared at it again. She wasn't sure if she should call yet. The phone made little clicking noises as she searched for his number under his new name, 'A-hole.'

"Cindy," he cried out, "I have been so worried. Are you okay?"

She hesitated. His voice was so hoarse, he sounded truly broken, and it made her heart ache, "I don't know."

"I love you. I am so sorry. I promise you, Cindy, I don't know what came over me. I'm under a lot of pressure. I try not to. Babe, please, I don't know what to do without you."

"Me, too."

"Then, come home. Where are you? I'll come get you."

Something was different this time, she could tell. He sounded really bad.

"Are you okay, Tracy?"

"No," he broke down, crying again, "I've messed everything up. Dad hates me. You hate m—"

"I don't hate you," Cindy rushed to say.

"I need you. No one else will even talk to me."

"How's Raini?"

"Dad said she's really worried over money right now," Tracy's voice skipped through a sob. "I've really made a mess of things. Dad's not been this mad since I accidentally sold the river property to Jeselle."

"That wasn't your fault. She tricked you. But… the stocks, well, is there any way to get the stocks back?"

"Not unless Dennis or Jeselle will sell them back to me and…" he left the rest hanging.

"But we have money, right? And other things? I mean Tracy, your dad owns a lot of other stuff. Plus, he still owns his stocks too right?"

"He said he won't pay for my way anymore, Cindy. He said he's done. He's got to worry about keeping Raini in the lifestyle she deserves and he said he's mortgaged to the hilt."

"What does that mean for 'us'?

"Is there an 'us'?"

"Of course, there is," Cindy heard him break down and start sobbing. "I'll come home in a few hours, okay?"

"Come now. I need you."

"I can't right now. Tracy, listen, we'll figure it out," Cindy reassured him.

When he finally let her hang up, Cindy sat on the sofa for a while looking out over the city. She felt suffocated half the time with Tracy, and degraded the other half. She knew he loved her, but he had no control over his anger. It seemed his anger was coming out more and more.

The sound in his voice, his true remorse, made her hopeful that this time was different. He needed her. She needed him, too.

The coffee went down her throat and soothed the dryness. Cindy wasn't like Camilla, she didn't have money of her own. She only had what Tracy had, and at the moment she wasn't sure that was enough either.

She had tried to warn Tracy over the years that keeping up with Dennis was a mistake. It would put them into the poor house. Tracy had always resented her help.

***

"She is in my condo right now."

"Why are you just now telling me this? She's been there for four days, and I am only finding out about it today?"

"I," Camilla huffed, "hardly think I have to tell

you everyone I have over to my place."

"My place, Camilla. You have yet to start paying rent, it is my place," Jeselle stood and walked around the desk to be closer to her. "So, you've had the wife of my biggest, newest business rival, someone who would love to get any info against me, in my business condo for four days?"

"I...guess I hadn't seen it that way. I thought of her more as a friend in need," Camilla appeared worried.

"Friend is a very loose word," Jeselle commented, then seemed to relax. "How is she?"

"Well, she is bandaged around her midsection. Tracy called the doctor to the house once he came down off his anger. Doctor said she had broken ribs, concussion. She is covered in bruises and two black eyes, Jeselle it is horrid."

"I have a well-trusted physician I can get her to. Leave early. Tell her I'll help."

"Not sure she wants the help. She seems close to going back."

"It has been the same cycle with them for so many years, she'll likely need counseling to truly leave, but if she wants to leave, I'll help."

Camilla started to rise when a knock on Jeselle's office door made Camilla jump.

"Why are you so nervous?" Jeselle asked.

"Are you kidding? I am harboring Tracy's wife. I've been scared to death since she stepped inside."

Rose walked in, "You asked for me?"

"Yes," Jeselle said, "Dennis is in the main lobby.

Please go down and tell him I am too busy to go to lunch. Then I want you to hang back and see if he asks Rachel to go instead. If she goes, fire Rachel on the spot."

"Oh, yes, ma'am. I will," Rose didn't hesitate. She turned and left.

Camilla looked at Jeselle in question, "Are you and Dennis finally dating again?"

"No," Jeselle offered no other explanation.

"I don't understand. Did he-"

"Camilla, I don't define my relationships to people, especially employees. I answered you because you are his sister. Rachel isn't, and she isn't privy to know that I am not dating Dennis. However, it is strongly rumored that we are. So, anyone who would take a lunch with the man I am supposed to be seeing has sold their loyalty to me for a mere hundred-dollar steak."

Camilla sank back down into the chair, "Jeselle, I am sorry about letting Cindy stay with me. Please don't fire me. I have nowhere else to go."

"Camilla, stand," Jeselle commanded and Camilla responded immediately. "Cindy has been a friend to you for years, and I am willing to help her also. Be clear that I do not think you intentionally did anything to me. However, I need you to weigh your every move when I am involved in it from now on."

"I will," Camilla answered.

"Good, now leave, and go tell Cindy I am willing to help."

The moment that Camilla exited the room, Jeselle looked around. The frayed rope that hung from so many places around her seemed to be mocking her then. She couldn't lose focus. She had worked so long for this moment.

CHAPTER 20

PAST

"The ignorance of the world leaves one at
the mercy of its malice."
-William Hazlitt

"Cindy!" Jeselle saw her coming up the sidewalk, "Mom! Dad!" she yelled back into the house.

She saw her mom rush from the back patio, her dad not far behind.

"Sherrill?" Jessica stood on the porch unsure of what to do.

"Jessica, call 911," he said calmly as he moved closer to Cindy.

"Cindy? Cindy, did Tracy do this?" Jeselle asked.

"Yeah," she sobbed.

Jeselle looked back at her dad. The

disappointment was clear. "You, you knew Tracy hit her?"

She blinked a few times, "No, but he gets mad at her a lot. Like jerks her arm and stuff, but he's never hit her. Nothing like this."

He tried to hide the disappointment, but it was still apparent.

"We broke up last night." Cindy said. "He came over after school and Mom made me go riding to talk it out with him. He only pulled down the street and started yelling at me. Jess, he was so mad. He said I humiliated him by talking to Todd. I, I was only talking to him on the phone last night about Tracy. I don't even know how he found out."

"From Todd, no doubt," Jeselle said under her breath.

"I tried to call her mom, too, but no answer," Jessica said from the porch.

"She's gonna be so mad at me," Cindy said.

"No, she won't. She's your mom," Jeselle tried to reassure her.

"You don't get it!" Cindy yelled, "She will lose her job. She works for his dad, Jess."

"That's stupid. His dad will likely beat him over this!" Jeselle said.

Cindy huffed, "You really believe that, don't you?" Cindy continued to cry.

Soon, sirens wailed in the distance and Jeselle wrapped her arms around Cindy, dumbfounded. The neighborhood security people weren't far behind the paramedics, who didn't take long to assess and bandage up Cindy's face and hands. They said she seemed fine, however suggested she still go to the hospital to get checked out.

Cindy declined. Adamantly.

"I'm so tired," she said as the ambulance backed out of the driveway.

Jeselle's mom walked closer, "I haven't been able to reach your mom yet, but the security guard is going to go to your house and wait for her. It'll be okay. Why don't you go lie down in one of the extra rooms, okay?"

"Yes, ma'am, Mrs. Parsons," Cindy said.

"I'll bring up some chamomile tea?" Jeselle said.

"Yeah, okay," Cindy replied.

In the kitchen, Jeselle started to fill the kettle when her mom stepped in, "Here, let me do this, why don't you go up with Cindy? She likely needs a friend to talk to."

"Mom, I don't know why she came here instead of…well, just about anyone else's."

"Maybe because she thinks you'll understand. Just listen, and help her carry a little of the burden while she's here. That's what listening is, it's us carrying some of the weight with another person. That's all God asks of you."

Jeselle left the kitchen and walked up the stairs slowly. She wasn't even sure she could carry any of Cindy's burden. What she really wanted to do was go beat Tracy up instead, which was nothing new.

"Knock, knock," Jeselle said softly at the open door.

Cindy was lying in the bed crying. Jeselle walked in and sat on the side closest to the door.

"You okay?"

"No," Cindy whispered.

"Want to talk?" Jeselle asked.

"Not really anything to talk about. I guess, I don't understand. He loves me so much sometimes that I feel whole, ya know? Like I'm right where I am supposed to be. But then…" Cindy let her words trail off as she sat up in the bed. "Then, Mom; she's so scared she's going to lose her job, but it sorta feels like she's using me or something. Ya know?"

"Yeah," Jeselle said.

"Do you? Do you think that, too?"

"Maybe, kind of, yeah," Jeselle said.

"Thank you," Cindy fell over onto Jeselle's shoulder and wrapped her arms around her. Jeselle felt uncomfortable for a second, but then she wrapped her arms around Cindy and hugged her back.

They stayed like that for a while, until they heard the doorbell.

Cindy jumped up, "Oh God, it's Mom!" she exclaimed.

"It'll be okay. Just give my parents a little time to talk to her. They'll call up the stairs when they need us. Okay? Relax."

Cindy sat on the edge of the bed tapping her foot. "Can't we go by the stairs and listen?" she asked.

"Yeah, I do that," they both sort of smiled at each other as they made their way closer to the stairs.

"Can you hear anything?" Cindy whispered.

"No," Jeselle whispered back.

They listened as intently as they could, but only heard mumbling.

"Cindy Jean!" Cindy's mom's voice startled them both.

"Coming!" Cindy quickly descended the stairs, Jeselle trailing in behind her. Once they made it into the kitchen, they were surprised to find Brantley Briggs standing near Cindy's mom.

"Mom?" Cindy asked, confused.

"Honey, are you okay?" her mom asked, but didn't move from Mr. Briggs's side.

"Not really," Cindy said slowly.

"Well," Mr. Briggs's voice bellowed through the kitchen in a much louder tone than necessary, "I can tell you, young lady, Tracy will be thoroughly reprimanded for this. This is unacceptable."

"Thank you," Cindy said quietly with relief. Tears started sliding down her face rapidly. Jeselle started crying also.

"Tracy told me that you called him a bunch of names, females are inclined to do that. It excites us men, but still no excuse. He is wrong to hit you." Briggs bellowed again, "Just wrong. I'm ashamed of Tracy."

Jeselle looked over at her parents, and they had as much of a confused look on their faces as she was sure she did.

Cindy's mom spoke up, "Luckily, Darryl stopped the police at the gate, misunderstanding, but they'll likely call back on the situation once the emergency people file their reports. What did Cindy say to them?"

Jeselle's parents remained quiet. Perplexed.

"Mom, I didn't say anything," Cindy said with obvious frustration, "I said I was hurt. That's all. They asked who did it, I said it was my own business. Geez. Are you seriously doing this? How embarrassing." Cindy walked right up to her mom, crying, "Want to lick his shoe while we're all here?" Cindy motioned to Brantley's highly shined shoes.

"That's what I'm saying," Brantley said in a huff, "See? Women and their mouths."

Cindy stormed out of the kitchen; the front door slammed soon after.

"I will be taking care of this, that I can promise you both," Brantley said to Jeselle's parents.

"It isn't me you owe a promise to, Mr. Briggs," her dad said calmly.

Brantley gave a quick nod and left, Cindy's mom followed.

The weekend passed, and Cindy didn't show up at the river. Tracy did, and he made it a point to add that Cindy wasn't feeling well. Jeselle called several times, but Cindy's mother said she hadn't wanted to talk to anyone. Monday, at school, no Cindy. Then on Tuesday Jeselle walked to Cindy's house to check on her. Cindy's mother wouldn't let her in the house, but again stressed that Cindy didn't want to talk to anyone. Wednesday, Jeselle wasn't sure what she had expected when she saw Cindy, the light bruise still visible under one eye. Maybe Jeselle expected a new friendship with Cindy. She definitely was surprised when Cindy purposefully ignored her at lunch with the others. The girls were sitting around the same picnic table they sat at every day for lunch.

Jeselle looked over at Cindy, "You okay?"

Cindy looked disgusted, "Of course I'm okay. Why wouldn't I be? Jess, seriously are you okay? You are always trying to start trouble."

Melanie laughed, but Jeselle saw the familiar look of remorse cross Camilla's face.

"Okay," Jeselle said, "Want you to know I'm always here if you need me."

Cindy stood abruptly and turned to Jeselle, "A lot of good that did me. No thanks. I think I'd rather wing it than to trust you." Her voice resembled a hiss, "You are nobody," Cindy bent closer to Jeselle's face, "and a nobody can't help anybody." Cindy stormed off and Melanie laughed again.

When Jeselle looked over at Camilla, she turned away.

CHAPTER 21

PRESENT

"Actions speak louder than words."
-Becca Fitzpatrick

The moment Camilla stepped in the door she knew Cindy was gone, because the oversized Daum Ultra Violet vase that Cindy had eyed a few too many times was missing. She immediately pulled out her cell.

"Cindy's gone. Looks like she took the Duam with her."

"She took it?" Jeselle asked.

"Looks that way. I mean I just stepped into the door, but it's gone."

Jeselle smiled. Maybe Cindy staying at Camilla's wasn't such a bad idea after all.

"Well, look around first, be sure it's gone and text me."

"Do you want me to call the police?"

"I don't think so. Let me think on it while you look around."

Camilla hung up and searched the condo. She expected to find a note, maybe saying *thank you* or even *sorry for stealing your vase.*

Jeselle's vase, she thought.

It hit her then, that nothing in that condo was hers, except her wardrobe. Not even the pots were hers. Camilla sank onto the floor and cried.

She realized she very literally didn't even have a pot to piss in.

How had she turned out like this? Her house in Wellgrove, the one Rick kicked her out of, was given to them by her parents on her wedding day. It was hers. It came with no mortgage, until Rick needed to get money for his first campaign. She'd agreed without a second thought. Worst case scenario, he didn't win, and her dad had to pay it off again. Only, he had won. Then the tide shifted.

She remembered the exact moment that it had.

She had worked her fingers to the bone helping run his campaign while juggling the kids. She called on every one she knew to help spread the word. Then finally, that night, the night Rick won the seat, her dad had thrown a huge celebration party. She was standing next to Rick in her flowered Oscar De La Renta gown and watched, almost giddy, as her mom and dad approached. Her dad had the biggest smile on his face and Camilla remembered thinking he looked twenty years younger. He hugged Rick and said, "Good thing my daughter married so well." Camilla almost cried in that moment.

That moment changed her. She saw it for the first time...she was just a girl.

From that second forward, it was always about Rick. Maybe it always had been from the beginning and she simply hadn't noticed it. She became numb to all the times she heard, "Where's my other boy?" and "Give Rick our love."

The first time she found out Rick was cheating and went to cry on her mom's shoulder, her dad burst into the sitting room and set her straight.

"Men are men, Camilla. You are whining about him sticking his Johnson in somebody else when he provides a nice life for you! You are the one he loves. Show him the courtesy and respect he deserves. He is giving you a good life." she remembered him throwing his hands in the air, "Spoiled girls. I never wanted spoiled brats and look at you sitting there crying over something so trivial. Men don't see it the way you women do. It's nothing to us. Come on, Girl. He is an assistant District Attorney as well as a State Representative. The man works hard."

She got angry and stood, which surprised her father, "I work hard too! I take care of his kids and his campaign! He wouldn't even be in office without me!" she screamed.

Her dad's face turned red and he stalked slowly toward her, "You listen to me. You go back to that man and you be the good, devoted wife your mother raised you to be. Do you hear me?" he spoke, his teeth clenched, "I will hold back every dime of your trust and make you penniless, humiliated. He works for peanuts to serve this state and you will not push me, Girl. He needs you and your money."

Her mother stood, "Now, Theodore, let me handle this. Go work or something."

He left, but that one glance backward before he did, drove his point home to Camilla.

She was just a girl.

They both stood there, side by side, silent until they heard the study door close.

"Mom?" she whispered, "Does Dad cheat on you?" she turned to look at her mom.

"Camilla, I … I learned … well, about the same as you did, that boys will be boys. My father had the same talk with me years ago."

"Grandad told you to let Dad cheat on you?" she was devastated.

"It's, well … Camilla, it's just the way things are."

"So, you being so depressed? It hasn't only been about Uncle Brantley screwing you out of your part of the business, has it?"

Her mother shut her eyes for a few minutes, took a deep breath, and then replied, "Some, but no, it hasn't."

She hugged her mother tightly, and they cried together.

***

"Camilla said she took it. She's looking through the place now to be sure, but likely she did." Jeselle said through the phone.

"Is this at all funny to you," Dennis laughed, "that it was hers originally?"

"Yes, I admit it is somewhat amusing."

"Surely she knew Tracy sold it. She must've taken it because she knew it was hers."

"Maybe," Jeselle said.

"Then again, that one was a popular one. I have two. It's why I didn't need another when he sold it in the first place."

"I think half the furnishings in the corporate condos came from their house."

Dennis laughed, "I guess he likes selling off Cindy's stuff out from under her. Hey, I meant to ask you, why did Rose fire Rachel? That young girl at the reception desk?"

"I figured Camilla would tell you."

"Camilla? No, wait … why would Camilla know?"

Interesting.

"No reason other than being here when I instructed Rose to do it. So how did you find out?"

"The little twit fired her right in front of me. In the lobby."

It was Jeselle's turn to laugh.

"Seriously, we were leaving, and she came right

up and told her that she was fired. Not to come back."

"Oh, poor Dennis, and let me guess you were there to pick up all the little broken pieces?"

"Hell, no. I hate crying women," he admonished.

They both remained quiet for some time, hard to tell how long. Although, Jeselle knew exactly what Dennis would be thinking of. She was thinking of that night also.

"I mean, you know, unless it's a good reason."

"Of course," Jeselle answered dryly.

"Jeselle..." Dennis sounded pitiful.

"So, let me guess, you cancelled lunch with her also, after her having been fired?"

"Yes, I said 'tough breaks' and left."

"You are a dreamboat, Dennis. However do I keep myself from groveling at your feet?"

"It sounds harsh, but I was really being compassionate. Would you have rathered that I used her in that state?"

"Are there only two choices? How about being a decent human," Jeselle moved quickly to the next comment, "Are you still picking me up for dinner?" she asked.

"That depends, am I allowed up yet?"

"No," she stated bluntly.

"So, no dinner?"

"You are trying to bribe your way back up before the week is out, with a dinner. Which would only be to see if you can manipulate me, since tomorrow is the last day. It's childish. So, no dinner then. See you day after tomorrow, Dennis."

"Wait, Jesel-,"

She hung up the phone, satisfied.

When she exited the front lobby, her car was waiting. Dennis's was also, parked right behind hers. In life, we get choices. We get to decide if we choose one path or another. Sometimes, the choices are hard, and require a lot of thought. Other times, they are very easy. She walked straight for hers, waited for her driver to open the door, before turning in Dennis's direction. She could see him watching her from the backseat. A touch of light from the building illuminated his face.

She waved to him, then got into her car and left.

***

He knew why she did it, why she pushed him away. It was when he pushed her and she had to prove that he couldn't. Dennis knew though, that he could. She'd loved him since middle school and that hadn't changed.

Ever since the kiss in her office, he could see the desire written across her face each time they were together. He saw it in her body language. He knew, like all women, Jeselle wanted him more than she could stand.

He imagined their first time would be a blur of clothes being ripped into the air. He pictured wiping everything off her desk and taking her right there, on top of the entire city. He would pleasure her beyond her wildest fantasies, and she would be his, one hundred percent.

He knew things about her that no one else knew. Her vulnerable side. Her secrets. Her pain. He knew her past and her future. Sometimes, in the right light, he could still see that sweet girl there inside her, wanting to be loved and accepted. Innocent and beautiful. He would treat her like the queen she was. He would love all the hurt away.

He'd also come to realize it wasn't going to happen until everything was done. He needed to be patient. She had to do this, and he was her willing and able accomplice.

Only a few more chess pieces.

The endgame.

CHAPTER 22

PAST

"Monarchs ought to put to death the
authors and instigators of war, as
their sworn enemies and as dangers
to their states."
—Elizabeth I

Christmas at the Stryker's played out with royal fanfare. Jeselle was so excited to be a part of it all, and that her parents were also invited. She stood by Dennis like she was a part of his family and greeted all the guests. Her mom and dad bought her a beautiful dress, red and full like a princess. When Dennis came to pick her up, he paused when she came down the stairs and stared for a long time. That made Jeselle feel even more like royalty. She was relieved when her parents arrived and was eager to introduce them around.

Melanie was really the only glitch in the whole

night.

"Melanie, this is my mom and dad, Mom and Dad, Melanie."

"I'm Mr. Parsons."

Melanie kept her eyes on Jeselle's dad, "So you are the one wreaking havoc at Stryker." It wasn't a question, but it was a statement.

"I'm sorry, what?" her dad asked.

"Wreaking havoc," Melanie said. Then she talked slower like she was talking to a child, "You know, like, making trouble."

Jeselle's dad was obviously taken aback by it, "Wrong person. I'm the one removing the havoc," he replied.

"No, you are the havoc. My mom runs the LAEPA, and from what I hear you are causing quite a stir."

"Ah, yes, the Environmental Protection Agency," her dad laughed, "Well, they like me, I'm making their jobs much easier, not more difficult."

Melanie talked even slower, tapping her fingertips together as she talked. "I said at Stryker, not at the EPA."

Jeselle stood shocked at how comfortable Melanie, a girl in the eighth grade, felt talking to an adult as she was.

"Ah, I see. Yes, well, that 'trouble' is saving Stryker multiple millions, so I imagine the only people who find it to be 'wreaking havoc' would be Stryker competitors."

"There you have it. Making powerful enemies

in such a short time, how bold," Melanie looked at Jeselle.

"We can be bold," Jeselle's mom stepped toward Melanie. Jeselle felt worried for her mom. Her mom didn't know who she was up against. Jeselle prayed to baby Jesus quickly that her mom didn't say anything that would cause Melanie to hate her even more. "No weapon formed against you shall prosper, and you will refute every tongue that accuses you," she said sweetly, "Hi, I'm Mrs. Jessica Parsons."

Melanie didn't smile, "Oh wonderful, Quakers. Exactly what we need," Melanie turned to Jeselle, sighed and rolled her eyes before walking away leaving Jeselle and her parents standing there.

"Jessie, I see now, wow … she is an awful child," her mom paused before adding, "*Is* she a child?" The look on her mom's face was so comical that they all burst into laughter at the absurdity of it. If the conversation with Melanie had shaken them, they definitely hadn't shown it. Jeselle, still smiling with amusement, looked toward Melanie across the room in time enough to see that Melanie had noticed, too.

***

It felt like spring in the park, even though it was February. It reminded her of California, but with a humidifier on high. If the other friends ever found out they met in the park so much, they'd probably get mad. She didn't care; it was worth the risk to sit on that bench and watch nature all around them. The geese were her favorite. They were always there, swimming peacefully. It didn't make any sense to Jeselle that none of the friends ever stopped to enjoy the park, especially since it was free.

The gift was wrapped in white, shimmery paper with a soft golden bow.

"I don't want to unwrap it," Jeselle said.

"Why not?" Dennis asked, shifting himself on the bench.

"It's so beautiful. It's ... wow. Thank you."

"I promise," he said, "you will love what is on the inside much more than the outside. Open it."

Jeselle took her time. She took the bow off and neatly folded it on her lap. She opened one side of the paper, then the other.

"Rip it off. Do like you did at Christmas," Dennis laughed.

"Oh God, did you have to bring that up again? How was I supposed to know you all didn't rip into your gifts? We do."

"Dad said it looked like he was watching a National Geographic special."

Jeselle slapped his leg, "Stop. I'm still so embarrassed about that."

She finally removed the wrapping from the small box and lifted the lid.

"Whoa, wow, is this..."

"Real?" he laughed again, "Of course."

"Dennis, I can't take this. It's so..."

"Expensive? I know. Hey, it's your first teenage birthday and Valentine's Day, so it had to be good. Here," he took it out of the box, "let me put it on you. It's called a rope chain. Mother told me to buy something special to us. The river is special, isn't it? The rope swing is both of our favorite, so I thought this would be perfect."

"Yes," she lifted her hair so he could clasp it on her.

"Then Mother said I had to get you something with a diamond in it; can't have my girlfriend walking around with no jewelry. That's when I picked this pendant. I hope you like it," he said.

"I do. It's incredible." She adjusted the chain on her neck and touched the pendant, something felt wrong about accepting it.

He smiled and leaned in for a kiss.

Jeselle and Dennis sat on the bench for a long while and watched the geese in the pond, the birds in the air, and all the elderly people walking together holding hands. It seemed sweet, not geeky, that the old people loved the park so much.

Sitting there on her thirteenth birthday with Dennis felt like they'd one day be one of those old couples walking together.

***

The morning light spilled so brightly through her window that it woke her from a cozy sleep. Jeselle looked at the clock and shot out of bed.

Late. She was up late. Why hadn't her mom awakened her?

She rushed to take a shower, comb her hair, and throw on a little makeup before running down the stairs.

"Mom! Mom!" she yelled through the house.

"Out here, sweetie."

Jeselle found her mother sipping coffee casually and reading the paper on the back patio.

"Why didn't you wake me up?"

"Jessie, dear it's only six o'clock."

"Yes," Jeselle stressed her words, "and I told you I needed to be to school early today because we are decorating."

Jeselle's mom flew out of the chair, "I forgot. I am so sorry! Oh, no!"

"It's okay, but we need to go now or I'll be late."

"Isn't Dennis picking you up?"

"Mom, really? I mean sometimes I think you aren't listening when I talk. Dennis's driver is on vacation today, so I need you to bring me."

Her mom walked up to her, "I am so sorry. I do listen Jessie, I just have a lot on my mind lately."

"It's okay. Me, too. It's the last day of school, and the decorating committee needs me. So, can we go?" Even though Jeselle wasn't trying to sound rude, she realized she had. Her mom looked sad, and she felt guilty. "It's okay Mom, I love you. It's okay. I'm sorry."

She hugged her mom, and then they made their

way to school. Dennis was already waiting for her.

"Bye, Mom, I love you."

"Bye, sweetie, hey, wait, are you and Dennis okay?"

Jeselle slid out of the seat and looked back at her mom, "Yeah, why wouldn't we be?"

"Oh, no, just asking. I guess I never thought about how weird it could be, you know, you dating the boss's son."

"Is…it…weird?"

"No, I guess not. Do I need to pick you up after school?"

Jeselle rolled her eyes a little, "Yes Mom, Dennis's driver is on vacation, remember?"

"Yes. Okay, see you then. Congratulations on your last day of middle school."

Jeselle smiled wide at her mom, shut the door, and walked away.

Dennis waved at Mrs. Parsons before putting his arm around Jeselle's neck.

"Big day. We will be high schoolers at three-thirty," he practically sang as they walked. "This summer is going to be the best."

***

Summer started with a literal bang. The moment the afternoon bell rang, fireworks flared across the sky.

Jeselle stood outside the front door of the school watching them in amazement.

STOP ME

"Never seen daytime fireworks before?" Melanie asked, coming to a stop beside her. "Figures."

She didn't care about Melanie's tone. She knew, after all the months of dealing with it, that it was more about who Melanie was, not about who anyone else was. Melanie put people down. Jeselle believed more and more it was jealousy. It wasn't only jealousy against Jeselle, it was against everyone. Jeselle found it was pretty easy to figure out once her mom explained why someone would always have such negative things to say to others: self-doubt.

When Melanie said anything negative about someone, after that talk with her mom, Jeselle found she could easily pinpoint what the issue really was.

Calling Camilla pathetic, which she did often, was always after Melanie found that Camilla had done something good, or spent time with other people, especially Jeselle. Camilla always cowered.

Telling Cindy that she was nothing but a pin cushion, which she did often, always happened when Tracy and Cindy were doing well. Or that Cindy was only a cheap whore and only in their world by the good graces of Tracy's lust. It always worked on Cindy, too.

Melanie was good at egging the guys on, like they weren't man enough for this or that, worked too.

Every time.

Not man enough to punch one of the others in the face. Done.

Not man enough to jump into the river without looking. Done.

Not man enough to break up with Cindy. Done.

Not man enough to steal a coke or bottle of wine. Done.

Jeselle was shocked at how much power Melanie actually did have. It also scared her sometimes. Even knowing why didn't curb the fear, it simply made it a bit more predictable.

"Hey, Lanie. You look great today. I meant to tell you earlier," Jeselle said.

Melanie looked at her with a frown.

"I'm serious. You do," Jeselle said again, feeling immediately like a coward herself.

"Thanks," Melanie's said flatly. "That beautiful display is thanks to old man Briggs. He always likes to one-up Dennis's Dad."

"How are fireworks doing that?"

"Jess, I swear you are stupid. Don't you see it? That ridiculously huge Christmas party at the Stryker's with the fireworks display ... you didn't think that was only because the Strykers love Christmas, did you? No. They did it because Mr. Briggs had that Memorial Day fireworks display in the park after that lame picnic. Wow, you need to open your eyes. It is cutthroat here and it's kill or be killed." Melanie walked away, but not before knocking Jeselle's purse off her shoulder.

Jeselle was shocked by it.

CHAPTER 23

PRESENT

"It's about time," Todd said arrogantly, "I had to dangle the money in front of you first, didn't I, Cam Cam?"

"Well, I've never lied to you about that. I need money." She walked into his house, nicely furnished, however not nearly as nice as her own place.

Jeselle's place.

"I am finding it hard to believe you live in your parent's old house," she said.

"Why wouldn't I? It does hold such fond memories of us."

She felt dirty already. "A different time."

He trailed a finger up her sleeveless arm. "Not so different. You still like it dirty, Cam?"

"Gosh, please don't call me that here. I feel like a prostitute, not a young girl in love."

His finger stopped. "Were you in love with me back then?"

"If that isn't obvious then maybe you shouldn't be an attorney, because your skills of observation are sorely underdeveloped."

He smiled at her. "I thought you were in love with Tracy."

"No, I thought I was too at times. But I think it was more because I knew I couldn't have you. You were in love with Cindy."

Even though he'd had no guilt that the arrangement had proved to be very beneficial, he made the decision that very second, before he led her into the bedroom, that he would use every tool he had, to drain every dollar out of her ex-husband, Rick Harrison. After looking over all the paperwork Camilla sent to him the day before, he had plenty. Getting her money back, and her house in Wellgrove, would be child's play. Then he would marry Camilla and finally be a part of the Stryker family.

Her destiny now, literally rested in her own hands, and Todd intended to use them very, very well.

***

STOP ME

The porch light was out. Cindy reached for her phone and used the flashlight on her phone to get the key in the door. She walked in and waited. She really expected Tracy to be there to greet her. She'd told him that she would be home in a few hours.

She walked further in, listening for sounds. She placed the vase on the table, where it belonged. When Tracy told her a year or so before that he'd broken it in a rage, she was devastated. She got more compliments on that vase than any other item in their house. Nearly everyone that was anyone had one. She was disgusted to think Camilla had one and she didn't. Camilla would likely not even notice that it was missing. If she did, she'd never say anything to her about it. That was the way Camilla was, a follower. She did anything to keep the peace, smile, and be pretty. Even let her husband screw half the women in his office without saying a word. Not Cindy. If Cindy ever caught Tracy with another woman behind her back, he'd be dead.

She adjusted the vase a few times, a little to the right, a little to the left. As soon as it was perfect she started upstairs.

The second she opened the door she started screaming. She went as quickly to the bed as the pain would allow. Piled high on top of it were all of her belongings, some of them burnt. Her clothing.

"Oh no! No! No!"

"I'm sorry," she heard him from across the room. She turned to find Tracy sitting in her vanity chair in the corner.

"Tracy, what have you done?"

"I was angry. Still angry," he said.

She tensed up. It was hard to tell if he really was. He seemed calm.

"I wasn't angry on the phone with you. After waiting here for hours, I became angry again."

"So you burnt my clothes?"

"No, that was the day you left. Luckily, the fire didn't really catch on well." He stood slowly and Cindy took a step back. "I put it out right before it truly caught and set off the sprinklers. I imagine I'd be more pissed had that happened."

"Tracy?"

"Hush it!" he took a deep breath, another. Then another. She could tell he was trying to remain calm and she wanted him to. "You clean this mess. Then you come down and have a late dinner with me and Dad. He'll be here in about two hours. Don't be late, be dressed with a smile on, and whatever isn't cleaned up will be thrown out. Do you understand me?"

"Yes," Cindy replied.

Then he walked out of the room. Cindy, still in pain, hurried as fast as she could to get everything back into the closet. She knew she'd never get it all, so she started with the jewelry and most expensive clothing first.

Her side, where the ribs were broken, hurt so badly that she almost gave up and let him throw it all out.

She couldn't.

STOP ME

She knew the pain was only temporary, but those things would be hard to replace now that they were having money troubles. She forced herself to push through the agony to save her dignity. How would she ever go out in public again without decent clothes and shoes?

She knew Tracy would do it too. He'd throw it all away. She was surprised he hadn't already and tried to be thankful.

Watching the clock on the wall she knew when she only had thirty minutes to make herself look decent. Her hair had frizzed badly being at Camilla's because she didn't have her Oribe Gold Lust Conditioner to tame it. She jumped in the shower and out within five minutes and slapped on makeup and a casual house suit that had remained mostly unwrinkled.

Once on the stairs she could hear Brantley bellowing in the foyer below. She put on her best smile and walked carefully down the grand staircase.

"Cindy," he looked toward her, "so happy to have you back. Are you okay, Dear?"

"Yes, Brantley," she kept her smile as normal as possible, "I am. Side is still hurting but its better."

"Good, good!" he put his arms out to greet her at the bottom of the steps, "What is that odor. Smells odd?"

"Oh, yeah, Tracy lit some of my clothes on fire when I left. Smelled up my room."

"He did what?" Brantley took a step back.

"Oh, hey it's no big deal. I'll have them cleaned."

Brantley stared at her like she had lost her mind, maybe she had. Telling Tracy's dad that had basically sealed the proverbial nail in her own coffin, but she'd made that decision in the shower, when the pain had been at its worst while she was washing her hair, that she'd answer all of Brantley's questions honestly, but with a smile.

That's why he was coming for dinner after all. To be sure she was back in the fold.

Cindy had done this a time or two.

"Do you think you need to come stay with me and Raini, Dear? For a few days?"

"I don't know. Maybe if you suggested it, Tracy wouldn't be angry."

"I think you may be right. Speaking of, where is he?"

"I haven't the slightest idea. I was getting dressed."

"Well, let's go look for him together, shall we?"

They made their way through the house, her father-in-law leading her like a horse to slaughter. They were almost to the kitchen where the staff would be preparing dinner. She felt more at ease then, until they stepped into it, and it was empty.

"Where is the staff?"

"Off for the night," he winked at her.

Cindy began to feel panicked. Something wasn't right. Brantley looked at Cindy, slipped his arm around her shoulders and guided her to the back door, "Let's go see what he's doing."

They passed through the patio and onto the side

of the house where the garage was located. The large spotlight on the edge of the garage shone brightly over the back driveway. There was Tracy, with a big smile plastered across his face standing in front of the new Mercedes-Maybach she had been wanting.

"Oh, Tracy," all of her anger slipped away. She walked toward it slowly.

"Tracy here felt you needed a proper apology. I had no problem helping." Brantley came up behind her and squeezed her around the waist.

She winced.

"Oh, sorry, I forgot," her father-in-law said ingenuously.

"Do you like it?" Tracy asked.

"Yes," Cindy felt confused, "I thought you were mad at me?"

She saw something flicker in Tracy's expression, and then he righted it again.

"I was. Still am, you had us all worried," Tracy replied, "Even Ken couldn't find where you were, but you're here now, safe, sound, and home."

Safe. Sound. Home.

All words that didn't ring true to Cindy. Not anymore. She wanted them to, but they didn't. She felt free at Camilla's. Poor, but free. She had decided that she'd rather feel rich than free. But now, standing in front of her dream car, she wasn't so sure anymore.

Tracy lifted the keys and dangled them in front of her like a carrot.

"Go for a spin?"

"Sure," she said, "You drive, my side kind of hurts."

He bent down to her waist and Cindy noticed he looked over at his father before he placed soft kisses on her.

Pins prickled up her spine. Something was off, really off.

"Well, let's go into dinner before you two shoot off down the street. You can take her later; we've got things to discuss."

Cindy felt as though there was a double meaning in old man Briggs' words and felt alarmed. Tracy grabbed Cindy's hand roughly and followed his father into the house, pulling her along.

CHAPTER 24

PAST

"If you want to make enemies, try to
change something."
-Woodrow Wilson

For the first two weeks of summer they had been to the river nearly every day. Jeselle had gotten comfortable with her body, especially since her breasts had finally started filling out. She was thankful that over the past six months they were already bigger than her mother's, but she also realized they would never be as large as her friends' were. At least she was in a B and a half.

She removed her shirt and heard Tracy's cat calls, the same annoying ones he did for all the girls when they took off their shirts or shorts. Jeselle still left her shorts on though. Probably more because she didn't have the hips the other girls did, but she was learning to love herself. Dennis made it easier with the way he showered her with compliments.

"Cindy!" Tracy yelled from the bank of the river. "Take off your bikini top and throw it up to me!"

Jeselle looked at all the other girls already in the water. Camilla was wading close to Melanie. Cindy was closer to the edge.

"Tracy," she pleaded, "I don't want to."

"I didn't ask you if you wanted to, Cindy. Just do it for me." Tracy said then turned to laugh with Todd.

"Make Camilla do it, too." Todd added and they laughed again. "Thirty bucks."

Tracy smiled, "Thirty? How about thirty an hour? Only Cindy. If you want Camilla's off you'll have to do the work yourself, Dude."

"Deal," Todd laughed.

"Don't pay attention to them," Dennis whispered in her ear as he threw his own shirt onto the pile of discarded clothing.

"I don't want to," Cindy replied.

"The water is so muddy, no one will see you," Tracy was getting aggravated, "Keep low. It'll make me happy knowing you're waiting down there for me like that."

They all knew she would eventually do it. That's what Tracy did; he bullied her until she complied.

"Tracy, leave her alone," Jeselle said.

Tracy turned toward Jeselle as Dennis whispered hurriedly in her ear again, "Hey, let it go. That's

216

between them."

"What did you say to me, Jess?" Tracy walked up to her.

Jeselle stood straighter, "I said leave her alone. She obviously doesn't want to do it."

"Listen, you litt-"

"I'll do it!" Cindy yelled from the water. "Look, Tracy," she took off her top and held one arm across her chest while she tossed the top onto the bank, she looked at Jeselle briefly and Jeselle couldn't help but think that Cindy saved her from something. "See, no harm done."

Tracy smiled at Jeselle, and then blew her a kiss. "Sometimes people simply need a little push."

"Come on, Man," Dennis said before Tracy backed up and went to retrieve the bathing suit top. He held it in the air and swung the top around in a circle like he was roping a bull. "Yeee haaaaw."

Jeselle looked back at Dennis, his head was bowed.

"It's not right the way he treats people," Jeselle said.

"I know. I know. Just can't cause any waves, okay? It's okay. Come on, let's go jump."

They did and soon they were laughing and having fun like they always did.

After a few hours, Tracy finally gave Cindy her top back, and she got out of the river to leave. It was obvious she was angry.

"Baby, come on, don't be sore with me. I showed you a good time, didn't I?" Tracy said.

"Lanie's right! You don't see me as an equal." Cindy cried, "You do things to purposefully humiliate me! I hate you!"

"Then get off my property!" he started to get out of the water. Jeselle moved quickly to stand by Cindy. She wrapped an arm around her shoulders, "You okay? Want to come to my house?"

"I'm coming, too." Melanie said.

"Wait for me!" Camilla added.

"You guys can't leave," Dennis said, "We're having the barbeque at my house, remember?"

Jeselle looked at Dennis, "We'll be there later."

The girls put on their clothes and started for the trail. Jeselle looked over her shoulder at Tracy, who was staring daggers into them. The other guys were trying to calm him down.

"Cindy!" he yelled, "You better not leave here with them."

She did. They reached the fork in the trail and decided to take the long way. They came out right at the bend of Grove Forrest Lane which led closer to the front of the neighborhood. Most of the houses up front were only an acres or so away from one another, unlike the back side, where some of them were tens of acres away from their neighbors. By the time they reached Jeselle's house they were laughing and having fun.

"We never do this. Only us," Cindy said. "We are always with the boys."

"Not true. Camilla and I spend the night at each other's houses all the time," Melanie said.

"Well, invite us. I need girl time," Cindy said. "I don't feel alone right now, like I usually do."

"I'd like that too," Camilla added.

Melanie didn't respond, but it was fairly obvious she didn't like that Camilla wanted to invite the others.

When they arrived at Jeselle's house, her mom baked cookies, and they sat around the back patio laughing and talking.

"I like your house," Cindy said to Jeselle. "I forgot how comfortable it felt to be here."

"Oh, it's not ours, it's a Stryker house, remember?"

"Not the house-house. I mean, I like how it feels here."

"Me, too," Camilla agreed.

"We need to go. Dennis's barbeque? The guys will be mad if we take too long," Melanie snapped.

Back to same old Melanie. Jealous and rude.

The walk to Dennis's was quiet. Different than the walk to Jeselle's. The mood had definitely changed. They pressed the button at the gate to get in and walked around to the back of the house. Smoke from two large pits rolled in the air, and it smelled delicious.

Dennis saw Jeselle and rushed to her. "I was worried you forgot."

"I kind of did, I'm sorry. We were having so much fun." Jeselle placed a small kiss on his cheek. "Mad?"

"Not at all. I'm glad you had fun! Food's almost

ready."

He grabbed her hand and led her to a large outdoor area where servers were cooking and laying out long gingham tablecloths on the ground. Jeselle giggled.

"What's funny?" Camilla asked.

"Oh, I've never seen a barbeque...be so formal, with waiters and stuff."

"Yeah, that's my mother for you," Camilla said. "You didn't think she was going to cook it herself, did you?"

"No, I guess I thought your dad would," Jeselle answered.

"Dad?" Camilla laughed, "He'll be at work until way after dark. You know he isn't here very much."

"Right," Jeselle looked at Camilla, then Dennis, and felt sorry for them. "I guess I never noticed."

"That's because a lot of times you come when it's a special occasion or also known as a 'public relations event.' He wouldn't dare miss one of those." Camilla said, and Jeselle felt even sadder for them both.

"Dude, did you see those steaks! They are huge!" William jumped in the middle of them.

"I love your parents' barbeques, Dennis," Todd said, punching Dennis on the arm.

"And Camilla," Camilla added. "They are my parents too."

"Are they?" Melanie said and everybody laughed at her expense, only Jeselle didn't get the joke. She looked around at all the friends. They had a lifetime together. When they all laughed about something she didn't understand, she was reminded that she was the outsider. They all seemed so happy. One after the other she watched as they smiled and joked together, then she saw Tracy. He wasn't smiling. He was glaring at her with hate in his eyes.

She probably should've listened to Dennis and kept out of it, but she couldn't. Not after Cindy came to her house that day. She recalled what her dad said afterwards, "There is power in numbers," and Jeselle wanted to stand with Cindy. She'd felt that she should've stuck up for Cindy countless times before, but she hadn't. Jeselle had decided that day, when she watched Cindy march out of her house soon followed by Ms. Labelle and Mr. Briggs, she felt Cindy was like a lamb being led to slaughter. She knew something had to change. Tracy shouldn't be able to get away with it forever.

She felt as if she'd made an important, empowering decision that day.

She also felt that she'd likewise made an enemy.

* * *

The looks didn't stop; they became almost like a secret between them. She tried to tell Dennis. Even when he saw how Tracy looked at her, Dennis would say it was nothing. Just ignore it. Simply Tracy being Tracy.

Melanie used it every time she could.

"Awww, poor Tracy can't control everyone. Looks like Jeselle might help your spineless lackey of a girlfriend find a back bone."

"I'll talk to her," Dennis would say, but it didn't seem to do any good, because it continued over the next month. Each time they were together, Melanie would say something about Tracy being weak, or pathetic and it would make him mad again.

"I'm only saying you let him get away with anything. He's not a good person, Dennis." Jeselle said walking home one evening.

"He's my cousin. I've told you, Jess, Dad asked me to deal with it until Mother gets her money. It's only another year or so. I can handle his crap until then," Dennis said, unconcerned.

"He knows it, too! What if I can't?" she asked. "What if I can't handle it?"

"You can…for me. He's harmless."

"He's not harmless to Cindy. He treats her awful," Jeselle started to raise her voice.

"She lets him. She knows how to handle Tracy, trust me. We've been watching that roller coaster for years, and she likes the drama," Dennis laughed. "Ask the others. She eggs it on."

He had a point. Jeselle had wondered so many times why Cindy did things that she knew would make Tracy mad. Also, Jeselle had seen them break up numerous times, and she'd only been living there for close to a year.

Wow, had it been almost a year? she thought. Still, even for a year, it was a lot of break ups. "You're right. It makes me mad the way he treats her."

"She must like it," Dennis said.

Later, in bed, Jeselle thought about the whole set of friends. When she had first moved, she was so thankful to have them. Then she started seeing how money ruled most of what the friends thought and did.

Then, power.

There was always a power dynamic that Jeselle couldn't quite put her finger on, mainly between Melanie and Tracy. But also Tracy over Dennis. Melanie over Camilla. Camilla over Todd. All the guys over William. Still, Melanie over everyone, even though Tracy fought for first place, she knew exactly how to play him, too.

They were her friends, and it was for the most part harmless, even if a little disturbing.

Dennis was by far the best of the group. He didn't want to cause waves. He was the peacemaker. She was excited for the weekend. It was going to be her first slumber party, and all the girls were staying over.

***

Jeselle woke up in the best mood. All of her girlfriends were going to spend the night. Dennis wanted to spend the afternoon with her for a few hours and Melanie asked to go to her house early so they could talk.

Jeselle knew, at some point, she'd get through to Melanie. She thought Lanie was rude, but at least she was pretty honest about it. Melanie had eased up on a lot of her prodding the others for the past week. Maybe she could change after all, like Jeselle's mom had said.

Hopping down the stairs she felt the temperature change and realized that her parents were up early for a Saturday, sitting on the back patio, with the back door open, of course. She would swear her parents were hippies sometimes, turning off the air and opening the doors as much as they did. They basically lived outside anyway.

She smiled, reached for a bowl and poured the cereal. Before adding milk, she thought to go say good morning first. When she got closer to the back door, she heard her dad first.

"Jessica, the royalties alone. We could live off only that," he exclaimed.

"Oh, Sherrill, I am so happy for you. You are finally seeing the fruits of all your labor through the years," her mom said sweetly.

"Well, I guess the positive environmental impact is the true fruit, but to be making that much money off my passion. My work," he said excitedly.

"Well, do you want to not work? Live off the royalties and travel the world?" her mom sounded whimsical.

"No, there is still a lot left to do. The world needs our help. Mr. Stryker is getting me a mobile phone Monday."

"Oh, important," her mother teased, then turned serious, "I really am so very proud of you. All those years of living on pennies when we were young."

"Yes."

Jeselle took the pause as a signal and she exited the back door.

"Morning!" she sang.

"Well, good morning to you, young lady," her dad said.

"You excited about tonight?" her mom asked.

"Yes, ma'am! Dennis is coming in a little bit so we can see each other before."

"Ma'am? Where did that come from?" her mom asked.

"Oh," she thought for a moment, "I guess from the others. They all say that here." Jeselle answered and turned to go back into the house when her mom said, "Blueberry muffins in the oven if you want to wait."

And wait she did, because her mom's homemade blueberry muffins were the best.

CHAPTER 25

PRESENT

Jeselle pointed to the chair in front of her desk, "Here, sit. So, he did reply by email?" she asked.

"Yeah, Mr. Reims doesn't care, Ms. Parsons, I've been telling you. He thinks he won't get caught," Desiree said.

"Well, that's more because William thinks you won't turn him in," Jeselle added.

"Right. Hey, as long as I let him-"

"Desiree," Jeselle interrupted, "you better not be doing what I think you were about to say you were."

"It's nothing, I've slept with hundreds of men," Desiree waved her hand around in the air.

"No, Desiree, you will not do that. I didn't have you go to the Haevn.E to get office skills so you would still be…" Jeselle let the rest of her words hang unspoken.

"Hey, it got you the information, didn't it?"

"At what cost?" Jeselle became angry.

"Look, I appreciate your indignance on my behalf, but it's wasted. I can have sex with whoever I want."

"I'm not saying you can't. However, I'm pretty sure you wouldn't pick William Reims as a sex partner given difference circumstances. And I don't want you sleeping with him to get information. You already have the job. You are worth more than that."

Desiree looked serious for a minute. "It really isn't that big a deal. I've slept with men for a meal, Ms. Parsons. It doesn't mean anything to me. Promise."

"But you mean more to me. Desiree, it is okay to love yourself, past and all. Learn and embrace every stage in your life, no matter where it is. But you don't need to have sex with men for meals anymore. You are educated and I pay you well, don't I?"

"Yes, you do," she said.

"I don't pay you to do that. I pay you for information. You are worth more than that. No more, okay?"

"Well, I can't stop now, he'll fire me for sure. Then you won't get the info you need."

"Print all those emails safely. Hold on," Jeselle lifted her hand, picked up the phone and dialed.

"Jeselle, I was wondering when you'd get with me," William said. "I would love to get more stuff transferred to your portfolio."

"Been busy," Jeselle said sweetly, "however, that's exactly what I was calling about. I need to add several stocks. Also, any high rate return investments you know of?"

"How high a rate and what kind of money are you looking at? I mean I've got a few on the line, they seem on the up and up."

"Perfect! Lunch?"

"How much we talking?"

"I think I want to invest around one, maybe one and a half."

"Yes, I can definitely get you going with that. Probably a thirty return, maybe higher."

"Thirty? Is that possible?"

"With a hefty investment, yes. Don't tell anyone though. It's only for special people."

"I feel so fortunate. Lunch? I'll order in."

"For you, I'll be there, Jess."

She hung up the phone.

"He offered you that fund thingy? He really is stupid," Desiree said.

"People who have always had power usually are. Tell me more about it."

"Like I said, I heard him talking about it, but I don't know anything really. It's all a bunch of numbers to me."

"Go back. I will keep him as long as I can and call you when he leaves. Print everything you can find on that. Can you do that?"

"You bet I can," Desiree smiled.

Once the door closed, Jeselle walked to the window of her office and peered out over the city. Setting people up to do the wrong thing was so easy when it was people like William. The ones who think their money and power will protect them forever. People who have hot shot lawyers like Todd Parrish. Or huge investors like Brantley Briggs.

The phone ringing broke thoughts, and she quickly picked it up.

"Ms. Parsons," Karli said, "lobby reception called, Camilla is off in a far corner of the main lobby, sobbing."

"Sobbing? Did anyone offer to help her?" Jeselle asked.

"I don't know. They are concerned though."

"I'll go."

It wasn't hard to find her in the large lobby sitting off to one end.

"Camilla," Jeselle's voice was stern, "Why are you in my main lobby blubbering like a baby? Get up."

Camilla looked up at Jeselle in her perfectly tailored suit. Jeselle was flawless in her understated, but expensive jewelry, and smooth long, golden hair, and Camilla saw a friend. Even though she didn't sound like one, Camilla knew definitely she was.

"I have made … such a mess … of my life."

"Well, messes can be remedied, stand up,"

Jeselle commanded and Camilla stood.

"Go up to my office. Tell Karli to have you wait in the break room and have her order us all coffees and blueberry muffins. I'll be there in a minute."

"Oh, I don't think I could eat anything," Camilla said through tears.

"They are for me," Jeselle stated bluntly.

Jeselle watched as Camilla walked to the elevators. She was disappointed when the accountants audited the books the week before in Camilla's department and not only didn't find any discrepancies; they also found that Camilla had saved the company money.

Jeselle had really expected her to steal.

Yet the accounting firm came up with nothing.

She had also assumed Camilla told her brother about Rachel getting fired, but he had only witnessed it for himself, even puzzled that Camilla would've known anything about it at all.

So, she'd kept that secret.

Jeselle could tell that Camilla had housed Cindy as a friend and not a foe. Camilla was so remorseful once it hit her that Cindy was actually a competitor's wife. She also called when she found that the vase was missing. That could've been to save her own hide; it was a sixty-five-hundred dollar vase after all. Yet, when Jeselle offered to buy another one, Camilla had said she'd found one at a yard sale she'd stumbled upon the day after.

Camilla at a yard sale?

Jeselle made her way up the elevators and

through the fifth floor reception area when her cell rang.

"Hello, Dennis," she said.

"My time is up. I intend to ride the elevator up to the fifth floor and to the lobby at least fifty times today, so heads up."

Jeselle laughed loudly, "You are so entertaining."

"I know. Can I entertain you for lunch?"

"Oh, I hate to do this, with you being unpunished and all, but I have other plans," she rushed to make amends, "Dinner?"

"Dinner sounds more promising. Pick you up after work?"

"No, I'll come to you."

"We need to go out. We have a waitress that needs firing," Dennis offered it as though it were a gift.

"Oooo, true. Okay, pick me up at my house, not the office," she said.

"Jeselle?"

"Yes?"

"I'm still going to ride the elevator in your building up and down all day, so if you see me, ignore, I'll be exercising my freedom."

She laughed again, and then ended the call. Entering the elevator that led to the upper floors, Jeselle got close to the mirror. She looked into her reflection until the elevator dinged announcing her arrival. She quickly exited the moment the doors opened. Camilla was in the breakroom with Karli, still crying.

"Are you missing your life that badly?" she asked, "I understand, but Camilla you must move forward."

Karli exited as Jeselle seated herself at the table. Camilla looked up at her.

"You don't understand," Camilla said.

"Let me guess, you simply cannot tolerate living like this. Having to work and…" Jeselle saw something that caused her to pause.

"No, it's not the work, I, well, never thought I'd say this, but I actually am enjoying it. It's fulfilling. It's not that," Camilla used a tissue to wipe her eyes.

"Well, spit it out," Jeselle grew frustrated, more likely because she was starting to like Camilla and that was disturbing.

"I hired Todd," she sniffed, "to help me with getting some of my money back from Rick."

"I thought the divorce was final, over and done with."

"It is, but I had boxes of stuff from the last campaign still in the back of my car the day he wouldn't let me come back in the house. He didn't realize I still had them. It had files upon files of transactions where he was transferring money from my trust into another account. Not…not his campaign one. One I didn't know about."

"Oh," Jeselle sat back in the chair, "go on."

"Also, where he had forged my signature on other documents that I had never seen. Loans mostly, but it showed that he could've done the same with the prenup. Dennis told me to go to Todd, and when

I did Todd said it looked like the exact signature, which would be easy enough to prove."

"Okay, then why are you crying? What am I missing? You should be elated that Rick will not only get booted out of office and disbarred, but will likely go to prison. That should make you happy."

"I guess it should, but I haven't really thought about all of that. I don't think I want to see him go to prison, broke maybe," she laughed bitterly.

"It's Todd," Jeselle leaned forward. "He is charging you?"

"Oh, well yes, I knew he would but, I don't have any money. And he said he couldn't wait, there was another way I could pay him."

The silence drew out.

"Oh," Jeselle breathed, "no."

Camilla closed her eyes.

"How do you feel about that?" Jeselle asked in a whisper.

"Awful!" Camilla started crying again. "I've been there two nights in a row. It's been awful. I feel so, ugh. He is telling me he loves me, but the whole time, you know, he's smiling. Like he loves that I'm, I don't know, at his service. I don't even know why I'm telling you this. You!"

"Camilla, listen to me. That is not love. That is someone using you. In fear of sounding preachy, which I certainly am not, I'll keep this short. My mom used to say *'Love is patient and kind. It doesn't envy or boast. It is not proud.'* What Todd is doing, isn't love."

"I know. I'm pretty angry about it, if I'm being honest…" Camilla sniffed a little and lifted her nose in the air, "Todd. of all people. How did I sink *that* low?"

A laugh slipped out, "Camilla, you are one of the few truly arrogant ones."

"Pardon?"

"Nothing. Let's see, okay, I say tell Dennis. He would be the one to help you. He can pay the attorney's fees and hold Todd at bay."

"That's the other reason I'm crying. I did tell him, this morning."

Jeselle felt her temperature rising, "And?"

"He laughed and said I deserve what I get. He said he found it comical that his snobby sister finally got the screwing she has given everyone else. Said he hopes it humbles me."

"Did he now?" Jeselle sighed, "Okay, then you and I will make a deal that is far better than the one you have with Todd. We need him to get you your money, but also not have you to debase yourself. Come to my office first thing in the morning. And Camilla, tell no one, not even Dennis. Do you hear me?"

"Okay, should I be worried? Am I going to have to be your maid for the rest of my life or something?"

"No. However, I do pay my maids much more money than I pay you right now, if you ever reconsider."

Camilla smiled, warm and honest, dropping eye contact, "Of course you do."

STOP ME

Jeselle left the room and went into her office. She'd have to leave early in order to look perfect for dinner.

She didn't want to ponder too much on the fact that she felt bad for Camilla, or why she wanted to help. She was sure it was the next part of the scripture her mother used to say all the time that she'd omitted when telling Camilla about love.

'It does not dishonor others, it is not self-seeking, it is not easily angered, it keeps no record of wrongs.'

Because Jeselle absolutely kept a record.

CHAPTER 26

PAST

"Destiny means there are opportunities to
turn right or left, but fate is a one-way
street."
-Paulo Coelho

Jeselle ran as fast as she could. The tears were
burning her eyes and branches were slapping her
in the face. The moon provided some light, but not
much and she wasn't very familiar with the trail.
She looked back.

No one was following her.

Then, she tripped. Pain exploded in her knee
as she hit the ground, but she got up and started
running again. She couldn't run as fast, simply
because her knee hurt so badly. She found that she
had to stop for a second to catch her breath. She
looked back at the trail.

STOP ME

No one was behind her.

She started sobbing. Jeselle couldn't believe what was happening. She felt her heart pounding in her chest and thought, it too had exploded. Just then, she heard the snap of a branch.

She took off running again. Her lungs started to burn. The humidity made it worse. She was sweating and sticky. Branches were clawing at her as she ran faster.

"Jess!" she heard Dennis calling her from far away. She ran faster and faster. Finally, she hit the opening to the trail. She realized, in trying to look around for light that one of her eyes was swollen shut. If only she could make it to a house.

"Jess!" She heard her name again, only this time closer.

She ran. She ran straight for the street.

The last thing she remembered before she woke up in Dennis's arms was a flash of bright light and his voice yelling at her in the distance.

* * *

"Oh God, Jess, please be alive. I love you, please," Dennis's voice cracked through her silence. Another man's voice was pleading to God for help.

"Letty, Wayne Letty! I didn't even see her! Oh God, she jumped right in front of my car! I swear!" he was hysterical, "Please hurry. No, no, not my house, I'm on one of those mobile things, we are in the bend of Grove Forrest Lane in Wellgrove Estates."

Dennis whispered in her ear, "He called 911, he called 911! Oh Jess, please, please be okay. I, I tried. I am so sorry Jess, I love you. Please don't die."

She must have passed out again. When she awakened that time, it was with noises flooding from every angle. Sirens wailed all around her, red flashes of light kept throbbing through the thick night air, a man was yelling.

Then Dennis. He was crying and pleading that she would be okay.

As they loaded her into the ambulance, they tipped the stretcher to one side by accident, and her life switched to slow motion. She saw each of them standing off in the distance, just inside the tree line. The red light from the ambulance flashed on them several times as they stood there.

Tracy Briggs.

Cindy Labelle.

Todd Parrish.

Camilla Stryker.

William Reims.

Melanie Wheaten.

Better known as her frenemies.

* * *

Dennis rode in the ambulance with her. She could barely see him out of the corner of one eye. She couldn't move her neck, and she wasn't sure why.

Still, even through the blur, she knew it was Dennis.

"I love you, Jess," he was still crying.

They came to a stop, and she was unloaded. People whisked around her as they wheeled her through double doors with a bright red sign that read EMERGENCY.

"Who are you?" a stranger asked.

"I'm her boyfriend, Dennis Stryker."

"Stryker Steel?"

"Yes!" he answered.

"My husband works there. Okay, what happened?"

They were moving her at a fast pace while they talked.

"We were playing a game, hide and seek, she got scared and ran through the woods into the street."

"She's pretty banged up."

"Yeah," Dennis said.

"Okay, we're gonna ask you to wait out here-"

"Uhh-uh," Jeselle grunted.

"I'm sorry?" the medical worker got closer.

"He...come."

"You, come," the stranger repeated louder.

"Thank you! Jess, I'm here," Dennis reassured her.

"Mom," she managed to get out.

"My..." he seemed frantic, "Mr. Letty still has my mobile."

She felt like she should be angry at Dennis, but she was also thankful that he was there. She really didn't know what to feel, but she knew deep down she could trust him.

After a number of tests and X-rays, Jeselle was put into a small area closed off by a curtain. The doctor came in briefly to let her know that her internal organs seemed to be okay, but physically, she had a few issues. A broken arm, two broken ribs, a fractured ankle, and three broken toes. "Lucky," he'd said, because that car could've killed her. They were keeping her overnight as a precaution.

Once the doctor left, Dennis sat next to the bed.

"It's going to be okay, Jess. I promise. Dad's on the way. He's going to help."

"My…parents," she said, although barely. Her throat was sore and scratchy.

"Please, please tell the police it was a game and you got scared and ran into the road. Please."

He could've punched her, and she would've felt it less.

"Jess, I'm scared," he whispered, "Dad said this could ruin all of our lives. If not, I understand. I'm here for you," he paused, "Look, say what you need to say. Okay? I'm here."

It was clear to Jeselle that his emotions were all over the place. She heard him break down sobbing and her anger dissipated.

* * *

"I have a proposition for you, Officer Hayes," Theodore Stryker stood off to one side of the large hospital corridor and passed him a small bundle. "I need some side investigations done and Chief Reynolds here told me you were the one to talk to."

Officer Hayes looked to the Chief who nodded, then he opened the package and saw a brown strap of cash. "I can do side work?"

"Yes, plenty of officers do it," the chief replied. "I need to head back, Theodore." The chief patted him on the back, shook the man's hand, and left through the emergency room doors.

"I need someone watched," Stryker focused back to Officer Hayes.

"Watched? How?"

"Your typical stuff. See where he goes right after work, his routine before work, that kind of thing."

"And how long does this five-grand pay for?"

"A week."

"A week! That's a lot of money."

"Chief Reynolds and Captain Kramer said your investigative skills are worth it."

"Then yes, I accept. I can only do it on my days off. I'm on four a week." The officer shook hands with Theodore and agreed to meet with him that following Monday morning. When he started to walk away, he turned back, "Hey, what about the girl?"

"I am here to help her. I know her dad, he works for me, and he's a good guy. We'll sort it all out. You know, we get stuff like this all the time, unfortunately," Theodore lowered his head and blew out a long breath, "That's the down side of having money son, somebody else always wants it."

"She seemed really upset."

"Oh, I don't doubt they scared her real good. They play this stupid game of hide and go seek in the damn woods back there by the river. They shouldn't have let her play alone the first time. It gets dark back there. Wish Brantley Briggs would sell that land off or keep the kids out of it. It's caused more trouble than it's worth."

Officer Hayes nodded in understanding, "I'll see you Monday."

CHAPTER 27

PRESENT

"A woman always has her revenge ready."
 -Jean Baptiste Molier

The door opened and Dennis was stunned into silence. Jeselle stood before him in a beautiful, red, silky gown. Simple and elegant. It hung off her shoulders and fell over her body, cascaded wonderfully around each curve. She was perfection, as always.

Under the massive diamond necklace, he noticed something else, "The pendant."

"Yes," she replied softly and touched it.

"Wow, Jess … Jeselle, it looks better on you now than it ever did back then. Does this mean something?" he asked hopefully.

"It does," she replied softly again.

"Should I have brought a special box with me tonight?"

She laughed lightly, "No, you still have Raini in your future."

"I don't need that though. That was going to be my last jab at dear Uncle Brantley, but I don't need to screw his wife." Dennis walked forward, almost ceremoniously, and placed a kiss on her cheek. "Dinner awaits, my love."

They held hands all the way to la Rousse du Coup. Of course, they were seated immediately. This time Jeselle sat next to Dennis and not across from him as she usually did. His approval was fierce.

"Are you sure she's here tonight?" she asked.

"Yes, George confirmed, and I requested her when I placed the reservation," he answered. "Funny thing is, there was no Melanie working here. After I described her, they knew exactly who I wanted. I laughed and said I simply must've gotten her name wrong."

"Well, you have it all thought out."

"We, you and I, we have it all thought out. Finally, Jeselle it's coming together. We will finally have the revenge we deserve."

"Yes, finally," she agreed.

A much younger, less worn Melanie appeared at their table.

"What can I get for you both tonight?" she asked, then recognition registered on Melanie's face and she appeared scared.

The satisfaction Jeselle felt moments before dissipated. For years they had chased her around town, making sure she got less and less with each job. Working in the worst of dumps, and now she has a crisis of conscience.

"Hello, Melanie," Jeselle said.

"So good to see you've moved up in the world. Really saves us from having to go to those junky cafés," Dennis added cruelly.

"Look, guys, please, don't get me fired. I need this job."

"Oh, what a pity," Dennis laughed flippantly.

"We were kids!" she yelled hysterically, "Please! Jess, we were kids!"

A manager appeared quickly and asked if everything was alright.

"No," Dennis gasped, "She was yelling at us. I am Dennis Stryker of Stryker Steel, and I have never been so insulted."

"I am so sorry, Mr. Stryker, I, I," the manager stuttered.

Melanie took off her fancy server's apron, tossed it onto the table and left.

"I don't know why she would do that. Lily has been a great server."

"Melanie, her name is Melanie, and when we were kids she got into a lot of trouble. Stole wine, cigarettes, that sort of thing. I guess she never forgave my dad for turning her in," Dennis said.

"Oh, well, sir, I am so sorry about that," the manager bellowed.

"Is it then safe to say we won't find her in here again?" Dennis asked.

"Yes, indeed, sir. Meal on the house today," the manager insisted.

"No, need. We appreciate your diligence," Dennis smiled.

After the manager left to find them another server, Dennis turned to Jeselle, "I think we've actually broken her this time. Bon appétit."

The meal was served quickly and Dennis and Jeselle had a host of staff at their service.

"This is a really good steak. We do need to come here more often."

"I don't know how you eat so much, Dennis," Jeselle said.

"I have a large appetite for all things."

"Let's discuss. Found out from William today that I can invest a mil, or mil and a half and get a thirty percent return."

"I knew it!" Dennis laughed, "And you taped him?"

"Of course."

"George is the best at finding out the dirt, isn't he?" Dennis asked.

"I don't know, is he?"

Dennis looked at Jeselle pleadingly, "Not tonight Jeselle, don't ruin tonight. If you would simply meet the man, you'd see he's a good guy."

"I think I had enough of him when I was a teenager, thanks anyway."

"Don't hold a grudge against him, he didn't

know. The chief told him to leave. He thought they were going to take care of you."

"Oh, they did alright."

"Jess, stop it! I said not tonight," he snapped and Jeselle knew to leave it alone. "Now I've already had the Chief and Captain fired, what more do you want."

"*You*, Dennis did not have them fired; their own corruption got them fired." Jeselle softly reminded him.

"Tit for tat. Leave it alone," he demanded.

"Fine," she whispered.

"Better. Now, let's continue. William."

"Yes," Jeselle seemed flustered, "while he was offering it to me, Desiree printed as much of the evidence as she could find."

"Then we have him. Don't do anything until he can sell Briggs stock for me right before they tank."

"I'm not going to be a party to that. Besides, too late, it's already been sent to the FBI."

"I hardly believe *the* Jeselle Parsons is getting a crisis of morals?" Dennis said mockingly. "Fine, I'll sell through someone else. You are willing to lose all that money? It's ridiculous."

"I simply don't do that and you very well know it…," she said, "illegal stuff, and you shouldn't either."

"And you know I don't lose money," he dotted the end of her nose with a finger, "that's why you are so sweet and we make a great team. I don't mind doing the dirty work. Yes, I could wait, but why when I'd lose so much. This way William can still take the fall if there are any red flags. I'll simply blame it on him. Win-win in my book. I guess you can afford to lose that much, but I certainly can't."

"Now on to Todd. He's despicable, Dennis. You know what he is doing to your sister and you told her she deserves it?"

"She does. Jeselle, she ended up not stealing from you like we thought she would, what else was there? You want to do this legally," he stressed, "let people fall into their own traps? Well, she didn't and after what she did to you," he paused to stroke her arm, "It's what we've worked for, isn't it? Her in prison and me taking over all of her money that Todd gets back from Rick. I mean, she has always brought full discredit on the Stryker name."

"But she didn't steal, and won't be going to prison," Jeselle pointed out the obvious flaw.

"Yes, who would've thought? Camilla, a good person? Please."

"She is doing a good job," Jeselle offered. "A really good job."

"Either way, Todd will still tie her money up in a trust with me as trustee. I'll bring the money back to Stryker, where it belongs, and she'll be penniless. She never really worked a day for it anyway.

"Why do you sound like your Uncle Brantley?"

"Are you trying push me," he smiled widely, "I may love you, but calling me anything like that old parasite is grounds for a parting of ways," he quipped, but Jeselle could tell he'd been hurt by her observation.

"What of Todd?"

"Yes, that plan worked like a charm, didn't it?" he smiled.

"What plan?" Jeselle asked.

"Getting him to make her have shameful sex with him in return for his help."

"Plan?" Jeselle scooted away from him, "You orchestrated that?" She was truly taken aback.

"Oh, please, Jeselle, save your morality crisis. She needed to be kicked off that high horse of hers. Todd was more than willing. He's been trying to get back into her pants for years, and she ignores him incessantly. Think nothing more of it. It was an extra, for me really."

"Wait, you planned that with Todd?" Jeselle asked with repulsion apparent on her face. "She's your sister."

"Yes, she is. One that not only abandoned you, but treated you mercilessly after. Also, she sucks the family of money at every turn. But, let's not forget why we are here. I did it for you," Dennis stated.

"You, Dennis Stryker, planned that far before the audit, so you did not do that for me. You did that because you are a hideous creature," she kept her words cool, "I didn't know you were hatching so many plans behind my back. I thought we were a team."

"Oh, come on, we are," he leaned in to kiss her cheek, "It was an extra bit of fun. No harm done."

"What of Todd?" she asked again.

"No touching Todd, for now anyway. He's done so many shady business deals over the years, George will find something, but I need him to get Camilla's money and assets back first. He'll file all the reports soon and Rick will not only be out of cash and a job, he'll likely be out of a life too," Dennis beamed with pure satisfaction.

"Then, that's it, I guess," she smiled wearily. "You have officially become the worst human being in the entire world."

"Yes, trumping only you, my dear," he assured her. "Soon you will be vindicated and the world will be set to rights again."

***

"George that is what I pay you for, and very well I might add. I need something on Todd Parrish," Dennis said into the air of his car.

"I'll look further, give me a few days. Old man in on this one?"

"Is he ever? No, still, never report to him. He's retired, living the good life. Mother is finally coming out of her nearly twenty-five-year depression, I am in charge now. Get me something, quick."

"I can only get what's out there. His office is tight-lipped, no one will talk. I've spent more hours in bars trying to pry information out of his drunk employees than I have at home."

"Then I'll add an extra ten grand, find me

something already." Dennis pressed the disconnect call button on his steering wheel.

Jeselle, sweet, Jeselle. She wanted revenge, but didn't quite have the stomach for it. No matter, that was his job. Since she was twelve years old, she had been his. Even through college. Even when they drifted apart at times, she remained pure as the driven snow. He got excited thinking of taking her for the first time.

Her true first time.

When she opened up to him, and welcomed him, it would be the best night of his life. A night he would be sure to consummate their nuptials. She needed respect, she deserved it. She had saved herself all these years. He now knew she was sexual, he'd seen it play across her face, and it made him happy to know it. He'd believed for years that they would have a sexless marriage, possibly having it only for the children she deserved, but mostly not on the radar. That was okay with him, he'd known years earlier it was part of his own penance, and he was willing to pay it. Since that kiss in her office coupled with tonight, he felt a new vigor.

Hope.

Soon, he knew. She was so close he could hear the church bells ringing. Married to his best friend; that truly was what life was about. The realization floored him.

He thought about the ring he'd bought years before. The one that sat in that tiny, perfectly gift wrapped box. It wasn't nearly big enough. He had considered several times through the years of trading for a larger diamond, but he knew the sentiment of that ring, that very ring, was what he wanted to slip onto her hand before saying 'I do.' Then, on their one year anniversary, he rapidly worked out the details in his mind, he could buy her an upgrade, maybe use the original to make another piece of jewelry.

He felt like a king already having taken back his family's stolen fortune, but soon he would truly be king when he married the only person he'd ever truly loved.

CHAPTER 28

PAST

"Not everyone has been a bully or the
victim of bullies, but everyone has seen
bullying, and seeing it, has responded to
it by joining in or objecting..."
—Octavia E. Butler

One of her eyes was glued shut. She tried to open the other one, but it was so painful she stopped trying.

"Ma'am?"

The voice startled her.

"Sorry ma'am, I'm Officer Hayes. George Hayes. I need to ask you a few questions."

Jeselle tried to sit up, found she couldn't without terrible pain.

"Sorry Ma'am, maybe you shouldn't try to move. Uh, I need to ask you some questions about the accident. Can you talk?"

"Yes," she whispered, her throat scratchy and sore.

"The man that hit you said you were already bloodied when you ran in front of his car. Is that correct?"

"Yes," Jeselle started crying.

"Okay. So, you were already hurt. Is that correct?"

"Yes."

"And you were running from the woods. Is that also correct?"

"Yes." With every answer her throat seemed to grow more and more inflamed.

"Can you tell me, what happened before Mr. Letty hit you?"

"Yes, I was, was with … friends," she started sobbing, then choking.

"Take your time, ma'am."

"I was with friends, we were doing what we always do on Saturdays, swimming in the river and then something changed," Jeselle coughed a few times.

"Do you need some water, miss?"

"Yes, please."

"Let me get a nurse, hold on."

Jeselle cried as she waited. The more she cried, the more she could open her swollen eye a bit. The tears were loosening whatever it was that had glued her eye shut.

Blood, she figured.

Jeselle leaned over a bit to look out of the opening

in the curtain and pain shot through her. She could barely distinguish Dennis talking to his dad and the doctor that had left after examining her. Where was her mom and dad? What was taking them so long?

The curtain was pulled open further.

"Hey, Ms. Jeselle, this is Trudy. She's real sweet. She brought you some water and pain medication."

"Hello sweetheart," The voice was soothing; Jeselle started sobbing again, this time with relief.

"Is … my mom … or dad here yet?" she asked.

"No, honey, but your friend who came with you said they are on their way."

"They hurt me," Jeselle heard nothing for a few seconds.

"Who did?" the policeman asked.

"My frie-, the people I was with at the river," Jeselle could barely get the words out.

"Honey," the sweet woman said, "here have a sip of water, your throat is dry. Are these people your friends? The ones who you were at the river with?"

Jeselle started crying even more. She heard the curtain being whisked open again and hoped it was her parents.

"Officer Hayes, Chief wants you," a deep male voice said.

"Okay, tell him I'll be out in a few. Need to finish this," Officer Hayes replied.

"Nope. Needs you now. I'm takin' over the interview." The deep voice stated. "Also, nurse lady, I need to interview her alone, if you don't mind."

The policeman was much larger than Officer Hayes, and didn't look nearly as nice.

Jeselle got nervous, "No! Don't leave me, please, Ms...Ms. Trudy can stay."

"No can do. This is official police business, she'll have to leave."

Ms. Trudy moved closer to her, "I'll be right outside of that curtain. It'll be okay. This policeman is going to help you. Then I'll come back in, okay?"

"Okay."

As soon as the curtain was closed again, the policeman started.

"I'm Captain Kramer. So, one of these boys is your boyfriend, right?"

"Yes, well, yes."

"And you'd kissed some of the others earlier in the day, is that right also?"

Jeselle let the tears fall as they needed, she didn't think she could truly stop them anyway. "It wasn't like that."

"Uh huh, tell me what it was like. And you better be sure you get this right, you are blaming some people for some mighty big crimes," he said sternly.

"We were playing hide and seek. The penalty, if caught, was...you had to kiss the one who caught you. Only a peck kiss, you know."

"Did you get kissed a lot?"

"I'm sor-, sorry, what?"

He cleared his throat, "Did you get caught a lot?"

"I guess so, I really don't know my way around the woods that well."

"Haven't you lived here for almost a year?"

"Yes, but-"

"And haven't you been goin' to the river nearly every weekend of that year?"

"Well, yes, but—"

"And you tellin' me you didn't know your way around?"

"No," she started coughing again.

"So you hid where they could find you? Wanted to be kissin' everybody?"

"Wait, no!"

"Don't you get loud with me there, Jezebel. You think I ain't seen your kind before? Trying to blackmail the rich kids. See it all the time."

Jeselle broke down, "No," she whispered. "Ask Dennis, he's the one that came with me."

"Your boyfriend?"

"Yes."

He paused a while. "Did you agree to play this game?"

"I did, but I didn't want them to hurt me."

"So, you didn't agree to be kissin' a bunch of boys…and girls. Expect anything else to happen?"

"No, I did agree to kissing, only peck kissing, you know, like light on the lips, not to anything else."

"You do know where kissin' leads, young lady?"

"Please help me," she sobbed again.

"I'm tryin' but you makin' it mighty hard. Dennis, your boyfriend said the game is kissin', then if you are caught more than eight times, you get spanked by the one who got ya last. That's the rules of the game. So, my question is, did you agree to play the game?"

"I only agreed to the kissing!" she coughed again.

"So, you didn't agree to the spank part?"

"I did, but-"

"No buts, ma'am, did ya or not?"

"I thought it would be play spanking, but it wasn't! And they — "

"Hold ya horses there, Missy," he got up and moved closer to the bed. "Sounds like you was teasin 'em. Got your other friends' statements and they all say you agreed to it. They all said you was laughin' the whole time, till — "

"No! WHY WOULD I WANT TO BE BEATEN AND RAPED!" she reached for the water cup before she coughed again, but he grabbed it.

"They said there was no beatin'. Said you'd wanted to go further, and everything was fine until you started feelin' guilty, then you took off runnin'. They said you must've got caught by trees, branches, they don't know. But they all, all seven of them, say you lyin'."

"That's not true."

"They said the car hittin' you is where all them bruises come from."

"That's not true, ask Dennis."

"We did. He and his dad's the one gave us the other friend's names to back up the truth."

STOP ME

***

Jeselle waited. She didn't understand why her parents were taking so long. The curtain opened slowly and Trudy walked in.

"Honey, they got your room ready, so you'll go on up there."

"Do … do you know where my parents are?"

"Your boyfr —, the boy that is with you said they are on the way."

"The policeman said that an hour ago," she cried.

"I know, honey. Look, you got to tell the truth. Your friend is real worried about you," Trudy lowered her voice to a whisper and moved closer to Jeselle, "I heard him tell his daddy what happened. Then how he tried to stop them. That he gave you a chance to get away. Tell the truth. He'll back you. He's real worried about you."

"One of them was his sister."

"I know, I heard him tell his daddy, but that doesn't matter. Tell the truth. Give your parents my name; I'll back you with what I heard."

"Thank you. Did … did you hear anything else?"

"Yes, I heard your friend's dad talking on his phone to one of the other boy's dad, said something about putting away their rivalry until this was all over. He told him to do whatever he needed to help this go away."

Jeselle cried harder and Trudy hugged her. "Tell your parents."

The curtain was thrust open and Captain Kramer stood there. "I'm done here. I left my card with your parents."

"My parents," Jeselle tried to lift herself, gasped in pain.

"Honey, lay back," Trudy said. "They are here now, you'll be okay."

"Hope ya learn your lesson with this, little Missy." The officer said before he retreated, leaving the curtain wide open.

Jeselle pulled the cover up to her chin, looked straight through of the open curtain and saw Theodore Stryker standing with Dennis by a nurse's station talking to her parents. Her dad briefly looked back at Jeselle with sorrow on his face.

It broke Jeselle's heart for the second time that night.

A few days after being released from the hospital, Jeselle found her parents on the back patio, exactly where they had said they would be when she was ready to talk. She had felt numb off and on since she'd been home, almost like it happened to someone else.

Dennis had visited her every day in the hospital, apologizing and begging for her forgiveness. He said his dad's attorneys, also Todd's parents, advised them to keep the truth to themselves. Too many people would get hurt over a silly kid's game that got out of control. He stayed every day, all day long. He fed her and read to her.

"Dad swears it would ruin the company," Dennis said.

Jeselle stared off into space.

"You know, we'd have to go bankrupt."

"Yes, Dennis," she said softly, "so you've said. Over and over."

"But he wanted me to tell you, it would also ruin your dad," Dennis waited.

"How?" she looked more alert and Dennis was thankful to finally be getting through to her.

"All his life's work, Jeselle. It would be worth nothing. His name would be worth nothing. I'm so sorry. I didn't know until Dad told me. I mean if we lose, your dad does too."

"And..." she closed her eyes, "your dad told you to tell me that?"

"Yes."

After being released she thought about what Dennis had repeated so many times. She knew the first step was to talk to her parents. She opened the screen door and they bolted out of their seats.

"Hey," her dad waved slightly.

"You need me, dear?" her mother asked.

"Can I talk to you both?"

They collectively said yes.

After she told them all of it, which she had contemplated doing for days, including what Mr. Stryker wanted Dennis to tell her in the hospital, her mom rushed to her and wrapped her arms around her. Tears were streaming steadily down all of their faces.

The sun was setting and they sat in silence.

"I am going to the police," her dad finally said.

"Dad, I'm not trying to be rude, but the men who talked to me in the hospital, one of them was the chief of police, the other was that mean captain guy. I already told you they basically accused me of lying and being out for money."

"Then, I'll go to the DA in the morning."

"And risk losing everything? Your job?"

"One, no one can take my work, Jessie. I'll simply go to another company with it, and two, you and your mother are my everything. I'll do whatever I can to protect you both." Jeselle started sobbing, "Do not worry over any of that do you hear me?"

"Yes, dear," her mother added, "Bullies don't win."

"Mr. Stryker said he wanted to talk to me in the morning. No doubt about this, so I'll go to his office first, at least give him a heads up, then the DA."

The phone rang, and her mother went to answer it. When she returned she looked somber.

"It's Dennis again, he said he really needs to talk to you. Something he needs to tell you."

"That he's sorry. I've heard it enough."

"He's waiting on the line. Jeselle, he says it's important." Her mother nodded her head.

Jeselle went into the kitchen and picked up the phone, "What?"

"Jess, listen quickly," he whispered, "Dad had

the District Attorney over here, Rick something ... Harrison, Rick Harrison. I can't talk long, but I think he's going to help you. I'll tell the truth. Have your attorney or, or the police, or whoever call me. I'll tell the truth."

"Thank you, Dennis, Thank you so much!" Jeselle cried. "What about Camilla?"

"I heard him say something about a deal, I think Camilla will be okay. I love you, Jess. I am so sorry. I'll never be that weak again, I promise. I'm sorry."

After she hung up the phone, Jeselle collapsed onto the floor and cried. Of all the things she'd lost over the past few days, Dennis was the most important one. It was crushing.

She went and told her parents what Dennis had said.

Maybe there was hope after all.

CHAPTER 29

PRESENT

"Get out!" Cindy yelled through her bedroom door.

"I'm not leaving! This is my house!" he said with another shove to the door.

"I will call the police if you don't leave. I have the phone in my hand!" she screamed.

"Cindy, if I leave here, when I come back you will be sorry. Do you hear me? Open the damn door now. When I count to three, I'm gone, you'll never know when I will be back, but I promise I will," he whispered in his calm and maniacal tone, "You humiliated me tonight. Open. Even if you have me arrested you know damn well Dad will have me out in less than an hour and then…it'll be worse. Now. Open. This. Door."

"I only want you to calm down first," Cindy said through the door.

"I'm only going to get angrier, Cindy. My advice is to open this door. One. Two."

She cracked the door slightly "Tracy, please-"

He pushed the door open violently and it sent her stumbling backward. He reached out and caught her by the hair with one hand while he punched her in the face with the other. Cindy pleaded as he dragged her toward the door, "Please, Tracy please."

"Shut the hell up!" He reached down and ripped at the t-shirt she was wearing. "You want to lock me out of a room, in my own house! This house belongs to me, not you!" he bellowed.

"I'm sorry, please, please don't," she cried.

Tracy finished dragging her to his bedroom and let go of her at the foot of the bed, "Get up there! Now!" he yelled. "You are going to be the proper little wife for a change!" He used the free hand to unzip his jeans as he pulled her head down closer to his zipper.

"Tracy, please my mouth is bleeding," she whispered, "Please."

"Show me how sorry you are, Cindy."

The beating would go easier after. She had no choice anyway.

So, she showed him.

Cindy waited until he was snoring deeply for a

while before she got up. She shoved a few basics in the bag. Thank God his dad had made him put her new car in her name as a faith offering. She always knew deep down it would come to this. Everything was so perfect when they married. He was perfect. But the pressure of maintaining his dad's approval was too much at times, and the only way to let off steam was to take it out on her.

Their perfect life. Everyone else saw their perfect life and wished they were the lucky ones. They had to be perfect. How well would it go for them if their stockholders knew the soon-to-be president and majority shareholder beat his wife? She'd heard it enough from her father-in-law to know they'd be broke within the year. She had to leave. If she didn't, the next time Tracy would kill her. She walked slowly through the hall with a bag that contained only the jewelry she could stuff into it with the few pairs of designer jeans and a few shirts. Though she only took the non-generational jewelry, of course. She would never risk taking the pricey heirlooms. They would easily be able to trace that; but all the "I'm sorry" jewelry they couldn't. She surely had earned every piece and more.

When Cindy got to the bottom of the stairs she heard his bedroom door open. Pain ripped through her body. She rushed as quietly as she could, around the staircase and through the hallway toward the back of the house. No doubt she'd taken this route before and no doubt he'd awakened and seen that she'd gone to her room and he was heading toward it for his typical apology and 'make up' sex. When he realized she wasn't there, he'd find her. She took off running the moment she rounded the large kitchen and grabbed both his and her keys. She was thankful she had grabbed his too when she saw him running after her car in the rearview mirror. She sped out of the garage. If she hadn't made it through the gate before he got to the phone, she'd have run straight through it. Luckily, she pushed the opener on her visor and glided right through and onto the main street.

*** *** ***

The light lit up his phone and Dennis quickly answered. "Must be something unexpected to hear from you this time of day."

"Yes, it is. Cindy left about an hour ago. She nearly ran over the gate getting away and now is settling into a room at the Biltmore," George said.

"The Biltmore? Why on earth would she be there?"

"Desk clerk said she paid with cash. Dennis," the man paused, "she looks pretty bad."

"Find out everything you can," Dennis said before he hung up the phone.

Dennis immediately tapped his second favorited contact, "George called, Cindy is running."

"Where?" Jeselle asked.

"She's at the Biltmore. He is trying to find the

specifics now."

"Biltmore is cash only. Probably so he can't track her credit cards," Jeselle said. "Is she okay?"

"Are there places that use cash only? How strange. Anyway, George said she looks pretty bad. I'm going to have him call it in. They can catch him on camera if we wait a bit," Dennis huffed, "I can leak where she is to Brantley's people and see how fast he makes it there. When the news shows him rescuing his daughter-in-law from a hotel, full of bruises, they'll know. They'll never forgive either him or Tracy, and the stocks will tank."

"I don't know. Shouldn't we get her a doctor or something?"

"No! Jeselle, this is perfect."

"No Dennis, it isn't. She's hurt."

He didn't respond for a few moments, "You knew someone was going to get hurt."

"Not like this. I told you, not this kind of hurt."

"It's the name of the game, sweetheart. People get hurt in the process."

"I remember very well, how people can get hurt," she snapped, "Dennis?"

"Yes?" he asked.

"Don't do this," she said.

"I've not heard you sound like my old Jess in years, nice to hear it," he said as she heard the click, Dennis had ended the call.

Jeselle paced the floor. What if Tracy went instead of Brantley? The phone rang, and she answered immediately.

"You heard?" the caller asked.

"Yes, I need you to please alert Brantley, not Tracy," Jeselle said.

"Already thought about that. Don't worry. I'll be sure to stress that Tracy needs to stay out of it."

"Thank you. Always. Thank you," Jeselle said.

"Doesn't feel as good as you thought it would?"

"No, but it doesn't make me want to stop either. I have to do this," Jeselle said.

"I get it, Jessie."

She hung up and paced the floors again.

* * *

As she knew it would, the ten o'clock evening news played out for all to see, nevertheless it was more damaging than Jeselle had expected.

Dennis proved to be shrewder at his plans because not one, but every news team, having received anonymous tips, had eagerly waited to catch the footage involving the President of Briggs International. It was unforeseen also that Tracy showed up in the limo as well. Also unanticipated, was footage of Brantley when he had rolled down the window to bark something at his son before the limo made a slow drive to the back of the parking lot.

Both Briggs men.

While it was impossible to hear what he snarled at his son, it was equally impossible to miss the words that poured off of his lips, *Get her.*

Of course, the news wouldn't have missed the moment the police cruisers began to appear at the scene, Brantley's limo slowly easing from the back of the parking lot, leaving his son to fend for himself. What the news caught next was Tracy dragging Cindy out by her hair, kicking her several times along the way. He was clearly observed on the dramatic footage pulling her through the lobby of the hotel and into the parking lot where six police officers, theatrically holding their weapons behind the open doors of three police cruisers, were waiting.

He dropped Cindy, immediately, put his hands behind his head and smiled his most cunning smile.

A smile that Jeselle knew well.

It was natural for Tracy, after the many years he'd gotten away with all his treachery, to believe he'd get away with this also.

Jeselle was held between elation at watching the smile Tracy wielded so effortlessly, knowing this time it wouldn't work, and guilt at watching Cindy scurry behind a police officer, scared for her life.

But Cindy was safe, she assured herself.

Jeselle called her lead broker and asked him to start buying as many shares of Briggs International through Tag.E Investments as he could. No doubt many of them would be the very shares Dennis sold off the day before to ensure he wouldn't lose money on the deal.

By noon old man Briggs, and his son, had been left in complete financial ruin.

STOP ME

Jeselle knew that while Brantley would've been able to bail his son out, chances are he wouldn't. Not this time. Not when the entire world had proof of all the years of lies the Briggses had told in court, and all the shaming and name-calling they'd so easily inflicted upon other people, especially women. Brantley Briggs definitely wouldn't emerge from it smelling like a rose. Jeselle knew how business worked, all the shady business deals, the many under-the-table loans and interest debts that Briggs had acquired through the years would be called in. Knowing Brantley, he'd sell out his own grandmother to preserve himself. No doubt everything that he owned would have to be sold to save his own hide.

At that point, Jeselle knew that it still likely wasn't going to be enough.

She needed to proceed with the last pieces.

Plans that had been years in the making.

CHAPTER 30

PAST

"No one ever told me that grief felt so
like fear."
—C.S. Lewis

She could hear her parents talking through the
screen, as she did often when she hovered at the
back door.

"Mr. Stryker said it was out of his hands."

Jeselle almost burst through the back door, but
her dad continued.

"Also, the way he sees it is his son may have
frozen up at first, but he ultimately did help her.
Camilla is on the way out of town to a mental
health facility, because she has been under so much
pressure at school. He said her participation was
minimal at best."

"And what did you say, Sherrill?" her mom asked.

"I let him know I was going to the DA's office. I wasn't really surprised when he said we'd have to end our relationship if I did. I mean, Jessica, I understand his side. He really seems like a good guy. His daughter did something awful, but would you want to lose your whole business over it? No. Only…I can't not help my daughter. I think of Tracy and what he did to Cindy that day. How his father did nothing, but cover it up…and her mother. I, I, just…I'd never be able to live with myself if I did nothing. What happened to Jeselle is eating me alive inside."

"Me too, dear. Me too. So, then you went to the DA? What did he say?"

"He said it is basically six words against two. Said Dennis called his office before I got there, and he told Dennis the same thing. Can't make a case when six are saying she fully participated, and have been for months, one saying she didn't. That one being her boyfriend who is desperate not to lose her."

"That was the DA? Who else can we go to?" Jessica asked.

"I don't know. No one."

Jeselle made her way back to her room and cried for hours. She had so many conflicting feelings. About everything.

* * *

When she awoke, she heard voices, loud voices downstairs. She tried to get up fast, but her body jolted in pain. She opened the door to her bedroom and heard Dennis talking.

"I'm telling you, the nursing assistant. Her name is Trudy Michaels. She heard everything. She'll testify. I just left the hospital. She was so worried about Jess."

"What did she hear though?" Sherrill asked.

"Well, she tended to Mr. Letty and heard his whole statement about Jess already being bloodied when she jumped into the road. She heard Jess's statement and witnessed how many injuries she had that night. She heard me call my dad from the pay phone in the waiting area, when I told him everything. The tests, like the swabs and stuff are missing, but she was there when they were taken and she delivered them to Captain Kramer herself. She copied her notes from the file that night, because she said he was really rough with Jess and she felt like something wasn't right."

"What about Mr. Letty?"

"He's a nice old man, I went to his house to get my mobile, he still had it from calling the police. Only he said that Uncle Brantley came to his house and really scared him and he simply wants to live and be left alone."

"Do you think that'll be enough?" her dad asked.

"I don't know, but we have to try," Dennis said.

"I think...I need to call an attorney."

"Yes, but Mr. Parsons, my advice ... pick

someone out of town. My dad and Mr. Briggs have a lot of ties here."

"Good advice," her dad said and patted Dennis on the back, "Thank you, son."

Jeselle had slowly walked until she made it halfway down the stairs when there was a knock at the front door. It was Dennis's driver.

"Sorry miss, but Dennis needs to leave here immediately. There has been an emergency at home."

"Dennis?" Jeselle called from the stairs.

"Jess!" He ran up to hug her, but she backed away before he could.

"You're still hurt," Dennis said sadly.

"You have to go, Dan's at the door. You have an emergency at home."

Dennis turned and looked at the doorway. "I'll come back soon, promise." Then he was gone.

After that she heard her dad make call after call, but no attorney would even listen to him past the names, Briggs and Stryker. She heard him break down in the kitchen again, but since she didn't know what to do, she simply stood outside the room and cried herself.

"Sherrill, it'll be okay. It will. Let's go sit on the back porch for a nice glass of iced tea. Take a break," she heard her mom say.

***

The days blended together, but Jeselle still knew it had been a week since Dennis had been by to see her. It was the longest they'd been apart since they had started dating almost a year earlier. She wanted to call him, but every time she picked up the phone, his face would flash through her mind, and she wouldn't call.

Watching the news with her parents, a bulletin came on about a local prostitute that had been found murdered in an alley known as a prostitute hang out. She had been a nursing assistant by day as well as attending nursing school at night. Trudy Michaels's picture flashed onto the screen and Jeselle screamed. She couldn't take her eyes off the evening news, even though she could barely see through her tears.

"She was so nice to me," she said. "She was murdered?"

"Honey, I can't believe this," her mom said to her dad. "This is terrible."

Her dad didn't reply.

"Sherrill?"

"Too coincidental…" he whispered.

The phone rang, and she heard her dad rush to pick it up quickly.

"Hello? Yes, this is he." A long silence hung in the air, "No, wait there is a mistake, those are mine. I own those patents. No, that's not true. I would never have signed something like that." Her dad's voice elevated, "Listen to me, I will not have…hello… hello?"

He hung up the phone.

"Sherrill? What is it? Sherrill?"

"Jessica, that was the law firm of Parrish & Parrish, Todd's parents. They represent Stryker Steel." He took a deep breath, "They said that I am terminated due to my breaking a morality clause in my contract with indemnity something or another by going to the DA. That I have forfeited my, my processes to Stryker."

Jeselle heard her dad collapse and she turned to go to him.

"Sherrill, they can't do that. They are all in your name," her mom sounded so levelheaded like she always did. "Sherrill, it will be okay."

"They said because I broke the contract, it states that the patents will be absorbed by Stryker Steel."

"Sherrill, that doesn't sound legal. We'll call some attorneys tomorrow. It'll be okay."

After talking to several out-of-state attorneys the next day, her dad was told that the contracts were likely air tight. Dad swore he hadn't signed anything like that, wouldn't have. He swore it, but it didn't matter, most of the attorneys said the same thing: a company as large as Stryker had money enough to drag the case out in court for decades. Several also added that an injunction against Stryker to stop use, probably wouldn't get awarded. His whole life had been spent doing that, only to have it all ripped away.

Adding insult to injury, the next morning they were served an eviction notice to vacate the house. They had until August tenth, the first day of high school.

"Dad," Jeselle opened the back door, "Can I come talk to you?" she could see his eyes were puffy and his face was swollen.

"Sure, Jessie, how are you?"

"I'm fine. How are you?"

"I don't know," he said honestly.

"I'm sorry," she cried, even though she swore she wasn't going to, "I'm so sorry." Her dad stood and hugged her. "I feel like this is all my fault. I only wanted to say I'm sorry."

"You have nothing," he held her arms and pushed back, "Nothing to feel sorry about. I'm sorry," he broke down again, "I brought us here. I thought this would be such a perfect opportunity for us."

"I love you, Dad."

"I love you, too, Jessie Bug. So much." He pulled her close and held her.

"You haven't called me that in years." Jeselle tilted her head and looked up at her dad.

He wiped his eyes, only the tears continued to fall. "You were so small. Tiny, tiny, when you were born. I knew, when I first saw you, that I'd do everything I could to protect you." He started sobbing again.

"This isn't your fault either, Dad."

"Yeah."

"We need to just focus on what we are going to do now?"

"We don't have any savings, I, I, had been set

to start get-" his voice cracked, "getting royalties off the lease of my patents, but," he stuttered through sobs.

"I love you so much. I'll get a job. Mom said she'd get one, too. We'll figure this out," Jeselle reassured him.

"All I keep seeing is what happened to you. I just can't wash it away," he replied.

"Me neither," she said honestly.

A week and two days later, after leaving a note on the kitchen counter, her father walked through the neighborhood carrying a sign that read "STRYKER IS A MURDERER — THIEF — LIAR" on it, placed it against one of the large brick columns at Theodore Stryker's front gate, and shot himself in the heart.

CHAPTER 31

PRESENT

"We can't be late to the meeting, Camilla will have our hides," Karli said.

"I don't understand how she can be so rude all the time," Rose commented, "Seems like a lot of work."

"She is one of the ones I was talking about to you Rose. Truly arrogant," Jeselle took a deep breath, "It may take a while. That type of arrogance is real, built from years of relating one's identity to being wealthy and powerful. Be patient with her." Jeselle looked over her shoulder, "Coming, Jed?"

"I wouldn't miss it," he said making his way to

them.

"Do people like her ever really change?" Karli asked.

"Do people like you change? Exactly. Don't look at me like that. I'm not judging you by your past, all I'm saying is that we all have one," Isabel said loudly, Jed agreed. "Any of us can change, it's more a matter of do we change. It's tough and many don't seem like they change, but they change in their hearts. I think she's had a lot happen to her, same as you."

Karli smiled knowingly, "Yeah, true."

"That's right, Ms. Isabel," Jed said.

Isabel looked at Jed, "I told you about that. Don't call me 'Ms.' again. I'm Isabel."

"Can't help it, you a lady." His eyebrows wiggled up and down.

Jeselle stopped walking and looked from Isabel to Jed and back again, "Am I missing something here?" she squinted in observation.

"Nothing to miss," Jed said, "Isabel is a mighty fine lady."

"Oh, stop it!" Isabel giggled and playfully slapped him on the arm.

Jeselle seemed extremely serious, "Okay, if you two start dating, there needs to be ground rules."

"For who?" Isabel asked, "You, young lady," she pointedly looked at Jeselle, "don't get to set that standard for me."

"I'm just saying, that...Jed here, needs to consider that you may not be very happy living in a church breezeway. That is all." Jeselle's honesty was mixed with playfulness, a trait she hardly ever showed.

Everyone was stunned for a second and then they all erupted in laughter, including Jed.

They all eventually made their way to The Alley and ate lunch together. They laughed and Jeselle felt years younger. It was apparent that Jed and Isabel exchanged more than a few passing glances.

Right before they stood to clean up and make it back in time to get to the corporate meeting, Isabel said, "Food for thought: I have a big, nice house in Wellgrove Estates fully paid for," Isabel winked and Jed smiled.

* * *

The stage lit up and the crowd of a little over twelve hundred stood and cheered. It felt more like a pep rally than a corporate meeting, but Camilla really had pulled out all the stops.

"Without further ado, our owner, Jeselle Parsons," Camilla said into the microphone.

Dennis kissed Jeselle on the cheek before she entered the stage. She waved and the crowd continued to cheer. She motioned for them to sit, but Camilla motioned for them to stand and cheer again.

And they did.

Jeselle heard her earpiece engage which meant

Camilla's was off. She leaned in and hugged her, then watched as Camilla exited the opposite side to stand on the sidelines of the stage.

"Everybody, our corporate coordinator, Camilla Stryker," Jeselle clapped her hands together and the crowd went crazy again. Jeselle looked over at Camilla, who was smiling.

"I'm going to jump right in. I know this was a mandatory meeting, and I'll admit most of my corporate meetings up to this point have been boring compared to this one. Door prizes? Why didn't I ever think of that?" Jeselle laughed along with the crowd and looked back at Camilla again.

"If each of you will look under your seats, there is an envelope taped under the bottom. I'll wait a minute for you to open."

The hum started and then cheers, some even crying.

"That is a voucher, you can't cash it, but it represents the three-thousand-dollar bonus you will each receive on your next paycheck!'

The crowd cheered again.

"I have always said that bringing people up is what having position and power is all about. Each of my companies here, represents a part of me," she paused, "the news is already out there, and yes, I did buy up a large portion of stocks in Briggs International Steel several weeks ago and again after the recent decline in value, I bought everything that came available. Which was pretty much all of it. Some people couldn't understand why I would do that since I am definitely not in the steel industry.'

A few people laughed.

Jeselle motioned behind the stage and a stool was brought out to her. "My dad was. His entire career was built around finding better ways to engineer and manufacture steel that make our world a better, cleaner environment. Many of you know Dennis Stryker, he's around a lot," a few claps went out. She motioned for him to come out on stage with her, and he did without hesitation.

"I am so proud that all of my dad's processes and patents are still held at Stryker Steel. They could've sold those off and made a hefty profit, or been stingy and kept it all to themselves, however instead, they lease to companies around the world to help create a better place for us all. I am excited to utilize those processes in my new venture with Briggs!"

She smiled up at Dennis, and he shocked her by bending down and placing a soft kiss on her forehead. His public statement did not go unnoticed, especially to Jeselle.

"Now, back to that voucher, the reason I am giving you, my employees and all the vendor employees, bonuses like this is to help me celebrate. Now that I own most of Briggs, I intend to buyout the last few smaller shareholders…"

Cheers went up again.

"…and as of this morning," she spoke louder over the crowd, "I implemented the process of privatizing Briggs International Steel!" Jeselle felt Dennis drop his hand from her back. She looked up at him and smiled warmly.

"Dennis here, as everyone already knows, is my biggest ally. We have been through so many ups and downs through the years, and I am so thankful for his strength, and his knack at being business savvy. We are not competitors simply because I bought Briggs, we are family I have now brought the company full circle," she raised her voice, "back into the family where it belongs!"

Loud cheers went up again. She thought about the Business Person of the Year gala and how scolded he felt at her put down. Now he was vindicated. She looked back at Camilla along the side of the stage, tucked behind a curtain clapping and crying. She felt Dennis's hand as he slipped it around her waist again.

"We have some changes coming soon! Be ready! We are moving up!" Jeselle said thrusting one arm in the air as she stood.

The cheering came with a standing ovation.

Dennis escorted her off the stage; she saw an admiration he'd never displayed before. He was deeply awed by her. The moment they stepped behind the curtain he said, "I have never been more mesmerized by you than I am right now."

"Yes, money does that to you, doesn't it?" she smiled.

He laughed, "See how well you know me?"

* * *

Cindy bit what was left of her fingernail. "I don't want your pity, Dennis," she said as she slurped her coffee.

"I'm not pitying you. I'm saying you won't be able to stay in the house. It's in Brantley's name." He waited to see if anything registered in her expression. "You do understand that Tracy did not own any of it? All of the assets are in his dad's name."

"I heard you Dennis! I heard you!" Cindy grew more frustrated, "I don't know what this even means."

"It means Brantley will sell it. He'll need to. His business is gone, his son in jail, his wife left him, and even his attorneys won't call him back. He is in debt up to his eyeballs, Cindy. He owes everyone. You'll need to get a job. Soon. It also means all your credit cards are likely now closed if they weren't already. It means, whatever cash you have on you is all you have."

"Tracy owns other land, you know."

"No, he doesn't. He's sold all of it over the years."

Cindy looked astonished, "Are you sure?"

"Yes, I bought most of it to help him out."

"I can't believe this. I just can't. What am I going to do?"

"You could ask Jeselle."

"No, no! I'll work for you," she stated.

He laughed, "Cindy, I don't hire lazy people with no experience, and I definitely don't hire friends. Learned that the hard way. Ask Jeselle."

"She would laugh in my face," Cindy pouted. "Besides, she'd probably have me scrubbing toilets or something."

"No, Cindy I *promise* she wouldn't. Call her." Dennis slipped her a business card. "But don't call her 'Jess,' call her Jeselle."

As he reached his car Dennis dialed, "She took the bait. Half down, half to go," he said to her.

"Hard to believe it," Jeselle responded. "What will we do after this is over?"

"Bask in all the money," he replied. "Speaking of, I need to go. I need to figure out what I'm going to do with all this extra money from the sale of Briggs stocks," he laughed. "That was quite fun. Mother and Father are still on cloud nine."

Dennis fantasized briefly about a warm, cozy day on the beach, Jeselle lying with her perfect, delectable body by his side, her wearing his enormous rock on her left ring finger. Living the life they deserved.

"It's her," Jeselle said.

"Already? Damn, I literally pulled out of the parking lot a few seconds ago," Dennis laughed.

"I'm switching over now. Call me later," Jeselle touched the button and put it on speakerphone. "Hello?"

"Umm. Jess-, Jeselle?" the voice sounded so timid.

"This is she," Jeselle's didn't.

"Uh, I don't even know how to say this but, well, it's Cindy. Cindy Briggs."

"Cindy! How are you? I saw on the news what

happened. I've been following it as best I could. Are you okay?" Jeselle asked hurriedly.

"No, Jeselle," Cindy started to sob, "I'm not okay."

CHAPTER 32

PAST

Dennis raced around the back patio, "Jess!"

He stopped short when he saw Jeselle and her mom sitting together weeping.

"Jess," he curled up beside her and hugged her from behind.

"Get off me! Go away!" she yelled. "Your dad did this!"

"No! It's a misunderstanding! I promise!" he pleaded.

"There is no misunderstanding that my dad is DEAD!" she screamed, "And if that happened over a misunderstanding I promise, as God is my witness

I WILL SEE YOU ALL PAY!"

"Jeselle," her mom's broken voice called to her, "It isn't Dennis's fault."

"It is his fault, Mom! He stood by and did nothing!" she turned around and glared at Dennis, "Where have you been for the last two and a half weeks, traitor?"

"I was with Mom! We went to see Camilla. She's in a hospital in Virginia. I left you a message! We left suddenly, as soon as I got home, my bags were packed. I'm here now, Jess," he broke down crying. "I'm sorry."

"You are sorry," she repeated with a scoff.

"I love you!" he said.

"Nothing you do can help us now. My father is gone, and we don't know where we will go. We have nothing!"

"Stay here, Jess, what do you mean where you will go? Stay here."

Jeselle stood up abruptly, went into the house and when she returned, she shoved a paper in Dennis's face. As he read it, his face lost all color.

"Wait, this is an eviction notice…," he said.

Jeselle's mom wiped her eyes, "I think that's what really did it. The straw that broke the camel's back. First, Mr. Stryker stealing Sherrill's patents, then the eviction."

"Stole?"

"Yes, Dennis," Jeselle yelled at him, "Stole! All because we told the truth. As soon as Dad got back from talking to the DA, he was terminated! Want to hear something funny, Dennis, he wasn't even mad about that part. He understood your dad trying to protect his business, his kids! But because he went to the DA, my dad supposedly broke some stupid clause in his contract which made all the patents my dad worked for his whole life, to automatically go into Stryker Steel's name."

"I, I ... there is definitely ... that's not right." Dennis looked down at the eviction notice again, and placed it on the patio. When he stood he looked at Jeselle, the hurt evident on his face. Then anger instantly replaced it as Dennis stalked off.

***

She would've known that voice anywhere, Theodore Stryker. Jeselle walked up the back patio steps and listened through the screen door to him talking in the kitchen to her mom. Anger built so swiftly that she thought her head would explode.

"For one I didn't know any of this, this is a board decision on behalf of the stockholders. I would never have done that," he said calmly.

"So, you didn't take the patents?" her mom asked wearily.

"No, I mean now that he's no longer here they do get absorbed into Stryker, but not before. I really don't know how this all got so messed up. When Dennis came home last night, I didn't know what he was talking about. Honest."

"I'm confused though; your attorneys told Sherrill that they had sent him the contract that he'd signed." Jessica said.

"Yes, he had signed one, but I wouldn't have done that. Like I said, the board may have initiated something, but I didn't. And the eviction notice, that was automatically generated when he was terminated. It's company policy for our corporate houses. I didn't do that. I wouldn't have done that. I hate that all of this got so messed up."

"I really don't know how to process this."

"I know how to process it," Jeselle spewed her anger, the back door popping loudly against a wall.

"Jess," Dennis said her name, but she was too mad to notice.

"My dad is dead because you stole from him. Where are the patents now, Mr. Stryker? Does my mom get the royalties?" Jeselle asked.

"I, I don't know, Jeselle. Look, we think of you as family."

Jeselle huffed, appalled.

"We do, really. I came by today to let your mom know that I've put this house in her name."

Jeselle was stunned. He sounded so sincere. She looked to Dennis for confirmation and he nodded.

"I know it won't make up for ... I know, but ple-please, I ... you Jessica, can come work at Stryker. I can make sure you are taken care of."

He was being sincere. That didn't sit well with Jeselle's anger.

"Thank you, Mr. Stryker, I can't thank you

enough," her mom said in her kind way, "We have to mourn. I'm sad that my Sherrill is gone."

"Sad? I'm FURIOUS!" Jeselle yelled.

"With every right," Theodore said, "I'll leave now. I will be paying all of his funeral expenses, don't want you to worry over a thing,"

He and Dennis left and Jeselle started slamming cabinets in the kitchen. Her mom walked up behind her and hugged her.

"I don't understand, Jessie. His death is for nothing."

Jeselle turned and collapsed into her mom. There was really nothing else to do.

* * *

Many people attended the funeral, including her frenemies and their families, minus Camilla. Dennis said she was still away in Virginia. That she was truly broken over the whole thing. He pled his sister's case, to no avail.

Mr. Letty and his family were there. When he passed through the line to give his condolences he was sobbing. "Please forgive me," he begged. "I should've come forward. I should've said something."

Jeselle's mom, who stood beside her, leaned forward and said through tears of her own, "We forgive you, Mr. Letty. Of course, we forgive you." He nearly collapsed in front of them. "You could've driven off, out of fear, instead you stopped and helped her, that's what matters to us."

Jeselle learned primarily that people may have their *reasons* for the bad things they do, but there really is no *excuse* for the bad things they do.

After they were home, her mother came to her room. "Hungry?" she asked.

"No thanks." Jeselle fell back on the bed and her mom joined her. Jeselle reached over and took her mom's hand.

"I was thinking … but we need to do it together. Make a decision," her mom turned to look at her. "We can sell this house, it's in my name, take the money and relocate."

They were both silent for a while.

"Yeah," Jeselle answered.

"You don't want to leave Dennis?" her mom asked.

"It's not that. Maybe it is. I'm confused though, Mom. He means so much to me still, even after."

"That's good, Jeselle, it means you have forgiveness in your heart. He's a good boy. He made a mistake out of fear." Her mom shifted onto her side to face Jeselle, who mimicked her mother's actions. "From all you told us," she paused and took a deep breath, "us," she repeated. "He felt like he couldn't stand up to Tracy, but … in the end he did."

"Yeah. I don't know."

"It's your decision. All yours. I can stay or I can go."

"Can you? Stay?" Jeselle asked, "Honestly."

STOP ME

"If it means your happiness, yes. God will help soothe my heartache no matter where I live. The question is can you stay?"

The next month flew by in a blur, but the pain remained steady. Dennis stopped by more often, and Jeselle was caught somewhere between anger and thankfulness. It was hard to get the look of his face when he'd read the eviction notice out of her mind. She was glad that at least it replaced the look she hadn't been able to get out before, which was him staring at her, for so long, then looking away.

He was weak.

She knew he was now.

A slave to Tracy. That's the most important thing she learned that day.

The day.

Melanie had control over everyone else, but only Tracy had control over Dennis. And they both knew it. It all boiled down to money. She'd sat for hours and thought about it all. Tracy only had control, because his dad controlled Dennis's mom's trust.

Money. The lust of money.

Power. The lust of power.

Her mom would spout off scripture after scripture, but it really seemed like a bunch of gibberish.

Especially the parts about forgiveness.

Her feelings about Dennis confused her, but more than anger toward him, she felt utter pity.

She walked onto the patio where her mom sat staring into the wooded area that barricaded their house from the neighbors.

"I've made a decision. I want you to sell the house to give us a fresh start, together."

CHAPTER 33

PAST

"If you want to keep a secret, you must
also hide it from yourself."
-George Orwell

Her mom started at Stryker about four months after the funeral. It hadn't taken long to find out that the insurance policy her dad had talked about in the note he left for them that day was voided since it had been funded through Stryker, and he was no longer an employee at the time of his death. Ironic, since part of the reason for his suicide was that he thought he was sacrificing himself to save them. Her mom also found out that she couldn't sell the house. Yes, Theodore Stryker had put it in her name, but he also put a lien against it with the clause that if it were ever sold, he'd get the money. Which meant technically he still owned it. With no other options, and no work skills, her mom accepted a job in the housekeeping department of Stryker Steel Corp. She hadn't complained. She told Jeselle it could've been much worse.

Most weeks they could barely pay the bills. Her mom and she decided to turn off the vents in two of the bedrooms in hopes that would lower the electric bill.

Still her mom was thankful to God.

Jessica met a friend at Stryker, Isabel, who came over from time-to-time on weekends to visit. Her kids were much younger, but Jeselle still loved playing with them. Dennis stopped by one day and was shocked to find Ms. Isabel there. Dennis and Isabel told stories and laughed about him following her around Stryker helping her clean, especially after his ninth birthday. Jeselle noticed he and Ms. Isabel had an ease to their relationship that he didn't have with his own parents. Eventually one day he stopped his visits. He started spending more and more time at work with his father instead.

Jeselle's mom told her she could home school if she wanted, but Dennis begged her to go to Eastdale High. It was weird, mainly because the frenemies acted like nothing had happened. When Camilla finally returned home two months into the school year, it was clear, that she too, like Jeselle, seemed simply a shell of her old self. Whatever good, happy traits Camilla had before that summer, were replaced with arrogance. At least with that, she was able to avoid Melanie's influence.

Dennis acquired a car, the first one of the friends to do so, but of course, he only had his permit. Soon after, the others followed close behind in getting cars, except Cindy. It was the same when Dennis had received his first mobile over that past summer, each of the friends had one within the week, except Cindy.

During the school year Melanie continued to be Melanie.

Tracy continued to be Tracy. He'd still flash a sly smile at Jeselle every so often when no one else was looking, and it would send chills up her spine. She stayed as far away from him as she could and never let herself be caught alone with him.

William was still the follower he'd always been. He dated one girl after another and the gay jokes finally wore off. He was elected freshman class treasurer, which made his parents proud enough to take out a full-page ad in all the local papers to announce it.

Todd went to a private school, his parents insisted, but he still hung out with the others on the weekends. Jeselle heard him say that his parents told him not to hang out with any of them anymore, but they were too busy to notice, and their biggest client was Stryker so they couldn't dare make their wishes public.

Jeselle never went back to the river with them; however Dennis said that none of them went much anymore anyway, except Tracy and Cindy.

It ultimately belonged to him anyway. It disgusted Jeselle to hear him talk about building a house on that land one day. He always looked at her when he added parts about letting his kids and grandkids swim at the very spot they used to.

Cindy was still the outsider trying to fit in. Snobby to everyone else, everyone on the outside, always trying to prove she belonged. She'd show up some days with bruises, always had one excuse after another as to why they were there. The friends knew why, everyone else had no clue.

Jeselle didn't go back to the Strykers, even for their annual Christmas party, no matter how many times Dennis pleaded. He came to her house often, but said his dad was getting frustrated that Jeselle wouldn't even try to understand his predicament.

She felt like a different person at school, smiling and faking her way through each day. At her house, she could simply be herself. It was depressing that her mom wasn't there when she got home from school like she used to be. Her mom still left notes for Jeselle on the refrigerator or counter every day, but it didn't feel the same as it used to.

Jeselle basically lived through the weeks as best as she could to get to the weekends when her mom, Dennis, and often Isabel and the girls were there. She found a new normal, which she felt guity about.

Missing her dad came in waves. Sometimes, it was numbed, and she didn't really feel it. Then other times it would crash around her until she was sobbing from the heartbreak.

STOP ME

Freshman year was soon over, and Jeselle was thankful for the summer. It was a much needed respite. Most days she spent sitting on the bench in the park, waiting for the geese to come back.

"Dad really wishes you'd come for dinner. It's been so long," Dennis said, right after he sat on the bench.

Jeselle ignored him, "Notice that the geese are still gone? Isn't that odd?"

"Maybe. I don't know. Never noticed," he said.

"Yeah, they were gone the first time I came here … after Dad, and they haven't been back."

"That is weird," Dennis shifted in his seat. He hated when Jeselle brought up anything to do with the past. "Let's look forward," he cleared his throat, "Dad asked if I'd bring you to dinner tonight."

"I can't."

"Jeselle, please, if we have a future, I need you to give my dad a chance. He's done everything he can."

"Dennis, I know he's your dad, and you give him the benefit of the doubt, but I don't have to. I don't owe him anything," she said harshly.

"For me. Look, I see he's tried to do everything he can. He didn't make any of those decisions about the patents."

"But he could make it right, he could at least give Dad's portion of the royalties back to Mom so she wouldn't have to work so hard."

"That's a board's decision, not his," Dennis stressed.

"I don't know what a board is!" Jeselle cried.

"Dad said it's like people that stockholders vote in to make decision that are best for a company." he explained. "And he did give your mom a job, Jess," Dennis pleaded his dad's case.

"Scrubbing toilets, *Dennis*," she retorted sarcastically.

"He gave her a house."

"That she can't sell, so basically it's still his!"

"He had to do that, because of the business," Dennis implored her to understand. "Look, I can't stand Dad either. I mean, I get it, his business is everything, but he's trying. Think, without it being your mom, if someone had no skills, no work experience, didn't even know how to use a computer, what job would you give them? On top of that, would you let them live rent free in your house?"

"I don't know. I don't know anymore. It's so unfair."

"It is. I agree!" he said, "It isn't fair. Your mom is awesome. Your dad ... too," his bottom lip started quivering, "I can't lose you, Jess."

"You aren't losing me."

"Then, please, see that my dad has done everything he can. Come to dinner. Mother misses you."

"Okay," she relented. Dennis refused to let her go home between her agreeing and dinner time for fear she'd change her mind, so they sat in the park watching all the old people holding hands.

She wasn't fully in the front door before Sissy, the Stryker's housekeeper, greeted her, "Hey Ms. Jess. How are you today?"

"I'm good, Ms. Sissy. How are you?" Jeselle replied.

"I keep telling you not to call me Ms.," Sissy smiled, "It's just Sissy."

"Okay, how are you, Sissy?" Jeselle repeated her words.

"Can't complain. God is still God, so nothing left to figure out I guess," she smiled warmly at Jeselle. Mrs. Stryker butted in quickly to hug Jeselle, "Sissy, will you get us some tea?" she said.

"Sure thing, ma'am," Sissy said kindly before turning toward the back of the house.

"So lovely you are here, dear," Mrs. Stryker said, overzealous.

"Thank you," Jeselle replied numbly. She noticed Mrs. Stryker looked impeccably put together. Unlike her mom, who came home smelling like strong cleaner and barely had the energy to put on makeup, let alone get fully dressed for dinner.

"I have worried myself sick over you and Justine. I've been meaning to call." Dennis's mother said across the table.

Jeselle looked at Dennis, her eyebrows crinkled.

"Jessica, Mom. Her mom's name is Jessica, not Justine," Dennis corrected.

"I knew that sounded wrong coming out, I am sorry. I don't think clearly sometimes."

"Well," Mr. Stryker's unmistakable voice

traveled through the dining room as he entered, "I am glad you are here. We have missed you, Jess. We think of you often. Dennis fills us in on how you are doing."

She simply nodded.

"We are going to erect a memorial for Sherrill in the park," his dad said.

"Not now, Dad."

"Okay, son, I only wanted her to know how we feel about it all. Horrible. Terrible tragedy."

"Not now, *Father*," Dennis said again, more sternly.

The dinner was served, and they ate in relative silence. Every now and then his parents would make small talk, but for the most part it amounted to nothing. All she could think about was the memorial in the park, to her dad, the one she sat in all the time.

What would it say? She wondered. *'A memorial to a man who was swindled out of his life's work by the wealthy, who easily get away with it. A man, whose daughter was also stolen from, by the wealthy, because they easily can get away with it. A man, so full of grief that he killed himself on the front lawn of the wealthy, in protest.'*

"We are planning our annual Christmas party. I do hope you'll come, be a part of our family again. We missed you last year. Would you?" Mrs. Stryker said.

Jeselle looked at Dennis, his expression hopeful.

"Sure, thank you." Jeselle said politely, then immediately felt like a sellout.

STOP ME

Just like Cindy.

* * *

Her mom was happy Jeselle had decided to give the Strykers a chance and also to go the Stryker's Christmas party. Jeselle had been to their house several times since that dinner and Dennis' dad couldn't help but to bring up the memorial every time he got the chance.

Every single time.

What happened to my dad doesn't go away with a simple memorial, she'd screamed in her head a billion times. Which was about as many times as Theodore Stryker had mentioned it.

"You're way early! I've got to go get dressed. You look beautiful," Dennis went to kiss her, but she turned her head, and it landed on her cheek.

"Sorry," she said.

"No," he looked dejected, "I get it. I'm sorry."

She smiled softly and he bounded halfway up the stairs before turning around, "Hey, there is plenty of food, the caterers came early, too," he winked. "You can go eat if you want. I won't be long."

She nodded and watched as he made it the rest of the way up the stairs, two at a time. She missed his kisses. She missed a lot of things.

Jeselle looked around her. She'd been in the house a number of times over the past two and a half years, but things looked different. Everything looked different. She peeked into the living room to the left of the foyer, then wandered across the foyer to the other room, the formal dining room and peeked inside. Commotion could be heard from the back of the large mansion from everyone bustling about getting ready for the party. Jeselle slowly made her way down the large hall. As she drew closer she picked up on Mr. Stryker's voice in his study, but couldn't be sure. She started to walk past it when her father's name startled her.

"Sherrill's policy? Yes, we did. There is another one we are waiting on, but for some reason they are saying it doesn't pay out for suicide and I am tired of waiting. It's been almost a year and a half. Get it done."

She gasped for breath, her heart pounded wildly.

"No, no, no, Parrish looked over everything. There is no such clause. I told them I'd sue if they didn't release that money. No, Brantley, it doesn't go to his family, it pays out to Stryker. He hadn't been officially fired yet. Parrish said he'd back me on that."

Brantley? Parrish?

Jeselle wanted to burst into the room and scream at the top of her lungs, only she couldn't even catch her own breath.

"The eviction notice? He said he'd take the blame for that, too. Well," Theodore demanded, "I pay him a hell of a lot of money, that's why. Plus, I'll cut him in on the insurance check if I have to."

Insurance check?

STOP ME

Jeselle moved away from the door, rushed through the foyer and out the front door. She ran home in her evening dress. She ran as fast as she could down the streets, through the park, and up the side of her house.

When she'd finished telling her mom what she'd heard, her mom said she was so angry she could spit. Like a foreshadowing of things to come, rain started pouring down in sheets as her mom backed quickly out of the driveway, leaving Jeselle standing in the rain in her evening gown.

It hadn't been long when her mom returned, Jeselle was still dripping wet, sitting on the back patio. She could see it was all her mom could do to keep her composure.

"What happened?" Jeselle asked.

"It's all a misunderstanding. It was a company policy, standard practice for top executives."

"It sounded shady though, like why would he be cutting somebody into the check if it were on the up and up? And why was he talking to Mr. Briggs when they can barely stand each other? And he said dad hadn't been fired yet," Jeselle saw her mom wasn't really listening, "Mom!"

"Jeselle, listen. Please listen," she grabbed her firmly by the arms, "I need you to finally listen. I have been trying to tell you for so long, your dad made that decision, do you hear me?" her mom shook her, "I didn't. You didn't. They didn't," she sobbed. "He did it because he was hurting. He'd lost everything he'd ever worked for. Then knowing what happened to you, he, he couldn't process it all, but he, he made that decision. Do you hear me?"

"No, Mom, he was driven to it," she fell to the ground and her mom followed.

"No, baby, there were bad circumstances. Bad decisions and yes, I can guess somewhere in there was some very bad dishonesty and greed, but no one made your dad kill himself. He had time to write us a letter, make a sign, and walk all the way back there to the Stryker's."

"Mom!" she wailed.

"I know honey, I KNOW," her mom wailed also.

They cried together as the rain poured down around the patio. Headlights appeared on the side of the house and soon Dennis showed up, his tux for the Christmas party, drenched.

"Jess, Dad told me."

"Dennis, something isn't right!"

He made his way up the stairs and sat beside her. "I agree. Something isn't right. I could tell Dad was lying to me."

She was shocked. He usually stuck up for his dad. She looked over at him and he hugged her and her mom. "I'm going to find out what's going on. I promise."

Dennis missed the Christmas party and slept on their sofa that night. His dad showed up the next morning, but Dennis told him he wasn't ready to talk. Jeselle could hear his dad pleading with him to come home and heard the strength in Dennis's voice when he refused again, saying that he'd needed time to think.

On the third afternoon, three days before Christmas, Mr. Stryker came to the door and asked if he could come inside for a minute. He sat with Jeselle and her mom and admitted to making many mistakes. He explained that so many of the decisions made were from the board of directors and he had no control over those things. The other episode, from that summer, was to protect his kids and the business. Mr. Stryker asked for their forgiveness and offered to pay for Jeselle and Dennis to transfer to private school together if they thought that would help.

Jeselle had witnessed Dennis crying for days and then, as his dad sat apologizing, noticed how proud Dennis was of his dad. Her mom said she recognized how hard that must've been for him to do and of course, she said she already had forgiven him. Still, there was an anger inside Jeselle that couldn't be alleviated. It was simply there. She knew it wasn't going to go away and she'd have to learn to live with it.

School seemed better after the holidays. Everyone was so shocked that Dennis not only missed the annual family Christmas party, but stayed at Jeselle's for three extra days. They saw how serious he was about protecting her, and for the remainder of sophomore year there were only polite smiles from everyone.

Except for Tracy, he still looked at Jeselle with his evil grin, reminding her of exactly who he was.

CHAPTER 34

PRESENT

"The best excuse is to have none."
-Ivan Panin

The mural seemed to loom over her and Jeselle couldn't understand why, of all days, it seemed unfinished. She thought of Trudy and looked down where the outline lay. She thought of all the accomplishments she'd had through the years, and still, it wasn't finished. She felt herself getting emotional, which she really didn't have time for.

"Well, look who's here early," Jed said.

Jeselle turned to see her friend and then returned her attention to the mural.

"You okay?" he asked, making his way to stand beside her. He looked up at the mural with her and waited.

"Yes, thinking,"

"Thinking can be good, and thinking can be bad. Which thinking you doing?"

"I guess a bit of both. Ready to eat? I brought the new subs you like. The ones with the marinara sauce."

"Well, I guess I am a blessed man," he said. "We going to eat them here, standing?"

"No," she laughed, "let's go sit."

"I did want to ask you something, if you don't mind. I'm feeling weird about asking though."

Jeselle sat next to him at the picnic table, "You know you can ask me anything."

"I was hoping you might still want to hire me to put flower beds around your office building?"

"Of course, I do!" she hugged him. "I've been so jealous of the church's flowers for so long. Now I'll have some of my own. Wait," she paused, "I guess being jealous of a church isn't so good now that I've said it out loud."

They both chuckled.

Jed had taken a large bite of his sub, so it remained silenced while he chewed.

"So, Jed, do you also want an apartment? I have several, you know. I mean the back room is still available, but I'd much rather one of the apartments if you were comfortable with that. They are really lovely and..." Jeselle wasn't sure why she rattled on, but she stopped herself. It was very much unlike her.

"Naw, I appreciate the offer, but this morning I asked the pastor if I could take that extra room he'd been offering me. I'll stay there."

"That's wonderful!" She meant it.

"Another question, which is likely rude. Against my first check, and you know I've never asked for money before, and it would just be-"

"Of course! No need to tell me what it's for. How much do you want?"

"Enough to maybe buy a new suit at the thrift store and dinner with Isabel."

"Oh," her eyebrows shot up. "Of course! Why not a new suit? You'll be making really good money. So, it's no problem. You can get a really expensive one if you want."

"Yeah," Jed said sarcastically, "because you always buy expensive suits, right?"

"Well...you deserve it." Jeselle replied.

"You do too," Jed paused. "No need, though. Got enough waste in the world. Figure I'd rather get a perfectly good secondhand one. Thank you, anyway."

"Of course, Jed! You are a dear friend to me and anything I can do to help my friends, I will."

"You are a good lady. I'm proud of all the good you do for people."

She didn't know, or expect, that Jed's words would ring in her ears, but they had. It had been so long since an older man, who she looked up to, had given her such approval. Yet, also it made her feel disingenuous at the same time. She shook the feelings off, all of them, and continued eating in silence.

"Found her!" Jeselle looked to find Karli yelling down the street at an unknown person.

"Looks like we've got company," Jed said.

Karli waved at them from The Alley's opening. Jeselle watched as Rose and Camilla came into view.

"Oh no, Jed, I'm sorry. I had no idea they were coming."

"No bother to me. Don't think so bad about that hoity-toity one. She is who she is."

Jeselle watched as Camilla lifted her chin slightly at the sight of Jed. The last lunch they'd all had together hadn't gone over very well. At least Camilla wasn't outwardly rude, like Dennis. It was in the nuances of her actions that made the truth of her discomfort over eating lunch with a homeless man apparent. Camilla definitely was who she was. At least she comes by it honestly, Jeselle thought.

The three ladies gathered at the table with them. Camilla made sure to take a seat on the opposite side from where Jed and Jeselle were seated.

"No lunch?" Jeselle asked the others when she realized they hadn't brought food with them.

"No," Rose said, "knew you were here and wanted to visit."

Suddenly, Jeselle stiffened at her own annoyance. She took on her usual cool demeanor, "I'm overly emotional today, for whatever reason, so let's not make it worse. Can everyone simply keep their sentiments to themselves? Save me the trouble of repressing."

They all laughed out loud, including Jed.

"I did bring something though," Camilla reached into her purse and pulled out a small box, wrapped neatly. She leaned over the table slightly, enough to place the box in front of Jed.

His eyebrows drew together, as did Jeselle's.

"I saw them and thought you could use them," Camilla added.

Jed unwrapped the paper delicately, as if it were a gift of gold. He understood what an offering like this from Camilla truly meant, a peace offering.

When he lifted the final fold, he smiled. "Thank you, Ms. Camilla. I love it."

"There are two," she added, almost excitedly.

Jeselle leaned in to see a handkerchief, beautifully monogramed with the name 'Jed.'

"I didn't know your last name," Camilla sounded insecure.

Jed lifted one of the white linen clothes, "Mighty fine," he looked up at Camilla, "They are perfect. Thank you."

She smiled. A true, happy, genuine smile.

Jeselle was perplexed over Camilla. She was becoming a monkey wrench that Jeselle was unprepared for.

After that day, Jeselle watched everything Camilla did. She looked over every report with meticulous determination. In every meeting, she questioned every one of Camilla's actions.

STOP ME

* * *

Cindy screwed up and it surprised Jeselle at how quickly it happened. Definitely sooner than she'd anticipated. She nearly smiled as she walked down the long hall to Cindy's office, a plush, high-end masterpiece she'd had especially made for Cindy. Jeselle remembered the look on Cindy's face as she opened the door the first time to her new office. Her expression had changed from the drudgery of being forced to work, to the superiority of being valued for the prize that she thought herself to be.

All a part of the plan, of course.

"Knock, knock," Jeselle said as she pushed the door open.

Cindy didn't even bother to stand, "Hello, Jeselle. I'm guessing you heard."

"Yes."

"And you came all the way down from the top floor simply to scold little ole' me?" Cindy said with clear derision in her voice.

"Scold is a bit strong, let's say discuss. I came to discuss what happened this morning," Jeselle said blankly.

"Fine. It's that horrid maid. The one you love so much. What, is she like your new mom now or something? You don't see how she treats other people, Jess," Cindy stood from behind her ten thousand-dollar Cocobolo desk.

Jeselle's expression remained blank on purpose.

"She walks around like she owns the place. She bosses people around and she's the maid, for God sake!"

Jeselle moved closer to Cindy, "Tell me what happened."

"I was telling the girl that cleans my offices that I didn't need her to clean mine. I don't want anyone in my personal business." Cindy looked to Jeselle and shifted on her feet when Jeselle's expression remained fixed. "I...I also keep my belongings in here. I have a few pieces of jewelry that I like to have with me. You know, safe keeping."

Again, no change in expression.

"Anyway, next thing I know Isabel is in my office saying that I can't talk to the girl that way."

"That girl's name is Kayla," Jeselle offered, "Continue."

"Well, I told her that I was only frustrated that the girl wouldn't stop dusting after I told her to stop. She wouldn't listen!" Cindy's voice started to elevate, "And damn it, this is my office! I'll not have a little pip squeak ignoring me in my own office! Period!"

"Let us be clear, Cindy," Jeselle said.

"Thank you! I knew you'd understand," Cindy flipped her hand around in the air a few times as if she were swatting at a fly. "They need to know who's boss, ya know? Make things clear."

To that Jeselle took two steps forward until she had reached the expensive desk that Cindy stood behind. Jeselle's voice was steady and low, "Yes, let's discuss. See, this," Jeselle made a slow swirling motion with her right hand as she rounded the desk slowly to stand toe to toe with Cindy, "This office belongs to me. Period," Jeselle leaned forward enough to cause Cindy to take a step back, "And you don't have 'personal business' here. You have my business here. And in my business we don't opt out of housekeeping. We also don't forget that you could be sifting through a dumpster to eat by now if it weren't for my business."

Jeselle took another step forward, causing Cindy to fall back into her chair. Jeselle leaned over her and grabbed both armrests.

"Because I learned a lesson years ago, on a very tragic night when you held my arms above my head, I learned that if one turns against you, they all do. Right, Cindy?"

Cindy looked immediately contrite, "I, I, we were kids, Jess."

"Yes. We were. And the way I see it is we can move forward or backward. It's your decision. But be very clear that if you move backward and act like that kid, you will be treated like that kid should've been then. However, if you move forward and act like an adult, then we can move forward. Right? You no longer have the money or power to hold anyone's arms down again. Do I make myself, what was it… clear?"

"Yes," Cindy choked through silent tears, which were streaming down her face.

Jeselle walked to the door of the office, seeing the

tears as nothing more than Cindy being the Cindy she always had been, anger or tears, whichever manipulation worked best, "Be up in my office in ten minutes. Don't be late."

Ten minutes later, Cindy sat pouting as Isabel and Kayla entered Jeselle's office.

"This won't take long," Jeselle stood to greet them.

Cindy didn't.

"Cindy…" Jeselle waited.

Finally, Cindy took in a deep breath and turned in her chair to face the open door where Isabel and Kayla still stood. "I want to apologize for my actions. I didn't realize that maid service was a requirement. So, I'm sorry if I was rude to you." Cindy's eyes were fixed on the wall around them, not directly at them.

Isabel looked at Kayla, "That's to you."

"Oh, no need to apologize," Kayla said quietly, "I understand."

Cindy stood and brushed off her pants, "Good, I didn't feel like there was a need to apologize either, but I did anyway."

"Actually, Kayla," Jeselle walked around the desk and toward the young girl, "There is a need. No one is to be disrespected in my business, especially housekeeping. You are new, so you don't know this yet, but housekeeping is the most important job here. I value it above all other jobs." Kayla's eyes widened. "You are important to us and we want to be sure you work in an environment that lets you know that every day. When Isabel hired you, she told you that my mother was a housekeeper after my father died, correct?"

Kayla nodded.

"She was one of the hardest working, most incredible women I have ever known." Jeselle turned and went back toward her desk. Cindy stood wide-eyed staring at Jeselle as she approached. "You may all leave now."

CHAPTER 35

PAST

"No woman is required to build the world
by destroying herself."
-Rabbi Sofer

The summer went by in a blur. She went with the Stryker family to their beach house on Martha's Vineyard for a week, and it was incredible. She didn't initially want to go, but Dennis had enlisted the help of her mom to persuade her.

"It's a once in a lifetime opportunity, Jessie," her mom said, "Go. Have fun!"

"What about you?" she asked her mom.

"I want you to go. Isabel and the girls are going to come stay with me for the week. They live in that small apartment, and it seems silly to have all this space for nothing."

"Mom, that's a great idea!" Jeselle said.

Isabel's friendship made her mom happy. Companionship was more important than anything else for her mom since her dad died and Isabel filled that gap in a way.

Jeselle walked along the beach at Martha's Vineyard a lot at night and thought of her dad. A few times Dennis joined her, though he remained quiet as they walked, as though he knew it was a special time for Jeselle. One night Camilla came out to join her.

"Hey," Camilla waved. The sun was setting, and it cast a warm glow over Camilla's skin.

"Hey," Jeselle said.

"Rick's here."

"Yeah, I saw that," Jeselle replied.

"He's really cute."

"I guess," Jeselle said.

"Does it seem like Dad is trying to push us together?" Camilla asked.

Jeselle laughed nervously, "Yeah, it does. How do you feel about that?"

"I don't know, he's cute, but," Camilla paused, "he's also like ten years older than me."

"Yeah, that is a lot. And has an ex-wife and kids, too. Don't *you* think it's all a lot?" Jeselle asked.

"I don't know. He is an attorney. Dad keeps correcting me, 'he's a district attorney.' His dad was too. I guess that's different. Dad was talking to him about politics and I think maybe he wants to run for something. That's cool, right? I mean he's not poor.

Poor would be hard."

"Camilla, can I be honest?" Jeselle waited.

"Sure."

"I think you are too young to be thinking that seriously about stuff like that," Jeselle said. "I mean sixteen and thinking about marriage?"

"Almost seventeen, and Dad said I needed to. He told me yesterday before Rick showed up that I wouldn't do well in college, so marriage was the only option I really have."

Jeselle could hear the hurt pouring through her words. "I think you are really smart, Camilla. I don't think marriage is your only option."

"Yeah, well, it's not like your opinion really matters, but still, thanks," Camilla turned slowly and went back to the house.

Jeselle could've taken the comment as a jab, but it sounded more like a resolution on Camilla's part. A depressing one. Jeselle also wasn't surprised at Camilla's comment. She'd hoped after that vacation, she and Camilla would be friends, start anew, only that wasn't what happened. Camilla was too conceited to lower herself to be friends with a maid's daughter, even though her brother was dating her.

Junior year started with Camilla as leader of the pack of all the rich, popular girls.

Camilla belonged there, Jeselle thought many times.

Still, visiting the Stryker's got more and more comfortable over the months. With her mother working long hours, Jeselle found being there, around Dennis's mother and sister, was better than being alone most days. His dad occasionally made it to dinner, but not often. Still, it was good.

Dennis never pressured her, but she could tell he wanted to get physical. He had tried to kiss her a few weeks before when he was at her house and her mom had gone to the grocery store, but she couldn't. He left with tears in his eyes, but returned the next day to pick her up for school and that afternoon they watched movies.

Everything resembled a normal.

They studied together and Dennis shared his aspirations for running Stryker one day.

"I'm going to give employee bonuses and make sure everyone feels a part of something special. I'm going to grow our profit so big that Dad will have to recognize how important I am."

"I don't doubt it. You are amazing," Jeselle agreed.

They walked around the park in the evenings, right alongside all the old, sweet, grey-haired couples. Unlike most kids her age, she almost couldn't wait to be like them. To be with *the one*. The one who has been there through thick and thin. The one who loves you above all others.

One evening, right before Christmas, Dennis brought Jeselle to their favorite bench and gave her a small box wrapped in white paper and a big gold bow.

"Déjà vu," Jeselle said.

"Except Sissy couldn't find that glittery white

wrapping, so we had to get this one."

"What is it?"

"Open it, just be sure you do it the right way," he smiled.

She laughed and ripped into the box. She lifted the lid expecting to find another necklace, instead found a ring. Her eyes widened.

"Do you like it?" he asked.

"Uh, I don't … know," she looked at him, "it looks like a wedding ring?"

"Only to other people," he laughed, "it's a promise ring."

"A promise ring? This big? My mom's wedding ring isn't even this big."

"Yes," he grinned, "Do you like it?"

"I, hmmm, don't understand why you are giving it to me," she said honestly.

"Do you love me?"

"You know I do, but-"

"No buts, I love you. I know one day we'll be one of these," he pointed to an old couple sitting on another bench across the pond, then he took the ring out of the box and slipped it on her ring finger. "Jeselle Kate Parsons, will you promise to be mine?"

"I'm scared, Dennis. I don't thin-,"

"Don't think. Don't overthink, is what I mean. I'm not asking you for anything you aren't willing to give."

"But I can't even kiss you, yet," she said.

"Yet, is the key word," he reassured.

She hesitated and he grew agitated, "Is there

someone else?"

"No!" she nearly shouted.

He calmed and grabbed her hand, "Then accept it, okay?"

"Okay," she agreed, but still something didn't feel quite right. She attributed those feelings to that night, but then again, she attributed anything negative to that night.

Jeselle's mom didn't have much to say about the ring other than to point out to Jeselle that she should never do something just because she thinks she is expected to do it, rather than because she simply wants to. Jeselle looked at that ring often and thought it felt more like an anchor, but she really didn't know why, because she did love Dennis.

Two weeks later, the Stryker family Christmas party was bigger than usual, which was saying a lot. Dennis showed off Jeselle's ring to everyone, and she felt important, predominantly because of how she was treated by everyone afterward.

She'd dropped some of the cheese fondue on a woman's fancy shoe, because she had hurriedly tried to get it onto her plate, ironically, to avoid that very thing. The older lady had huge diamond rings on every finger and large earrings that were so heavy they weighed down her earlobes dramatically.

"I am so sorry!" Jeselle turned, put her plate on the table and frantically grabbed a napkin to help clean the woman's shoe when the woman stilled her arm.

"No need, dear, it seems I may be wiping your

shoe soon enough." The old lady snatched the napkin and tossed it onto the floor before grasping Jeselle's arm again.

"I'm sorry?" she giggled out of nervousness, "What?"

"That ring on your finger," the older lady motioned, "Look around the room, dear child, all these pretentious people dressed in thousand-dollar dresses and tuxes, everyone you see will soon be bowing at your feet. Use it well." The lady tightened her grip on Jeselle's arm and looked much older all of a sudden, "Don't be an old crow like the rest of us. Do you understand me?"

"Yes, yes ma'am." Jeselle was a little scared of the woman. When she told Dennis later, he laughed, "That's Old Lady Rowe, she's like everyone's grandmother. Rare, one of the good ones. She doesn't have any kids, so I guess that makes her a little awkward."

She noticed the woman several times throughout the night, squinting her beady eyes and tilting her head in reminder. Jeselle wasn't sure if she wanted to be in a room full of people where that lady was a rare, good one.

Before she left the party, someone grabbed her arm. When Jeselle turned she found Old lady Rowe holding on tight, "I'm sorry about your dad."

It was the most sincere condolence she'd been given. It startled Jeselle, who simply nodded as she whispered, "Thank you."

Christmas at Jeselle's house was perfect. Isabel

and her daughters spent the night and on Christmas Eve, it snowed. It rarely snowed in South Louisiana, so it was extra magical. Dennis showed up as soon as the flurries started and they all drank hot chocolate and played in the snow together. Winter in Louisiana wasn't much to speak of, but since they'd gotten snow for Christmas Eve, no one complained after that.

Christmas break, as it always did, flew by all too quickly and when everyone returned to school they found that Cindy had received a ring from Tracy that was twice the size of Jeselle's, of course. The days of January melted into one another in the same routine.

Dennis and Jeselle stepped inside the front door, "Mother?" Dennis called up the staircase.

"Sssssh," she answered from the top of the stairs.

"Jeselle's over. We're going to get some stuff and go in the guest house, okay?"

His mother, dressed to perfection as always, rushed down the stairs cheerfully. "Ssssh, the attorneys are here. It's time."

"Time? Like time, time?" Dennis asked.

"Yes!" she said excitedly.

Jeselle looked puzzled and Dennis explained, "Her trust. Her birthday is tomorrow."

"Happy birthday," Jeselle said.

"You must come. We are having the biggest birthday bash this city has ever seen," she squealed.

Jeselle had never seen Dennis's mother so giddy, it definitely made her look younger. Dennis grabbed

Jeselle's hand, and they basically took off running through the house, slowing only as they passed his dad's study. Dennis put his finger over his mouth as they tiptoed past the study door, then they took off running again.

Jeselle looked back, right before they rounded a corner and saw Mrs. Stryker straighten herself and walk into the study.

"I don't think I've ever seen her so happy."

"She hasn't been. Ever," He laughed. "I can't believe I didn't remember. We've been waiting so long for today."

They loaded their arms down with stuff from the pantry and refrigerator to take with them and were almost to the back door when they heard a blood curdling scream blast through the house.

His mother.

They both dropped everything and ran to the study. His mother was on the floor gasping for breath.

"Dad, what's happened?" he asked, but the answer was already written on his face.

The other men in suits stood and apologized to his dad again and left.

"Dad?"

"Her trust. He drained…Brantley drained every dime," his dad was stunned.

"Oh no," Jeselle rushed to Mrs. Stryker.

Theodore was startled by Jeselle's sudden movement. He cleared his throat, "You need to leave, young lady, this is a family matter."

"Don't you ever talk to her that way again, she is family," Dennis walked toward his father.

"I, I am sorry, of course. I am just upset," he responded to his son as he allowed himself to fall back into his large leather chair.

"Tell me," Dennis demanded.

"The trust attorneys said there was some sort of clause that stated it could be liquidated if the company was in trouble and needed it. Briggs was in debt, so Brantley emptied it a year before he bought her out of the company."

"A…year…before? Wait," Dennis sat in the nearest chair. "We were eight."

The devastation descended over all of them.

"That means," Dennis started breathing heavier, "that all this time, all these years of kissing Tracy's… there was no money."

His dad sat back into his own desk chair, "And they didn't even have the decency to tell us."

"Tell us! Dad, they held it over our heads! Every time! Every day!" Dennis yelled. "All this time…"

His mother fell onto Jeselle and she simply held Mrs. Stryker as she wailed. Dennis and Jeselle's eyes met and all Jeselle heard after that was Tracy's chant echoing through her mind:

Your. Mother's. Money.

Your. Mother's. Money.

Your. Mother's. Money.

CHAPTER 36

PRESENT

"Perhaps everyone has a story that could
break your heart."
-Nick Flynn

When Isabel, Kayla, and Cindy left her office, Jeselle thought back to the day, after seeing Rose get out of the luxury car and how unsteady she had felt, knowing something was off. She had had good instincts about Rose initially, yet one step out of a car had changed that. The contrast of instincts and truths get muddled when you have little trust for others. Jeselle's original instincts were that Cindy was truly broken, contrite, and in need of help. Jeselle had felt sorry for her role in the situation. The truth became apparent the day she hired Cindy, when she said she'd do anything, except scrubbing toilets. Or anything in the sun, since her skin burned way too easily.

Nothing "too degrading," Cindy had said. She was "still a Briggs, afterall."

When Jeselle had found out that Cindy was mistreating the housekeeping staff, she knew it had been cemented. Cindy's future was cemented by her own actions, like the others.

Sometimes, we can be wrong about people and it's hard to correct ourselves, because it makes us feel weak. Stupid. Not in tune enough to the truth. Inexperienced.

Yet with Rose, Jeselle had thought her instincts were telling her that Rose wasn't who she said she was, simply because of seeing her get out of a car. Truth was, Rose was exactly who she said she was. Rose would have been happy with cleaning toilets. Also, when asked, Rose told the truth. She thought back to the day that she had doubted Rose and had called in Isabel to share her story. It was a stark contrast from the experience when Cindy had been confronted.

Jeselle remembered her own words to Rose: "From this day forward, if you need help, ask me. I am loyal, but I am also skeptical. I have enough frenemies; I'm not looking for more. However, they are always looking for ways to use someone loyal to me, against me. If you find yourself in trouble, come to me. Take no favors from anyone. Owe no one."

"I, I am not, I won't, owe I mean, I promise," Rose had put up her hand in oath.

"Rose, put your hand down," Jeselle had snapped, "Now, is there anything you need to tell me?"

Rose had quickly answered, "Maybe."

"If you think you maybe have something to tell me, best to do it now." Jeselle had said, taking in a deep breath.

"It's that, well, my dad, he's real sick. He has so many medical bills. And my parents ... well, they've fallen behind on a lot of their regular bills and I, he said he could help them, but Ms. Parsons, I swear," Rose had lifted her hand in the air in oath, "I haven't told him anything. He said he would help them if I would just watch for anything weird, but I swear I haven't-"

"Who?"

"Please don't be mad, I swear I haven't told him anything."

Jeselle had taken another deeper breath, "Rose, who asked you to watch me?"

"Mr. Stryker," she had all but sobbed, "I promise you though, you can see all of the texts. I haven't told him anything. I mean I don't really know anything, I've only been here for four days, but I haven't, not about anything you have told me."

"What did he offer you?"

Rose had lowered her head, "He said he'd pay off my parents' house and medical bills if I brought him anything worthwhile, but, I," Rose had moved forward in her chair and had looked back at Isabel, "I promise you, I wasn't going to tell him anything."

"Rose, do you remember what I said on your first day here? You can't buy loyalty. Someone is either loyal or they aren't."

"I am-"

"Let me finish. Because no matter how much you pay someone, there is always someone else who can pay more. Do you agree with that?"

"Yes."

"And if there is anything I've learned the hard way, it's that Theodore Stryker will pay whatever you ask,"

Rose had stood quickly, "Oh, no ma'am... Dennis. It's Dennis Stryker."

Jeselle had been shocked for a millisecond, then she had laughed in sheer amusement. "Really? Oh, this will be fun. Okay Rose, start from the beginning."

"It was the night of the gala."

"That quickly," Jeselle had made more of a statement to herself than anyone else, "Extra points for him. Continue."

"I had gone to the bathroom, and when I came out Mr. Stryker...Mr. Dennis was there. He said he loved my dress, which was really nice, because I could tell once I got there I probably didn't fit in, but my momma made it and I am so proud of it, ya know?"

Isabel and Jeselle had smiled, "We know," they had both said together.

"He said that he knew my parents were in debt and that he could help them. Only," Rose had sunk into the chair, "that it had to be a secret because you didn't like when he stuck his nose in your business."

Jeselle's smile had widened.

"He said he was worried you were making big mistakes that would cost you everything. He said he worried you were nearing bankruptcy. He also knew that my parents were close to getting their house repossessed, which I didn't know about!"

"Is that why you left early?" Isabel had asked.

"Yes, but he stopped me in the foyer and said that he needed to know that I wouldn't tell you, so for good measure," Rose looked back down at her lap, "he said he would make sure it was repossessed if I said anything to you. I didn't know what to do, but I knew … I knew I wasn't going to tell him anything. Then,"

"Pause. For one, I won't tell him you told me, but I understand why you would assume so. Continue,"

"Well, so then I went to my parents' and told them what he said, and they told me to let him take the house. They'd rather that than to have me compromise myself."

Jeselle had thought of her own dad and felt her nose burn.

"Daddy said a person who bribes is never satisfied and that his threats likely wouldn't end there. Then, Momma said to simply play it cool and not to directly refuse him until I had to, so…so they could make other arrangements." Rose's tears had reminded Jeselle of being on the back porch with her dad, both of them defeated.

"I wonder how he knew about you. Your first

day was the same day of the gala. He hadn't met you before then."

"Oh, yes ma'am he was in the main lobby when we left. You were making him wait and he seemed a little upset. Karli sorta laughed about it because Dennis is always coming on to her, so she thought it was funny."

"Hold," Jeselle picked up the phone, "Karli, come in here please."

The moment Karli arrived Jeselle asked, "Does Dennis come on to you?"

Karli laughed, "You know him," she waved a hand in the air, "He's harmless though. I don't pay any attention to him, why?"

"Because Rose told me he did, and you've never told me."

"I thought you knew, I guess, I mean everyone knows he thinks he owns everyone else. And to be honest, Ms. Parsons, for the greater good, I can deal."

"Has he ever touched you?"

"Oh, no! He'd already be dead if he had."

"Okay, Karli, thank you. Stay with us, here. You can probably help. Now, Rose, continue."

"Like I was saying, he stopped me and Karli and asked if you were coming down soon. She said she wasn't sure, but then he introduced himself, and I introduced myself."

"Oh," Karli had laughed, "the day of the Gala. Yes, that was funny, you making him wait," she had said to Jeselle.

Rose had continued, "Then, he asked something about was I kin to the Fontenots of New Orleans and I said I didn't think so, we were from Brusly."

"Ahhh, okay. So, we know how he found your parents then," Jeselle had looked to Isabel.

"But I didn't tell him their names, and there are a lot of Fontenots in Brusly."

"Rose, listen carefully," Jeselle had risen from her desk, "people with money can find out a lot of information the average person wouldn't be able to. They pay people to do that sort of thing," Jeselle had paused and thought for a moment, "However, he probably got his secretary to call around. Would've been easy enough with a small town and a daughter named Rose." Jeselle had smiled, "While this is a surprise, we can certainly use it to have a little fun. I'll feed you what information to feed him. Nothing important, but also nothing untrue. Your parents gave you good advice, and it is to your credit that you've followed it. Do your parents have an income?"

"Yes, ma'am, my dad gets social security disability."

"Which isn't much to be sure." Jeselle had thought for a moment longer, "I want to pay off your parent's medical bills, but it would send a red flag to the Strykers if I did it now. Just be sure," she had looked to Karli and nodded, "it's on the 'list of things to right.' "

"Done," Karli had made the mental note.

"Let no one else know about this. Only the four

of us. Can you do that?"

"My parents..."

"Yes, well of course. Do you feel they could keep their mouths closed about the fact that I know? Your mother doesn't have a best friend she tells all her gossip to?"

"Oh, no. She wouldn't gossip. Strict Southern Baptist."

Jeselle had nodded, "Well, best to keep it between us then. Let Karli know what their mortgage is, and she'll give you a new raise to reflect that amount. Pay it every single month. How far behind are they?"

"I ... Ms. Parsons, I already told you I wouldn't tell him anything. I promise."

"And I believe you. Again, I don't buy loyalty. That still doesn't change that your parents are facing foreclosure, does it?"

Rose had started crying, "No, ma'am."

"There. Done. Now, Karli, would you mind?" Jeselle had motioned toward Rose and Karli nodded. "Rose, you've heard Isabel's story, now Karli's."

Karli had started slowly, "I was a runaway... you know, bad home situation. Mom was always hyped on the next guy, thinking he was the one. The one that would finally come rescue us, when most of them only made her worse. I never knew my dad, but I wanted one so bad. I would've done anything to have one of them love me, you know," Karli had noticed Roses eyes widen, "Oh no, nothing like that. None of them ever did anything to me. Most of them never paid me any mind at all. I was only the annoying baggage most of the time. When I was fifteen, Mom told me the new one, the one, didn't really like me being around as much. She asked me, temporarily until he married her, if I could maybe go stay with my Aunt Mae in Baton Rouge. I was hurt, but sure, if it made her happy. I wasn't really happy anyway, to be honest. So, I packed up what I could in two suitcases and found my way here."

"I'm sorry," Rose had whispered.

"Aunt Mae was my mom's aunt, and she was old and really strict. My first job came quick, modeling 'off the radar' for cash. Friend from school knew a guy. Thought it was pretty fishy at first, but he had a company address and a studio. I told Aunt Mae I was working for a local grocery store. She'd drop me off there, and he'd pick me up. Danny, the man I worked for, promised me that the manager of the store was in his back pocket, and he'd vouch for me if she ever went in. Worked pretty good, decent pay. One day, I was hired by a man to be an escort to some business meeting. It was four hundred dollars. I turned it down, no way. Sounded like it was, you know, prostitution. Danny swore it wasn't. Still I felt weird about it, so I didn't do it. Then Danny was late dropping me off one afternoon. Looking back, I realized he did it on purpose. I had told him how strict Aunt Mae was, and he knew how scared I was every Saturday that she'd find out. But that day, we were late and Aunt Mae was waiting. She kicked me out. Got me a bus ticket back to Mom's. I called Danny to come pick me up and take me to the bus station. On the way, he essentially told me about the escort job again. No sex. Basically, dressing up in nice clothes and accompanying men to dinners, meetings, etc. He said most of them were rich losers, needing some attention from a woman. I could support myself. Be my own boss. He'd help me get my own apartment, under his name of course, because I was underage. So…" Karli took a deep breath, "I took the job."

Rose's breathing had slowed.

"Don't feel sorry for me, I made those decisions. Biggest one was when Danny told me he had a 'job' for me that could potentially pay me ten thousand dollars."

Jeselle had walked from her desk to one of the sofas.

"All I had to do was, on this date, if, and he stressed only if, I wanted to let things get physical, the guy would pay me ten thousand. I was disgusted at first. But then I asked how physical. That's when he dropped it, my virginity," Karli laughed but it was clear nothing was funny, "I went. The guy was cute, there was some chemistry, not to mention that ten thousand dollars kept blinking in my mind. Freedom. *Just this once and I'd be free.* I knew I could probably enjoy it too. Heard friends talk about sex a lot. Didn't seem so bad. So I did it."

The office had been quiet for a minute.

"It was though, and I bled a lot, which seemed to make him happy. I kept my eyes closed mostly, but when I did get the courage to take a peek, he was smiling." Karli had seemed lost in the moment as she continued, "He was on top of me, moving, and smiling. I started crying because I felt so awkward. Then I started apologizing to him for crying. I was worried he wouldn't want to pay, but he kept moving and smiling. Seems like it took forever. The longer he took, the more I cried. I felt so humiliated. Still, he smiled. I don't think I'll ever forget that smile," Karli shook off the thought. "I was nearly hysterical by the time he finished. He got off me, called Danny and I heard him say 'Dude, best yet, worth the whole fifty grand.' And I was only offered ten of that."

Rose had cursed, then quickly apologized for cursing. Isabel had moved closer to Karli, "I'm sorry, again."

"No need," Karli had replied. "Truly. I made those choices." They had all listened as she continued, "After that, I lost all self-respect. Started sleeping around at school. I avoided Danny as much as possible until the day he showed up at my door, really his door because he rented the apartment. Basically told me he knew, through my friend at school, that I was 'throwing it around to every guy for free' why not make money at it. I didn't care anymore. I really didn't. That week I dropped out of school, and Danny started setting me up. Rich guys at first, one a week. I could do that. Then, it got to be not so rich guys and two or three a week. Then to one a day, then two or three and barely making rent and utilities to Danny. What they, the people who promise all that money at first, don't tell you is at some point you are used up, just can't do it anymore. Only, you have to, then you get desperate for having been around the block one too many times. So, you end up stuck, giving yourself away for ten, twenty bucks."

Rose had cursed again, only that time she hadn't apologized.

"This is that part of the story you need most, Rose. Listen well. When Jeselle bought the buildings around Prostitution Way, she immediately, the next day, converted them into temporary housing. She brought in beds, furniture, lots of people to help. She had a sign put up on one that said *Haevn.E, a Place of Refuge.* You know it was spelled weird with her capital E thing, but we all knew what it meant. Another building's sign said *Haevn.E Foundation, Education for Financial Freedom.* I'll never forget the excitement most of us felt. I walked in that first day, and it changed my life. I was treated like I was important. I enrolled in the education program and over the first month had met Jeselle a few times when she came to volunteer. Not long after I got my certification in clerical, Jeselle hired me here. Here, for her. Right at the top."

Rose had felt the tears bubbling up. Jeselle had quickly pushed away her own feelings.

Jeselle had stood and looked at Rose, "Now me. I was watching the Powerpuff Girls marathon. My mom had recently died. I was angry and afraid; no need to go into details. Isabel's kids and I were watching the episode where King Morbucks buys Townsville from the Mayor for Princess."

Rose had wiped her eyes and spoke softly, "Oh yeah, I love that one. They used the new law to steal and get the town back,"

"Yes. It was then that it hit me: you have to play by their rules, their laws, to right the wrongs," Jeselle had clapped her hands together, "Okay, time to get back to work. Enough reminiscing for the day." Jeselle had looked at Rose, "We good?"

"Yes, ma'am," Rose had sniffled, "we are."

Sitting at her desk, Jeselle knew Cindy was that first type of person, the one who knew she was no better than anyone else, but acted as though she were in spite of it. She mistreated people to show power. She was the traitor for money, mortgaged to the hilt, bought name brand shoes she hated to wear, and did just about anything to keep up with the Joneses. She may change at some point and be a better person, but Jeselle didn't see it happen often.

Jeselle sat back in her chair, a smile spreading across her face, she was even more satisfied that she gave Cindy the job.

CHAPTER 37

PAST

"...and trust is where the real power of
love comes from."
-Diane Keaton

It was the end of January and Jeselle was excited that her birthday was only two weeks away. She'd be seventeen. Dennis kept telling her he had a huge birthday present for her. Something she'd never forget and she freely admitted she couldn't wait so he decided to give it to her early.

Her mom stood in the kitchen with Jeselle when Dennis gave her the envelope.

"Mom and Dad wanted me to do it at our house, but I couldn't wait any longer," Dennis said.

Jeselle was confused, "I kind of expected a puppy."

Dennis laughed, "This is better, much better. Promise."

Jeselle opened it and pulled out what looked like a check. It was made out to Louisiana State University. Her eyebrows shot up and she slowly handed it off to her mom.

"It's for college. From Mother and Father."

"Now, I'm really confused," Jeselle said.

Her mother, dumbfounded, gently passed the check back to Dennis.

"I don't think you understand what this is. They are paying for your college," he smiled bigger.

"Dennis," Jeselle took in a deep breath, "I already got a full scholarship."

He was obviously disappointed, "Why didn't you ever tell me this?"

"Well, we don't ever really talk about that kind of stuff, I guess," she replied.

"Still, that's ... great," he replied.

Jeselle could see it wasn't great. "Dennis, your parents don't have to do anything for me. They know that, right? Like, we're good."

He slanted his head and looked at her quizzically.

"I mean I know, the house," she stumbled over her words, "and, I guess the job," she looked at her mom. Jeselle noticed her mom was put off by it all too. Which was unusual for her.

"Okay," Dennis said, "Good, good. Okay. I guess I need to go get you a puppy," he laughed nervously, then quickly righted his insecurity. "LSU is awesome. I'm excited to go there, too."

Her mom took a deep breath, patted Jeselle, nodded, and left through the back door to sit on the patio.

"Dennis, I'm realizing just now that we haven't talked much about the future at all, except yours. I, um, I, my scholarship is for Tulane."

He took a step back. Then another. "I have to go to LSU, it's my family's alma mater."

She smiled knowingly, "We don't have to go to the same college, Dennis."

"Right," he sighed then rubbed his face, "Right. Okay. Then I guess I can drive down there on the weekends."

"I'll be here on the weekends," she took a step toward him.

"Even better," he said, "I guess I can get them to get you a car. You'll need a car."

"I have Dad's truck," she said as if it were a no brainer.

"But, driving all that way every weekend, I mean you'll need something dependable," he continued without thought, "good on gas."

"Nothing would be better than Dad's truck. Dennis, I have Dad's truck."

The rest of the visit was awkward, he left not long after. They hugged, but Dennis still seemed perplexed.

Jeselle met her mom on the back patio,

"Sorry," her mom said.

"No, this was good. I realized today, that we only really ever talk about him. What he wants.

What his future is. It's weird that I hadn't noticed, but I was standing in the kitchen now, and I can only remember a handful of times he's asked me what I wanted. None of it was about my future, my career. It all mostly centered on his life. Like, did I see us together? Or stuff like I'll make a great addition to the Stryker family. Stuff he hated in eighth grade has transitioned to the stuff he wants like having big family picnics for all the workers, etc."

"I love you, Jessie. Be you. You make sure, no matter who you love and where you are in life, be who you want to be. You know your dad always knew he would help the environment in one way or another. I really admired that in him. He knew all through college that he'd do it, and he did."

"What did you want?"

"I wanted kids," her mom answered.

"Why didn't you ever have more than me?"

"You know, I hate to say it like this, but you were enough. Sounds weird, but it's true."

"Mom, is it weird that I don't want kids?" Jeselle asked.

"Not at all. Be open to change though, because you may change your mind when you get older, or meet the right guy."

"Wait, do you think Dennis isn't the right guy?"

"I think only you can make that judgement call," her mom smiled.

"But, do you?"

"I'm not going to answer that for you, Jessie. You have plenty of time to figure it out," her mom pointed to the promise ring, "Don't rush anything."

Jeselle sat on the back porch for several hours trying to figure that out. It was fairly late when headlights appeared in her driveway. It was Dennis.

"I saw your light on back here, knew you were probably still up. Here." He pulled one hand from behind his back, a gift.

"Dennis, you didn't have to get me anything. Really."

"Jeselle Kate Parsons, I looked everywhere for this, open it," he laughed as she ripped open the box.

In it was a Tulane t-shirt.

"Oh, Dennis! I love it! Thank you!" she jumped out of the chair and hugged him tightly.

"Okay, okay, one more," he pulled the other arm from behind his back and extended another gift toward her. "This one you won't like as much, because I know they freak you out, but...we'll be able to keep in touch."

She ripped that box open and found one of the phones she had just finished telling her mom she'd never own.

She smiled politely, "Thank you, Dennis."

"Let me show you how it works. Press and hold the number one and it calls me." He did it and the one in his pocket rang.

"You would put yourself as number one," she laughed.

"And you are number one in mine." He showed her, pressing the one down and hers rang.

"It's pretty neat. Your house is number two, my

house number three," he said.

"Cool," she said.

"See you tomorrow," he leaned in to kiss her lips and she turned her face away instinctively. The kiss landed on her cheek.

When his headlights disappeared, Jeselle sank back into the chair and looked at the ring on one hand, the cell in the other. She knew his intentions were good, but the cell phone also felt like another anchor somehow.

She had no way of knowing that the next day, she would be making a call from that very phone, from a police car on the way to the hospital where her mom was being treated with severe injuries. A car had sideswiped her on her way to work.

***

She felt so lost at the hospital without Isabel's number. She closed her eyes and pictured it on the hand written note under a magnet on the refrigerator, but couldn't remember the number. Dennis called his dad to get it.

"Jess, we are so sorry," a deep voice echoed through the waiting area.

"Dad?" Dennis stood, "I didn't expect you to come."

"Of course we came, she's family," he blurted out.

Dennis was clearly appreciative, "Thank you,

both," he hugged his mother.

"No need," Theodore bent down in front of Jeselle, "Jess, we discussed it on the way over, you come stay with us."

"I'm staying here with Mom," she said.

Dennis's dad looked up at him and Dennis knew. "Has Dr. Daniels come out to talk to her yet?"

"No."

"Okay, stay right here, I'll go see what's going on."

"Oh, Dad, did you get in touch with Ms. Isabel?"

"I have Sissy taking care of it."

Mr. Stryker disappeared for a few minutes and when he returned, he had the doctor with him.

"Jess, this is Dr. Daniels."

"Hello, Jessica Parsons was your mother, correct?"

"Is!" she said, but then it hit her...and her legs gave way, Dennis caught her.

"I'm sorry," the doctor said, "we did all we could, however the injuries were too severe."

"I don't believe you. I want to see my mom."

"You can, but I don't recommend it. She was in bad shape," Dr. Daniels said.

After crying and screaming and getting her mom's belongings in a clear plastic bag handed to her, she was ushered out through the emergency room doors and into Dennis's car.

"Bring her to the house, Son. Sissy has a room ready for her," his dad said.

"No...I want to go home," Jeselle insisted.

"I'll stay with her," Dennis said.

"Well, short term, but she needs to think long term also. She can't stay in the house alone."

Either they had made it to her house really quickly, or she had zoned out. She walked straight into the kitchen, lifted the paper off the refrigerator, and dialed the number.

"Ms. Isabel?"

"Honey child, what's wrong? It's late, everything okay?"

"Did no one call you?"

"No, why would … Jessie, what's going on?" she asked.

Jeselle blurted it all out through sobs. Dennis rubbed her back while she was on the phone. Then, as they waited for Isabel and the girls, Dennis attempted to make her tea. Jeselle thought how absurd it was that he had to read the directions on the tea box. Then, conversely how sweet it was.

She couldn't wait to tell her mom, she thought.

Her mom, Jeselle broke down in sobs again, her mom was gone.

CHAPTER 38

PAST

```
"Liars ought to have good memories."
         -Algernon Sidney
```

Two days later she woke up to the smell of bacon cooking. Only a few moments, that's how long it took for her to remember, as it did each morning, and she cried again. She got into the shower and stayed until all the hot water was gone. Isabel was pouring her a cup of coffee when she finally did make it downstairs.

"You got to make decisions today, honey. No matter how hard. Can't put it off again." Isabel said.

"I know."

"I can't stay forever, and Mr. Stryker has called a few times worried, asking when you were moving over there."

"I don't want to go over there," Jeselle said.

"I know, Jessie, but you have no other choice. You can't stay here,"

"Why not!" she yelled. "This is my home, or is it his?"

"You gonna be angry. That's okay, be careful who you direct it at," Isabel said.

"I'm sorry."

"No need to apologize to me, I'm not talking about me. You still have issues you haven't gotten past. That thing that happened, your dad, now your mom. You be careful, okay? You are still a child and cannot stay here alone. You are welcome to make a pallet at our place, but I doubt that would be better for you than the Stryker's big mansion and our public schools aren't nearly as nice as yours over here. You have to think it out, Jessie. You have another year of high school before you go off to college." Isabel placed the steaming mug of coffee in front of Jeselle.

She took a few sips. "Wait. Why not stay here."

"What are you talking about, child?"

"You all stay here. Why not? There is plenty of room. The house is mine. I'm not selling it. So isn't it going to be mine?"

"I don't think you can legally own anything, baby," Isabel said.

"Isabel! There is a way."

"If there is a way, we would gladly move into this swanky place, but realistically I'm not sure there is. Go talk to the Strykers, find out, okay. I'll take you myself if you'd like."

"I'd rather not be thinking about anything," Jeselle started crying again, Isabel went around the island and hugged her.

* * *

Four days after her mom's funeral, Jeselle was more than ready to talk to Mr. Stryker. Dennis was glad she finally decided to see his parents. He knew they would help her.

"Well, honey it's good to see you," Sissy said as she opened the door.

Dennis peered around her, "I told you I'd come get you," he said toward the open door.

"I know, Isabel offered to bring me, too. I just needed the walk, I guess."

Dennis led her into the formal living room, sat, and she settled next to him onto the sofa, which seemed abnormally stiff to her. She had never sat in the room before, and it made her feel like she was in a strange place rather than a comfortable one.

"Sissy, please bring us some tea," Mrs. Stryker said to the older lady.

"Right away, ma'am," the housekeeper said.

Mr. and Mrs. Stryker and an unknown person sat across from her on another sofa, staring at her.

"I'd like to stay in the house," she said.

If his parents were stunned, they didn't let it show.

Theodore spoke first, "Unfortunately, that isn't possible. I'm sorry, Jess."

"You are underage and have no job, dear," his mother chimed in, "you wouldn't be able to pay the bills on such a big place, plus you are going to college soon, what then?"

"Actually it is possible," Jeselle noticed the surprise on Dennis's dad's face first. "I spoke with one of the law professors at Tulane, and he said the court can designate a custodian over my mom's assets and insurance money."

Oddly, Jeselle noticed Mr. Stryker relaxed quite a bit, "Yes, we could do that, but we aren't going to move in that direction. Jess, it would really be putting more on us than we need right now, you know, to make it easy on everyone. Staying here is the best option. Plus, the insurance policy is a Stryker policy, and I'm sorry to say the board will likely vote to return it to Stryker. You understand, that's just business. Like with your father."

That struck a nerve. One that hadn't been plucked in a while.

"Dad," Dennis huffed, "You are majority shareholder and on the board, so, I do believe you could persuade them otherwise, she needs the money."

Jeselle let his words sink in.

"And we will provide any financi-," his dad was saying when she interrupted.

Jeselle looked at Dennis, "He controls the board?"

"I just found that out in business class," he whispered it like it was nothing, like he hadn't even realized what that really meant yet. That two and a half years before, things could've gone differently.

Theodore Stryker could've helped them.

She collected herself, as she had promised herself she would do on the long walk there. "First, I was talking about my mother's own insurance policy, not the one through Stryker. After what happened with my dad, she never wanted to leave me vulnerable like she was." Jeselle could tell the moment Dennis registered his dad's lies back then, when his arm grew tighter around her waist. He was obviously processing the domino effect like she already had.

"She got her own policy?" Mr. Stryker cocked his head sideways, dumbfounded.

"Yes, sir," she answered, "and I would never want to put any more on you than is already there." It was obvious everyone in the room understood her meaning. "The professor already filed for me to designate Isabel."

He squinted his eyes in assessment before talking again, "Jess, this is nonsense. Isabel works for me, and there is no way I can pay her to do that."

She wasn't sure, but it sounded like he'd added a threat somewhere in that statement. Luckily, Isabel and she had already talked it out that morning and decided Isabel could work anywhere. That was the best part about being in housekeeping, her mom and Isabel used to say, everyone needed it and no one wanted do it.

Jeselle inhaled, somewhat melodramatically, "She wouldn't expect to be paid. She's my mom's closest friend. We worked it all out. Isabel and her daughters will live there with me, and then take care of the place for me when I go to college." As wretched as it was to admit to herself, Jeselle immensely enjoyed the collective gasps that spread through the room.

"Jess," she hadn't expected Dennis to talk at all, "she's a maid," he whispered.

Jeselle stood abruptly, "My mother was a maid, *Dennis!*" she put extra emphasis on his name.

"I know, I'm sorry, I didn't mean that, I'm sorr-" he stood and slipped his hand around her waist.

"Do you mean Isabel is black?" Jeselle moved away from his grasp.

"That's an outrage, Jess," Dennis's father bellowed indignantly, "We aren't racist. I have many black employees, even in my own household."

"Yes," she turned to look at Dennis, "*the maids.*"

Just then Sissy came in with a tray full of tea, stopped, wide-eyed, then stood a bit taller as she walked between them and laid the tray on the coffee table.

"Stop this nonsense," his dad held up a hand as he stood also. His wife and the other man followed. "I know you're angry, and I'll excuse this. Jess, there is a problem with that plan of yours. The boar..." Mr. Stryker paused and looked at Dennis briefly, "The board has already voted, I'm afraid. The process to call in the lien has already been started. I'm sorry there is simply nothing I can do. You'll have to stay here." He turned to leave the room.

"I somehow expected that, and not sure why, but no, Professor looked over the lien paperwork and found that the lien can only be fulfilled through a title owner sale, not a forced sale, so board vote or not…"

"The house," he blubbered rudely, "is mine, Jeselle! It's something about the law, it can't be transferred now."

"Also, not true. Mr. Stryker. Respectfully, sir, it is transferrable … to me, Mom's heir."

"Dad?" Dennis sounded like he was a young boy having just found out that his father wasn't the hero he'd always thought. The benefit of doubt, gone.

Jeselle walked out of the house feeling empowered like she never had before. She'd lost nearly everything. Everything that mattered, except Isabel and Dennis. Halfway down the walkway she heard the door slam, looked back, and Dennis was rushing toward her.

"Company?"

"I don't know, Dennis," she said with indignation, "I *am* the daughter of a maid."

"I am sorry. I did see Ms. Isabel that way, but not your mom. In any case, I love Ms. Isabel, but…but I shouldn't see anyone that way, should I? I feel … uneasy about how I feel, actually."

"Well, today Dennis, this isn't about your feelings. Today it's about me."

They walked down the middle of the road,

toward her house in silence. All his life, Dennis had been taught to categorize people: The rich and the poor. The deserving and the undeserving. Her family had started off somewhere closer to deserving. Then, because of the rich, they became the undeserving. Only Dennis probably still saw her as deserving…merely having a run of bad luck.

"Why did your dad put the house in my mom's name?"

Dennis was stunned by the question. "Why?"

"Yes, why? He was set to evict us. Obviously, since I heard that he actually did do it, but covered it up. He could've chosen to simply not evict us. Why put it in her name?"

Dennis stopped walking, took in a deep breath and let it out slowly. Jeselle turned to face him, standing in the middle of the street.

"Because, after I heard about your dad… and then the eviction notice, the patents," he took another breath in and let it out, "I went home and told him I'd leave, I'd live with you both in an apartment and work at a gas station, do whatever it took to support you. I was so mad. He said he might be able to persuade the board to let you guys stay as long as you needed until you found another place, but…I told him that wasn't good enough. I intended to marry you, and if he wanted a daughter-in-law who lived in Wellgrove, he'd better come up with a better plan. Then I left and went to your house."

Jeselle stood in silence.

"The night of the Christmas party, when you

disappeared I knew something was wrong. Dad said he'd been on the phone when he heard a cry in the hallway right outside the door."

Jeselle didn't remember making any noise.

"Told me that you possibly heard him talking about the insurance policy, how it couldn't be converted to your mom. I knew he was lying. I made the point that he had more than enough money to donate whatever the amount was to your mom from his personal account," another breath. "He said it was impossible, that nearly every liquid asset they had was tied up. Jess, I looked around at all the decorations, new ones because Mom wanted to do white instead of the blue, all the catering and… Camilla's new dress that I remember Mom saying was only a thousand dollars and Camilla was mad, hoped it would measure up to the other girls dresses. I felt … disgusted."

Jeselle started crying. She had held it back, thought maybe she was in that numb place again, but after his confession the tears started flowing.

"I yelled at him and said that he hadn't even apologized to you, really apologized. Then I left and went to your house."

She remembered him crying for days at her house. Jeselle walked slowly to Dennis and wrapped her arms around him, maybe it was about him too, after all.

He was losing his family as well.

Only in a different way.

CHAPTER 39

PAST

"It's no fair. If we do good, we'll be bad, and we'll have to be bad if we want to be good."
—Bubbles, Powerpuff Girls

"You better suck up whatever problem you've got and get busy living." Isabel threw a large box onto the floor in the foyer, "You better get back to school, smile at your enemies, and let your anger push you to do better. Graduate. Then go to college, and let nothing stand in your way."

Jeselle reached for the box, but Isabel stopped her, "No, you go, get your clothes ready to go back tomorrow. I can move our stuff in by myself. You go take care of your stuff. You lucky Dennis convinced his daddy to get you both that tutor so you wouldn't fall behind this month, but it's time, girl."

"I'm not ready."

"I'm not asking."

"Ms. Isabel, stop. I really am not ready," Jeselle started to cry and Isabel kept working, unloading box after box off the back of Jeselle's dad's tailgate that was parked up against the front porch.

"I don't know how many times I need to tell you, stop calling me Ms., it's Isabel. And nobody is ever ready. You simply do it. Now, look at me," Isabel stopped just inside the front door, "Life don't stop when tragedy hits. You got a lot of good in you, Jeselle, don't you let the bad win. You hear me?"

"Yes, ma'am," Jeselle replied.

"Good, go up in that room of yours and get to preparing."

That night she sat with Isabel's daughters watching a Powerpuff Girls marathon, not knowing how she would go back and face everyone at school the next day. An episode that seemed eerie in the way it reminded Jeselle of her own life in ways. King Morbucks had bought Townsville from the Mayor for his spoiled daughter, Princess. As Jeselle watched, something hit her. The only way to truly win is by playing by their rules, their laws. Use what they've created against them to right the wrongs.

Jeselle and Dennis returned to Eastdale High School to finish out the last three months of their junior year. It wasn't as hard to smile at her enemies as she thought it would be. She'd done it before, somehow, after that Powerpuff Girls episode, it became more fluid.

A plan started coming together.

Same dynamics continued, except with Dennis. Jeselle could see he had changed. He saw the hypocrisy and greed all around him. They never discussed it, but she could see it on his face when he noticed something new. The friends, 'frenemies' as Dennis started calling them when it was only he and Jeselle, continued on their selective paths.

Camilla made sure to let everyone know that while her brother was dating Jeselle, she was still only a maid's daughter with thirty-dollar pants. She pointed out often that the only valuable pieces of jewelry that Jeselle had were the ones her twin brother had given to her. Jeselle loved the necklace and promise ring, but knew her mom and dad's wedding rings were worth a hundred times more in sentimental value than the jewelry that Dennis gave her. The jewelry Dennis gave her was to bring her up to his standard, her mom and dad's rings represented theirs; a life of love, commitment, even pain and loss.

Tracy was still Tracy. Cindy continued to show up at school with bruises clearly displayed while she doted and hung all over Tracy. Most rewarding was when Tracy initiated his slow, evil sneer at her after her return, she grinned back just as slowly, and it unnerved him. Jeselle thought there had never been a better feeling than the one she felt after Tracy's face went blank. She kept smiling and found that there was a better feeling...the one she felt when fear flushed across his smug face.

STOP ME

Melanie continued to be Melanie, only she amped it up a notch or two. Seemed the higher the class level, the more she got off on the power. Unfortunately, Jeselle had four of the seven classes with her and the frenemies, so she got to experience them all firsthand.

One random morning Melanie, in the middle of class, said loudly, "Everyone remembers their first time, it's special,"

Jeselle responded immediately, "Yes, we do." Smiling, Jeselle looked slowly at each of the frenemies. Once she landed on Tracy, she smiled even wider. That must have shaken Melanie up a bit, because after that, when she spoke out in class it was, "Kids do stupid things when they are young," or "Don't be a baby, can't live in the past forever." To which Jeselle would always agree wholeheartedly.

William, still the follower, had a steady girlfriend who was best friends with Camilla. She didn't live in Wellgrove Estates, but she did live in the new neighborhood that the Briggses had started next to it named, Hedgefield Court Estates. Same neighborhood, different name. It was rumored, that venture required the Briggses to mortgage everything in order to fund it. Jeselle found that interesting. Also, interesting was that the back half of the planned, wealthy-living neighborhood had gotten an injunction that prohibited building on it from the LA Department of Natural Resources, because it was deemed protected wetlands.

Todd was back at Eastdale, he had insisted and

his parents finally relented, he claimed. But it was also rumored that his parents' law practice was suffering a bit financially and public Eastdale was about fifty thousand a year less than the private school with the same test scores.

Jeselle went to Dennis's for dinner and family functions and it was as if that day, the one where she took charge over her life in their formal living room, hadn't happened. They all went on with life as usual…and business as usual.

One night, at the end of the school year, on her back patio when they were saying goodbye, Jeselle leaned forward and kissed Dennis on the cheek. It had been the first time she'd initiated a kiss since the incident, and it was evident it meant something to him.

Over the summer, Dennis worked at Stryker, and Jeselle thought about taking on an additional major. She already had the scholarship for Mass Communication, but she also wanted to major in Business. Dennis always seemed so busy, working late hours a lot. Even on the weekends, his dad always had something he needed Dennis to attend to. When they finally did get to spend time together, he seemed more business-minded and less aware of the things he'd started noticing about wealth and power. He did still talk about changing the world and using his money one day to help others, so Jeselle wasn't really worried. Still, she thought of that extra major, and wanted it more than ever. Toward the end of summer, while she prepared for her senior year, she asked Isabel if she could use some of the insurance money to fund the business major.

"Honey, that is your money," Isabel said, "All you got to do is tell me how much you need."

"Well, how much is left?" Jeselle asked.

"All of it," Isabel said.

"How can that be? What about all the bills?" Jeselle was surprised.

"I pay them. I still have a job, Jeselle. Hey, we are thankful to be here, but what, you think I'd come live off you? I don't need your money."

"No! Ms. Isabel, I thought I'd be paying the house bills. Do not pay those yourself, use the insurance money."

"No need, honey. You missing anything? Need better food? Better clothes? The way I see it, I'm paying about what I was in that one bedroom apartment, 'cause here I don't have rent, and I am closer to work."

"But you could be saving," Jeselle pointed out.

"Who says I'm not? When you live with little, you learn how to make it stretch. I'm not a millionaire like all our neighbors, but if I get a flat tire, I can replace it. Don't you worry about us. You hear me?"

"Yes, ma'am."

Dennis wasn't happy about the idea of her having double majors.

"When will I get to see you? I mean, Jess, I work all week, barely off on the weekend."

"And...I'm supposed to come at your beck and call? Did I miss something here?"

"No, but I will be supporting us one day. My job is important."

"Who says I won't be supporting us one day, Dennis? What is going on with you?"

He laughed, "Jess, you know I'll be making the most money, come on, don't get irrational. I'll be in charge of one of the largest corporations in the South," Dennis said with confidence.

"Are you seriously saying I'll need to change my life to fit around yours?" she exhaled.

"No...maybe, I don't know. When Dad says it, it makes sense," he said honestly.

"If you are listening to anything your dad says at this point, I am worried for you."

"He's a smart businessman Jess, of course I listen....you're right though, that does sound a little self-centered. I don't know. When are we going to see each other?"

"We'll work it out. We'll find a way," she grabbed one of his hands and he kissed her forehead. It was always something he did when he was proud of her, when she'd yielded or let him take the lead.

The next day, Jeselle enrolled in the extra classes.

CHAPTER 40

PAST

"When you close your eyes to tragedy, you
close your eyes to greatness."
-Stephen Vizinczey

Senior year started as a near replay of the end of junior year, with the exception that Jeselle took all AP classes, and none of the other frenemies did. She felt relieved of not having to be around them as much.

It was also a relief that Dennis worked at Stryker after school. She was able to get much of her school work completed early and knew if they were hanging out the way they always had before, she wouldn't have.

She was finishing up an English essay when the sound of a car in the driveway caused her to stop.

Isabel and the girls left to go get their school supply lists, so she assumed they had forgotten something and returned.

Dennis appeared around the back of the house, running, frantic, "Did you see? Katrina?"

"Yes, Dennis," she laughed, "I saw the branch that fell in the neighbor's yard across the street.

"No, New Orleans!" he ran through her back door and she followed. He grabbed the remote, and turned the TV on. The news flashed with flooded streets and people on rooftops.

"Oh my God," Jeselle sat down on the sofa and watched,

"I know," Dennis sat next to her watching the screen, "Do you know what this means, Jess?" he whispered.

She was speechless.

"It means you won't have to go to Tulane," he said softly.

"Tulane?" she jumped away from him on the couch. "Tulane? Are you kidding me? Look at the TV, Dennis. Look, people are dying, losing everything. Everything they own…dyyyying. Oh my God, New Orleans is flooded and all you can think about is I won't have to go away to Tulane?"

She heard the back door open and Isabel crying, "My sister, I have to get my sister,"

"Ms. Isabel? Your sister lives in New Orleans?" Dennis asked and then looked at Jeselle. The reality of it hit him. "I'll call Dad, he'll help." Dennis pulled his cell phone out and went out the front door.

"What am I gonna do? I don't know how, I was getting gas and I heard, oh Jessie, how did this happen?"

Dennis rushed back in, "What's her full name and her address, Dad's going to get some guys and the company helicopters to go down there and get her,"

"Thank you, Jesus!" Isabel cried. "it's her and my nephews."

Jeselle heard the voices trail off as they walked to the kitchen. She couldn't move. She sat watching the news, watching all the devastation. The girls came and sat beside her.

"What's happening, Jessie?" Patricia, the eldest asked.

"Yeah, Momma was crying. What's goin' on?" Tina, the next oldest asked.

"I think I'll let your momma tell you that, okay? Why don't you guys go up to your room, take Mikelyn with you. I'll make some blueberry muffins, okay?"

"Yay!" The girls raced each other upstairs and Jeselle went into the kitchen. Isabel seemed calmer. "Thank you, Dennis. I don't know. How are they going to find her?"

"Father has the best investigators working for him, they'll find them." He looked up at Jeselle and she mouthed the words, "Thank you."

He nodded, "I'll keep you updated. The cell phones aren't working, so I'll call the house phone, okay?" he looked to Jeselle.

When he left, Isabel took one of the seats at the island.

"I'm making blueberry muffins for the girls, comfort food. They are asking questions."

"I hope they find her," Isabel covered her face with her hands, "I don't know what she's going to do. Her house, from what the news is saying, flooded."

"Well, they'll stay here for now. Let's worry about the rest later."

"Here? Jessie, you sure?"

"We have five bedrooms here. The girls can share a room for now. That'll give your sister her own room and the boys can share the other. It'll work," Jeselle assured her.

Isabel broke down again, "Thank you, Jessie. Thank you. I'll help them find a place as quick as I can."

"Why do you feel rushed, Ms. Isabel? This is your house too. You have been so good to me. You were so good to my mom." They hugged and cried together, until Mikelyn came down the stairs asking to "go potty." They laughed briefly.

Jeselle started the blueberry muffins. She was so angry at Dennis about the Tulane comment. Worried and disgusted that his first response was so selfish when so many people's lives were being devastated. He redeemed himself to some extent when he convinced his dad to help, because Jeselle knew, Mr. Stryker helped no one but himself, unless forced.

STOP ME

She also knew life didn't stop when tragedy struck.

* * *

It hadn't taken long after Isabel's sister, Truth, and her two sons moved in, that the homeowner's association of Wellgrove filed a suit against Jeselle and Isabel as her representative, for having too many families living under one roof, a grievance clearly stipulated in the HOA's Covenants, Conditions, and Restrictions and By-Laws. Jeselle and Isabel attended the following meeting. The board consisted of, of course, none other than Mr. Stryker, Mr. Briggs, Mr. Parrish, and Mrs. Wheaton, the latter two of whom were controlled by the former two.

Jeselle stood to state their case, "Truth Davis and her two sons are seeking temporary housing with us following losing their home in New Orleans, during the flood." Jeselle spoke into the microphone.

"Yes," Mr. Briggs was the first to respond, "we understand that, and did not file anything until past the thirty days, Ms. Parsons. The restrictions clearly state," he cleared his throat and looked down at a booklet in his hand, "no one can house another family on their estate past thirty days without the written approval of the HOA."

"Then, I am filing for approval," Jeselle said.

"Denied," Mr. Briggs responded, Mr. Stryker remained quiet.

"What else can I do?" Jeselle asked.

"I already said denied," Brantley Briggs said, "That'll teach you not to follow the rules around here."

His meaning was well understood. She looked from Mr. Briggs to Mr. Stryker and noticed he had a small, almost unnoticeable smirk.

Powerpuff Girls flashed in her mind.

"Then follow your rules, I must," When she stood, Jeselle bowed down as a person would to a king. The look on her face would've scared all of them, had they even been smart enough to understand what they'd decreed.

That next weekend, Isabel and the girls followed in her car behind Jeselle who was in her father's truck to help Truth and her boys move into an apartment across town. Isabel had gone earlier that morning and stocked the kitchen.

"I know it's not much, but I want you to use it as long as you need it," Jeselle passed the truck keys to Ms. Truth and they both cried.

"I expect the insurance to pay pretty soon. I know what this means to you, Jessie. Thank you," Truth said.

"I'm sorry."

"Don't be sorry for what those others did, Cher, you are not them. We'll come for dinner on Saturdays, right?" Truth asked.

"Yes," Jeselle said.

They all hugged and Jeselle left her dad's truck behind when she climbed into Isabel's car. She knew it was the right thing to do.

Nothing really changed much with the kids at Eastdale, many of them didn't talk about the flooding at all, except to say how sad it was going to be not having a Mardi Gras. Several new kids showed up, because their parents had relocated, but they all fit in as if they'd always been there. Isabel helped Jeselle find an affordable older car, and it was obvious that none of the kids at Eastdale approved.

Senior year went on as usual, because outside problems didn't affect the areas of Baton Rouge that nestled around Wellgrove and Hedgefield Court. Same Halloween celebration at the park. Same extravagant Christmas parties.

The frenemies had the same fallouts between them and other people. Cindy still wore bruises, along with her faked arrogance. Camilla still ousted a friend or two and replaced them with the next Camilla follower. Melanie, of course, still had her new set of followers as well.

At the library, located next to Eastdale High, Jeselle was thumbing through books on the shelf, searching for her homework assignment, when she heard conversation. Loud for a library. She saw a couple of people through the bookshelf on the other side.

"Her mom was a maid. Seriously, you are giving her way too much credit. Her dad did some stupid, like, new way to produce steel that would've been worth nothing had my dad not hired him. His company was about to go bankrupt. Dad did him a favor."

Camilla.

"Doesn't she live in your neighborhood?" one girl scoffed.

"Yeah, but my dad owns the house. He's done nothing but try to help her. Get this," Camilla paused and lowered her voice, although not low enough to be a whisper, "she has another one of Dad's maid's living there with her, okay? I mean, he doesn't want her living in squalor because her parents died, right?"

"Yeeaah," another girl said overdramatically.

"So weird, though. If your dad owns the house...?" another girl asked.

"He's not going to kick her out on the street," Camilla defended.

"But I mean playing devil's advocate, I heard y'all used to be friends," another said.

"No," Camilla answered quickly and loudly, "not friends. You didn't live here then, so you don't know what you are talking about. She seemed cool at first, only she wasn't. She's not like us. Dad says she's always judging us. Us! Like who is she to judge us?"

"But she's dating Dennis."

"He takes pity on her for something that happened years ago." Camilla drew in a deep breath, "Dad says it won't last past high school. I mean, really, how could it?"

Jeselle walked around the bookcase and stood in the opening. When one of the girls saw her, she hit

Camilla on the shoulder and Camilla turned to see Jeselle.

Full of true arrogance, Camilla walked toward Jeselle, the other girls followed. Right as she was passing Jeselle, Camilla said, "Well, it's true."

It didn't bother Jeselle at all, that was exactly what she'd learned to expect from Camilla. Saddest part was that Camilla really believed all the things she said. It also crossed her mind that Dennis heard all the same stuff his dad said too, but at least he had seen the truth.

William, Todd, and Tracy were the three musketeers. It was weird to think that Dennis had ever been one of them. Especially, with him working long hours after school and on weekends at Stryker, Dennis grew more and more "over" being a kid in high school. Jeselle and Dennis still spent time together, but the times were few and far between.

At graduation, Dennis and Jeselle stood for formal pictures together, done by an exclusive photographer, paid for by the Strykers. Then Camilla and Dennis stood together for theirs. It was always obvious that they tolerated Jeselle more than accepted her, but that was okay with Jeselle.

She did the same.

His mom had been pretty much an empty shell since she found out about the trust being stolen, and she was the only one Jeselle felt there was any hope for, other than Dennis.

Tulane University initiated a new plan to get the university up and running for the spring semester, so

Jeselle was able to start that fall on schedule. Dennis wasn't happy about that, even though he worked so much she barely saw him. It was Isabel and the girls who helped her move onto campus. They went shopping for her dorm room decor, clothes, and supplies. She thought of her mom and dad and how proud they would be of her. Jeselle was thankful to have Isabel. Isabel was her family.

The first weekend home, Jeselle waited on the back patio for Dennis. He'd made her come even though she felt it was best she stayed that first weekend and got to know her roommate better. He'd insisted, said that was how it started, her not coming home one weekend, then it turned into another. After dinner and a movie with the girls, Jeselle decided to go to bed. Her room felt comfortable. She'd laid in bed and wondered if what Camilla had said was true and that Dennis was over her now that they were out of high school. She cried herself to sleep.

In the middle of the night her cell phone rang out. She jumped up and answered it, "Hello?" she whispered.

"Jess, so sorry. Got caught up. So sorry. Coming now."

"Now?" Jeselle pulled the phone away from her face, looked at the time, then returned it, "It's three twenty-two, Dennis."

"I know, I'm sorry. I have meetings tomorrow, and I want to see you."

"You have meetings? I thought you said you'd have the whole weekend open," she said.

"I thought so too, but Dad needs me. We have been working on this big deal for a while, and I need to be there," he was excited, "This is big for me, Jess."

"Okay fine, but not now, I don't want to wake up everybody, and I'm a little mad. What time tomorrow?"

"I really want to see you...okay. Five, promise."

She went shopping the next day and picked up a new sundress to wear for dinner, one that showed off the rope chain. She hung out around the house the rest of the day and helped Isabel cook a big dinner with all the trimmings for Dennis. Starting at five fifteen, Jeselle called Dennis several times, but they all went straight to voicemail each time. They all waited to eat until six, then finally gave up and ate.

Ten o'clock her cell phone rang. She knew who it was and ignored it. When it rang again, she turned it off, went up to her room, packed her bags, kissed the four of them goodbye and drove back to Tulane. Sunday, she was hoping to at least get some time with her roommate.

CHAPTER 41

PAST

"Little rabbits have big ears."
-Virginia C. Andrews

"This is so fun!" Jeselle yelled over the crowd.

"It is, I didn't expect it to be this crowded," Lakshmi jumped up and down.

"How did Neal even hear about this?" Jeselle continued to move up the line.

"His mom lives here. He said Slidell is pretty boring most of the time, except twice a year when they have the street fair. I think it's awesome!" Lakshmi finally made it to the ticket booth and slapped her money on the counter.

"I just want to ride the Ferris wheel all day," Jeselle said. Her phone rang, and she saw it was

Dennis. He had left three messages before she finally talked to him after her last weekend home. She understood, and told him so, but the expectation of her sitting around all weekend waiting for him was a ridiculous waste of time. He tried to guilt her into visiting with Isabel, but Isabel told her to stay and have fun with her friends; that was part of the experience of college. So she decided to stay in New Orleans that weekend.

"Hey!" she said into the phone.

"Are you coming hom-? What is all that noise?" Dennis asked.

"I'm at a fair," she answered.

"In New Orleans? Do you understand how dangerous it is there right now? Dad said it is worse than ever," Dennis was talking so loudly that he drowned out the crowd around her.

"I'm not in New Orleans," she said.

"Where are you, then?"

"A huge fall fair in Slidell," she giggled, "I haven't been to a fair in years. It's like an all weekend thing. Lakshmi and I are staying the whole weekend," she explained.

"Who?"

"Dennis, my roommate, Lakshmi. Remember?"

"Well, maybe I can come up there tomorrow, spend the day with you and meet her," he said.

"Yeah, right," she tried to talk louder than the crowd, "Okay, let's see if that happens. Come."

"Okay, what hotel?"

"No hotel, my friend's parents' house,"

"Your roommate's parents?"

"No, another friend, Neal. Neal Stewart. I'll text you the address," she didn't hear a response so she hung up. "Hey, what's the address at Neal's house?" she asked Lakshmi.

"Hold on, let me look." Lakshmi took out her Blackberry, and pulled up her messages, "2131 Betty Road."

Jeselle started clicking buttons on the Nokia and Lakshmi laughed. "You need to get a Blackberry, so much easier."

"Well, I didn't buy this one, Dennis did. He's coming tomorrow, by the way, so you can meet him."

"It'll be so much fun!" Lakshmi squealed. "Neal's coming tomorrow, too!"

Jeselle did spend nearly all day riding the Ferris wheel. When she was at the top, she'd look around for Lakshmi. Sometimes she spotted her right away, and it made Jeselle giggle. She felt free. Happy and free.

The next morning, bright and early, Dennis showed up at Neal's parents'. Jeselle laughed when she saw him in a suit and tie walking up the driveway. She walked out to meet him and resigned herself to the fact that he was probably going to be going to work later and wouldn't stay long.

"Hey, let me guess, not staying long?" they hugged.

"I am," he said, "All day."

"You came here, to go to a street fair, all day...in

a suit?" she asked.

He smiled, "Yeah had a meeting before I came. I packed the Diesels."

"Do you have to say the brand? Can't you be normal and simply say jeans?" she rolled her eyes.

"What fun would that be?" he laughed.

When they walked into the kitchen, Neal's mom was pouring a cup of coffee.

"Mrs. Stewart, this is Dennis, the boy I was telling you about," Jeselle said.

"Boy?" she asked in a heavy Cajun accent as she pointed toward him with her thumb, "Don't look like no boy to me."

"Trust me, he only looks mature," Jeselle joked.

Dennis went to shake her hand, "Good to meet you, Mrs. Stewart."

"No need to be so formal," she hugged him and left the kitchen.

"I only look mature, huh?"

"Yeah," she said with a slight smile.

By the time he had changed, Lakshmi was awake and dressed, and they were off to the fair. Dennis had insisted he drive, and Jeselle felt it was more of the name brand matter that he was preoccupied with. It bothered her for him, because she knew how much he detested when Camilla did that.

The three of them rode the Ferris wheel four times in a row and intentionally placed Dennis in the middle, which Dennis hated at first. Halfway through the day he finally started to relax and enjoy himself.

They walked down the alley of booth games. Sounds and excitement filled the air. Kids were laughing, one was crying because he didn't win. Dennis walked up to the boy and handed him a bunch of tickets and it made the boy smile. Lakshmi stopped to play at a booth where yellow duckies were floating in a large vat of water. She paid and picked up one with numbers on the bottom, then another and squealed as she tried to decide which stuffed animal she wanted for her prize. Dennis laughed, really laughed, and Jeselle looked at him. He was so beautiful when he laughed, when he was being Dennis. Lakshmi started to reach for the fluffy dog when Neal crept up behind her, his finger over his mouth so Jeselle wouldn't ruin the surprise, and took the stuffed toy from the attendant.

Lakshmi turned around like she was going to punch someone, "Neal!" she screamed. "Yay!"

Dennis immediately grew serious, slipped his hand into Jeselle's. They were introduced, but Dennis made it seem more like a business transaction, than friendship. He made sure to emphasize his last name, but it was obvious it meant nothing to Neal.

They all continued on, playing one game after another, except Dennis.

"So, uhhh, Roommate," Dennis leaned forward as they walked so he could see her, "Are you in one of Jess's majors also?"

"It's Lakshmi," Jeselle corrected. "pronounced kind of like, 'lock-sh-me."

"So…Lak..shmi?" he tested the waters.

"Yes?" she answered with amusement, "I know it's hard. It's okay."

"You in Mass Comm or Business?" Dennis asked again.

"Oh gosh, neither. I'm in for Security Studies."

"Oh, let me know when you graduate, we are always looking for good people."

Something about the statement bothered Jeselle. Dennis was being nice, but for some reason Jeselle felt it was more condescending than helpful. She quickly shook off the thoughts.

They walked for a bit more before Dennis asked, "Lockshoni, what country are you from?"

"Dennis!" Jeselle was embarrassed.

Her roommate leaned forward to look at Dennis who stood on the other side of Jeselle, "America. Born and raised."

Dennis didn't skip a beat; he wasn't embarrassed at all. "I thought with the name."

"Whoa," Neal said in disbelief.

"Yeah," the roommate replied with a touch of discomfort.

They came to a booth that was larger than the others. The prizes were, too. The back wall of the game booth was covered in oversized, overstuffed toy animals.

"Oh bunnny!" Jeselle said. "Stop, stop, guys, I'm going to win the bunny. Here," she shoved her cotton candy to Lakshmi.

"Here, let me," Dennis said, stepping in front of her.

"Oh, no, no, I wanna do it," Jeselle said stepping around him.

She gave the tickets to the carnival worker, picked up the gun, and aimed at her target. Water squirted on just about everything, but the target. Lakshmi and Neal laughed.

"Poop," Jeselle said, "Again, again," she handed over more tickets. She aimed and again water squirted everywhere, except the target.

Lakshmi and Neal laughed louder and started making jokes about Jeselle's lack of killer instinct. Jeselle laughed with them then handed over more tickets.

"I am not leaving here without that bunny," she told the worker.

"I don't know … it's been up there for a while. Don't think you can do it," the worker prodded with a smile.

Jeselle tried again, this time hitting the target some of the time, only not enough for the bunny.

"I want the bunny," she play-acted as she pouted like a little girl.

"Here, take my tickets," Lakshmi offered, "You must have that bunny."

Dennis went around the booth, through the opening and grabbed the bunny off the wall.

"Yo, dude?" the worker said.

"Two hundred cover it?" Dennis threw two one hundred dollar bills onto the counter as he exited the back.

"Whatever, dude," the worker said.

"Not cool," Neal whispered.

Jeselle stood, mouth open, watching as Dennis did what he always did, whatever he wanted.

"Here, you deserve it," Dennis held the bunny out to her.

"Dennis," she pleaded quietly; it was obviously mixed with pity.

"I would buy you the moon," he smiled. He had no idea what he'd done. She looked at Lakshmi and Neal, both as aware as she was, their faces full of pity for her also.

She regained her composure, "Dennis, the whole point is in the fun. Well, and me doing it for myself."

"Is it fun to not win, Jess? I'm pretty sure it's not," he laughed.

No one else did.

She slowly took the bunny, looked at the worker, "Thank you."

After that, the day was ruined. The worst part was that Dennis hadn't even noticed. He could have whatever he wanted, and he bought it without regard. She felt the weight of it on her like a lead balloon. For the first time, she honestly believed he wanted her mainly because he couldn't have her.

What would he do if he ever really did?

CHAPTER 42

PRESENT

"We make a living by what we get, but we make a life by what we give."
-Winston Churchill

Jeselle looked into her own eyes as the elevator made the descent to the fifth floor. She often walked around the main building to take a look around, especially before heading to the *Haevn.E Foundation* for her monthly volunteer day.

The plants scattered around through the office building in large pots appeared healthier than usual. Jeselle stopped in front of one for a closer inspection. Isabel ran housekeeping so well that Jeselle never had to worry over anything. She suddenly felt selfish that she'd never thought Isabel to be lonely, until she noticed the spark between her and Jed.

How had she never noticed it before? Maybe it wasn't there before. Still, Isabel seemed happier than Jeselle had ever seen her.

Maybe they hid their connection. Jeselle was well aware of how hard that could be, but in a way she felt betrayed about not knowing. She surely didn't deserve to know all of Isabel's secrets, nonetheless, she did feel like they were close enough to share those kinds of things.

Jeselle shook her head as she also shook off the thoughts. Isabel had been like a mother to her, then a friend. A confidant. Still, she felt she needed to ask and she knew Isabel would understand why.

She continued through the fifth floor reception area and took the next set of elevators down. The moment she stepped out onto the first floor, she knew exactly where she would find Isabel. She walked to the back of the main floor to where the housekeeping offices were located. She'd originally wanted them located on the fifth floor or higher, for importance sake, but Isabel had insisted when they were mapping the office space on the blueprints that housekeeping should always be located on the main floor. One, for deliveries, since they would regularly be getting large amounts of supplies. Two, the main floor consistently received most of the activity in a building and needed the most upkeep.

She opened the main door and proceeded through to the housekeeping reception area.

"Good morning, Eunice," she said to the younger girl behind the desk.

"Good morning, Ms. Parsons. Isabel is in her office," Eunice responded.

"Thank you," Jeselle probably sounded sarcastic most of the time since she made it a point to be overly thankful to all of the housekeeping staff. She walked down the ample hallway until she reached the double doors at the end. She smiled, remembering Isabel's disgust when she'd first seen the expensive solid mahogany doors covered from top to bottom with mirrors. They not only reflected a person's image, but also replicated Jeselle's exact walkway and doors that led to her own office on the top floor. Years before, when the office building was completed and Isabel saw it, she nearly went into a fit.

"What the he-" Isabel had exclaimed.

"It's your office," Jeselle said, the smile playing along the corners of her mouth. "You deserve it."

"Girl, if there is one thing I been trying to get through your thick skull since you were sixteen, is we don't deserve anything we haven't worked for." Isabel turned to look at Jeselle, "Not one thing."

"And you have worked for it," Jeselle said as she opened one of the doors for Isabel.

"I haven't worked for this door..." Isabel pointed at her, "you worked for this door."

"So, I can give it to whomever I want," Jeselle smiled cleverly.

Isabel didn't take a step forward; she bent at the waist and looked into the office. A large space packed with expensive furniture filled her sight. In her own judgment it appeared to be about as big as Jeselle's office.

"Nuh, uh, Jessie, This is not my office."

"It is."

"It isn't. I can't work from here. This is ridiculous for a ma-"

"A *maid*," Jeselle finished. She grew slightly agitated, and it showed in her change of tone, "A maid? That's how you see yourself after all these years? I would gladly support you, but you won't allow it. All these years you've been a mother, a friend. Try not to spoil the only repayment I can give you."

Isabel grabbed Jeselle by both of her arms, stood on her tip toes, and looked Jeselle directly in the eyes, "That's what you aren't getting, child. In all these years, all I ever asked of you was love and respect. Not money."

"Well, this is respect. It's proving to the world that you are owed as much respect as I am. If it weren't for you, I wouldn't be here," Jeselle said, small tears forming in her eyes.

"Don't you dare give me credit for what you are doing here. This was born out of revenge, not love. Gladly you seem to be doing some good with it, but you still got that vengeance in you, and I want no part of that. When you get done, then we'll talk."

"Okay," Jeselle said, "but take the office please, for me. It's something I have to do." Isabel nodded in agreement right before Jeselle turned and left back down the hallway.

Isabel had worked out of that office ever since.

Jeselle walked closer to the doors and looked at herself in the reflection. She couldn't lose focus. She felt as if she had recently. She was having trouble processing her compassion for Camilla. Said more accurately, she was having trouble processing the revenge toward Camilla, because unexpectedly she had transformed into a great employee. A solid worker with a really good head for business. Jeselle put a hand up to her own face and smoothed it across one cheek where a tear had fallen.

She was definitely losing the edge.

Suddenly the door opened, and Isabel's image quickly replaced Jeselle's.

"You going to stand there all day or come in? Eunice told me you were headed to me five minutes ago."

"Thinking."

"Then I don't want to know," Isabel laughed and turned to go back to her desk.

Jeselle wasted no time the moment she shut them inside, "What is going on with you and Jed?"

"Jessie, I promise you I will let you know the minute I know."

"Well, something is. He's changing, obviously because of you, or for you, and I am uncomfortable not knowing."

"As am I. But life doesn't spell out all of its mysteries like that. Life's a journey and most times we don't get to see all the answers at the beginning of it." Isabel took her seat at her desk and Jeselle sat in front of her, leaning back into the chair like a child would. Isabel sighed, "I know why you are here. It is less to do with Jed and more to do with you feeling out of sorts altogether. It's okay to walk away from it, Jessie. You don't have to do it."

"I do, though."

"Then?"

"Then why do I feel this way about Camilla all of a sudden?"

"Because she isn't who you thought she was. Maybe because underneath all that pomp and circumstance, she's what you always talk about. You know that 'there are only two types of arrogant people' talk you are so wise to know about. Be wise. Possibly because under all of that privilege-taught ego, she's good."

"Maybe," Jeselle thought. "Shouldn't change anything."

"Sure, it should," Isabel stood, "Look at how what happened to you changed things. You are exactly what change makes. Only thing is Jessie, you can use that change for good or bad. Your choice."

Jeselle stood, straightened her jacket, "I am not bad," she said with indignation.

"Didn't say you were."

"I am simply playing by their rules. *They,*" she stressed, "They determine the outcome." Jeselle turned toward the door and started walking.

"If that were true, dear, then Camilla should be safe, and you should have no conflict about it."

Jeselle made it to the main lobby at the front of

the building before realizing she knew no more than she did when she started the trek to Isabel's office. Soon she found herself rounding the corner with a steaming cup of coffee. She only had one, for Jed, because they were hotter than usual and she had to switch hands to keep it from becoming too hot to hold. For that reason she'd quickly tossed hers into the garbage along the way. She needed to see him, for whatever reason, selfish or not.

As she drew nearer, she saw Jed sitting against the wall of the church across the street. A young lady was sitting next to him. Jeselle moved along the sidewalk of her office building and slowed her pace as she watched. The young girl opened a brown paper bag and pulled out a sandwich and offered half of it to him. Jed easily took it and smiled.

The brown paper bag brought back memories of simpler times. Of peanut butter and jelly, blueberry muffins, and notes from her mom. Jeselle watched as Jed and the young girl laughed. She sighed deeply, took a sip of the coffee and turned around to go back inside the building again.

Upon reaching the front doors, Jeselle decided to pass up the entrance and continue through to the covered breezeway between her two buildings that housed a line of patio tables. She spotted Rose reading and eating lunch.

Out of a brown paper bag, no less.

As she got closer, she could see Rose was reading a Bible. Jeselle always thought how odd Bibles were in the fact that they always looked distinctive;

recognizable. Immediately, thoughts hit her about her mom leaving notes in the morning before school. She thought back to finding her mom's devotional after she passed away. Jeselle had been sleeping in her mom's bed, to smell her scent on the pillow, because it was almost gone from the house.

She turned to smell the pillow and saw the devotional laying on the side table on top of a Bible and a notepad.

Jeselle took all three of them to her room. When she left for college, she left them behind, stacked neatly on her night table. When she moved into her own big house in the back of Wellgrove, she put them on her stand by her new bed.

Never once had she opened either of them.

Rose looked up, "Hey," she said with a mouthful of food. She quickly put her sandwich down and stood, "Did you need me?"

"No," Jeselle replied.

Rose smiled while she resumed chewing, "Okay. Want to sit?"

"Sure," Jeselle wasn't really certain why she said yes, or why she actually sat, it seemed like the right answer.

"Why are you reading that?"

"My Bible?"

"Yes."

"Are you being condescending, or do you really want an answer?" Rose asked.

"Answer."

"Well, I get encouraged with it, mostly. It's

interesting, especially Proverbs," Rose flipped a few pages, "I mainly stick to the New Testament though, which I don't think I'm supposed to do, but I do. Except Proverbs."

"Okay."

"Well, no, I take that back I do like some of the stories in the Old Testament. You know, like the baby cut in half."

"The what?" Jeselle was horrified.

"I … thought … I mean, Ms. Isabel said your mom was … you know, a Christian. Didn't she read to you?"

"No, not really. I mean, yes, some, but not the Bible." Jeselle fully realized what Rose had said, "Wait, why would Isabel tell you my mother was a Christian?"

"Because I asked if you'd fire me if I brought a Bible to work."

"Oh."

"Did she ever talk about God?"

"My mother? Yes," Jeselle became defensive which was a fairly odd emotion, one that had been missing mostly throughout the years. "I mean she would leave me little notes, scriptures. I know about God, but my mother wasn't a Bible thumper. Neither is Isabel."

"That's good."

"Agreed."

"Bible thumpers have a place though."

"I think extremes are needed in anything," Jeselle affirmed Rose's comment. "My mother was sweet, a lead-by-example kind of person, but she loved God. So does Isabel, " Jeselle relaxed a bit.

"All we can really do is live better ourselves, I think. I know we're supposed to go out into the world and preach or something, but I don't think that's right for everybody. I think we live and be decent people and other people want to know why maybe. I mean, I'm probably wrong because I'm a nobody. No one asks me why," Rose laughed.

"I asked why."

Rose's smile spread, she sat up taller, "You did, didn't you?"

"Yes. Now tell me about the baby."

In what little was left of lunch, Rose told Jeselle the story about King Solomon.

Long after Rose left, an idea started to form.

CHAPTER 43

PAST

"Life consists not in holding good cards,
but in playing those you hold well."
—Josh Billings

Weeks turned into months, and Jeselle hadn't been able to make it home much. She spent Christmas Eve and Christmas Day at home mostly with Isabel and the girls. Dennis's parents had their big Christmas party, but it had been the weekend before and she wasn't able to make it, although, she wasn't upset over it. Dennis couldn't make it to her house for Christmas Eve, he had a big deal he was closing. She made sure to go to the Stryker's for a few hours on Christmas Day and as always, it was a formal affair centered on gifts. Opposite of her time at home that she spent with Isabel, her sister Truth, and all the kids enjoying one another; cooking together and laughing. Dennis never made it to her house for Christmas dinner either, work of course.

Carrying the workload of a double major was harder than she'd expected. Isabel and the girls visited her at Tulane a couple of times. While the visits seemed short and sweet, they were breaks that Jeselle had needed.

Dennis had called several times, and they texted a little. But he was busy also, and their schedules never meshed well. After the fall fair, she'd felt differently about their relationship anyway. She couldn't pinpoint what that difference was, but it was there.

"Jess, hey, can you text me instead, I'm right in the middle of something," Dennis answered, in a rush as usual.

"No, text is too hard and takes forever," she replied, "I wanted to tell you that I can make it to the block party for Memorial Day."

"That's great news! But isn't school over, why not come today?" he asked.

"There's a speech I've been waiting months for. I can't miss it. It's Maso—"

"That's great, Jess. Look I'm sorry, I really have to go. Want me to pick you up at your house for the picnic?" Dennis offered.

"We'll meet you there."

"We?"

"Yeah, Isabel and the girls. I'm coming in that Friday to visit with them since I haven't been home in a while. You know?"

"I know. Just as Dad predicted," he said in a lower tone.

"What?" Although Jeselle knew she'd heard him properly.

"Nothing. Look Jess, I have to go. Meeting is starting. See you then." He ended the call.

Jeselle went about her day. She made it to the lecture hall early. One of her professors was already setting up a display at the front of the auditorium.

"Good morning, Professor Lobrano," Jeselle waved.

"Good to see you here, Ms. Parsons. My star student," he smiled.

She unpacked her notebook and pen, pulled down the desk on the back of the seat in front of her, and waited. She looked up as an older man, with grey hair and a grey suit, the same exact color of his hair, glided across the stage. The grey seemed misplaced with the way he walked. Grey was bland and reserved, whereas his walk was stimulated and confident. He was well-built and attractive. Not in a sexy way, in a magnetic way. She knew without ever having seen a picture of him, it was Mason Vinton. He sat at the front of the auditorium and observed student after student as they filed into the room. He made eye contact with her briefly and then moved on to the next student. Soon the small class-sized lecture hall was packed. Some students lined the side walls.

Professor Lobrano stood onstage, "Today we

have several guest speakers who have distinguished themselves in the world of media. Many of you in Mass Comm are familiar with our first speaker, since I've spoken of him often and the impact he's had on Louisiana. For those of you that don't, owner of Vinton Publishing and Media," the professor extended his hand toward the man, "everyone Mason Vinton."

The distinguished man stood, glided to the microphone, and thumped it hard with his hand. The sound loudly burst through the speakers and everyone jumped, including Jeselle.

"Hear that?" he asked, but didn't wait for an answer, "That is the sound of a lie being told." He thumped it again, that time as light as a feather, "that is the truth. Our world consists of three types of things. The third of those three is nearly worthless, leaving only two that are worth any importance. One is the lie, the other is the truth. Now, I know what many of you are thinking, you are thinking that truth can be different, depending on the perspective; that perception is reality, right? No, that one is the lie. Some of you may even be saying to yourself that truth is relative to one's own reason, but no, that also, is a lie. Others are thinking truth falls between moralities, again a lie. Those...all those things you thought, those are opinions, and opinions are the third thing, and it is nearly worthless. Neither truth, nor lie, opinions in today's world may very well be considered one's own truth. However they are typically worthless to anyone but you."

The class laughed.

"I hated the color orange. It was ugly," Mason said.

The class laughed again.

"Seriously, I remember as a child my mathematics workbook was orange. I hated that book. It made no sense to me, and it was a total waste of time. Also, my father's car was orange, and when it drove up the driveway, I hated it, because I knew more than likely one of us was getting a beating that night. Typically me since I never stood by to watch my mom or younger brother get it. Carrots..." he paused, "you get it. Orange, yuck. Disgusting." Mason covered his mouth like he might vomit.

The class laughed again.

"Then, one day a woman, the woman who would become the love of my life, was married to her for thirty-seven years before she passed, walked into the back door of a small country church one Sunday wearing a bright orange dress with a big, bright, orange bow in her hair ... and suddenly orange became my favorite color." He took a deep breath, "My point, opinions are fickle and can change. Many of them are based on variables, or age. Preference or personal attachment. Truth ... stays the same. Was it the law that women couldn't vote before Congress ratified the 19th amendment on August 18, 1920, granting women the right to vote?" he waited while several students agreed. "So then, that is a truth?"

"No," Jeselle spoke up instinctively.

Mason was surprised, then he smiled, "And

your name?"

"Jeselle," she said.

"A last name...Jeselle?"

"Parsons. Jeselle Parsons," she said.

"Very well, Ms. Parsons, why is that statement not the truth?"

"Because some women could vote ... unmarried or widows who were land owners or worth a certain amount of money could," Jeselle said, thankful her mom and dad were the feminists they were.

"What of those who were married? Surely the law prohibited them, because they could, in fact, not vote, right?" he asked.

"They couldn't vote because, one, they had no worth. Once they married, any money or land they had, transferred to their husbands and, two, they were no longer considered individual people," she said with confidence.

"Then why did they have to even ratify the 19th amendment at all? Was it simply for married women to then vote?" he smiled, clearly amused.

"No, because women's, the unmarried ones and widows, rights to vote were revoked by many states, spurring women's suffrage."

He smiled wider then looked over the entire class, "So, then the statement you've likely heard all throughout your lives, that women *couldn't* vote before the 19th amendment was passed, is a lie. That doesn't change. Truth. On to the next one. A recent headline read: New Orleans man shot to death the moment he walked into local convenience store."

Mason held up a newspaper with the headline clearly displayed, "True?"

Nearly all the students, including Jeselle, quickly agreed.

"Yes, those are the facts. All true. What the headlines left out was that the man who was shot had robbed that store six times over the past year, killing the last clerk that worked there in cold blood. The man was unable to get the cash register open and ended up leaving with only the twenty dollars he was able to get out of the kid's pocket and a small bag of Fritos. This headline incited violence against the store owner and the worker before the rest of the truth could be revealed. When it was revealed, it was tucked quietly inside the paper," he laid down the first one and opened a second newspaper, "here on the bottom of page twelve in the general section. One can use the truth enough to tag a great headline and still be telling the truth. But that, young people, is a lie. The greatest lie you'll ever be told is the partial truth of anything."

Jeselle was mesmerized listening to Mason Vinton. He paced the stage a round or two then stopped back at the microphone, "A little over two weeks ago while on a family vacation, Madeleine McCann, a three-year-old, went missing when her parents left her sleeping in their room at a resort while they went out to dinner? True?"

A few agreed, skeptical.

"Yes, those are all facts, but not all of the facts. What the original stories didn't tell you was that their room," he emphasized the word room, "was actually their apartment. The resort, one they visited regularly and the restaurant was at the resort itself, approximately sixty yards away. They also didn't add, in the earlier news reports, that the McCanns were with friends who frequented this resort with them as a group, seven other people. All who took turns checking on their sleeping children, every fifteen minutes or so, eight children in total. All of the apartments close by one another's. The group, who the staff knew very well, said to be good people, had done this many times before. So, they were comfortable there, like you are in your own home town. Like you would be walking next door to a neighbor's house, while your child took their nap," Mason took a few steps away from the microphone, then back again.

"Truth is this couple's child went missing and they had solid alibis. Problem is, all the other information to that story is interpreted through personal opinion. Whether you believe they were right or wrong, anything you think past those facts is worthless. Moral judgement. The base facts, as it stands right now, is their child was kidnapped, and they had solid alibis. Whether your opinion is that they shouldn't have left their sleeping children in their apartment is only that, your opinion. It isn't against any law, and they weren't charged with neglect. That, young people, is the greatest folly you'll ever do to yourself, is to believe your opinion must matter to anyone else."

Mason Vinton reached behind him to a table that Professor Lobrano had set up beforehand, turned on a large fan, and lifted a pillow. With a pair of scissors he ripped it open at one side, sending a few feathers flying through the air. He turned back to the audience, "Most important thing to remember about these three things is that, and this is a truth people, so listen well. What you say, whether truth, lie, or opinion, if you took this pillow to the top of a mountain and let all of these feathers go," he opened the pillow in front of the large fan and hundreds upon hundreds of tiny feathers flew throughout the hall, "you could never recover every one. In this auditorium, it is possible. Difficult, but possible," he paused. "Always consider that every word that comes out of your mouth are the feathers in this pillow on a mountaintop. Watch your own integrity carefully." Before he left the stage he thumped the microphone lightly as a whisper, then thumped it hard.

Jeselle smiled. She knew in that exact moment that she would work for Mr. Vinton Mason, somehow.

Someday.

CHAPTER 44

PRESENT

"You're not free in life until you're
free of wanting other people's approval."
-Dawn Steel

"I don't like you."

Jeselle thought often how funny it was that people say anything and everything as if by holding cell phones to their ears makes them invisible or makes everyone else deaf. People fighting, gossiping, and talking business strategies. Many of the conversations that were spewed through a tiny mouthpiece were the very ones that her people targeted for information. *Need to sell asap, Can't be tied to him any longer, I'm mortgaged to the hilt,* were easily some of her recent favorites. Of course she loved that people talked so freely, it made for easy pickings.

"I said, I don't like you."

Jeselle shook her head, the boring conversations never ceased to amaze her. She didn't mind standing in line for her and Jed's coffee, but the number of people on their cells in The Bean Bean line were always ten to one. Twenty to one with the line being as long as it was that day. She was always the one.

"Hey, you, media lady," the voice behind her said, "I don't like you."

Bingo, Jeselle thought, *that would be me.*

She slowly turned to face the younger girl, who was located three people behind her in line. She knew the instant she turned around, because the young girl was one step out of line, with a proud smile plastered across her face.

Jeselle smiled back at her, "Okay." Jeselle turned back around.

"Don't you want to know why I don't like you?"

Jeselle turned again, this time she could see the girl had her cell phone held to her own chest, face forward, no doubt taping. "Your reasons wouldn't matter, because you don't have to like me," Jeselle smiled, this time she didn't turn around. She simply stared at the young girl.

"I wasn't asking for your permission," the girl spewed.

"Simply put, I'm okay that you don't like me," Jeselle said, the smile still locked on her face.

The young girl raised her voice, "Well, so everyone here knows, she is an awful person. She buys a homeless man coffee, one that costs six dollars, but doesn't really help him. She's throwing her wealth in his face every day!" the girl screamed, "She could be taking that money and buying him food!"

Jeselle looked at the other people in line instead of the girl, "Only because my name is being attacked with such a lack of integrity or truth, in my own office building no less, I will say that homeless man is a dear friend of mine, by the way. He lost his beloved wife, the love of his life, years ago and has had a hard time recovering from it. I offered him a job, which he refused, a place to stay, which he won't use, and shoulder to cry on, which he offered back," Jeselle then locked her smile and cool disposition in place as she stepped out of the line and one step closer to the girl, "You are about to buy a six-dollar coffee yourself, yet have you ever offered him a job or a place to live? More importantly, a shoulder to cry on?" Jeselle looked directly at the girls phone still nestled against her chest, "I didn't think so. You undoubtedly are the one who tapes him and posts to your social media how awful the homeless man is and how we must help the homeless in our community, without ever having had one conversation with him. Without respecting him enough to not use his photo or image. So, again, you don't have to like me, your opinion means absolutely nothing to me. Moreover, whoever made you feel like your opinion mattered in this world, young lady, has grossly misled you." Jeselle took another step forward, her smile still fixed, "The next time you want to accuse someone of something you so hypocritically do yourself, you might want to get the whole story. That way you don't butt your little nose into something you are one hundred percent ignorant about, to keep from disliking yourself more than you dislike me."

The girl stepped out of line and left. Jeselle got to the end of the line to wait again. Each time a person went to pay for their coffee, they would be told it was free of charge that day. Isabel always said that it was one of Jeselle's ministries, blessing people who probably didn't need it, with six-dollar coffees and twelve-dollar deli sandwiches.

Only Jeselle knew that the food court located in her office building was meant to be a gift to more than just her employees. It was also meant to bless the shop owners.

Patricia, the founding owner of The Bean Bean, stood a step behind the cashier, waved slightly and smiled back at Jeselle.

CHAPTER 45

PAST

For reasons she already knew, but hadn't thought too deeply about, Jeselle was dreading the Memorial Day picnic at the park in Wellgrove Estates. She had spent the night with Isabel, Patricia, Tina, and Mikelyn.

"I can't believe you are already fourteen," Jeselle said to Patricia, Isabel's oldest. "That's how old I was when I first met you."

"Well, I can't wait to be an adult like you. Have my own apartment at college," Patricia replied.

"It's a dorm, and not really an apartment, but one day," Jeselle smiled wide.

"Well, I want a dorm then," Patricia corrected.

"You might want to bring those grades up if you planning to go to college, young lady," Isabel said to her daughter.

"I only want to go so I can learn business," Patricia said. "I won't need great grades to run a business. I need grit. Isn't that what you always say?"

"You better not be getting smart with me child. I say that to make it in this world you need grit." Isabel raised her eyebrows, "but to make it into college and pay for it, you need good grades. Which, by the way, also requires grit."

"Well, I don't want to own a business. I want to be a lawyer," Tina said.

Isabel looked at her middle child, "You keep your grades up, and I have no doubt you'll do it."

"I want to have a car," the youngest said.

"Now Mikelyn, that's a goal," Jeselle laughed and the others joined in. "What kind of business do you want to have, Patricia?"

"I want a coffee shop that sells bagels and cream cheese-filled donuts," she replied confidently.

"That sounds great!" Mikelyn said, "I'd go to it every day!"

"Me too," Jeselle said.

"Well, I might also. I happen to love coffee," Isabel added.

Patricia felt validated and smiled at her mother.

"Are you all excited about tomorrow?" Jeselle asked.

"I'm not. When we went to the Halloween one, most of the people wouldn't talk to us," Tina said.

"I told you there is no need in complaining," Isabel said to Tina, "Some people are going to treat you that way, and you can't let that define you. Do you hear me?"

"Yes, ma'am," she pouted.

"Wait," Jeselle looked at Isabel, "What is she talking about?"

"Nothing we hadn't encountered before." Isabel looked at each of her children while she spoke, "We are blessed to live here."

"No, seriously, I want to know," Jeselle pressed the issue.

Isabel remained quiet.

"Some of the people in the neighborhood don't like us, I think." Tina said.

"Well, they are idiots. I like you." Jeselle replied.

"You have to like us, we're your family," Mikelyn said.

Jeselle teared up.

"Well, one of the best lessons you'll learn in life is realizing other people don't have to like us," Isabel paused and looked at Jeselle.

"I know … it's different … here," Jeselle said.

"There is nothing different about hateful people, all the same if you ask me. There are other black families in this neighborhood that fit in fine. It's more about who they think belongs, versus who doesn't."

"You belong," Jeselle said more firmly than she

meant to.

"Again, I don't listen to hateful people. We are happy here, aren't we girls?"

They all enthusiastically agreed.

"But I still don't wanna go to the picnic," Tina moaned.

"Well, I'm not going to let anyone stop me from going where I belong, no matter what they think, so you don't have a choice, young lady." Isabel said bluntly.

She looked around the circle they had formed on the floor in the living room and smiled at each of them. This was her family, and she was proud to be a part of it.

The next morning, they all got dressed and walked together to the park. The water rides were full of screaming children. The smell of meat cooking filled the air. Jeselle noticed some of the looks, a few snubs, but she'd also encountered those same snubs before. She knew that Isabel and the girls being black had something to do with it, of course, still she felt it mostly boiled down to power and money.

Jeselle had noticed that there were prejudices of something everywhere you went. In Bakersfield it was who you knew. In college it was your intelligence or education. In the South Baton Rouge area it was social class and manners. There were several other black families in Wellgrove and Hedgefield Court who were accepted and included. Not many of them, though there were a few.

Still, all of those variables included power and

money.

Dennis found them immediately and rushed over, "Hello!" he hugged Jeselle tightly. "Mind if I whisk her off for a minute?" he asked Isabel.

"No, I don't want to leave them. They can come," Jeselle said.

"It would only be for a moment, Jess. I'm sure they can manage," he seemed insistent which did nothing more than irritate Jeselle.

"No, I'm good. They can come," she insisted.

"Fine," Dennis clipped his lips together tightly.

Jeselle looked at Isabel, who had her eyebrows raised.

They walked through the park, past food stands and painting stations. Through a line of rambunctious kids running around the water slides and amusements splashing water everywhere.

Jeselle saw the gazebo, the large one with the platform that Theodore and Brantley used every Memorial Day and Halloween to talk to the crowd. She spotted Theodore Stryker looking at them, blank-faced as they approached. She put on her best smile and waved slightly. It caught him off guard and he looked confused. The moment they were standing in front of Dennis's mother and father, Jeselle didn't hesitate; she hugged each of them tightly.

"Hello," Jeselle said enthusiastically. She looked at Dennis and saw the happiness written all over his face. Then she looked back briefly to see Isabel's eyes squinted in question.

"Well, it, it has been a while," Mr. Stryker

stumbled over his words a bit. He gazed over Jeselle's shoulder and nodded toward Isabel, "Isabel, good you could come."

She nodded back, "We wouldn't miss it," she replied.

"Jess," Dennis's mother looked down at the promise ring still on Jeselle's left hand. "We thought you two might have broken up. It's been so long since we've seen you."

Jeselle looked at Mrs. Stryker, "No indeed," Jeselle said, as eagerly as she had in greeting them. "How could I ever give up such a great guy?"

Dennis perked up with her statement. She thought that maybe he'd also wondered.

Dennis's mother touched Theodore's hand, "We are glad to hear it. I guess I worried you'd get sick of his long hours. It takes a special kind of woman to understand."

"Oh yes, ma'am, I agree. I'm so proud of him. He's busy making Stryker Steel the best it can be," Jeselle shifted her gaze to Mr. Stryker, "Who could blame him for that? It's what he was raised to do."

Dennis's mother settled on that answer and seemed satisfied. Mr. Stryker was obviously appraising.

She saw it and bowed down as a person would to a king, mimicking her actions from the HOA meeting a year and a half earlier. "We must follow the rules, after all."

When she stood, she saw a flicker of appreciation, if not admiration, in Theodore Stryker's expression.

Then she turned to Dennis, grabbed his hand, and walked down the steps of the gazebo to where Isabel and the girls waited.

"Everybody ready for fun?"

The girls all agreed loudly, and they hauled Dennis off with them for a day of water rides and face painting. He was reluctant at first, but after a few rides, he seemed like the old Dennis she'd met in middle school, and Jeselle was thankful that he was still inside there somewhere.

CHAPTER 46

PRESENT

"Within the hearts men, loyalty and
consideration are esteemed greater than
success.
-Bryant H. McGill

Rose entered the house slowly. The key that
Jeselle had given her the week before made her
a little uncomfortable, but also trusted. She wanted
to go to the back door, like most people in the South
did, but for some reason Jeselle's house seemed so
formal on the outside, it made you feel compelled to
enter through the front.

Rose was struck by how simply the large foyer
was decorated. An understated round table stood
at the center with an enormous bouquet of white
flowers arching out of a black vase that sat directly
in the middle. Taking out her phone she quickly

tapped a text to let Jeselle know she was there. She heard a ding in another room, but nothing else. Rose crept her way through the foyer, around a large abstract painting that caused her to pause and admire it.

"Do you like it?" Jeselle startled her.

"You scared me," she took a deep breath and clutched her chest, "Yes, I like it very much."

"It hung on the wall at Vinton the whole time I worked there. It was the first thing you saw when you walked in. Right behind the large security desk."

"And when you bought the company all the furnishings came with it?"

"Yes, and no. The furnishings did come with it, except this painting," Jeselle walked closer to it, and Rose followed. "His wife, who died long before he did, painted this soon after they were married. Both young and broke, she took the last bit of money they had for the week and bought this canvas, then painted it and gave it to him for their first anniversary. She said that one day when he was successful, he would put this in his office, and it would be the first thing people saw when they walked in. He called it his *good love charm.*"

"Good love charm?" Rose seemed like a child as she listened to every word.

"Yes, it is a symbol of love and hope."

"That's beautiful," Rose whispered. "She must've been a wonderful lady."

"So I've heard. I'm simply sad I never got the chance to know her personally."

"If he didn't give it to you, how did you get it?"

"I didn't say he didn't give it to me. I said it didn't come with the company. One thing you won't hear about in all the articles you've read about me is that Mason was like a father to me. He gave me a chance, yes. But more than that, he was good to me. I took care of him at the end. He said he felt that I was the daughter they never had. He believed in me and my goals," Jeselle stopped.

"What did he say when he gave it to you?"

"Well, let's see…" Jeselle tapped a finger against her chin, "the attorney read a letter to me before the formal reading of the will. There were several other people in the room, so it felt invasive to have it read, but I guess in those circumstances we don't get to choose. In the letter, Mason said that of all he owned, the *Good Love Charm* painting was his most prized possession. It was worth more than everything in the world, and he wanted me to have it. To hang it somewhere and to remind myself that love, true love, can rescue any of us."

"That's beautiful."

"Yes, and then the attorney read on. Mason said that he loved me and had only wished Evelyn could've met me also. Then the will was read," Jeselle sighed, "Mason had allowed me to acquire Vinton Publishing and Media with a private loan that I made payments on every month. After the first two years, I renamed it with his blessing, of course. Anyway, the will stated that the business debt was to be forgiven. I was astonished, and very appreciative."

Rose looked at Jeselle, really looked, and saw the tenderness in her eyes as she talked about Mason Vinton. She also saw the tears starting to gather there.

"That was nice," Rose said softly.

"Yes," Jeselle sighed again, "Then he left some of his other possessions to some of the others in the room. His wife's entire jewelry collection to her sister. His car collection, which I didn't even know he had, to his nephew. His gun collection to his brother-in-law. A few other items to others. I had expected the loan to be demanded for by his family, even had a formal loan ready to sign. I was doing well financially then and honestly, nothing compared to that painting. I knew what that painting meant. He kept it in his condo after I bought the company."

"When he was with you, at the end, did all those people he left stuff to come visit him here?"

"Well, we weren't here. I had another house before this one. But no, not one of them. I think at the end of your life you are seen as irrelevant. Old. Outdated. Forgotten. He never felt that way, that I could tell thankfully."

"That's pitiful though. He gave them all that expensive stuff, and they hadn't even come to see him."

"Yes, it is pitiful, but," Jeselle turned and faced Rose, "it's only stuff. The lead attorney continued by saying that they all, all eight of his attorneys present, knew Mason's wishes and any attempt to contest the will would be met with such incredible force that it would drain whoever contested it down to the very last cent they owned. I thought it was excessive. Well, truly because I didn't think he had much left. We never really talked about money. He had come to live with me by that time; he'd already sold his condo. I figured whatever he had would go to charity, since his heart always followed the less fortunate. So, I was just as shocked as all the others to learn I was sole beneficiary of Mason's entire remaining estate."

"Oh, I never read that," Rose said, stunned.

"Yes, again, not that I thought it was much. I think I really believed it was more to let me know how much he knew I would use it to help others."

Rose waited.

"It's all a matter of public records of course," Jeselle waved her hand in the air flippantly and then started walking through the foyer leading to the back of the house, "but his estate was worth a little over eighty million."

"Whoa…"

"Yes, I agree, whoa," Jeselle repeated the sentiment.

"Did his family freak out? They probably weren't happy about it."

Jeselle brushed off any feelings she'd been experiencing and replaced it with her normal coolness, "It was obvious they didn't like it, but no one said a word. Wouldn't have mattered anyway. His attorneys all knew his wishes and no amount of complaining or lawsuits would've changed the outcome. That's how I fund all the community organizations. *The Geno Prett.E Suicide Alliance, The Heavn.E Foundation, The Alley, Lett.E Learning Center*...all of it is because of Mason Vinton's kindness."

"Did he want to start those before he died?"

"No, it's all because of my parents and their influence that those particular organizations exist. It's Mason's generosity that pays for it all." With that Jeselle walked away from the painting and Rose followed.

CHAPTER 47

PAST

"Men are taught to apologize for their
weaknesses, women for their strengths."
-Lois Wyse

Starting at Vinton Publishing and Media the same
month she started her sophomore year at Tulane
was easier than Jeselle had expected. She wasn't
really quite sure what she had expected at Vinton
initially; only she hadn't thought it would be such
a positive environment with everyone smiling.
Enough big business had been thrown in her face to
know that people often didn't smile in business. She
knew right away that there was something special
about Mason Vinton's company, and she intended
to find out what made it that way.

Months flew by in a blur. Dennis rarely answered

his phone. Then again, she rarely called. When he did "find a few minutes" here and there it was mostly to talk about himself and his life; less and less did he ask about hers. Camilla had married Rick, which she hadn't expected either. Jeselle thought for sure that Camilla would've been honest with herself and backed out. Jeselle guessed after their parents put several hundred thousand dollars into a wedding, it became harder to say no. It was not so unexpected that Cindy and Tracy announced their wedding date, which had been planned secretly, and fell only two weeks after Camilla and Rick's. As usual, the Briggs's family wedding was far bigger and much more expensive than the Stryker family's latest happy nuptial. Jeselle often wondered when they'd ever get tired of it all. The competition, the rivalry, the jealously. Likely never.

Her phone rang, she glanced at the screen for a moment longer than normal, puzzled.

"Hey," she answered, "I was thinking about you and poof, you call."

Dennis laughed, and Jeselle noticed his voice seemed deeper, more grown up than she somehow remembered. "Well, I like that news. I happened to be thinking of you also. Hence, the call."

"What's up?"

"I was hoping to get you to come home this weekend."

"Why?" she asked.

"It's a family thing."

Jeselle took a deep breath, "I knew your

good mood was too good to be true. So you want something from me."

"Yes," he became aggravated, "I want to see you."

"You know where I am," she said, making sure she kept her voice even.

"You know I don't have the time to go there."

"A flight would take no time at all."

"Are you kidding, Jess? After check-in and security, then the flight, it would be faster to drive."

"Then drive." She waited for a response, but all she heard was a sigh from the other end of the phone. "I tell you what Dennis, you pick me up, and I'll come."

"Deal, I'll send the car."

"No," it rushed out more quickly than she'd intended, "*You* pick me up, and I'll come."

"This is an important weekend, Jeselle. I need you by my side," he stated.

"You know where I am."

* * *

Jeselle sat on the patio of a coffee shop on Magazine Street to enjoy the weather and thought of Patricia. It had been a while since Jeselle had a day off during the week, from work and school together. New Orleans was experiencing a major rat issue, and Mr. Vinton insisted that everyone take off for a few days so he could have a company come in and catch the "little buggers." She'd heard from other employees all day, after the announcement, about how much he hated killing anything. So, everyone was off with pay for three days before the weekend to give the exterminators time to actually catch and release them elsewhere.

Jeselle didn't want to let Dennis know that she was off, because then he'd have every reason in the world not to come get her. Why was she making him come? To prove that he would. Jeselle felt petty. She knew how busy he was since he'd taken on more authority at Stryker.

She clicked on his name and waited for three rings before it was forwarded to voicemail.

Yeah ... *he could come get her after all.*

She spent the next two days reorganizing her mini dorm closet and packing boxes. With one year left of college, she could stay in the dorm, but with the job at Vinton, she was finally able to afford her own place. She didn't see much of Lakshmi anymore anyway.

Friday afternoon, Dennis arrived early with a smile on his face. She was a bit taken aback at his appearance. She was shocked to see how much had changed in the four months since she'd last seen him. He'd bought a new car also, which was surprising to her because his last car was fairly new. They talked easily on the drive back to Baton Rouge. She tried to call Isabel again to let her know she was on the way, but the call went unanswered.

"Something wrong?"

"No," Jeselle sighed, "Just Isabel hasn't answered her phone in a couple of days and hasn't called back. I wish she'd use the cell phone I got her."

"She may be overly busy. I know Dad has had housekeeping working overtime, because we have a big summit coming up after Thanksgiving."

"A summit? Sounds important?"

"It is. That's why I've been so busy also."

"What's it for?"

"To be honest, the company is struggling a bit. Briggs is playing dirty, and we are hemorrhaging. I came up with the idea of an investment summit to raise capital. It's highly vetted though, to be sure old man Briggs can't get in."

"What do you mean 'get in?'" Jeselle looked toward Dennis.

Dennis had changed for sure. He not only looked different, he talked differently. Older. Jeselle felt as undeveloped as she had when they sat on the park bench years ago discussing how young she was. That insecurity made her angry.

"Well, we don't want him buying up stocks with dummy corporations, or through associates, so we are vetting everyone through a series of security steps. I mean, we aren't selling enough to lose control, but still it would kill Dad for Brantley to own any portion of Stryker."

"What about Mr. Vinton? He's always looking to invest in companies," she suggested.

"That," he looked over at her with admiration, "sweetheart, is a great idea. He's trustworthy?"

"One hundred percent. He believes integrity comes before anything else. I'll ask him Monday."

"You? You'll ask him directly? Do you see him often?"

"Yes, Dennis. I've told you several times, I've been promoted again. I work directly with him every day."

"Oh," he seemed overly stunned. "Then, I guess ask him."

The conversation died after that, and Jeselle wondered if Dennis was embarrassed for having not paid attention before, or jealous that she had been promoted again so quickly. Maybe, a little of both.

They arrived at Wellgrove Estates, and he drove past the first street which led to her house.

"I kind of want to go home first, freshen up. Is that okay?"

"Yes, there is plenty of time. First, I want to show you something."

They drove to the back of the neighborhood. She thought they were going to his parents' house, but instead they drove a few driveways further and turned in.

"Who is this? Dennis, I look horrible."

He smiled wide as he pressed a button on his sun visor. "Our neighbor, old Mr. Morris. He recently went to live closer to his daughter."

"Okay," it became obvious, since he had the gate remote, that his dad was looking to buy the house. She'd heard he'd bought one somewhere in the neighborhood for Camilla and Rick. Naturally, he'd buy one for Dennis. It made her new lease on the apartment seem contrary. It shouldn't have, but it did.

The driveway wound between a tight set of trees. The leaves were turning; a sure sign of fall that Louisiana doesn't get every year. Some years, a hard freeze kills everything, and there is no warm transition into winter; only barren, prickly trees. Jeselle admired the beauty. It felt like Thanksgiving.

Suddenly, the trees parted and the driveway led to a mansion. She had expected no less, but this was much grander than she had envisioned. Seemed her expectations were constantly getting obliterated.

Dennis must have seen her thoughts written across her face, "We don't get to pick. We take what comes for sale here."

"It's … it's huge."

"Yes, will need lots of babies to fill it," he said.

She chuckled uncomfortably. "So, Daddy Morbucks is buying you a house?" she said.

The Powerpuff Girls reference clearly went over his head, "No, Dennis Warbucks is buying a house."

"You?" she asked with a laugh. "How are you buying this?"

"Jeselle, I make good money." He seemed amused by her question, "I own over a third of Stryker stocks. Did you think Dad wasn't paying me?"

"I knew you had money, kind of thought it was his money."

"Not anymore, babe." He opened the door and

waved to her through the windshield to follow him. Once inside, Jeselle was startled to see it was furnished. She expected to find it empty.

"Has he not moved yet? Mr…"

"Morris? Yes, he moved."

"Then, whose furniture?"

"Ours."

Jeselle felt like someone had slapped her in the face. "Ours? As in your parents?"

Dennis walked up to her and lovingly placed his hands on her arms, "Jeselle, you and me, ours. Isn't it great?"

"Dennis, I have a house."

"Really," he laughed out loud, "and you thought I'd move in with you? In the *front* of the neighborhood?" he laughed again, "Oh, Jeselle, you are so sweet."

She took a step back unintentionally and felt a wave of dizziness. She was forced to steady herself against a wall. "Dennis?" she said softly. "I don't…I didn't ask you to move in with me. I live in New Orleans. I don't live here anymore."

"But now you can. I know you are too sweet to simply take the house back from Isabel. I get it. You needed a place of your own."

She looked around the expansive living area. "This," she started, then stopped and took a deep breath, "This is not my own. This is your own. This is your stuff. I, I," she stuttered, pointed toward the sofas, "I wouldn't have bought gilded anything. Or, or crystal chandeliers."

"Babe, this is the formal living room, where we host parties and stuff. It has to give off an air of luxury. All of the other spaces, minus the dining room, are waiting for you to furnish. Whatever you want." He looked at his watch, "Oh, wow, we are running late. Here," he shoved his keys to her, "go get your bags and we can get dressed."

"No, no, I am going home. I want to see Isabel and the girls for a minute."

"Okay," he contemplated, "take my car then. Come back and get me. We can't be late. Be here in, say, an hour?"

"Sure," Jeselle said as she walked toward the front door in a haze of confusion. She made it to her driveway in time to see Isabel and the girls getting out of their car. They stopped as soon as they saw her and ran to greet her.

"Oh my God, where did you get this car?" Patricia yelled excitedly.

"I want a hug," Mikelyn giggled.

"So good to see you." Isabel smiled warmly. Jeselle noticed that Tina stayed back. She also noticed that she looked angry.

"Well, hello Tina," she said.

"Why haven't you been home?"

"Tina, don't be mad at me. I talk to you all the time. You know I have two majors and a job." When Jeselle saw she wasn't making any headway she added, "Please don't be mad at me."

"Oh, ignore her, she's getting her hormones. Come on in, I'll make some coffee."

Jeselle rushed to say, "I can't stay right now, but you guys have me the whole weekend if you want."

"We want. We want," Mikelyn chanted.

"If you have plans, I understand. I tried to call. I left messages."

"I know, my honey, I've been so busy. But you know, this is your house. You come home any time you want. We'll always make room for you."

Jeselle didn't understand why, but she started to cry. Isabel stepped forward and hugged Jeselle. The girls followed, even Tina.

"Don't cry. I'm not mad anymore," Tina said.

After spending time with the girls, Jeselle rushed to get dressed. She looked in the mirror and saw it was obvious she had been crying, so she lightly concealed her swollen under eyes and red nose and put on a thin layer of lip gloss, then headed back to Dennis's house. Absolutely, it was *Dennis's house.*

The second the car turned around the tree line, Dennis opened the front door of the ridiculously large house, and darted for the car. He was dressed in a simple black suit. Thankfully, she knew enough about his family to dress accordingly. She opened the driver's side door and went to go around to the other side.

"No, don't have time. You drive." He quickly got into the passenger side, and she slid behind the wheel again, wondering what was so important that it had Dennis so frazzled.

From the second they arrived at his parents' house, Dennis disappeared, leaving Jeselle at the mercy of his mother. Mrs. Stryker carted her from person-to-person to say hello or be introduced. Glancing around, Jeselle spotted Camilla standing next to Rick. She looked so sad. The same kind of sadness that Mrs. Stryker had. Also, the same fake smile.

A clinking noise startled her from her thoughts and she turned to see Mr. Stryker tapping a glass with what appeared to be a money clip. Dennis stood proudly by his side.

"Everyone, hello!" he bellowed, "Tonight is an important night for us all."

Business, always business, Jeselle thought. She knew many of the new faces were likely potential investors.

Everyone stood in the large living room. She looked around and recalled what Dennis had said to her earlier about a formal living room; it was for hosting stuff. She looked up to see Camilla staring at her, and she waved slightly. Camilla simply lifted her chin and looked toward her husband and smiled that fake smile. She noticed something move off to the side and saw that Dennis was making his way to her.

Thank God.

The moment he stood in front of her, he simultaneously reached in his jacket pocket and lowered to one knee. It happened so quickly that Jeselle didn't have time to put two and two together.

She noticed all eyes were on them.

"Jeselle Kate Parsons, I have been in love with

you for many years and am extremely glad you are mine. Formally, and for my lifetime, will you marry me?"

She was stunned a moment or two, "Oh, um yes." Had she just said *yes*?

The room erupted into joyful congratulations. Dennis removed the promise ring he'd given her years before and replaced it with the much larger diamond engagement ring. He then slipped the promise ring onto her right hand, stood and wrapped his arms around her as he whispered in her ear, "You have made me the happiest man on Earth."

The party went by fairly well like all the others. People mingled, laughed, and talked about business of course. It was getting late, and she hadn't seen Dennis in a while. Strangers kept touching her on the arms and congratulating her. It was overstimulating and felt very invasive. She wanted to leave, go home, and take a bath. Jeselle moved through the large room, searching until she spotted Dennis. He was facing a group of men, and they were all laughing. She wished badly that she could see his face, because his laugh was so beautiful. It reminded her of his goodness. Moving slowly toward them, she was overjoyed in hearing his voice when she got within earshot. He was so blissful. His words earlier came back to her, *You have made me the happiest man on Earth,* and she smiled. She shrugged off whatever worry she had and walked closer.

"He begged," Dennis laughed as did the others.

433

"literally got on his knees right in front of me, and begged me not to bankrupt him." They all laughed again. "I could've dropped my pants right there, and he wouldn't have hesitated. I don't think I've ever seen Dad so proud."

"Seems he's not the first," another one of the men said, "I heard you tossed Fleming and Little out on their asses as well." They all laughed again.

"I love it. Especially when they try to manipulate me with their sob stories, 'My wife has cancer,' 'or my babies will starve' please. It's pathetic."

The room went quiet to her.

All Jeselle saw from that moment, until the moment she found herself on the back patio of Isabel's house, was a mansion she hadn't chosen, a formal living room full of gold furniture she would never have bought, a crystal chandelier that she'd forever be worried would fall and kill her, a long gone cell phone, and now two rings that seemed more like anchors than treasures.

Also, she saw a family full of women who had sad eyes and fake smiles.

***

The next morning, she made blueberry muffins and visited with Isabel and the girls for hours. She really had missed them so much, although she didn't regret working so hard.

"I see you looking at that ring. Now you got

two." Isabel said flatly. "What are you gonna do?"

"I don't know. I was so stunned. I mean, I'm still wearing the promise ring, I guess this was the next logical step."

"Yeah, well that *'promise ring'* could buy a car."

"I know," Jeselle put her hands over her face, "What am I doing?"

"I don't know, but you better figure it out. You love him?"

"I do, but in a weird way. I love who he used to be, maybe. Or maybe, I love who he is deep down, I don't know, Isabel. It's just, when I heard him last night and how happy he was at bankrupting all those people. How calloused. I feel that the old Dennis isn't even in there anymore, except in my mind. I do know one thing, I can't hurt him."

"Well, you gonna hurt yourself?"

"Isabel," she demanded, "he stood by me. He almost sacrificed his family for me."

"No, Jessie, I hate to be the barer of the truth to you, but I know Dennis; known him nearly his whole life. I've watched him take the wrong road too many times now to count. He knew his dad would back down. Dennis knows how much power he holds. Don't ever think different. You hear me?"

A knock at the door startled them. Tina ran from the living room to answer it. As soon as Dennis walked in, Jeselle stood up from the barstool.

"I told you I want to spend time with them today," she said.

"I know, relax, I'm not taking you away. I came

to join in the fun, but I only have an hour," he shrugged, "work."

"Dennis," Jeselle looked at Isabel, and then back to Dennis, "can I talk to you outside?"

"Sure," he had no worries at all, she noticed.

When they reached the patio and sat, Jeselle started before she lost her nerve, "I, Dennis, I don't' want kids."

"Whatever?" he laughed it off as a joke.

"Seriously. At least, not anytime soon. I mean maybe one day, but I don't know for sure that I will."

"You will. You're still young, in college. You'll get there."

"What if I don't," she asked.

"You will. We are definitely having kids," he said emphatically.

"See, that's the problem. I really, seriously, don't know that I want kids. To be honest, I'm not even sure I want to move back here. Too many bad memories."

"Jeselle, are you kidding me? I have planned everything. I have worked hard to provide everything for you. Are you seriously telling me, what? That you don't want to marry me? You sure said yes pretty fast last night!" he stood, clearly angry.

"Okay, this is going off the rails. I am saying that I have stuff to do first."

"Like what? Finishing college? Okay, I gave you that much."

"You *gave* me that much?" she grew angry.

"I mean, I get it, Jeselle, you have a job, you are in college, but you only have two years left. Then what?"

"Dennis," she stood, "I signed a year lease on an apartment."

"You signed for an apartment?" he took a deep breath, "Didn't want to ask me first?"

"*Ask?* Did you, or did you not," she walked up to him and pressed a finger into his chest, "buy a house?"

"For us!" he yelled. "An apartment is for you!"

"That house is not for us, if it were, it wouldn't be so close to your parents!" she yelled back.

"You are so ungrateful," he whispered. "What do you want, Jess?"

"I'm ungr-" she stopped and thought for a minute. "I don't like your father."

"I know that."

"Then why would you think that a house practically next door to him would be okay for me?"

"Jess, he … he can't undo the past. He's tried so hard to make it up to you."

"It's not only him. Dennis, it's this place, I guess."

Dennis huffed like he was a bull ready to charge, "You have to let it go."

She was stunned. Of all the harsh things he'd ever said, that one took the cake. "You know what Dennis?" she took a deep breath and somehow it felt like relief, but she wasn't sure, "You're right."

"It is about time. I'll tell you, I was starting to worry you'd never get over it."

She laughed sadly, and then slipped the promise ring off her finger followed by the engagement ring. It was his turn to be stunned when she slowly placed them in his hand.

"I need to let go of the fact that I'm not the same girl I was then. Not Jess anymore. I am not okay with what happened, and you shouldn't be either. I'm in college, have a great job, and I'm not ready for sad eyes and fake smiles."

He appeared desperate, "What are you talking about, Jess? You aren't making any sense."

"I can't move forward, because no one has paid, but me."

"I've paid!" he yelled. "I've paid a thousand times."

"I need this, Dennis. I need this independence."

"What am I supposed to tell everyone?"

She shook her head in disbelief, "If the truth isn't good enough, I guess tell them whatever you want."

His laugh was a mix of defeat and astonishment. "Pathetic. Seriously, Jess, it's pathetic. Of all the stuff my family has been through and you don't see us whining about it. You don't see us giving up the best thing in our lives over it."

She grew angrier, "The best thing being you?"

"Hell, yes, me!" he started pacing, "I've bent over backwards to love you, and you keep throwing it back in my face. *Damn it!*"

Jeselle turned, walked through the back door, slammed it as hard as she could, and locked the door leaving Dennis outside.

CHAPTER 48

PRESENT

> "It is impossible to inhale new air until
> you exhale the old."
> —T.D. Jakes

Camilla fell into a perfect pattern. She was surprised at how much fulfillment she gained through each event. Planning corporate meetings, luncheons, and fundraisers was what she had been doing for Rick's campaign for so many years that it was second nature to her. Only it was a completely different job, because she was being paid for it. Camilla felt appreciated, instead of taken for granted. Important, instead of neglected. The bitterness of being left for a younger woman was dissipating with each new accomplishment. The sting of having her money and house stolen from under her would likely never go away, she thought often.

Sleeping with Todd had made her feel dirty. Giving him one excuse after another, she hadn't been back to his house since talking to Jeselle, even though Todd had called that morning and insisted. He said he'd put a lot of work into her case and refused to be brushed off. No matter the reason she was required to be at his place that night with bells on.

As she pulled out of the parking lot from work, she thought of all that Jeselle had done to help her. Real help. Help that Camilla knew she certainly didn't deserve.

When she'd shown up at work that morning, having already talked to Todd and cried all of her makeup off, Jeselle stepped in like a momma bear.

Now she was headed to Todd's house, having to pass her own house that Rick was living in with his new girlfriend, along the way.

Camilla knew it was time.

Time to take her life back.

She knocked on the back door. Silence. She knocked again. After waiting a long minute or two she started to get anxious. What would he do if he found out? She took her phone out of her purse and texted.

I'm at the door.

I'm waiting in bed.

Come down for a minute. We need to talk.

No talk cam. Only touch. Come on in.

She waited a minute, scared he would know.

Then she did as she was advised to do.

No, come down now.

A few minutes later a naked Todd opened the back door with so much force that it slammed against the interior wall. "I am tired of being played with, Camilla!" he shouted.

"I have money," she said quickly, "A down payment."

Todd walked closer to her. She could see his eyes were squinted under the moonlight. She started feeling increasingly more and more anxious. He leaned into her and whispered, "Get upstairs, Camilla. Money isn't what I want, and you already agreed to this."

"Well, technically I didn't agree, you gave me no choice."

"Yes, and you still don't have one. Besides, wouldn't you rather be screwed by me than your pathetic ex-husband? Camilla, I'm not kidding. There is no space for negotiation. Besides," he kissed her on the cheek, "It's not only about sex. You know we belong together."

"Then why not help me for free?" she asked.

He grabbed her arm, "I didn't get where I was by doing favors, Camilla. Get. In. Bed."

"I'm not asking for a favor, Todd. I told you I have money."

Todd laughed, "Wow, growing a backbone, are we? Good for you. I hate to do this, but I need to drop you as a client. This obviously isn't a good fit." He turned to walk into his house when the sirens started. The closer they came, the more he understood. He looked back at Camilla in disbelief.

"Yes, Todd, I *do* believe I have grown a backbone."

$$* * *$$

The news hit the next morning like a bomb. Local respected attorney, Todd Parrish, had been arrested the night before on extortion charges.

"He kept his records too clean. They'll never make it stick," Dennis said. He lifted the glass of water off the table then remembered where they were and set it back down "Pity. I always said he'd be the toughest one to get, being a lawyer and all."

"Oh, I don't know, I'm pretty sure these charges will stick," Jeselle said confidently.

"Oh yeah? Do tell, you little minx. Doing stuff on your own now, are we?"

"Dennis," Jeselle used her wonderfully cold demeanor to her advantage, "I don't need to set anyone up, remember? All I have to do is remove the tools they used to get away with all of their dirty deeds."

"Oh, so what *tool* did you remove? Jeselle, you must keep me in the loop."

"Like you did when you set Camilla up to be used by Todd? Is that keeping me in the loop, Dennis? I really thought you were more loyal to me than that. I must admit, I'm rather disappointed to see I was wrong."

"That, dear Jeselle, was more for fun," he laughed, and then he noticed she remained still, staring at him. "Wait ... his arrest doesn't have to do with Camilla does it?" he looked a bit scared.

"Of course, it does. Did you think I could pass up the opportunity? I mean, unfortunately you did set it up, which was against our rule, but he is ultimately responsible. He is the one who went through with it."

Dennis looked even more worried. "What have you done? He could implicate me. Hell, he will implicate me."

She sat for a moment relishing in his discomfort, "Do calm down. Worry over things that matter. For example I still have your father."

"He has nearly nothing left."

"He has his legacy," Jeselle pointed out with a sly smile.

"Stryker?" he laughed, "do your worst. It would serve him right. Besides, I own most of the trust so I'd simply liquidate it all, and ride off into the sunset. Seeing the look on his face when the company he sacrificed everything for goes up in flames would be the coup de grâce."

Jeselle somehow figured he'd say as much, "Well, with Todd, I wouldn't worry because it wouldn't matter if he did out you. Who would really believe you set up your own sister to be used like that? Not the great Dennis Stryker. Besides, Camilla is far too loyal to you, she'd never give you up herself."

"True." He seemed to ease up.

"Unless…"

He grew worried again, "Unless what?"

"Unless Todd taped you," Jeselle let that soak in for a moment.

"I … don't think he would … do that. Do you?"

"I don't know Dennis," she paused for effect, "he is an attorney."

Dennis turned pale.

"But, then again that would simply make you immoral. At a stretch, complicit, but likely not put you in jail."

"Well," he smiled, a little uneasily. "I hardly see where a bad name would ruin me, no one ever really thought I was a good person to begin with."

"Someone used to."

"Pardon?"

"Someone used to think you were a good person," she simply stared at him.

He looked back at her with an intensity she hadn't seen in years. A longing. Then he turned away.

"Yes, well, I guess that's why I still tolerate you," he laughed, although there was no humor in it.

"Yes, I guess so." After a few moments, Jeselle slid out of the booth, "Have a good one, Dennis."

He waved at her, barely. She almost felt sorry for him. Anytime she let that emotion hit her, she conjured up the list of things he'd done to others that salved her guilty soul.

Dennis chose his path. Not just once, he chose

over and over and over again.

With every dirty deal.

With every dollar.

With every action.

With every turn of his head.

* * *

Rose entered with confidence. That was always the transition Jeselle loved to see. They start off scared, unsure. However, as they learned and worked, they became more and more assured in themselves. Poised, even.

As Rose walked toward her desk, Jeselle thought of the many girls that she'd helped through the years. Today, she was about to bestow her crowning gift to Rose. Exactly like the others, she was offering something that only Jeselle could offer.

"Good morning," Rose said as she sat.

Jeselle slid the folder across the desk to Rose. She watched with pure satisfaction as Rose opened the folder. A confused look washed over Rose's features.

"What, what is this?"

"She has a nice house on the south side of town, participates in all of her children's school activities, and has been married for a little over two years. However, it's rumored that her marriage is on very shaky ground, because she has a huge gambling problem."

"Why...Ms. Parsons, I'm confused. Why do you

have this file on Trisha?"

Jeselle stood, "Why else? She's your frenemy. And any frenemy of yours is a frenemy of mine," Jeselle waited to watch the moment Rose got it.

Rose stood, carrying the file with her, "I don't understand. What do you mean?"

Jeselle gave up hope that it would finally click with Rose. "Revenge, Rose," she leaned toward her, "For her misdeeds against you." Jeselle hadn't meant to sound so forceful.

Rose's voice was barely over a whisper, "Why on Earth would I want revenge?"

Jeselle was rocked to her core, she swayed slightly. "Because she hurt you. Horribly."

Rose's eyebrows drew together. She walked around the desk to meet with Jeselle. "I think that your heart is in the right place, only..." Rose threw her arms around Jeselle and hugged her, "I don't need revenge."

Jeselle stiffened in the embrace.

"Mom always says," Rose whispered in Jeselle's ear, "the best revenge is in not needing any." Rose stepped back and looked at Jeselle, "I am the happiest I've ever been in my life, and that has nothing to do with Trisha."

"Well, that's good," Jeselle brushed the front of her suit, sat behind her desk and made herself busy. "Lucky for you, you didn't lose a parent to anyone."

"True. But my parents were saved by someone. You."

"Yes, okay," Jeselle waved her hand to dismiss

Rose.

"You save people, Jeselle. Lots of people. I think revenge is a waste."

"Is it a waste, Rose, to have revenge because you are trying to save other people from horrible people, hmm? Answer me that." she replied coldly,

"No. But Trisha isn't that situation. In my opinion, saving her marriage or her family for her children by helping her get counseling for her gambling problem would save people."

Jeselle sighed deeply, "Go away, and let me go save the world then."

CHAPTER 49

PAST

"You get whatever accomplishment you are
willing to declare."
-Georgia O'Keeffe

It surprised Jeselle to see Dennis plastered on the TV with a beautiful blonde hanging all over him. The Louisiana Business Gala made the news every year and she hated that she was glued to the screen. He, of course, looked meticulously happy. The speaker barely spit out the name Theodore Stryker and Business Person of the Year before she got disgusted and clicked the remote leaving the room bathed in darkness.

Throughout her junior and senior years she'd continued to move up quickly and garner more and more influence at Vinton. She loved spending weekends with Isabel and the girls once a month. and every now and then they would all go to New Orleans and spend weekends in Jeselle's one bedroom apartment.

She also formed a deeper relationship with Mason. She'd shared her darkest secrets with him, as he had shared his deepest regrets with her. He warned her many times to stop walking toward revenge, because one day she'd have it, and her life would become empty. Revenge never filled a void, it created one.

Nonetheless, Jeselle really didn't have any, or know of any way to truly have the revenge she craved. All she knew was if she were ever going to have a chance at it, she had to work harder to make a name for herself.

Graduation ceremonies went well. Mason was sitting close to the front with a "proud Dad smile" spread across his face. For nearly three years he had been a mentor, but for the past year, he had also been like a father. After retrieving her degree and taking the picture, Jeselle made her way back to her seat to watch the rest of the ceremony. She thought about how quickly she'd moved up in the company and how suspicious she was about it at first. She also laughed to herself, which she did often, when she recalled after the first year she'd worked directly with Vinton Mason, asking him bluntly what it was that he wanted from her.

"I'm never going to sleep with you," she'd said.

Vinton looked up from his large mahogany desk

and smiled, "I'd throw up, young lady, if I'd had anything to eat today." He was amused.

"Wow, I'm *that* bad?"

"No, you're *that* family."

Jeselle was blown away by the statement.

"Jeselle, do you not know how much you mean to me? I only wish Evelyn was alive to know you. You are like the daughter we never had." He looked off into the voided space of his office.

"I, I, don't guess I thought that, no."

"You are guarded. I understand you have reasons that made you this way, but you need to understand what makes you stay. You are smart and a hard worker. You treat people well, which says a lot about you, but you are hardened also. Too young to be so hard."

"Yes," she placed the reports on his desk. "One learns to survive," she stated plainly.

"Yes, one does. Never thought I'd make it the first year without Evelyn. You?"

"Me, what?" she stood still.

"Sit and tell me, who have you survived without?"

She really didn't know why she sat, maybe she felt he deserved the answers. "My parents."

"That's tough. I am sorry about that."

"Thank you," she said quietly. It only took a week after that conversation for her highest wall to come crumbling down. As clumsily as she had spilled his morning coffee on her mentor nearly every day, she soiled onto him all of her darkest secrets.

STOP ME

The shattering fanfare around her brought her back to graduation. She'd missed the tossing of the caps. It didn't matter, because she probably wouldn't have participated anyway.

When she found Mason, he hugged her tightly. "I am so proud of you! Here," he shoved an envelope in her hand, "Happy graduation! Go on, open it."

"Right now? Here?"

"Yes, here, I've been waiting for this moment," he said.

She ripped open the envelope and inside she found a check, a personal check, for fifteen thousand dollars. "*What?* Oh, I can't take this. Why?"

He smiled at her again, "Get a decent car, okay?"

She felt overcome by emotion and wrapped her arms around him. "Thank you, thank you!"

"You deserve it. Now, go party with your friends, and I'll see you at work on Monday."

As she watched him walk away, she felt sad. She looked around at all of the people in the large auditorium hanging out with their friends and family. Jeselle took a deep breath and made her way to her car, which was definitely on its last leg.

When she got close, she looked up and found Dennis leaning against it. She hadn't seen him in person in almost a year. It caught her off guard. He looked nothing like the boy she'd left behind, he looked hard and mean.

"I see you've got a sugar daddy. Should've guessed."

"You would think that." Jeselle walked past him

to the other side to unlock it.

"I saw you hanging all over him. Geez, Jess, he could be your grandfather."

She turned toward Dennis, "You are disgusting. He's like a father to me. I need one, remember? Mine was stolen from me."

His face softened quickly, remorse washed away the anger. "I'm sorry, I guess I was jealous." He came around the car to be near her.

"You don't have the right to be jealous!" she spit at him.

"I can't stop thinking about you."

"Well, the host of women hanging all over you at every newsworthy function begs to differ." She started to open the door when he put his hand on it to stop her.

"Look, can't we talk?"

"I have a phone."

"You don't answer it."

"Oh, yeah," she looked up at him, "that's right. Guess that means no, we can't talk."

"You have changed," he said.

She looked up at him defiantly, "No Dennis, I haven't changed. I've stopped lying. This," she motioned around herself, "this is me now." She tried to yank the door, but he had a firm grasp on it so it didn't budge.

"Wait a minute, please. Jess, I, I, came here tonight because I didn't want to miss it, your moment. I'm proud of you."

"Great. Thanks." She jerked the door again.

"*Wait*," he repeated, more desperately, "just, can you go get a coffee with me? Just for a few minutes, *please*."

"Fine," she jerked again, this time hard enough to knock off his arm, "but, I'll drive."

He quickly got into the passenger's side of her old car.

***

"You look good. Mad, but good." He smiled across the table at her.

"What do you want?" she asked bitterly.

"What do you want?" he responded.

"Ultimately? Revenge?" she said matter-of-factly. "You?"

"You. I want you back in my life. I miss you."

"And it is all about you after all, right?"

"Jess, please," he reached across the table and touched her hand. "I, I know I was horrible. Without you I'm worse. I'm better when you are with me. We don't have to be together, together. We can be friends. Friends?" he asked skeptically.

"And how long will that last? Only until you get tired of me not giving you what you want."

"I've never done that to you," he said it so honestly she nearly believed it.

"I have one problem with that. One hold up."

"What's that, Jess? Anything, we can work it out." he stated quickly.

"I can't very well get revenge on everybody if you plan on standing in my way."

He looked puzzled for a moment. Then he squinted his eyes, not sure if she was joking with him or not. "Revenge?" he asked slowly.

"Yes, Dennis, revenge," she stated plainly.

"Like…killing people?"

"Maybe," she said with a straight face, then laughed when he looked scared, "No, not killing people." She saw the instant relief when the tension left his shoulders. "But when I'm done with everybody, they are going to wish they were dead."

"You scared me there for a minute. Well, luckily for you, not only am I the perfect person to help since I know them all, I so happen to benefit from each one of their downfalls."

"And Camilla? Your sweet, baby sister?" He nodded his head slightly, "And, dearest Dad? What of him? Because he's on the top of my list."

"I really thought you were joking at first, but you aren't, are you?" he asked.

"No," she folded her arms and rested back in her seat.

His eyes squinted again, "I don't doubt for a minute that you could do this. Okay, as long as you and I are good, and … Stryker Steel stays together. I'm game. I'll help you. I need the old goat out of Stryker so I can move the company into this century anyway."

"Also, don't call me Jess. I've told you, I'm not that girl anymore."

CHAPTER 50

PRESENT

"If you love only those who love you,
what reward is there for that? Even
corrupt tax collectors do that much."
                    —Matthew 5:46

"Oh look, there's our friend."

Melanie walked out from two doors that hung sloppily behind a greasy counter. She saw them instantly and closed her eyes.

Is she praying? Jeselle thought, and immediately felt a heaviness weigh her down. Removing all the obstacles people use to hurt other people is different than this. This was targeting. This wasn't letting her fall into her own consequences.

This was calloused.

Right then, a small child ran from the back and hugged Melanie around the legs.

"Mommy, Mommy, come look, Mr. Frank is letting me help make the muffins." Melanie bent down and hugged her daughter tight, and started crying. A memory from Jeselle's past about her mother and their baking muffins together flooded in. Her mother talked often about people changing and how we ought to forgive and love. Jeselle lowered her head.

"Well, let's get on with it, the food here is worse than all the others, I think she's hit rock bottom with this one," Dennis said.

"Yes, Dennis, I think you're right. Let's leave." Jeselle started to shuffle out of the bright blue booth.

"Are my eyes deceiving me, is Jeselle taking pity on someone?" Dennis asked.

Jeselle took in a deep breath, "Dennis, if you'd have ever really looked at me through the years, you'd know … never mind, let's go. You are right, she has hit rock bottom."

Jeselle didn't finish the day at work. She went home. She walked into the front door and sank onto the floor and cried. She thought of her dad. Then her mom. Isabel. Vinton. Jed. She was angry that she'd wanted to forgive Melanie. Melanie was the worst of them all, yet she'd felt sorry for her earlier. She was also angry that she helped Camilla. Angrier that Camilla deserved the help, because after all, she wasn't the bad person Jeselle knew so many years ago. True that she was haughty, but even that had begun to melt away.

Jeselle looked up at the painting on the wall.

The *Good Love Charm* seemed to almost reach out to her. She had spent so long trying to remove all the money and power from her enemies that she'd forgotten some of the most important parts of her life. She stood, wiped the tears away from her face.

All the betrayal, she thought, she couldn't simply let it go. Her dad. His life's work, his life. The pain he felt knowing what had happened to her. Her mom, the life insurance, working, barely scraping by on a housekeeper's wage.

She slowly walked upstairs, into her own room, and through it to the large walk-in closet. She moved a few boxes around, until she came to the one that she needed. On it was written the words: *my old stuff.* She wanted to leave it at Isabel's house years ago, but Isabel wouldn't have it.

"You need to bring that with you. You got your own house now, and it belongs with you."

"I don't want it in my house," Jeselle remembered saying.

"Doesn't matter. It's that or the burn pile. Same with all your stuff." Isabel said.

Jeselle knew Isabel was simply being her tough self, and she'd guessed back then she needed it.

Jeselle carried it to her bed and lifted the lid. In it was a file with a bunch of old documents. Wills, court-ordered guardianship, titles, an eviction notice, and a copy of the newspaper from the day after her dad killed himself. She put the file aside and raised the old backpack from high school. The one before her mom's accident. The one she shoved into the back of her closet and didn't look at again until she'd shoved it into that box.

She unzipped the large section and pulled out old notebooks, a pack of tissue and a smaller zippered bag full of colored pencils and stickers. She looked at the front pocket for a bit, knowing what was inside. The zipper moved easily to reveal a bunch of strips of paper. The notes, her mom left her every morning, especially after her dad died.

Back then, she simply shoved them into the pocket without reading them. After her mom died, guilt prevented it. Now, she was drawn to them like a magnet.

She put her hand in and drew out one. Tears started streaming down her face again as she carefully opened it, fifteen years since she packed this backpack away.

The first one, written in her mother's handwriting, read:

You have to do it, Jessie. Let it go! I love you!

"If you love only those who love you, what reward is there for that? Even corrupt tax collectors do that much. If you are kind only to your friends, how are you different from anyone else?" –Matthew 5:46-47

One after another, Jeselle read her mother's words until she'd cried herself to sleep.

Later that night, the ringing of her phone startled her awake.

"I know it was you," Dennis said.

"What?" she asked groggily.

"On the news tonight the lead story was about

a waitress who received a mysterious tip of twenty thousand dollars," he laughed.

"And?"

He laughed again, "Maybe you do truly have a heart after all."

"Maybe," she said flippantly.

"Jeselle, do you ever plan to marry?"

"I've considered it a time or two," she stated honestly, "I had stuff to do first."

He smiled to himself, "We…" he corrected, "We had stuff to do."

"Yes."

"Do you ever plan to marry *me*? Because I've never made it a secret that I love you, and your money, of course," he joked. "Seriously, together, no one could stop us."

"I'm tired Dennis. Ask me again in the morning."

He smiled wider, perhaps wider than he ever had, "Done."

CHAPTER 51

PRESENT

"In sorrow he learned this truth, one
may return to the place of his birth, he
cannot go back to his youth."
—John Burroughs

Dennis was in a frenzy to reach his office after the early morning phone call he'd received from his assistant. She said the FBI was seizing the Stryker offices and shutting down the business on a warrant. Dennis pulled to the side of the road to take a few moments to think. He tried to call his father, but there was no answer. He tried the home number, nothing. Then he dialed Jeselle's number, again no answer.

"Crap," Dennis cursed. *Camilla,* he thought quickly and started to dial, but before he had the time to finish, Theodore's face appeared on the screen of his cell. Dennis answered immediately.

"Son, what have you done?" his father's voice was harsh.

"Nothing. I, I don't know," Dennis was frantic.

The FBI said something about conspiring to manipulate the market. "Dennis," his father bellowed loudly, "What in the hell is happening?"

"It's nothing, really. I sold some stocks. It so happened that it was the day before all hell broke loose with Briggs. If I recall you were happy about it then. I saved us millions."

"But you didn't tell me you set the whole thing up!" he bellowed again.

"I, I, look, I can't think. I'm on my way." Dennis hung up the phone and sat for a few minutes. He'd wanted to call William immediately, but knew it would look bad, so he dialed George.

"George, thank God! No one seems to be answering the phones this morning. I need you to call William. Let him know that the FBI is at the offices, and they think I tried to do something illegal. Ask him to please sort it out, and fast."

"No can do," George replied in a lower than usual voice. "Already here,"

"At the office?"

"Yep, and my advice, better hurry before the news catches wind of it." then George hung up.

"No! No, no, no!" Dennis screamed and slammed his fist into the steering wheel repeatedly. He took another deep breath, and then reason returned. He knew his father would get him the best legal team, if nothing else, for the sake of the company. Theodore would be sure to get the entire team on it. Relieved a bit, he shifted the car into gear and drew many deep breaths on his way to Stryker Steel.

Once he arrived, he was arrested and read his rights. An agent let him know he was being charged with insider trading on the selling of his Briggs International Steel Corp stocks, as well as conspiring to manipulate the market. Dennis looked up at his father, and Theodore abruptly looked away.

The moment he sat down, in what he imagined was an interrogation room, the door opened and a tall man walked in.

"Hello, Mr. Stryker," the man had a warm smile and put his hand out to shake Dennis's hand.

"Hello," Dennis said as he placed his hand in the man's.

"My name is Agent Jansen. You okay? Want some water? Coffee?"

"No, I'd like a lawyer," he said.

"No problem, lawyer coming," Jansen sat and opened a thick file on the table in front of him. "I'm not really here to question you, my job is to stay with you. Some call it suicide watch. You sure you don't want a cup of water or something?"

"I can guarantee you I won't be killing myself," Dennis shifted in his seat, "Can I use a phone please?" Dennis asked.

"No, sorry," the man seemed like one of the low guys on the totem pole of agents. Dennis figured that the fellow didn't have the authority to do anything but sit here and offer water.

"I can call someone for you though," Jansen seemed genuinely helpful.

"Oh," Dennis was taken aback by the gesture, "yes, good."

Agent Jansen pulled a slender notepad out of his inside jacket pocket and opened it on the table between them.

"Jeselle Parsons, at — "

"Wait, wait," Jansen looked around, then patted his jacket, "Here it is." He reached in again, pulled out a pen, and held it up proudly for Dennis to see. "Found it."

Dennis' forehead crinkled in question. *Is this guy for real?*

"Jeselle, how do you spell that? With a 'G' or a 'J'?" he asked.

"Does it matter?" Dennis was obviously annoyed.

"The number?" he asked casually.

Dennis sucked in a sharp breath, "I don't know, you have my phone."

"Not me," Jansen said, "They. They have your phone." Silence fell between them momentarily, "Look I'm tryin' to help." Jansen leaned closer to Dennis over the table, "I'm probably not even supposed to be doing this."

"Fine," Dennis blew out a breath and sat forward, "reach her, Jeselle Parsons, at E. Rindre Corp."

"*E, Rinder Corp.*" Jansen took his time writing down the name.

Dennis watched, "It's, no, no, it's E, dot, R-i-n-d-r-e." Dennis pointed to the notepad and watched as Jansen wrote it down properly. "Be sure to at least get to her secre—"

"Remember," the agent said, a smile spread across his face.

"I'm, sorry ... remember what?" he waved his hand in the air in front of him, "Look, it's her secretar-"

"Remember," the agent repeated, pointing to the pad with his pen. "Sorry," he shrugged, "grew up with my grandmother, she was an immigrant from Denmark." Jansen laughed slightly, "hence the name, Jansen." The Agent saw the bewildered look on Dennis's face. "It can also mean remind, but remember is more common."

"Look dude, I seriously, don't know what your problem is, but I," Dennis stood from his seat, "really. Need. You. To. Listen." He emphasized each word for the agent. "Call her there, and let her know I'm here."

Agent Jansen slowly folded his notepad, placed it and the pen back into his jacket pocket, stood and walked to the door. He took one last look back at Dennis before opening it to leave.

***

"Dad, why the hurry? What's going on?" Camilla asked as she sat in a chair on the patio of the coffee shop.

"Dennis has been arrested."

"What? When? Why?" Camilla stood.

"Sit down, Camilla. He's with the FBI right now. Sit," Theodore demanded.

"What is going on, Daddy?"

"Seems your brother has put the company at risk. I've had to conference with some of the board members and we all agree that Dennis needs to be separated from the company immediately, until all of this can be sorted out."

"When did this happen?"

"At six o'clock this morning. I've been able to keep it out of the news for now, but it won't be long until somebody gets a whiff of it."

"This is horrible. Oh, Dennis must be so scared."

"He's not scared, Camilla. He knew exactly what he was doing. He set up that fiasco with the Briggses, which would've been fine by me," his voice started to trail off, "If he hadn't sold the Briggs stock the day before."

"Oh, no." Camilla gasped.

"Oh, yes, and he's made his bed for sure, now."

"Did Jeselle agree to fire Dennis?"

"What?" I don't need her approval for anything!" he raised his voice again.

"Dad, you said you talked to the board, that includes Jeselle, does it not?"

"No, it doesn't. For goodness sakes, Camilla, the damn woman doesn't even own a fourth and if it weren't for her whoring herself out to Vinton, she wouldn't even have that. I don't need her approval and she is definitely not a part of the board. Do you even listen to me?"

Camilla felt her face start to heat up, "Do not talk about Jeselle like that," she defended.

Theodore ignored her, reached down under the table and withdrew a few papers from his briefcase. "Here, sign these, damn it. I am sick and tired of snotty-nosed children who think they know everything. I have to sign over Dennis's shares to you."

"Is that even legal?"

"Yes, Camilla," he said sarcastically, "it is legal. I, unlike your brother, do not break the law."

"No, you simply let everyone else break the law and reap the benefits," she said forcefully.

"Do not push me, child. Sign." He tapped his finger heavily onto the papers in front of her. "The stocks belong to the trust; I'm simply removing his name and adding yours. Someone has to be on it."

She shoved the papers back at her father, "I'm not signing that!"

"Ungrateful. You have never been a grateful child, but I'll tell you this Camilla. You will sign these papers, right this instant. That," he grew despondent, slumped in his chair defeated, "or Stryker Steel dies. It'll be bankrupted, sold for parts. We'll lose everything."

She felt terrible about not considering that Stryker would be in jeopardy. Even though she had been left out of every company decision and every opportunity, always second class to her own twin, she couldn't bring herself to watch what her dad had worked so hard for, and sacrificed so much through the years to build, fall apart. Camilla reached for the papers, "I'm going to read every word first."

"Whatever, just do it," he said.

CHAPTER 52

PRESENT

"We know the truth, not only by the
reason, but also by the heart."
-Blaise Pascal

Jeselle sat and listened as Camilla told her
everything. Everything about her father. The fact
that she brought her mother with her, said a lot too.
She'd told her mother what Dennis had done to her
with Todd, amongst other things.

The one quality Jeselle valued above all else, was
loyalty. Astounding, even to herself, she found that
characteristic in Camilla.

"Hold a second please," Jeselle looked at Camilla,
then to Mrs. Stryker before pressing the button to
call for Karli. "Karli, can you bring the Theodore file
please?"

"Did you ever sign a prenup Mrs. Stryker?"

"No, indeed. I had more money than he did when we married." Mrs. Stryker took a tissue from her purse, "I tried, for years, to believe that Dennis wasn't like Theodore. I tried to make excuses, but I'm devastated, Jess. I have nothing. Even years ago, when I thought I should leave, for the kids, I couldn't. All my money I brought into the marriage was long gone. My trust was still under my brother's care. I had nothing."

When Karli put the thick envelope on the desk, Jeselle looked directly at Mrs. Stryker, "You are only going to do what you think is right for yourself, and that's okay. However, if you feel it is the right thing to file for divorce, in this file is everything, spanning years, that you would need to get a hefty piece of the assets in a divorce settlement. Mrs. Stryker, I am going to be frank with you. After the news hits, it won't be much. From this moment forward, you cannot think about what people will say, or how they will look at you if you choose to leave. You must think of yourself. This folder contains photos, receipts, and a load of other proof of Theodore's many infidelities over the years. You've probably known about them, but proof is different." Jeselle slid the folder to her, "And if you find that you need a job in the meantime, I can help you. For that matter, here is a card for my top attorney," Jeselle reached into the top drawer and pulled out a card, "Her name is Tina, and she's one of the best. She'll work with you about payment arrangements. She's very trustworthy." Jeselle looked at Camilla, "She's Isabel's daughter."

Camilla was stunned, "Okay. Thank you so much for helping. We don't deserve it. What now?"

"Well, you said you took pics with your phone of the signed trust papers. What exactly does that entitle you to? May I see?"

"Of course," Camilla pulled out her phone. "It gives me controlling interest over Stryker."

"Why would Theodore ever give anyone controlling interest?" Jeselle asked.

"I can answer that," Mrs. Stryker said. "He trusted Dennis, a lot, and wanted him to take over. Dennis demanded the trust so he felt comfortable about his future. Then Theodore would still get profit share without any liability and remain as co-chair on the board. Basically, an early retirement."

"Next, I am going to try to see Dennis. I was told that I could get in with an attorney, so I'll take one with me. I'll let you know the results."

Mrs. Stryker stood, "Tell him I love him and will visit him in prison."

* * *

Agent Jansen returned with two cups of coffee, "I didn't know what you take in it, so I put cream."

"Did you reach her?" Dennis asked.

"Yes, got her right here with me. She came with a lawyer for you," he said

It was easier to get in than Jeselle had imagined. She walked behind the attorney into the room where Dennis sat.

"Jeselle!" he sprung out of his chair, and one of the agents instructed him to sit back down. After the agent left, Jeselle began, "Dennis, are you okay?"

"No! I'm not okay! Do you know what they have?" he asked the lawyer.

"Not everything, but I know enough. It's bad."

"How long, if I'm convicted?"

"You are looking at twenty years, Dennis. The amount you sold was well over five million. The SEC will likely want to make an example out of you."

"I cannot believe this." When he started to cry, Jeselle felt guilt pour through her.

"Well, I'll sell out whomever. I don't care." He looked up at Jeselle, then back to the attorney. "Not to be rude, but Jeselle knew about the news being there at the hotel, why isn't she in here?" He looked her way again.

"I didn't sell my stocks, Dennis," she said straightforwardly. "Your mother wanted me to tell you she loves you."

"Oh, Jeselle," his tone changed, "I am so glad you are here. Being in here, my mind started playing tricks on me. I guess I thought, you know, that you…" he let his voice trail off.

"I get it. I understand," she said.

He looked to the attorney again, "I was told the arraignment is in the morning. So how long until I'm out of here?"

"They are not going to let you out, I'm afraid. A flight risk, and with your resources, the judge will undoubtedly keep you."

He sat back in his chair. "I can't believe this."

Jeselle spoke up, "I do need to discuss one thing with you. I'm sorry, but your father put Camilla on the trust and—"

Dennis started laughing; quietly at first then it grew louder and more hysterical. "Her? Wow, the company will go under in a month."

"I'm worried the news will do that within the week," she said.

That sobered him, "Right. Well, good riddance. He'll be shocked to find all that I've transferred through the years out of his name and into that trust. My trust," he laughed again, "The man's own house doesn't even belong to him."

Agent Jansen came back in to tell Jeselle and the attorney that it was time for them to leave.

"I don't care what it takes, Jeselle, get me out of here." Those were his last words to her as they left.

Jansen closed the door and looked at Dennis, "Need anything?"

"No," he said.

"No problem. Well, I'll be back to check on you in a few." Jansen rose to leave.

"Wait," Dennis said. "What did you mean earlier, it can also be 'remind?'"

The agent looked a bit confused, then he shook his head in understanding, "Oh yeah, the name of the company. It reminded me of my grandma."

"Oh, okay, you said remember, then remind. So, it reminded you of her," Dennis said conclusively. "Got it."

"Yeah, Danish is a hard language, but she beat it into me," Jansen laughed.

"The language? Okay, I'm confused again." Dennis wondered how in the world that guy ended up working for the FBI. Don't they have standards? A test of some kind?

"Yeah, erindre…" Jansen walked back to the table, pulled out his notepad, and opened to the page that he'd written the company name on, "it means remind."

Dennis shook his head, "That's E and Rinder. Not whatever you said."

"Oh, I know, like I said," he folded the notepad, "it reminded me of—"

"My grandmother," Dennis said in sync with Jansen, "Yes, so you said. Over and over."

Agent Jansen took that as his cue and stood.

"Just … out of curiosity," Dennis motioned for Jansen to give him the pad.

"Can't do it. The pen, you know."

"Right," Dennis replied. "Well then, do the letters m-i-n-d-e mean anything to you?"

Jansen face lit up, "Yeah! Remembrance."

Dennis squinted his eyes, "What about h-u-s-k-e?"

"About the same, remember. Hey, how do you know—"

"What about t-a-g-e?"

"It means take."

Dennis sat back and took a few deep breaths. "t-r-y-d-e?"

"Aww, that's a sad one, means regret."

Dennis's breathing grew deeper, "G-e-n-o?"

"No, nothing I know of."

Dennis inhaled one slow, deep breath, "G-e-n-o-p-r-e-t-t-e?"

"Yep. That's a good one, means restore. It's weird that you know all these words."

"Yeah, hey, umm what about l-e-t-t-e?"

"Rise."

"One more, h-a-e-v-n-e?"

"That one? That one means avenge."

Dennis's head started spinning. Another agent strode into the room whistling, which rubbed him the wrong way.

"How long are you going to keep me in here?" Dennis demanded. "Where is my attorney?"

"Oh," the new agent said, "I don't have any answers. Far as I know, attorney's gone already."

"Where's my father?" he demanded.

"No father either. You're not going anywhere, anyway. Got your buddy in a room few doors down, spilled his guts about everything."

"My buddy?" Dennis said condescendingly.

"Yep, got a Mr.," the man turned, stepped outside of the room and then returned a few moments later, "a Mr. William Reims. We have a file two inches thick on him. Seems he's been a bad boy. Tsk tsk." The agent moved his finger in a 'naughty' motion.

Dennis squinted his eyes in observation. "What about Theodore Stryker? He here yet?"

"Nope, like I said, no father. Seems everybody's busy little bees trying to clean up your mess. You know, you are under arrest, been read your rights, and your bond will be set in the morning in federal court. Until then, you're stuck with us."

When Dennis was finally left alone, the room was spinning out of control. He kept talking himself out of the doubt he felt, but then the memory of that night continued to flood back in and made him doubt all over again.

CHAPTER 53

PAST

"It is not only for what we do that we
are held responsible, but also for what
we do not do."
-Jean-Baptiste Poquelin, Moliere

"She thinks she can boss everyone around like she owns us." Melanie said.

"She's not bossing everyone around," Dennis said, "We don't need the hot dogs?"

"Well, according to Jess, Tracy was supposed to bring them," Camilla answered. "Still think she's not bossy?" Camilla asked Dennis. "No one likes her. She's poor."

"Yeah, she is," Cindy agreed.

"Who are you saying is poor, Cindy? You're here by our good graces too, so don't ruin it." Melanie said it, and Camilla giggled.

"I'm not going to let her boss me, Dennis. You hear me? It's my land; I shouldn't have to bring anything," Tracy declared.

"It's no big deal, we'll roast the marshmallows," Dennis said, thrusting another fluffy white confection on the end of the stick.

"She's still a virgin." Melanie said.

"Stop it, Lanie," William dropped his stick into the fire.

"Shut up William, you are pitiful. Why don't you at least be honest about yourself?" she said and William lowered his head.

"I get it dude, I'm pretty hot, but you ever come at me with that thing, I'll cut it off," Tracy said and most of the group laughed.

"All I'm saying is that she's awful. We've done nothing but fight since she's been here." Melanie stated. "She doesn't fit in."

"Seriously, all of you stop it. She's been here a year, and she's here to stay." Dennis said.

Melanie sneered in her usual way, "Tracy, are you seriously going to let Dennis dictate who stays and who goes in our group?"

"Hell, no. She's got to go."

"Guys," Dennis said, "I'm not joking, she'll be here any minute and I don't want her to hear you all talk about her like that. Her father is important here."

"Not for long," Tracy laughed.

"What's that supposed to mean?" Dennis asked.

"You don't know anything, Tracy. Besides, he works

for us, not you. She stays."

"Dad's hiring someone to mimic her Dad's crap and as soon as he does, she's gone."

"Well, tell him to hurry," Melanie said, "I can't take much more of watching all of you bow down to her like she's a queen or something." She knew exactly what to say to stir trouble.

Tracy stood and got directly into Melanie's face, "I don't bow to anyone."

"Prove it," she taunted.

"Hey guys. Chips are here," Jeselle's voice flowed over the group as she rushed forward, lifted the two bags high in the air to show them, "So sorry I'm late, it's getting dark and usually Dennis is with me. I got a little lost."

"Too bad you didn't stay lost," Cindy whispered and everyone in the group laughed, except Dennis.

Jeselle plopped down beside Dennis and kissed him quickly on the cheek.

"Cute shirt, Jess," Melanie said.

"Lanie," Dennis warned.

Jeselle looked to Dennis and then back at Melanie trying to figure out what was going on.

"Hide and seek anyone?" Melanie asked.

"I'm starving, I need food first." Jeselle looked around the fire. "Where are the hot dogs?"

"Tracy forgot them," Dennis said.

"Not forgot," Tracy said as he lifted his shirt over his head. He stared at Jeselle, "Nobody tells me what to do."

She looked at Dennis and whispered, "I wasn't

trying to be offensive."

"Please ignore him," Dennis said.

"Rules for hide and seek are easy," Melanie looked directly at Jeselle, "when someone catches you, you have to kiss them." Jeselle was obviously uncomfortable with that, so Melanie added, "Don't be a baby, it's only a light kiss," then she laughed. "The first person to be caught eight times gets a spanking by the one who catches them."

Dennis was the one who laughed then, "Hope you get Camilla, she's a weakling."

"Whatever!" Camilla snorted.

He leaned into Jess, "Melanie's the worst. Whatever you do, don't let her catch you," he chuckled again.

Melanie continued, for Jeselle's benefit, "You can hide anywhere in the woods or the river, but you can't use the trails. When you catch someone, you have to call out their name, then the person caught has to call out their own number. If you forget to call out your number the person who caught you gets to spank you the number of times you've been caught already. No cheating or everyone gets to spank you."

Jeselle noticed everyone was already up and poised to run when Melanie yelled, "Go!"

Jeselle took off running, following Dennis. When he turned around and found her, he screamed "JESS!" He kissed her quickly on the lips. "yell 'ONE.'

"ONE!" she did as he told her.

"Now, you better run away sweet Jess, or I'll be

the one spanking you," he laughed. She turned and ran in the opposite direction.

"CAMILLA!" the name rang out.

"ONE!" Camilla added.

The over brush was scratching her legs, but she kept going deeper and deeper each time she heard someone call out.

"Gotcha!" Tracy's voice sent a chill up her spine. He pinned her against a tree, "I'm going to make sure I get to be the last one. Don't worry, you'll enjoy it. JESS!" he yelled.

She was petrified when he pressed even harder into her. Jeselle could feel the bark of the tree prick against her back like little needles.

"NO CALL! Tracy yelled again and grabbed Jeselle by an arm, dragging her through the woods to the clearing where everyone else stood. They all seemed happy, but Jeselle was afraid.

"It's nothing," Dennis said to her. "Two licks, you got off easy."

Dennis seemed so nonchalant about it, Jeselle was obviously panicking for nothing.

Tracy sat on the ground pulling Jeselle over his lap, "You're lucky I only get two," he said in a low voice over her.

Jeselle was thankful that she'd worn her blue jean shorts, instead of thinner ones.

"One," she heard right before she felt an awful sting from the blow to the upper thigh. She elbowed Tracy in the side, "Ouch! That's my leg!" she cried.

He cursed. "You hit me!" Jeselle felt blow after

blow to her legs and butt before Dennis stepped in.

"Dude! That's enough!"

"Swim now?" Melanie suggested cheerfully.

Everybody else made their way into the river while Jeselle and Dennis stayed behind by peering over the fire at everybody in the water.

"He wasn't supposed to do that," Dennis said, "...Then again, you weren't supposed to elbow him, either," he laughed.

She didn't think it was funny.

"Oh, come on, it's a silly game. We always play games, you know that."

"Yeah, but usually they are fun," she retorted.

"Come on, let's go swimming. It'll ease the sting."

"I'll be out in a minute,"

Dennis took his shirt off, and got into the river with the others. The campfire made her feel exposed. She could see Melanie and Tracy talking off to one side, they looked back at her and she felt chills go up her spine again.

Melanie rushed out of the water and stood over Jeselle, dripping water onto her, "Coming in, Jess?"

Jeselle looked up, "Oh, yeah, um, sure." Jeselle stood and removed her shirt that she had on over her swimsuit. Melanie put her hand out in front of Jeselle.

"Shorts."

"I'm ... going to keep them on. Like usual," Jeselle said uncomfortably.

"Not this time. You want to be a part of the

group? We don't wear shorts to swim. Only fat people do that" Melanie lifted her hand closer to Jeselle's face. "And we don't like fat people."

Jeselle looked around for Dennis, but he was too far into the river.

"Jess, it's stupid to wear shorts. Off," Melanie demanded.

Jeselle slowly unbuttoned, unzipped her shorts, slipped them off and gave them to Melanie.

"Oh, wow!" Melanie turned her to where the firelight lit her backside for all the others, "Guys, Tracy really got her good! Look at these marks!" Melanie yelled.

Jeselle turned quickly and when she looked over at the river again, she saw Tracy smiling. It made her uncomfortable, and she couldn't wait to be hidden beneath the water.

She felt safe once she made it over to Dennis.

"Game time!" Melanie said loudly.

"Game time?" Cindy asked. "Which one?"

"Melanie and I came up with a game to see how well we know each other. Since we are all so close," Tracy said.

"Lame," Todd said.

"Bet I'll win," Camilla chimed in.

"Come closer, let's make a circle." Melanie instructed. "Me first, since I thought it up. The rules are a question to each of us about all the others and the person who gets the most answers wrong, goes home at the end of the game."

"Come on, guys," Dennis said, knowing what

the purpose of the game really was.

"Aw, that's sad though," Jeselle said, "I wouldn't want to stay and have fun while somebody else has to leave. What about something else for the loser? Like they have to cook us each a marshmallow," she smiled.

"Yeah, no," Melanie said, "Person with the most wrong answers, leaves. First question to Cindy. Cindy, how many dolls does Camilla have on that shelf in her bedroom?"

"Oh, that's hard," Cindy answered, "I guess twenty?"

"Wrong." Melanie looked at Jeselle, "How many?"

"I hate to say this, but—"

"Fine, Tracy, how many?" Melanie turned to Tracy.

"How would I kn—"

"Oh, no, I have the answer," Jeselle interrupted, "I hate to admit that I do, it's only that they are so pretty. It's fifteen, one doll for every birthday. Right, Camilla?"

Camilla ignored her.

"Fine, whatever, okay, Jeselle you get another question then. What happened to William with a girl named Belinda at the beginning of eighth grade?"

"Oh, I don't want to say it," she looked at William, "and I'm sorry they did that to you."

"I'm not gay!" William got out of the river and went to sit by the fire.

Melanie punched Dennis in the arm, "Group

secret, remember!"

"She's a part of the group. Besides, if you thought she didn't know, why did you ask her?" Dennis became enraged.

"Shut up everybody! This was supposed to be fun!" Tracy yelled. "Cindy, go talk to William. Everybody else, out of the river." Tracy was mumbling a few things, when Jeselle hadn't moved, he looked at her and yelled, "Out!"

She moved so quickly that the discomfort she felt for not having shorts on left her. As soon as she stood up from the river, Melanie came up behind her and pulled her bathing suit bottom down and off Jeselle's feet, causing Jeselle to fall forward.

Melanie held the suit bottom high in the air and twirled it around, the same way that Tracy had that day with Cindy's top.

Dennis rushed over to Jeselle and helped her up, her lip was bleeding. Jeselle used her hands to cover herself.

"Camilla, bring me my t-shirt," Dennis said.

Camilla attempted to stand and Melanie stopped her. "No, we've all been skinny dipping together, we've seen each other naked, if she really wants to be a part of the group, then she can prove it."

"Yeah," Tracy sneered.

William and Cindy sat still by the fire. Camilla looked as though she were about to cry, but remained beside Melanie, Todd stepped forward to stand next to Tracy.

"This is stupid," Dennis said.

"Dennis, Camilla's crying, go to her." Tracy said.

"Tracy, please don't do this." Dennis pleaded.

Jeselle began to sob then, "Please, just give me my shorts and I'll go. It's obvious you all don't want me here anymore. I'll leave."

"Yeah, that's good, Tracy. Let me give her the shorts." Dennis made his way closer to the fire where everyone else stood.

"No," Tracy said. He walked to Jeselle, "No shorts. No leaving." He put his hand up to her mouth and smeared some of the blood with his thumb. "You are in our group now. Dennis reminded us that you've been here a whole year. Doesn't seem like it." Tracy put his thumb to his mouth and licked her blood from it.

Jeselle tried to escape, but Tracy easily grabbed her around the waist and threw her to the ground.

"Tracy!" Dennis yelled and moved toward them.

"Don't," he taunted, "Think of your mother,"

"Dennis, don't. Mom..." Camilla pleaded.

"William, come here! Time to prove you're a real man. Todd come help!" Tracy yelled.

Jeselle punched Tracy as hard as she could in the face. He punched her back.

"Tracy!" Dennis called out to him, "Stop, I'll do anything."

"Yeah, you will." Tracy retorted mockingly. "Todd, take that arm, William, the other one, and get ready 'cause you go next."

Jeselle's face felt like it was on fire, she tried to squirm away, but Tracy slapped her face viciously and her lip felt like it exploded again. She started pounding Tracy's back with the heels of her feet.

"Cindy! Melanie! Come here!" Tracy yelled. Cindy rushed forward, her face burning from jealousy. She wanted to object, but the throbbing she still felt in her own eye from a few nights before kept her quiet.

"Take her arms, above her head and kneel on them. Guys, come get her legs!" Jeselle couldn't help but stare into Melanie's eyes as she was hovering over her head. Something about Melanie's satisfied sneer, she knew, would be burned into her memory forever.

"Please, help me," she whispered, barely choking the desperate plea out through her own sobs. Which prompted Melanie to roughly cover Jess's mouth with her hand.

She turned toward the fire and felt the warm blood flow down the side of her face. She saw Dennis, crying, pleading with Tracy. Although she really couldn't hear him anymore.

She saw Camilla crying.

She noticed that the rope swing was swaying behind them. It was moving so gently back and forth, that Jeselle thought it was somehow trying to soothe her. She looked above her head, this time at Cindy, who was looking away. Then she saw Melanie, who was smiling. Melanie pressed down on Jeselle's arm and suddenly everything started to spin faster and faster.

She felt a sharp pain between her legs and saw

STOP ME

Tracy hovering on top of her. He was flanked by William and Todd. William threw up on her leg, but it barely registered to Jeselle. because Tracy was looking at Dennis with a sinister smile on his face. And with every thrust he made, all she heard was Tracy's chant:

Your. Mother's. Money.

Your. Mother's. Money.

Your. Mother's. Money.

It seemed to go on and on. She looked at Dennis again, but Dennis wasn't looking anymore, he had turned away. The pain in her head was pulsing. Finally, she noticed Dennis inching closer and closer, and heard him tell Tracy he'd never forgive him for taking what was his. When Tracy laughed, Dennis charged him, shoving Tracy off Jeselle. When he and Tracy started to fight, Jeselle got up and ran. She ran as fast as she could down the trail.

CHAPTER 54

PRESENT

A loud noise woke Dennis to a sore back and neck. When he lifted himself from the small cot, reality flooded him that he wasn't waking from his Grand Vividus bed. The door to the small room was already open. He was thankful, at least, that he wasn't in a regular jail, or whatever they housed other prisoners in. He'd always imagined doors made of steel bars and people vomiting in the corners.

"You're on the news this morning," someone stuck his head around the cell door. "The TV's out here."

When Dennis didn't budge, the man said, "That pretty lady that came yesterday is on it, too."

Dennis got up and made his way to what he surmised was a common area for individuals of white collar crimes. Dennis watched the TV screen as Jeselle walked to the front of the Stryker Steel press room. She looked beautiful. More beautiful than he'd ever noticed before. She was stunning. She also looked pensive.

"It is with such sorrow that I am here today. I have always known, since I first moved to Baton Rouge, that there was bad blood between the Briggs siblings. I had recently hired Tracy Briggs's wife, solely because she needed a job after Tracy was arrested, and the Briggs stocks subsequently plummeted."

"Did you know that was going to happen?" a reporter asked.

"Well, being in business, yes, I knew it would happen. Cindy had shared intimate details with me in the previous months, so it was truly a matter of time."

"Why didn't you sell your stocks in Briggs International Steel Corp, like Dennis did?" another reporter asked.

"I'm not going to lie, I was tempted, as anyone would be when faced with losing millions, but in the end, I couldn't do it."

Dennis watched in amazement the way that Jeselle handled the reporters. He knew somehow, some way, she'd help him. It wouldn't be so bad.

He'd likely be able to choose where he served time, if he even served at all. Another reporter asked Jeselle if she had hired Cindy directly after that incident at the hotel, to which Jeselle answered that she had, in an attempt to help her.

"Unfortunately, she was fired and arrested two days ago, to little fanfare, for stealing funds from my company. I thought Cindy was having a hard transition to living on such a modest income, maybe that was the motive, but I can't be sure. Fortunately," Jeselle said as she looked at the camera, "truth always wins."

Dennis was mesmerized.

"It's hard when you go from having money to having none," Jeselle continued. "I know, I've been there. It's hard to watch the bad guys win, again and again. I've been there, too. I could file charges, but it really is up to the District Attorney's office on what they intend to do."

Dennis found that he had hot tears falling down his cheeks. He quickly wiped them away.

"What about Stryker Steel?"

"Yes, that is ultimately why we are here," the crowd laughed a bit. "I have, *legally*," she stressed the word, "purchased stocks which, combined with the stocks that I already owned, makes me the majority shareholder. Camilla Stryker is the next largest, and as of this afternoon, we are here to announce that she has been appointed CEO of Stryker Steel Corp. She is more than capable. She's been around the business her entire life."

STOP ME

Dennis felt the tears flow faster, as he watched.

"For now, I'm going to leave for my honeymoon. After many years of him asking, I've finally said yes." Jeselle held up her hand to show off a beautifully understated set of wedding rings, then she motioned toward the crowd and the camera followed. Dennis was knocked over as if someone had landed a blow to his gut, the force causing him to vomit all over the linoleum floor, because he saw none other than George smiling back at Jeselle.

"This man has been my rock for years. I honestly wouldn't be where I am today, without him," Jeselle looked to the back of the room, directly at the cameras.

He continued to dry heave violently as her words permeated through him.

CHAPTER 55

PAST

"And now you know the rest of the story."
-Paul Harvey

"Ms. Parsons, there is a man in the lobby to see you."

"Oh, I'm running late for a meeting with Mr. Vinton. Did he give you a name?" Jeselle would've thought Dennis, except, even though she'd broken up with him, she knew he had the new position at Stryker and would never jeopardize that, even for her.

Especially, with his pride.

She'd closed her eyes a few times over the last two weeks since then, and she could still see the devastation in his face when she returned his rings that night. She felt relief. Also she felt melancholy.

"Yes, ma'am, I called Mr. Vinton first, expecting you to already be there, he said he could wait."

"Oh, okay then, did he say he was a client?"

"He didn't, ma'am, only that he was willing to wait as long as he needed to."

"Okay then, be right down."

Jeselle knew the moment she saw him, who he was, "What do you want?"

"Please listen. I didn't know."

"You knew. You saw me that night. You knew." She started to walk away.

"I didn't though. I swear. Mr. Stryker told me you all had done this before, it was a game. Some people try to get money when they get hurt, even when it's their own fault. That you were dating his son and I, I, look, I was new on the force. Had recently graduated from the academy. I was only eighteen."

"Oh and, let's see, you finally put two and two together after, what? Umm ... five years?"

"I would never have thought about it again. I mean, Chief Reynolds and Captain Kramer confirmed it and told me to let it go. I was only eighteen. Plus, I knew you were still around, knew you were dating Dennis. I believed. I mean, why else would you stay with him, if he'd hurt you?"

She saw his logic, "Okay, why now?"

"Because I heard them talking about it."

"Who?"

"Mr. Stryker and Dennis. They were talking

about your new boss buying stocks or something at the upcoming summit."

Jeselle walked toward a sitting area in the lobby and George followed.

"I always knew Ms. Trudy's death was weird somehow." He sat. "I mean I'd only been on the job for a few months, but I got all the crap jobs like ER, so I was always around Mrs. Trudy. She wasn't a prostitute. I knew it. I knew something was wrong, but nothing else ever came out of it."

"Okay…" she waited.

"Mr. Stryker asked him, right before you came home for the engagement party, if Dennis was sure you were trustworthy, after what happened all those years ago."

"Wait!" she put her hand up, "How would you hear them talking about it?"

"Mr. Stryker hired me … *that* night … to do odd jobs, like private investigations and stuff."

"What else?"

"Dennis said yes, very sure. He said that you were so loyal to him; that you would never betray him because he was, after all, the only one who stood by you. And he intended to keep doing that as your husband. Then, Mr. Stryker laughed and told him that at least Briggs wouldn't have to get overzealous with you and make the same mistake he'd made with Trudy."

"What? Oh my God! Go to the police!" she demanded.

"And say what? Trust me, it wouldn't do any

good." He lowered his head again. "That's not all and...I'm sorry to say it, Mr. Stryker told Dennis that at least he was able to keep you in line until after your eighteenth birthday."

"I'm nineteen, why my eighteenth?" Jeselle asked, truly puzzled.

"I'm so sorry," George offered again before continuing, "when Dennis asked him, he said because eighteen was when all of your rights to your father's processes were up."

"My rights?" Jeselle stood, then felt as if she were falling, she'd lost feeling in her legs. George caught her.

"I'm so sorry." he said again. "Any way, the last few days Mr. Stryker has been throwing fits about you breaking up with Dennis and that he hadn't gotten back together with you yet. He's angry that Dennis refuses to go after you."

"Really? ...So, George, you are only, what? Twenty-four?"

"Twenty-three. Almost twenty-four"

"Why are you here?" she asked again, with much more bitterness in her voice than the first time. "I don't trust you. What's your reason?"

"I don't really know. I guess, I thought you should know. My momma always said there is truth, lies, and opinions, but truth is what matters most of all."

There was a long silence.

"George, can you come upstairs and meet my boss?"

CHAPTER 56

PRESENT

Jeselle and George stood in The Alley with Jed, Isabel, and the girls. Karli was there and so were Camilla and Rose. They all watched as the faces of the man carrying the steel pipe on his shoulder and the police officer in the mural were being painted over to reflect her dad's face and George's. George looked at Jeselle. "I love you. It's a real shame that Dennis's face had to be there for so long."

The others agreed.

"Yes," Jeselle responded, "but somehow I feel like Mom and Dad understood why."

They all stayed until the mural was complete. The

police officer, standing strong in the background, with his arms folded, representing an honest man who did the right thing. A nurse stood beside him, a bloodied shirt dangling in one hand, representing a woman who put her life on the line for the truth. Sitting on a bench behind the nurse was another man with his hands grasping a steering wheel, who represented all the people who stop and help when they could simply drive away. Two men, one carrying a large steel pipe on his shoulders, which now looked like her dad, a man who loved her so much that he put his own life on the line to save her; the other was Mason Vinton, holding a large book. He was the man of reason who told her that no matter how much information you have about someone's secrets, it can all be manipulated by opinion and power. It's their own actions that ultimately prove to be their downfall, not the secrets. Secrets can stay hidden, truths can't. Then, there was the woman, her mom, leaning on a wall with one foot propped against it, beyond the images of her dad and Mason. She was the backbone of it all; the strength. Lastly, in the forefront was a woman kneeling down running her fingers over her own reflection in a water puddle. The reflection was rippled, but you could clearly see that she had two different faces, split down the middle. One was angry, one was peaceful.

Jeselle still wondered which one she truly was.

* * *

That night, sitting on her sofa with her fresh blueberry muffin, Jeselle turned on the news. She had been replaced as the lead story by the next headline. George sat beside her right as the news started.

"In our top story tonight, Erin Young, an administrative assistant for Hamilton Financial Services was arrested today after an FBI investigation discovered that she had stolen nearly 3.8 million dollars from the owner, Thomas Hamilton's clients. Mr. Hamilton and his associates released a statement soon after the arrest apologizing to his clients for the former employee's actions and expressing his hopes that Ms. Young be prosecuted to the fullest extent of the law."

Jeselle leaned forward. Hamilton Financial Services was located in one of her buildings, the one next door to hers. The screen changed to a video of a man being chased down by reporters as he was getting into his car.

"So, Mr. Hamilton, what caused you to start looking into missing money?" one of the reporters asked.

The man, distinguished looking, an air of arrogance floating around him, stopped at the open door his driver was holding for him, "One of my clients needed to cash out due to an illness, and when I looked into their account, the amounts weren't adding up."

"So, it was you who called the FBI to look into the discrepancies?" another asked, shoving a microphone into his face.

"Actually, my client did, but I was glad. I would've had to report it if they hadn't. It's tragic, because I really trusted Ms. Young."

The screen went back to the desk reporter, "Ms. Young was arrested when she showed up for work this morning."

Footage played in a small square beside the announcer's head that showed a young woman, one that Jeselle recognized as the girl she'd seen sitting and sharing her lunch with Jed. She was being led from the building with her hands cuffed.

"I didn't do this," she cried, "I swear. I didn't do this. I don't even know how to do what they are saying I've done. Please someone help me."

Jeselle sat back and watched the rest of the footage with heightened curiosity.

"The FBI has seized records, some of which they have revealed in an earlier press briefing, where Ms. Young had signed out money from several client accounts and transferred into other accounts, titled none other than her own name."

The screen went back to Erin being put into the back of a black SUV, her head was lowered and she was crying. Then it flashed back to Mr. Hamilton, shaking his head and talking about how betrayed he felt.

All Jeselle saw, though, was his arrogance and lies. Another wrong that needed righting.

"And that's our top story for tonight," the reporter stated. "In other news Todd Parrish, prominent Baton Rouge Attorney, has been officially disbarred. As we reported yesterday, his records have been seized following a plea deal and the District Attorney's office said the files contain recordings and records of illegal dealings on behalf of several prominent Louisiana business people. His plea deal is still undisclosed, however someone close to the investigation told us that Parrish will still serve a heavy sentence. No other details have been released at this time."

She had been warned throughout the years that revenge, once achieved, would leave her with no purpose. She stood and walked to the large frame hanging on the wall. It was a collection of all of her mother's notes. She read a few. When she got to one, one she'd read many times before, it meant something different to her than it had before.

"Jessie, We're proud of you for helping Cindy. Remember, you can only control yourself. You did the right thing. ' Rescue the weak and the needy; deliver them from the hand of the wicked.' Psalm 82:4"

Jeselle realized a new mission was forming. A new purpose. Because there were plenty of wrongs that needed to be righted.

And she intended to change the order of billing.

NOT THE END...

ACKNOWLEDGEMENTS

One of the greatest moments of my life was my wedding day. Since that day, I find I am spending one great moment after another of my life with my husband. Thank you, Larry, for encouraging me to chase this dream. Thank you for pushing me to let the stories be what they are and not falling to the pressure of making them fit anyone else. You are the best person I've ever known, and I am so thankful to spend my life with you.

To my parents, who sacrificed so much to raise and protect me. I only wish you were still here to see it all happen. Dad, thank you for teaching me how to walk away. Mom, thank you for teaching me how to stand and fight. Both lessons have a place in my life and I use them regularly.

To my second set of parents, my in-laws, thank you for taking me in and loving me as one of your own. Ms. Nelda, thank you being the example of learning from mistakes, and then leaving them behind. Mr. Lester, thank you for being such a man of God and putting Him and us, your family, first. You both help me be a better person.

ACKNOWLEDGEMENTS

I am surrounded by incredible women every day! Women who stand in the gap with me, pray with me, and share their lives with me and my family. You all keep my head filled with encouragement and I treasure each of you!

My editing and marketing super-heroes: Alexis Jester, Nelda Spurlock Arnold, Taylor Voisin, Deborah Dawn Hall, Mallory at Tell It All, and Ann Purvis. Thank you for tolerating me and my clutch words. You are my literary moms. (Yes, even you, Alexis. ;)) Giselle at Xpresso, Carrie at Valor, and all the bloggers who participated, thank you from the bottom of my heart. You are all phenomenal!

Thanks to the city of Baton Rouge for locations that were featured in the book trailer. Special thanks to Rene Green at Hotel Indigo, Downtown Baton Rouge, for the hospitality. Also, to all the actors/models who worked on the trailer and promos: Caroline Scrantz, Erin Vavasseur, Lauren Parrott, and Sadie Fontenot. You ladies are all beautiful inside and out. Thanks for bringing the attitude.

To my amazingly talented daughter, and Producer Chuck Brooks, thank you for making my song Paper Dolls come to life! I love it!

Big shout out to Rachel Dugas, and her crew at Down and Dirty Cleaning Services, LLC, who keep my house in tip top shape for me!

As always, thanks to the readers for all the love and support!! I appreciate that you take your time to read!

Most importantly, thanks to God for giving me a purpose that includes my passion! You Lord, are the author and finisher of my faith.

Love to you all!!

ABOUT THE AUTHOR

Michelle Jester lives in Louisiana with her husband, high school sweetheart, and retired Army Master Sergeant. Together they have a son, daughter, and daughter-in-law. She is a hopeless romantic and has been writing poems and stories since childhood.

One of her prized possessions is a bracelet with only a yellow, rubber duckie charm on it; which she wears every day to remind her to enjoy the fun and happy things of life!

Feel free to connect with her, and sign up for her quarterly newsletter.

www.michellejester.net

RESOURCES

On average, one person dies by suicide every 13 hours
in my home state of Louisiana.
In the United States: 123 suicides per day.
An average of 44,965 suicides a year.
Only 1 in every 25 attempts,
Which means that in America alone, 1,124,125 people attempt to
commit suicide each year.
Globally, 800,000 suicides every year, one every 40 seconds.
Thought to be only 1 in every 20 attempts,
Which means around the world 16,000,000 people attempt to
commit suicide each year.

(American Foundation for Suicide Prevention and World Health Organization)

The highest risk period is 3 months following a suicide attempt.

SUICIDE

Deciding to commit suicide doesn't happen overnight. It starts
when a person adds death on their list of solutions to a problem
and it grows over months or years until death becomes the
only viable option left in their mind. Someone you know, if not
yourself, may be thinking today that suicide is your only option.
If you feel it is, please seek help, you have nothing to lose but
the pain.
Call The National Suicide Prevention Hotline:
800-273-TALK (8255)
Visit online:
www.suicidepreventionlifeline.org

SEXUAL ABUSE

Victims physical and sexual abuse often times live with guilt and
shame. Unfortunately, many never receive the help they deserve
because of it. If you know someone, or if that someone is you,
seek help today. I have seen firsthand the positive transformation
that can happen in you and/or your loved one's life.
Call The National Sexual Assault Hotline:
800-656-HOPE (4673)
Visit online:
www.rainn.org

Also from Michelle Jester

Olivia Brooks has been able to keep her life in Sugar Mill, Louisiana held perfectly together, far away from the small town where she grew up. Even though her past still haunts her, she has found a perfect process of surviving, until a string of events brings Luke Plaisance to Sugar Mill and turns her organized life upside down.

While Olivia fights to hold on to the life she's created, unraveling it may be exactly what it takes for her to truly survive. She must accept her past in order to live, or let it threaten the only future she's ever wanted. Because some secrets can't stay buried... and shouldn't.

An inspiring and heartbreaking tale of abandonment, survival, and purpose. A harrowing journey of self-discovery and perseverance.